NAMA Mia!

NAMA Mia!

ROSS O'CARROLL-KELLY

(as told to Paul Howard)

Illustrated by
ALAN CLARKE

PENGUIN

IRELAND

PENGUIN IRELAND

Published by the Penguin Group
Penguin Ireland, 25 St Stephen's Green, Dublin 2, Ireland
(a division of Penguin Books Ltd)
Penguin Books Ltd, 80 Strand, London WC2R 0RL, England
Penguin Group (USA) Inc., 375 Hudson Street, New York, New York 10014, USA
Penguin Group (Australia), 250 Camberwell Road,
Camberwell, Victoria 3124, Australia (a division of Pearson Australia Group Pty Ltd)
Penguin Group (Canada), 90 Eglinton Avenue East, Suite 700, Toronto, Ontario, Canada M4P 2Y3
(a division of Pearson Penguin Canada Inc.)
Penguin Books India Pvt Ltd, 11 Community Centre, Panchsheel Park, New Delhi – 110 017, India
Penguin Group (NZ), 67 Apollo Drive, Rosedale, Auckland 0632, New Zealand
(a division of Pearson New Zealand Ltd)
Penguin Books (South Africa) (Pty) Ltd, 24 Sturdee Avenue,
Rosebank, Johannesburg 2196, South Africa
Penguin Books Ltd, Registered Offices: 80 Strand, London WC2R 0RL, England

www.penguin.com

First published 2011
I

Copyright © Paul Howard, 2011
Illustrations copyright © Alan Clarke, 2011

The moral right of the author and illustrator has been asserted

Penguin Ireland thanks O'Brien Press for its agreement to Penguin Ireland
using the same design approach and typography, and the same artist,
as O'Brien Press used in the first four Ross O'Carroll-Kelly titles

Grateful acknowledgement is made for permission to quote from 'Summer in Dublin',
words and music by Liam Reilly / (P) Bardis Music Co. Ltd © 1979

Set in 12/14.75pt Dante
Typeset by Palimpsest Book Production Limited,
Falkirk, Stirlingshire
Printed in Great Britain by Clays Ltd, St Ives plc

A CIP catalogue record for this book is available from the British Library

ISBN 978–1–844–88226–7

www.greenpenguin.co.uk

Contents

Prologue   vii

1. We are where we are   I
2. Pack of bankers   35
3. Are you trying to seduce me, Mrs Rathfriland?   75
4. Darkness falls over Ticknock   III
5. Goin' courtin'   151
6. Dead man walken   193
7. The getaway package   231
8. Where there's a will . . .   270
9. The Battle of the Boyne II   312
10. 2G2BT   355

Epilogue   396
Acknowledgements   399

Prologue

The snow is coming down out there like I don't *know* what? And we're all freezing our nuts off in the church here. I'll say this for the old fart – he picked some time of the year to die.

Erika is in ribbons, we're talking literally bawling. Which is weird, in a way. I don't want to come across as, like, horsh, but she didn't actually *know* him that long? Except maybe that *is* horsh. She's got regrets, I suppose. Same as we've all got regrets.

I hand her a tissue from the wad she asked me to stick in my pocket. She dabs at her eyes where the mascara is spilling out, then she looks at me sort of, like, side-on and asks me if her face is okay and I tell her it's fine, roysh, even though it actually looks like a focking tanker disaster.

'If you need to step out,' I go. 'You know – if you're upset and blah blah blah . . .' but she just shakes her head, determined, like everyone else, to just get through it.

The thing I can't stop staring at is the actual coffin. It just seems so, I don't know, *small?* So then I stort having one of my famous deep thoughts, about how it doesn't matter how big any of us is in, like, life – our bodies, personalities, whatever – we're all going to end up in a box pretty much that size.

'Ross,' Erika goes, then I suddenly snap out of it and realize that the organ music has stopped and I'm the only one still standing. So I sit down.

There's, like, a whole line of people waiting to step up to the, I suppose, pulpit to pay tribute to him.

One dude goes, 'The Horseshoe Bar on Christmas Eve will never be the same again without his highly vocal drunkenness,' and of course everyone laughs, 'and his hysterical jeremiads on subjects as diverse as the saintliness of Michael Fingleton, the unsightliness of modern kick-and-rush rugby, the folly of energy-efficient lightbulbs and the national scandal that was the failure to exempt a seasonal *Romeo y Julieta* from the smoking ban.'

There's, like, more laughter.

The next speaker – who, again, I don't know – goes, 'He wouldn't have claimed to be the perfect husband and he wouldn't have claimed to be the perfect father,' and I suddenly feel Erika's hand tighten in mine. 'He could be terribly self-absorbed. Terribly opinionated, as we've heard. But he was what he was. A man. One with an enormous capacity for life, for love, for happiness. But human, with human failings. But who among us, gathered here this morning, can say we loved him any less for those?'

When they've finished, no one knows whether to clap or not. It's, like, *awkward*? In the end, some do, some don't. The priest mentions the name of the cemetery where he'll be laid to rest but I don't catch it. He says the family would like to thank everyone for the wonderful kindness they've been shown since their loss and extend an invitation to everyone to come back to the house afterwards for basically refreshments.

Then a tenor appears at the top of the church and while the coffin is carried down the aisle, he sings what was his favourite song, the one he asked for in his will.

I remember that summer in Dublin,
And the Liffey as it stank like hell,
And the young people walking on Grafton Street,
Everyone looking so well.
I was singing a song I heard somewhere,
Called 'Rock and Roll Never Forgets',
When my humming was smothered by a 46A,
And the scream of a low-flying jet.
So I jumped on a bus to Dun Laoghaire,
Stopping off to pick up my guitar,
And a drunk on the bus told me how to get rich,
I was glad we weren't going too far.

I know the song but it's, like, so random to hear it *sung* like that?

Erika peels out of her seat like she's determined to be the first out of the church. She *is* actually the first. When I manage to get to the corpork – twice nearly slipping on my orse – she's already sat in the cor, staring at nothing. She doesn't say a word during the drive to the cemetery, except when we drive through the actual gates. That's when she goes, 'I wish we'd had more time.'

'More time?' I go. 'Time for what?' except she doesn't answer.

Father Fehily used to tell us not to waste our lives away thinking about all the things we might have done but didn't. 'What *did* you do?' he'd say. 'Is *that* not the point of life? Is that not the *only* point?'

But then I feel like I've suddenly burst her bubble, so I end up going, 'He loved you,' I suppose for the want of something else to say.

She's there, '*I* don't know that he did. And *you* certainly don't,' and what can I say to that? I couldn't exactly claim that I knew him.

We get out of the cor. The path is like a basic icerink and I link her orm to stop either of us slipping. We ask this, I presume, gravedigger for, like, directions. We end up being the first there. There's, like, a hole in the ground and a big mound of earth beside it. I look at Erika, to see if she's okay, but she's got this look of what you'd have to call determination on her face. That'd be the Mount Anville thing again. There's a reason they've won . . . well, *all* they've won.

The headstone's already been engraved. It's like, '12 March 1940 – 31 December 2009 – Toddy Rathfriland', and that's the first time I cop that it happened on, like, New Year's Eve. A time for taking stock – is that the expression?

There's, like, a quote underneath from, I don't know, Shakespeare or one of that crew and it's like, 'Food to one man is but bitter poison to another', which is, like, seriously dark, it has to be said.

On the news they said it was a legally held shotgun. He supposedly put both barrels in his mouth before pulling the trigger and there was literally nothing left of him above the shoulders. But then you don't know if that's, like, horseshit.

He supposedly left a note for his wife, apologizing for everything – for doing the dirt, basically – but nothing for Erika, who he, like, supposedly *loved*? At least that's what he said that night in the Galloping Green and I heard it with my own ears – asking her to run away with him.

So I go, 'Maybe we shouldn't be here when the actual hearse arrives. Should we maybe watch it from, like, a safe distance?' a not unreasonable thing to say, I would have thought, given the circs. Except she looks at me like I'm a cat in a focking food blender. I'm like, 'All I'm saying is that sitting at the back of the church is one thing. But you do not want to be here when the old grieving fam shows up.'

She doesn't even bother responding – like it's *beneath* her? – and I'm there thinking, yeah, where's your actual boyfriend? At least *I'm* here – came running as soon as I got the call, when Fionn decided he wasn't focking man enough to handle seeing her at her ex's funeral. I said she was way out of his league and, not for the first time in my life, I've been proven spectacularly right, even though it gives me very little pleasure to say it.

She takes a couple of steps forward, then drops the rose into the hole in the ground. I don't know if I've already mentioned that she actually *looks* really well? Black always suited her. I'm on the record as saying that.

She stands there with, like, her head bowed, staring into the empty grave and I wonder what kind of thoughts are going through her mind. There'd be, like, a fair bit of guilt, you'd have to think. The shit she said to him. Just as an example, that she was only ever interested in him for the moo and that having sex with him was like being trapped under rubble with no hope of the Red Cross coming. Again, I heard all of this, the night he tried to get her to come away with him to Val-d'Isère.

The dude knew what he was doing, wanting to hop on a plane and fock off out of the country. He's supposed to have lost a fortune in Anglo shares and it's a well-known fact that his restaurant business – he had, like, fifteen or sixteen of them at the height of the whole Celtic Tiger thing? – was pretty much focked.

In the end, though, it's like my old man and Helen and Hennessy and everyone else has tried to tell her – he had, like, loads of reasons to want to actually kill himself. See, I heard a thing on the news – it was the day they found his body, in his cor on Bissets Strand – that the whole current economic thing is thought to be responsible for up to ten suicides every week in Ireland. But I suppose Erika is always going to wonder was it something she basically said.

I hear a cor approach, then the crunch of gravel, then voices coming closer.

'Erika,' I go, 'I really think we should make like shepherds and get the flock out of here. Either that or watch it from behind one of those trees over there,' and she looks at me like she's realized that I'm actually talking sense for once in my crazy life.

But it's suddenly too late.

There's a girl – eighteen, maybe nineteen, and an absolute ringer for Summer Glau – and she's, like, walking towards us at speed. And from the look on her boat, she's definitely not happy in her nappy.

'It *is* her,' she goes. 'I focking said it was her,' and there's, like, four or five people I recognize from the church following her, trying to calm her down, except having to run to match her stride.

Erika seems a bit, I don't know, in shock – like a rabbit about to take a bull-bar full in the face.

'Hedda,' they're all giving it, 'this isn't the time *or* the place,' and then I remember hearing that Toddy and his wife had a daughter – late in life, as well. He must have been in, like, his fifties?

She walks straight up to Erika and hits her *the* most unbelievable slap across the boat – even the sound of it is like the perfect focking tee shot.

Of course I'm immediately between the two of them, going, 'Okay, that's *one* – some would say you're entitled to it – but that's it. You heard them. It's hordly the time *or* the place.'

The rest of the, I suppose you'd call them, mourners arrive and stort to gather around us.

Hedda – it's *such* a random name – just looks me up and down like I'm a big sack of nothing. 'Oh my God,' she goes, 'don't tell me *you're* the latest.'

I'm like, 'Hey, we're actually brother and sister. Although I don't think either of us would deny there was a definite attraction there before we found out that fact.'

There's a few shocked faces at that one, it has to be said, as if no one here has anything better to do than stand around judging *me*. In the distance, I can see the pallbearer dudes lifting the coffin out of the back of the hearse. 'Let's not forget,' I go, nodding in their general postcode, 'that this is *supposed* to be an actual funeral?'

Erika, if you can believe this, is pretty much hiding behind me, using my body as a human shield to keep this girl beyond reach. That's when this woman steps forward and lays, like, a hand on Hedda's shoulder. I straight away recognize her from her photograph in the paper – Regina Rathfriland, in other words, the grieving widow.

She's obviously a few years younger than Toddy – think maybe Catherine Deneuve.

She says something to her daughter, which I don't quite catch, but Hedda is not going to be – I think it's a word – *dissuaded*? She's got shit to say and she's going to say it. It's me she actually aims it at.

'Your sister is an actual whore,' she goes, practically spitting out the words.

I stick my bottom lip out and pull a face, as if to say, 'Okay, that's an opinion,' my intention being to try to keep the peace here.

'Don't call her that,' I suddenly hear this voice – a man's voice – behind me go. I spin around, roysh, and who is it – speak of the devil – only Fionn McFocking Spectagoggles himself, suddenly determined to be the hero of the hour.

'Erika,' he just goes, 'I'm sorry.'

This is in response to the major borney they had last night over him refusing to come today. The old Erika, I don't need to tell you, would send him on his way with a couple of achers. Except this time she doesn't. She practically swoons into his orms, then *he* goes, 'Come on, let's get out of here,' and he – get this – leads her off, leaving me there on my Tobler, surrounded by all these angry friends and rellys.

And weirdly, it's, like, *I'm* suddenly their focus?

'He was happy until *she* came into his life,' someone goes. Then someone else is there, '*She* killed him – that's the fact of the matter.'

Which is bang out of order, even though she's already out of earshot. And I suppose it's in response to that, roysh, that I end up going, 'Hey, it takes two to tango,' and suddenly, roysh, everyone is immediately on my case.

'I beg your pardon,' it's Hedda – the daughter – who goes.

I just, like, shrug my shoulders.

'Yeah,' people are suddenly shouting at me. 'What *do* you mean by that?'

In the background, I can hear an engine storting up – Fionn's Honda Accord, from the sound of it – then disappearing down the road, leaving me to face this hostile crowd alone. It's nothing new for me, of course.

'I'm just saying,' I go, 'there was a pair of them in it.'

'He was going through a hard time with the business,' Hedda tries to go. 'And she took advantage of that.'

I actually laugh. I'm there, 'Took advantage? I'm sorry, no offence, but I'd say your old man couldn't believe his luck.'

There's, like, a collective intake of breath. Which is understandable, I suppose. They haven't put him in the ground yet. I look at the widow, Regina, wiping away fresh tears and I feel instantly bad.

'Look,' I go, 'all I'm saying, I suppose, is that it's easy to blame Erika for everything. But Toddy was no saint.'

Hedda makes a sudden lunge for me with her focking claws primed but her mother holds her back.

'You bastard,' Hedda goes – top of her voice.

'Hey,' I go, not knowing, as usual, when to shut the fock up, 'you didn't hear him that night in the Galloping Green. He said he'd his private jet at Dublin Airport – they could go anywhere in the world she wanted. She's the one who said no dice.'

'You're a liar,' Hedda practically screams.

'Hey, that's the only reason he went back to your mother.'

Some huge dude steps forward then – think of a Subaru Forester in a black Members Only jacket – and, without saying a single word, he punches me full in the face.

It honestly feels like I've run head-first into a train.

For a second, roysh, I'm just, like, stunned. Then I feel myself suddenly falling backwards, like I'm falling through space. I seem to be falling forever. It's only about ten seconds after I hit the ground with a thud that I realize that I've fallen backwards into the grave.

'The bastard,' I hear someone go and somehow I know it's the dude who decked me.

I'm, like, lying there, looking up at this hole in the sky, with twenty or thirty angry faces just staring down at me.

Someone storts kicking earth down on top of me.

'Let's just bury him,' I hear – I'm pretty sure – Hedda go. 'I doubt if anyone will miss him.'

1. We are where we are

So I'm in the old Hilary Swank, making a lodgement. You'd be surprised at the number of people availing of a confidential document-shredding service who insist on paying in cash. Or maybe you wouldn't. Maybe that's the point.

'How was your Christmas?' the bird behind the glass goes.

If I had to say she was a ringer for anyone, I'd say Jessica Michibata.

I'm like, 'Quiet,' because that's what you stort to say, isn't it, when you find yourself reaching the age of maturity. 'I was shit-faced from Christmas Eve until about three days after Stephen's Day. We've got to keep the old traditions alive, that's what I say.'

She flashes her veneers at me. A fake smile. She's big-time into herself, this bird – you can see it. One of those girls who thinks Michael Bublé just hasn't met her yet. Which is, like, an immediate challenge to me, of course.

'What about yourself?' I go, pretending to read her name badge while checking out the sweater meat. 'Er . . . Aithne?'

She's there, 'Quiet, like yours,' then she picks up my wad and storts counting off the fifties.

'Sounds like we could *both* do with some excitement in our lives,' I go, at the same time giving her a big, filthy wink.

She's seriously gumming for me. I can tell because she suddenly storts actually *mouthing* the numbers to stop herself losing the count?

I'm just on the point of asking her whether or not she's ever eaten in Bentley's when all of a sudden it happens. And by *it*, I mean she grabs one of my fifties from the top of the pile and just, like, holds it up to the *light*?

I'm just there, 'Whoa, whoa, whoa – what do you think you're even doing?'

'I'm sorry,' she just goes, 'there were a lot counterfeit notes in circulation over Christmas and New Year.'

I'm like, 'Er, how is that any of *my* beeswax?'

'Well, obviously, we can't be *too* careful.'

I suppose it's that line that pushes me over the actual edge.

'Can't be too careful? Hello? The focking mess that your crowd have made of this supposed country.' To be honest, I haven't a clue what I'm talking about – just parroting the kind of shit that everyone's saying. 'Er, I think if anyone's entitled to have trust issues, they're going to be standing on *this* side of the counter, don't you?'

That's when I hear what would have to be described as a small smattering of applause behind me. 'Quite right,' this old dude in a flat cap goes. There's two or three others nodding in agreement as well. 'Our taxes are going up to bail out this useless shower of cowboys – and they're throwing people out on the street for not being able to pay their mortgages. You give her hell, son.'

I wouldn't have ever seen myself as, like, a champion of – I don't know – consumer rights, but, as everyone knows, I've always been a sucker for the roar of the crowd. So, loving an audience, I turn back to Aithne and go, 'Look, you're a really, really good-looking girl – no issues there. But if you hold another one of those notes up to check it, I'm closing my focking account.'

That seriously shocks her. Her mouth is suddenly flapping open like she's bobbing for apples. It's like, oh yeah, she had all the confidence in the world thirty seconds ago – letting *me* do all the heavy spadework – but now she's looking over her shoulder for her supervisor, who suddenly arrives over.

'What seems to be the problem?' she goes. *She's* not even worth describing, other than to say that she's a seriously heavy battery.

I'm there, 'The problem? The problem is me being treated like a common focking criminal by – of all things – a bank.'

'They've got away with murder,' someone behind me goes. 'If only the Government had the balls that this fella has.'

I love any kind of boost to my confidence.

Aithne's there, 'He's lodging thirteen hundred euros, most of it in fifties. I was checking them like you told me to.'

The supervisor looks at me then – again, the fake smile, like a monkey eating shit out of a light socket. 'Sir, there *were* a lot of counterfeit notes in circulation over Christmas and New Year.'

'So I've been told.'

'Well, that's why we have to check every note that . . .'

I just, like, raise my hand, roysh, to cut her off. 'Look, I don't know what your name is. I'm not interested. All I'm saying is, I'm a customer of this bank and I'm not prepared to be treated like a basic crook, recession or no recession. And I'm telling you now, if you insist on checking whether those notes are real, Shred Focking Everything will be doing its banking elsewhere.'

'That'll soften their cough,' I hear the dude in the flat cap go.

There's, like, a stand-off then. She knows I'm serious. She also knows, I presume, that she's dealing with one of the few companies in, I suppose, Ireland that's still in the serious black. She looks at Aithne, roysh, then just nods, as if to say, look, whatever, he's right, he *is* holding all the cords.

I end up walking out of the bank with shouts of 'Well done!' and 'You could teach Brian Cowen a thing or two about how to treat these bastards' ringing in my ears.

To be honest with you, I'm not even a hundred percent sure what just happened, but I walk out of there, it has to be said, with a definite spring in my step.

He's got a cigor wedged between his teeth that's big enough for Victor Costello to pilot. Of course I end up having a total shit-fit when I cop it. 'You're unbelievable,' I go, leaning against the door – the door of his ward in, like, Vincent's Private. 'Er, do you remember *anything* the doctor said?'

He's delighted to see me, in fairness to him. Sits up in the bed. Gives it, 'Hello there, Kicker!' and all the rest of it. Then he whips the thing out of his mouth and storts, like, examining the other end of it. 'Oh, this? No, I shan't be lighting it, Ross. Good God, no. No, this is what we veterans of heart bypass surgery like to call a *placebo*.'

'Er, *excuse* me?'

'Well, I pop it in my mouth – like so. Or I hold it between my index and middle fingers – like so. Or sometimes I just run my nose along the outer leaf. *Vegas Finas de Primera*, as they're wont to say in Havana. Allows me to elicit at least some pleasure from it. Without any of the dangers, of course.'

'Well,' I go, 'all I'm saying is exactly what the doctor said – you've had your warning.'

I hear a voice behind me go, 'Hello, Ross!' It's, like, Helen.

'Seems he's worried about his *old dad,*' he goes to her.

I'm like, 'Don't go patting yourself on the back. I didn't actually say I was worried.'

Helen gives me an amazing hug. She was always a huge fan of mine. 'There's nothing to worry about,' she goes. 'He's on the mend.'

The old man's there, 'And it's not just Helen saying it either, Ross. It also happens to be the considered medical opinion of Mr Joel Vaszary, Consultant in Cardiothoracic Surgery, AKA the bloody miracle-worker who saved my life. You know he plays off a handicap of three, Helen?'

She's like, 'Three?' and she looks impressed. I know she golfs herself.

'Three!' *he* goes. 'There was even talk of he and I *playing* nine holes,' then he looks at her – sheepishly, it could be said – for a reaction.

She shakes her head. 'Charles, they had to open up your sternum to get to your heart. It'll be months before it's properly healed. Joel explained *all* of this to you – there'll be no golf until at least the end of the summer.'

I go to get Helen a chair.

'That's right,' the old man goes. 'And that's when the *real* work begins, of course – to try to reconstruct my swing. He did say, though, that in the meantime, there's no harm in a bit of – inverted commas – pitch and putt. Although heaven knows what the famous Hennessy will have to say about that. Working-class golf is what he calls it. Well, you know what he's like for the banter and the raillery and friendly badinage. Might need to keep it from him . . . Ross, you're limping!'

I go, 'Yeah, whatever,' just trying to, like, play it down.

'What happened?' it's Helen who goes. Again, she's actually *genuine*?

This might *sound* bad but I like her way more than my *actual* mother, although that's not saying much, considering that my *actual* mother is a bet-down, sex-storved whelk and a disgrace to the human race.

'I fell into an open grave,' I go. 'It's not a major deal,' and the two of them just look at each other like they wouldn't even know *how* to respond to a line like that? 'I've got, like, a bruised tailbone. I'm not going to go into the ins and outs of it, except to say that Erika walked off and left me in a basic jocker – her supposed brother.'

Neither of them asks what we were doing in an actual graveyord,

4

although they must know about Toddy topping himself. Half the country's talking about it and the funeral was on the actual news. There's, like, an awkward silence, then it's the old man who moves the conversation along.

'Well,' he goes, 'I think I can speak for both Helen and I when I say that we're very much thrilled with the choices that Erika's been making of late.'

I laugh. I'm there, 'I presume you're talking about Fionn.'

Helen smiles, I think the word is, like, *fondly?* 'Oh, he's so good for her,' she goes. 'I know she hasn't always made the best decisions when it comes to men. But I've seen such a huge change in her since she started going out with him.'

'Well,' I go, 'I still say *he's* heading for a major kick in the genitals. And that's no offence to Erika. The opposite, in fact. I'm just saying *he's* punching well above his weight. In some ways it'll serve him right – and I'm saying that as one of his best mates.'

'Well, speaking of mates,' the old man goes, 'I was reading about poor old Bernard McNamara's travails in this morning's *Times*. One point five billion in debt, if the old lady of what's-it is to be believed. I nearly threw a few quid into the Irish Glass Bottle site myself – except I listened to Hennessy's wiser counsel. The Ultimate City Seaside Development indeed! Poor old Bernard, though. That wonderful house on Ailesbury Road.'

I get this sudden memory of the old man in the hospital in Monte Corlo, lying there in the bed, unconscious, his face the colour of pretty much porridge, his head turned away from me, at an angle, his mouth slung open, sucking in the air like it was a major effort. Every breath – I swear to fock – I thought was going to be his last. And all I kept thinking about were all the things I said to him over the years and all the things I didn't say to him. And the weird thing was that – like Erika at Toddy's funeral – the shit I didn't say seemed so much worse than the shit I actually did.

'Of course,' he goes, 'Bernard's not the only one in trouble. The rate at which it all unravelled – it took more than a few of the chaps by surprise. Look at your old friend and mine, old Dunner. And poor Sean Quinn. Terrible, terrible business. Still, at least we have NAMA now, to help the victims of this thing.'

This is probably, like, a totally random thing to say, but I think I pretty much matured ten years in the month I spent out there by his bedside, watching him improve, then disimprove, wavering on the edge. Watching the weight just fall off him. Watching him struggle to find the breath to tell me that, well, at least he lived long enough to see Frank O'Driscoll's young chap lift the RBS Six Nations trophy.

There was another night he squeezed my hand really tight – it was a genuine shock that he still had that amount of strength in him – and went, 'I shouted some things at Declan Kidney, Ross . . . It was on Morehampton Road one day – just after he walked out on Leinster. I was never certain if he knew it was me . . . If you see him, Ross, tell him I was wrong . . .'

I feel, I don't know, lucky to still have him here. Like *I've* been given a second chance as well as him. And utter embarrassment that he is a lot of the time, if the worst *had* happened, I don't know what I'd . . .

'Now,' he goes, 'you can take that sorrowful look off your face this instant. I know what you're thinking.'

'What?'

'Why all this talk of economic doom – to say nothing of gloom!'

'I wasn't thinking that at all.'

'Just don't let it get you down, Kicker – this current economic what-are-you-having. No, if I may be permitted, just for a moment, to draw an analogy between my own situation and that of this country, what Ireland needs to do now is to change its lifestyle. Live more – yes, I'll say the word – *frugally*. Cut back on the *pâté de canard* and the Romanée Conti. Get out and about more. Breathe. Like me, Ross, it'll emerge leaner, healthier and wiser for the experience.'

'I suppose.'

'No suppose about it. The signs of recovery are already there. Did you hear what Brian Lenihan said yesterday? The worst is over!'

Helen sort of, like, laughs. She'd be pretty up on current affairs, see. 'I'm not sure I believe that, Charles.'

'Well,' he goes, 'if Brian Lenihan said it, then it's good enough for me. He's the man looking at the figures, remember. I know that I, for one, breathed an enormous sigh of relief when he said it. I trust the markets will do likewise.'

'I was in the Merrion Shopping Centre,' I go, mainly for the want of something to say. 'I saw the shop. It was, like, *weird* seeing it all closed up?'

See, that cheesemongers *was* their pride and joy. You could go further and say that it was their dream, from when they first knew each other, back in the – I suppose – sixties. It was only open, what, a year? I'm looking at *him* for a reaction.

'Well,' he just goes, 'I'm afraid that people are going to have to look elsewhere for their Idiazabal, their Langres and their Knockdrinna Snow. Yes, our erstwhile jousting partners in Sheridan's of South Anne Street can have the field to themselves now. And good luck to them – eh, Darling?'

Helen's there, 'Good luck to them is right.'

'You don't seem sad,' I go. 'Either of you.'

'What have we to be sad about?' *he* just goes. 'I thought that was it, Ross. Thought my number was well and truly up. It was how my own father went, remember. You know, when I was lying there, outside the casino, on the road where I fell . . .'

'Don't,' I hear myself go. 'Seriously, don't.'

'I was thinking, This can't be it. *Can't* be. Well, it's so soon. So bloody soon . . .'

You can see him, roysh, getting a bit upset himself, so Helen just, like, holds his hand. She's amazing. 'But you *didn't* die,' she goes, 'you silly great lump. And now you're well on the road to recovery.'

'Like Ireland, eh?'

'If you say so. Just try to stop reliving it.'

'I'm only reliving it,' he goes, 'because I want to make sure I remain grateful for every day I'm alive. My still being here . . . well, it's a gift I've been given and I'm going to treasure it. And anyway, it's well I can afford to retire, with my son and heir at the helm of the shredding business. Erika tells me you've been working all hours.'

I just shake my head. 'Don't get me storted. I put in, like, four days last week. Pretty much full days as well.'

'Four full days!' he goes. 'Did you hear that, Helen? Of wage-bearing work! Oh, that's one in the eye for the doomsayers who say we should write the country off as a bad job and invite the bloody IMF in to tell us what's what! He's a go-getter and no mistake! I knew I needn't have worried. I said it to Hennessy – didn't I, Darling? – I said, "The boy is ready to assume the mantle. I can kick back now and enjoy my retirement, watching him make a thundering success of the business." Naturally, we hoped Erika might take over the helm of Cheeses Merrion Joseph . . .'

I actually laugh at that. 'Sorry, the idea of Erika running an actual cheesemongers. The idea of Erika doing any actual work at all. No offence, Helen.'

Helen just smiles. She obviously knows what I'm talking about. The girl's always been better at spending money than actually earning it.

'Although,' I go, 'she might end up *having* to work? I mean, Fionn's hordly going to keep her in the style to which she's accustomed. A focking schoolteacher – albeit in the Institute.'

See, the more you think about it, the more ridiculous it seems. I'm just going to make sure I'm there when she eventually red-cords him, firstly to laugh in his face, then to help the poor focker pick up the pieces. Because he's one smitten kitten.

The old man – big, major ceremony, of course – goes, 'Ross, I have a gift for you.'

I'm like, 'A what?'

'Well, it's your birthday tomorrow – and don't think it's escaped my attention that it's a significant one. The big three-oh, what? Now, I must apologize, Ross, that due to circumstances, etcetera, etcetera, Helen and I haven't been able to buy you something, as such.'

'I told you – a cheque would have done.'

'Well, I've got something here for you that I hope is better than that.' He reaches down into his bedside locker, groaning with the pain. They said his ribs and chest are going to hurt for a while.

Helen goes, 'Charles, let me do that.'

He's like, 'No, no, I've got it,' and he pulls out this basically folder, which is bursting with, like, sheets of paper. 'Here you are,' he goes, handing it to me. 'Happy birthday, Kicker.'

I'm like, 'What's this?'

He laughs. 'It's the company, Ross.'

'What?'

'That's right. I think you're finally ready. You're about to enter a new decade of your life. And I think I can safely say, on the evidence of the past few weeks, that you've become a man at last. And it makes me very proud to tell you that you are now the chief executive and sole shareholder of Ireland's newest and fastest-growing document dis-posal service, Shred Focking Everything.'

I'm literally speechless.

He turns to Helen. 'Look at his face, all lit up there! You mark my words, Helen, the chap's already thinking about expansion – the views of these know-it-all economists, go hang!'

What I'm *actually* thinking – if I'm being honest – is how much could I flog it for in the morning and how many years could I live off the proceeds.

He goes, 'You have orders there, Ross, coming out of your ears. Like I said at my trial, that economic miracle of which we were all so proud – it didn't come about without a whole bunch of people doing a whole lot of things that they'd prefer stayed out of the public domain. This is your moment, Ross. Your time to shine. And I can spend my retirement staring happily at cloud formations, content in the know-ledge that Shred Focking Everything is in safe hands. The company, well, I know right now it's only a van, a mobile phone and a shredding machine, but in a year's time – given your undoubted skill and busi-ness acumen – you mark my words, it'll be worth literally millions.'

Literally millions? So what can I say, except, 'Er, whatever. Thanks.'

He's waiting, like he said he would be, outside Dr Quirkey's Goodtime Emporium and I can tell, even from a hundred yords away, that some-thing's up.

You *could* call it a father's instinct.

I'm like, 'Hey, Ro,' the hand primed for the old five in the sky, even *though* it's O'Connell Street. He gives me some skin, except he does it without any real, I suppose, *feeling*?

'Alreet, Rosser,' he just goes. He doesn't even wish me a happy birth-day, even though it's today. 'How's tricks?'

'I'm actually in cracking form,' I go. Except something is definitely eating him, because two cops pass by and he doesn't make an oinking sound under his breath, or even go 'A.C.A.B.' like he usually would.

I decide not to grill him, though. Giving your kids the heavy parent routine, I'm on the record as saying, is like wrestling with a hog – no one learns anything and all you do is make a mess. My attitude is that he'll tell me what's on his mind in his own sweet time.

'Are you still off the cigarettes?' I go.

See, he was actually scared off them when the old man had his hort attack. It's one of the few times in his life that I've seen Ro genuinely frightened. He honestly loves his granddad. He slept in the hospital waiting room the night of the operation. I had to carry him out of there the following night – fast asleep in my orms – and drive him home to his mother.

Now I'm thinking, yeah, whatever he *is* going through, it might be nothing more serious than nicotine withdrawal.

He goes, 'Still off them, yeah.'

'And how's that working out for you?'

He pulls a face. 'Ah, Ine fooken gutten, man.'

I give him one of my famous understanding looks. 'Look, do you want me to buy you some baccy? A pouch of your usual. Moore Street's only around the corner.'

He shakes his head. 'Nah, it's a doorty habit, Rosser.'

'Well, that's one way of looking at it. Another is that it's given your voice that gravelly edge – which is a major port of your image, don't forget,' but he doesn't answer, roysh, so I just let it rest.

We're heading for the Sinn Féin shop in Pornell Square, if you can believe that. I promised to buy him a Fenians Silver Signet Ring as a belated Christmas present. He's been banging on about having one for ages, although suddenly he doesn't seem as excited about it as he *originally* was?

'So,' I go, switching the play, coming in from a different angle, 'how's school?'

Notice how I phrased that? 'How's school?' instead of 'Why the fock aren't you there, by the way?'

That's when he suddenly stops, at the pedestrian crossing opposite the Ambassador, and I watch his little eyes fill up with tears.

'Hey,' I go, putting my orm around his shoulder, 'what's all this about, Tough Guy?' hoping to God he's not going to say he wants to leave Castlerock – what, two days after I shelled out seven Ks for him for the new term?

'It's Bla,' he goes, meaning Blathin – in other words his ex? I was actually happy when he finished it with her. Much as I liked her, he was way too young to be settling into something.

'What about her, Ro? Jesus Christ, you're not back with her, are you?'

'No,' he goes.

'Well, that's something at least.'

'She's arthur telling everyone in Mount Anville about me, but.'

'Telling them *what* exactly?'

'That Ine a bastord to women.'

I laugh – I *have* to? – because he's still at that age where he thinks that's an actual bad thing. I'm like, 'Okay, first of all, how do you know all of this?'

'Because we're doing a musical with them this year – the audishiddens were yesterday.'

'Auditions! Oh my God, that brings me back. What musical is it, by the way?'

'What?'

'As in, which one?'

'*Seven Berrides for Seven Berutters.*'

I end up just shaking my head. 'That's the exact same one *we* did. Did you get a port, by the way?'

'Yeah – Adam.'

I'm there, 'Adam?' literally unable to believe my own ears. 'Oh my God, this is, like, history repeating itself. Whoa, hang on, Blathin's not playing the actual main bride, is she?'

'No.'

'As in, you don't have to throw the lips on her, do you?'

'No, she's the director, Rosser.'

'The director?'

I'm thinking, Clonskeagh? Old man's a doctor? Yeah, she's the definite type. She's heading for Theatre Studies just as surely as we're on the wrong side of the river.

I'm like, 'So, what, presumably she's spreading the poison among the rest of the cast?'

He nods. 'She told them I broke it off with her cos she was in a wheelchayer.'

'Jesus, what a bitch – and that's not me being anti the whole disabled thing.'

'So everyone was pointing at me, Rosser, whispering.'

'Whispering? What kind of shit?'

'Just, you know, stay away from *him* – that type of a thing. Thee all hate me, Rosser,' and that's when the tears really stort to come. 'Thee all hate me, so thee do.'

The pedestrian lights turn green but I think, fock it, let it go. I put my hands on his two shoulders and I crouch down to his level. 'Ro,' I go, 'I'm obviously biased, but how could anyone in their right mind hate you?'

'Thee do, but.'

'They don't. You've got yourself a reputation, that's all. Already! At *your* age! Do you know how long it took me to get mine?'

'I don't want a reputation, but.'

I smile at him. It's, like, the innocence of youth.

I'm like, 'Look, Ro, I think I may have mentioned to you once or twice how focking embarrassing it is to have a kid who's already, like, five times more intelligent than I'll ever be. I mean, you're, what, two IQ points away from being considered officially gifted? There's literally nothing that I can teach you. Except maybe this stuff – relationships and women and blah, blah, blah.'

He nods his little head. Poor kid.

'I told you, didn't I? If it's, like, facts and figures – sums, dates, all that shit – you go to see your teachers. If it's *this* kind of thing? – you might even say affairs of the hort – you come to me.'

'I'm *coming* to you now, Rosser.'

'And I'm going to help you. Okay, first things first. You say that all these girls, like, *hate* you? Well, what you have to learn, Ro, when it comes to the old deadlier of the species, is that love and hate are just two sides of the same agenda.'

He nods, this time, I suppose you'd have to say, *thoughtfully*? See, this is me in my element, playing to my actual strengths.

'Look, take it from me,' I go. 'Yesterday, I was in the bank, where I reduced the bird behind the counter to literally tears. What I'll do now is, I'll give her a few days, maybe a week, then I'll ring her up and offer to take her out to dinner to apologize. By next weekend – you mork my words – I'll be bouncing her about the aportment, with her screaming her *attaboys* loud enough to wake the focking dead in Deansgrange.'

He still looks Scoobious, so I flash my phone at him. 'Do you want to *see* the kind of names I've got in here on speed dial?'

'No,' he goes. 'You've shown me loads of times, Rosser.'

'That's good. Because it proves I know what I'm talking about. What girls love more than anything, I can tell you from previous experience, is a whiff of danger, especially the daughters of the old Society of the Sacred Hort. And you have that whiff, Ro. Thanks to Blathin, you *have* that whiff.'

He nods. I give him a big smile, because I've suddenly thought of something. 'Actually,' I go, 'do you know what *I* did when I played Adam?'

'What?'

'Okay, I'm not shitting you, because this is actually how I got my rep in the first place. I ended up being with all seven brides.'

He's like, 'What?' and you can tell straight away, roysh, that he's seriously impressed.

'Yeah,' I go, 'all seven. In horseracing, it's called going through the cord. And of course every single one of them . . .' and I make the little – you'd have to say – punctuation morks with my fingers, '*hated* me.'

He suddenly smiles and I instantly feel like the best father in the world, although obviously that's for other people to say.

'Come on,' I go, 'let's get you this IRA ring before the shop closes.'

Oisinn says he can't believe the ad he heard on the radio this morning. Super Valu are offering a family meal – we're talking meat, we're talking potatoes, we're talking *even* veg – for seven focking euros. We all agree that it's a disgrace but what can you do? But *he* just shakes his head. He says that two years ago Aer Lingus were doing direct daily flights from Dublin to Dubai and that he can't believe that *this* is the country he's come back to.

'I feel like Charlton Heston in *Planet of the Apes*,' he goes. '*You finally did it! You maniacs!*' and then JP joins in, the two of them at the top of their voices – this is in the middle of Krystle, by the way – going, '*You blew it up! God damn you! God damn you all to hell!*'

Everyone laughs, but I feel actually bad, being the one who persuaded him to come back to face the muesli – to face the seventy-however-many million he owes to the banks. I mean, he's right. Seven yoyos for a dinner for four. A couple of years ago, you'd have dropped that in the bucket of whatever focking GAA club was packing your shopping.

'Hey,' Oisinn suddenly goes, turning to me, like he wants a private word, 'you can take that look off your face, Dude.'

I'm like, 'What look?' but we've been mates for too long for me to even *think* about trying to shit him. 'Okay, I'm just worried that you're going to, like, split again. Do another Park and Hide. And that this time I might not be *able* to find you?'

He laughs, then he gets suddenly serious. He's wearing a humungous black afro wig, red-tinted shades and a zebra-skin suit. 'I'm not going anywhere,' he just goes. 'This is where I belong, Ross,' meaning, presumably, the *whole* of South Dublin, rather than just Horcourt Street.

The theme of the porty, I should have mentioned, is pimps and hos.

I'm there, 'That sounds very much like fighting talk to me.'

We're both having to shout to be heard over the sound of the music, in other words Katy Perry.

'I don't know about fighting talk, Ross. I'm prepared to face it, though – whatever *it* is.'

'Dude, don't give me that. The word on the grapevine is you've got Hennessy Coghlan-O'Hara on your case. End of discussion.'

'Well, not exactly. I mean, all he's done is set up a meeting between me and my creditors.'

I'm there, 'Er, *how* many penalty points has he managed to get – I don't know – expunged for us down through the years?'

'This isn't doing a hundred and twenty Ks on the Rock Road, Ross.'

'I know, it's seventy-something million snots.'

He smiles. 'And the rest.'

'Well, I for one have faith in that focker.'

'Either way,' he goes, raising his glass, 'this is *your* night. So let's forget about it. Happy birthday, Ross,' and I'm like, 'Thanks, Dude.'

I look – it *has* to be said – amazing. And I think even my critics would admit it. I'm wearing, like, a purple silk shirt, open to the navel obviously – any opportunity to show off the old squeezebox abs – ridiculously tight trousers, shades, a white stetson and – the crème de la focking mer of the entire outfit – a white seal fur coat. And don't even *ask* me where I got it.

Anyway, I'm sitting there, roysh, letting my drunken eyes do a sweep of the place. That's when Chloe, Sophie and Amie with an ie arrive over, all three of them dressed the same, we're talking denim minis, pink boob tubes and the old PVC slag wellies. Middle-class skanks dressed as working-class skanks.

They each air-kiss me – of course, I've covered them all in my time – then Chloe goes, 'Thirty! That's like, Oh! My God!'

I can tell from her body language that Sophie is going all out to try to be with me tonight. She's cracking on to be all interested in my dollar-sign medallion but what she's really doing is checking out my bod, her little mouth working like a trout about to take a fly.

I'm a fan, don't get me wrong – she's got a cracking little tail on her and she handles you like a Dublin Corporation rental bike – but I'm happy to just keep knocking back the old Amsterdamage and see if something better comes along.

Chloe says she saw me the other day on Dawson Street in the shredding van. I tell her thanks very much, then I realize that she hasn't actually *paid* me a compliment?

Her face takes on a suddenly bitchy look. I'm sure you know women as well as I do. 'It was like, *er*, Ross doing *actual* manual labour? *Random!*'

'Well,' I go, 'if you must know, I actually *own* the company now? In other words, everything I earn goes to me. And as it happens, I'm coining it.'

She's there, 'Oh my God, Ross, I was only saying. Why are you being so defensive?'

Out of the blue, roysh, Amie with an ie goes, 'Oh my God, we went to visit your dad today!'

I'm like, 'What?'

'Yeah, in like, *Vincent's?*'

They're un-focking-believable. All they're doing is looking for goss.

'What the fock are you going to see my old man for – you don't know him?'

'Yes, we do. Everyone knows Ross's dad. We were like, "Hey, there, Ross's dad!" He was actually delighted we came to see him.'

'Okay,' Chloe goes, 'I'm *not* being a bitch, but he looks – oh! *my* God! – *so* bad.'

'Yeah, that's because he just had a focking bypass, Chloe.'

'What even is a bypass?' Sophie goes. 'And I'm not being a bitch either.'

I'm there, 'All I know is they take, like, a vein out of your leg and they put it in your hort.'

Amie with an ie's there, 'And how much weight has he actually lost, Ross?'

I just shake my head. 'Two, three stone – something like that.'

All their jaws just drop. Chloe and Sophie, especially, look at each other and I'm sure you can focking guess what's going through their minds.

The next thing, roysh, Erika arrives over – yeah, with Fionn in focking tow – and the three girls suddenly scatter like, I don't know, hyenas scared off by a lion.

Erika looks incredible, even dressed as a prostitute, and I'm saying that as her brother.

'Happy birthday!' she goes, then she gives me a really, really nice kiss on the cheek – which is *all* good.

He offers me a handshake and, being honest, I apply a bit more pressure to his hand than I usually would, although he doesn't actually *comment* on it?

'Sorry we're late,' he just gives it.

Then JP, who's been hanging off the edge of the conversation, goes, 'Did you get everything moved?'

He's standing there with Danuta, by the way, that stunning Russian headcase who he's still seeing. She's giving me serious filthies as per usual. There's just something about me that rubs her up the wrong way.

'Not even nearly,' Fionn goes, then he turns to Erika and smiles. 'I wouldn't have considered it possible for one person to accumulate that many clothes in *seven* lifetimes.'

Everyone laughs and, of course, I – in my focking innocence – just happen to go, 'Er, what's all this about?' which is the only reason I even find out.

'Erika and I are moving in together,' Fionn goes, as happy as Coolock on supplementary welfare allowance day.

I'm just like, 'What?' even though I'm trying my best to *not* let my anger show? 'Would you mind actually repeating that?'

Fionn laughs. He can well afford to. He hasn't worked out what her angle is yet. 'We're going to live together,' he goes.

I'm like, 'Where, though?'

He's wearing, like, a purple trilby with a fake goatee, although if you want my opinion, it's a pretty poor effort at an actual pimp. All I'm saying is there's, like, way better here tonight. 'We're going to live in my apartment,' he goes.

I'm there, 'Pilot View?' and I pull a face, like I'm not one hundred percent convinced. 'Bit on the small side, isn't it?'

'No,' he goes, with a definite tone in his voice. He's trying to make me feel bad for actually giving a shit.

I'm there, 'Hey, I'm just wondering will it not be a bit on the cramped side, that's all.'

'It's got three bedrooms, Ross.'

'Okay, fair enough. And am I allowed to ask whether you'll be sleeping in the same one?'

Erika just, like, closes her eyes, like she's trying to keep her cool. She's like, 'Ross, you are so focking weird,' the happy birthdays and blah blah blahs of a few minutes ago suddenly forgotten. There's loads of shit I *could* throw back. I could, just as an example, go, 'Well, I hope you treat each other really well and that neither of you leaves the other one to get knocked into a focking open grave by a practically lynch mob, then get very nearly buried alive and end up having to crawl out.'

Except *she'd* probably get a major kick out of that. In fact, I'm beginning to suspect it was her who asked the DJ to stick on 'Thriller' a minute ago.

My phone rings and my caller ID says it's, like, Sorcha, who I suddenly remember is supposed to, like, *be* here? I tip upstairs and step out onto the street to take it.

'Ross,' she goes and I can tell from her tone that it's instantly bad news. She's like, 'I'm, like, *so* sorry, Ross, but I'm not going to be able to make the porty.'

I'm all, 'Hey,' and, 'Ain't no thing but a Chandler Bing, Baby,' not wanting her to see my actual disappointment. 'Is it the snow? Are the roads still bad out that way?'

'No, it's actually Honor,' she goes and of course I'm suddenly having, like, a freak attack? I'm there, 'Is everything okay?'

'She's fine, Ross. She's just thrown one of her little tantrums. She's turned into such a little madam, God forgive me for saying it.'

'What was it about?'

'She just refused point-blank to eat her Thai fish cakes.'

'What? She focking loves Thai fish cakes.'

'Well,' she goes, a definite note of hesitation in her voice, 'the reason she wouldn't eat them, Ross, was because they were Tesco's own brand.'

I don't actually respond – possibly because I can see both sides of the orgument.

Sorcha ends up pretty much flipping. She goes, 'Like everyone else in this country, Ross, our daughter is going to have to learn to adapt to a reality-based lifestyle.'

'I know,' I go, only supporting her because she's still my – technically – wife. 'Some of that own-brand stuff can actually be good.'

'Quite often, Ross, it's the exact same product as the better-known brand – it's just how it's packaged.'

'Yeah, I'm backing you up here. These fish cakes, though, were they from the Finest range?'

'No – the Value. That's not the point, Ross. It's her attitude. She said own-brand food was for knackers.'

I actually laugh out loud. I'm like, 'Knackers?' because she's still only, like, four and a half, remember?

'I don't want her using words like that. I want our daughter to respect inclusivity – that was the whole idea of *sending* her to Montessori. I'm beginning to think we might have spoiled her.'

I'm not sure it's even possible to spoil kids. But I'm freezing my tits off at this stage, so I decide to, like, hurry the conversation along. 'So the upshot of all this is . . .'

'Well, she needs to learn, Ross – so I've cut back her mobile phone credit privileges to twenty euro a week.'

'Twenty yoyos a week?' I go. 'That's gotta hurt.'

See, personally, I'd have been against the idea of letting Honor *have* a phone? That's if Sorcha had bothered even consulting me.

'Well, I'm sure you can imagine how she responded to that,' she goes. 'You know how much she loves that phone. But I'm going to be firm with her. I don't care how many tantrums she throws. But obviously I can't ask my mum to look after her now – just in case she starts up again. I'm so sorry.'

'Look, it's cool, Babes. Cool as a bucket of free beer.'

'Let's celebrate your thirtieth another night.'

'Yeah, whatever.'

'No, seriously, Ross. Let's go out to dinner soon – just the two of us.'

'Er, yeah – look, I'm good with that if you're good with it.'

'Of course I'm good with it. Come on, Ross, we said – didn't we? – that we wouldn't let things ever get weird between us.'

'I suppose we did.'

'We said we'd handle our break-up like two adults. I think we still like each other too much to ever seriously fall out.'

'Of course. Jesus, we shared a toothbrush for two and a half years, didn't we?'

'What?'

'Er, nothing. Anyway, listen, I better get back inside. I'm freezing my towns off here.'

'Okay. Have an – oh my God – *amazing* night. And I'll see you soon.'

I wander back into Krystle and back to our table. The whole crew is sitting around, reminiscing about the – you could call them – *good* old days?

'Do you remember,' JP goes, 'people driving to work at, like, five o'clock in the morning just to avoid the traffic? You'd see all these cors porked on Baggot Street, Fitzwilliam Place, Pembroke Road, the drivers asleep in the front seat, catching a couple more hours before they went into the office. Our kids aren't going to believe that even happened. That's kind of sad.'

'You know what I miss most,' Oisinn goes, 'having come back? This is going to sound weird. But restaurants where they stacked your chips like Jenga pieces and charged you twenty euros for the privilege.'

Everyone laughs, which is fair enough, roysh, because it's one of those lines that's true *and* funny?

But then Fionn has to get in on the act. 'You might be onto something there,' he goes, as if we all need *him* to focking tell us. 'The *Economist* uses the Big Mac Index as a financial indicator. You've just invented the Thick-Cut Chip Stack Index.'

Everyone laughs, roysh, so as not to appear stupid. I'm thinking, he's not going to keep Erika long if *that's* the kind of banter she can look forward to during the long winter evenings.

'Okay,' I hear myself suddenly go, 'let's not forget whose actual porty this is supposed to be,' and everyone suddenly looks at me. 'Okay, I've an idea. Let's do what we did at my twenty-first. Let's stort lining all the birds up to give me my thirty kisses.'

I'm looking around me for a chair, roysh, to drag out into the middle of the dancefloor when Erika all of a sudden cuts the legs from under me. 'Ross,' she goes, 'when are you going to grow up?'

I'm like, 'What?'

'I'm just asking out of interest. You're thirty now. Do you have any plans to become an adult – as in, ever?'

And everyone at the table just looks away, roysh, the way they always do whenever Erika's, like, savaging someone. Oh, except for Danuta, who just stares me out of it – her pretty face all curdled, like bad focking milk – and under her breath goes, 'This fuggin eediot man!'

'The rest of us have all grown up,' Erika goes. 'We're getting on with our lives. You're still living in the nineties.'

JP – fair focks to him – changes the subject. He says that it said on the news tonight that the Government is now borrowing €4,500 each day for every man, woman and child in the country, which is a really nice thing for him to say, because it suddenly takes the heat off me.

Then Oisinn mentions that there are actual *Irish* people working in Spar now, which has got to be another sign of how royally focked the country is.

I get suddenly depressed, which is why I end up deciding to blow my own porty. I take the easy option and go off looking for Sophie. She's on the dancefloor, giving it loads to, I don't know, 'Bad Romance' – something by Gaga anyway. I catch her eye, then sort of, like, indicate the door with a flick of my head and she's suddenly nodding like a focking dashboard doggie.

I'm turning to leave when I suddenly think, fock it. It's my birthday. So I give Chloe the nod as well.

Then I give Erika and the rest of them the serious guns and a dirty big smile, as if to say, er, who needs to grow up now?

I step outside onto Horcourt Street. It's honestly freezing and I pull the seal fur more tightly around me as I hear the two birds clip-clopping out behind me in their F.M. boots. It's not exactly how I envisaged my thirtieth ending – a standard threesome with two faces from the past. But it's a lesson we're all suddenly having to learn, what with negative equity and the rest of it – you don't always get what you deserve. Sometimes you just get what you get.

The old dear's gaff smells of bad plumbing. I'm tempted to ask was it something she cooked, except I'm too taken aback by the sight that greets me in the kitchen. It's literally *the* most hilarious thing I've possibly ever seen.

Every morning, bear in mind, for as long as I've been alive, the old dear has had a nine o'clock hair appointment for – at the *very* least – a blow dry? So you can imagine my reaction when I see her sat at the table with a pair of latex gloves on her hands and a towel around her neck – *doing*, I believe the expression is, *her own hair*.

I kid you not.

The pen is only Padraig, of course, because there's bleach and all sorts of other shit involved.

I pick up the box – it's one of these, like, home colour kits – and I crack my hole laughing. 'Reduced to this,' I go. 'I think I'm beginning to see the funny side of this whole recession.'

She's just like, 'Bastards!' a word I've only ever heard her use to describe the paparazzi. The papers, I know, are still giving her a hord time over her still extravagant spending.

'They're outside Foxrock Hair Design,' she goes. 'They're outside Pamela Scott. They're outside the Lord Mayor's Lounge. Waiting – just *waiting* – to get a shot of me enjoying myself. Bloody sackcloth austerity – that's what it is.'

I honestly haven't seen her this angry since some kid mistook her for Twink coming down the steps of the Westbury two Christmas Eves ago.

Of course, *I* don't help. I'm like, 'You smell like a poodle that's been left out in the rain.'

She's got this, like, clear cellophane bag over her head, with strands of hair pulled out through the holes in it. And she's painting them with a brush.

'Well, sadly,' she goes, 'this is the sad pass that Ireland has arrived at. It's considered socially unacceptable now to spend money. Oh, yes – keeping *down* with the Joneses, that's the new obsession.'

Her voice is all high-pitched and she's got liquigel and developing crème dripping down her face.

I'm only actually here because there's fock-all to eat in my gaff. This is an added bonus.

'Well,' I go, opening the fridge, 'Sorcha seems to think it's the way forward. Reality-based lifestyles and blah blah blah.'

'That's all very well for Sorcha. I *happen* to have a sensitive scalp, Ross. And let me tell you, this thing is burning – *burning* – my head.'

'I still think it's hilarious to see you taken down a peg or six.'

This last line I say with my mouth full of Santa Fé pork stew. It's one of the most incredible things I've ever tasted. She can cook – I think I've always said that in her defence, the scabrous bagoon.

She goes, 'I heard some awful statistic in the National Gallery the other day, from one of the girls – that seventy percent of Irish people say they are now prepared to *haggle* over the price of goods and services. Haggling, Ross! The idea! And do you know what Marks & Spencer have started selling?'

'Reusable teabags?'

'Worse! Bread and jam! Bread and bloody jam! Oh, it's like something from *Oliver Twist*.'

I'm there, 'Well, Sorcha's storted giving Honor own-brand fish-cakes.'

The old dear just shakes her head. 'And I bet social services do absolutely nothing. I love Sorcha, you know I do. It just breaks my heart that she's joined everyone else in this . . . this race to the bottom.'

She suddenly cops her good fur coat on the back of the high stool where I hung it. 'Did you *borrow* that?' she goes.

I don't bother my hole answering her either way.

She's like, 'Ross, I'm asking you a question – did you borrow my coat.'

I'm there, 'Are you deaf or something? I said yeah.'

She's like, 'Whatever for?'

She's not even flattered that I'm eating her food.

'I wore it to my birthday porty to make me look like a pimp. Sorry, what's your issue here?'

She doesn't know what to say. She realizes she's being petty, of course.

'Well, what's that spilled on it, there?'

I barely even look at it – wouldn't give her the pleasure. I end up just, like, shrugging. 'It looks very much like red wine to me.'

'Red wine?' she goes, having a sudden conniption fit. 'It's genuine Arctic mink, Ross!'

I'm straight on the defensive, though. 'Well, while we're on the subject of my birthday, what the fock did you buy me?'

'I *beg* your pardon?'

'You heard me. Where's your gift? Even the old man managed to get me something and he's just come back from the brink of death.'

She tries to go off on a tangent then. 'I saw him this morning in the hospital, by the way. Oh, I'm glad they've decided to close that bloody cheese shop – his poor arteries.'

She suddenly stands up and makes her way over to the sink.

I'm there, 'Don't try to change the subject. You didn't even ring me to *wish* me a happy birthday.'

'Well,' she goes, taking off the cellophane bag and sticking her head under the running tap, '*we* can still do something. I could take you to *L'Ecrivain*. Just you and I – and who cares what the bloody newspapers say.'

'I'd rather eat roadkill off a focking bus tyre than eat with you. Jesus, you could have even just stuffed a few grand in an envelope – that would have done me.'

'I'm sorry,' she goes, continuing to wash the shit out of her hair, 'it slipped my mind. I *have* been busy, you know.'

'Busy?'

'Yes, working. On my new book. Hand me that towel, would you?'

Which I do. But I also laugh. I'm like, 'So-called book,' because this is her new recession-based misery lit novel she's talking about. They're building it up to be her big comeback book after her year off with supposed writer's block. I'm like, 'What do you know about misery anyway?'

She's there, 'What I see every day with my own eyes. There are four hundred thousand people on the live register, Ross! Delma's nephew is driving one of these minicabs. He's a qualified auctioneer!'

I laugh. 'When did you stort caring about the unemployed? You used to say they should only be allowed to have one child, like in China.'

She hates to be reminded, of course – but that's the Rossmeister, once again, telling it like it is.

She's there, 'I have a responsibility,' still rubbing her hair with the towel, '*as* a writer to try to encapsulate – in so far as a writer ever can – what is happening at this, well, terrible, terrible juncture in our history. And also to give people a message of hope – yes, things *are* bad, but we don't all have to start drinking tap water and eating our own excrement.'

I'm like, 'Yeah, yeah, save it for the *Late Late*,' and I go to walk out.

It's when I reach the door of the kitchen that I hear her suddenly scream. It's a noise that'd honestly strip the enamel from your focking teeth. She's, like, checking out her reflection in the stainless-steel, two-door, American-style fridge-freezer and she obviously doesn't like what she sees.

I laugh my head off. Her hair is literally red. It's not *even* red? It's, like, redder than red. She all of a sudden bursts into tears. I take a look at the box and it's pretty obvious she picked up the wrong packet in the shop. It says on the front Radiant Ruby.

'The bastards,' she goes. 'I hope they're bloody happy!'

And let me tell you, she's far from focking radiant.

She's skulling the old West Coast Cooler rosés. Don't get me wrong, she's giving me plenty of tude as well, in between flirting with me. 'I've heard things about you,' she even goes.

I'm there, 'What kind of things?'

She shrugs. 'Just things.'

I knock back a mouthful of Responsibly, cracking on that it doesn't really bother me. I'm like, 'We can all hear things, Aithne. Are we going to talk specifics, though? That's the big question.'

'Okay, I've heard that you fancy yourself as a bit of a player.'

I actually laugh out loud. 'Sounds to me like someone's been doing their research.'

'It pays to,' she goes, then takes another sip of the old giggle juice. This is us, by the way, in the Morket Bor. 'You were with a girl I used to work with in, like, graduate finance?'

I'm like, 'Oh?' all ears.

'I don't really care. She's actually a bitch. But you were with her, I think, twice, then you just never returned any of her calls. She was actually really, really hurt.'

I haven't a focking clue who she's talking about, of course. Could be any one of a thousand, but I pull a face. 'Well, if she's as big a bitch as you seem to be saying, maybe that was the reason I dropped her like a hot snot. Maybe I like nice girls.'

'And there was another one as well,' she goes, and I'm suddenly standing there thinking exactly the same thing as you – if the likes of her had applied their obvious research skills to actual *banking*, the country might not be focked seven ways till Sunday. 'She's, like, the friend of a girl I play tag rugby with . . .'

'Okay, let's hear about this one.'

'You were with her – as in *with* with? This is the story that's going around. You're supposed to have got up in the middle of the night – you said you were going to the toilet – and you went into her actual sister's room and tried to get into bed with her.'

I don't even bother denying it. Instead, I go, 'Hey, it's like the Spice Girls used to always say – if you want my future, forget my past.'

Birds, in my experience, are suckers for that line. Which is why it's one of the few famous quotes I've ever bothered my hole learning.

'Whoa,' she tries to go, 'slow down. I never said I was interested in getting into a relationship,' but you can tell, roysh, that she focking loves it – loves it like lemon pie. I don't want to come across as, like, cruel, but what else is she hanging on for? I had a root in her bag for her driver's licence when she was in the shitter. She's, like, thirty-six. Believe me, the Mark Wahlberg dream has long gone.

I'm there, 'I agree it's too early to, I suppose, *define* whatever this is. But I'm putting it out there – I'm actually attracted to you. If that's a crime, hey, lock me up.'

She laughs in my face, although don't ever believe that that's instantly a bad thing. 'You are *so* full of shit, do you know that? Do you find these lines actually work for you?'

'I've had a few in the woodshed over the years, yeah.'

'I bet you have,' she goes, then she just shakes her head. '*You're* not interested in a relationship.'

'Maybe I am finally.'

'No way. You're not the type.'

I'm there, 'You know, up until recently, I'd have possibly agreed with you? But I turned thirty there about a week ago. I know you're probably a good few years away from that yourself,' because I'm smoother than two eels humping in a bucket of snot, 'but it honestly changes your whole – I think it's a word – *prospectus*?'

'Oh, really?' she goes, except still Scooby Dubious.

'Yeah, I've been thinking, you know, I'm pretty much an adult now. It's maybe time I grew up, settled down, maturity, all the rest of it.'

'Bullshit,' she goes, smiling but still loving what she's hearing.

I'm there, 'Hey, you came here tonight didn't you?'

'I came here tonight to hear an apology – for the way you spoke to me in the bank. And I still haven't heard one, by the way.'

Timing was always one of my favourite qualities about myself on the rugby field. So you can probably guess what happens next. I go, 'Okay, here's your apology,' and I lean in, roysh, really romantically, and I press my lips against hers.

She tastes of, I don't know, exotic fruit flavours – whatever the fock they are – and the hot chilli nuts she was wolfing into her when I arrived. After three or four seconds, she storts responding, then I feel her hand running through the back of my hair and I instantly know that my work here is done.

I'm there, 'My place is, like, twenty minutes away in a cab,' and all she can do is, like, nod dumbly, obviously off in focking dreamland.

It's all too easy. Like beating a drowning dog.

I ask Sorcha how the food is and she says she – oh my God – can't believe she's eating hamachi crudo, soppressata and cacciatorini, what with everything that's going on at the moment – presumably meaning the whole current *economic* thing? Me, I'm, like, horsing down the raw succotash, telling her to just chillax.

'In a way, I actually agree with my old dear,' I go. 'There's, like, way too much of that going on at the moment – we're talking guilt and whatever else. It's like even Oisinn was saying at my thirtieth. Two years ago, if you weren't buying an investment property in Abu Dhabi, you were considered mentally unstable. Now you can't have a plate of charcuterie without some focker quoting the jobless figures at you.'

Not that I even *like* charcuterie? I'm throwing it into me like a focking orphan here but I'm still storving. If this really is what the Spanish consider a meal, it's no wonder they can't get through a working day without putting the old noodle down.

'I'm just making the point,' Sorcha goes, 'that it just feels wrong – as in, I'm, like, sitting in the bank this afternoon asking for a twelve-month moratorium on the rest of what I owe them. Now I'm in, like, Dax, eating from – oh my God – not even the early bird menu.'

I'm like, 'Sorcha, do you think Derek Quinlan, Gerry Barrett and all these mates of my old man's who are supposedly in trouble, are eating pot noodles every night in a focking petrol station forecourt? Er, I don't *think* so?'

She snaps out of it then, knowing that what I'm talking is basic sense. 'I'm sorry,' she goes, 'I've turned into *such* a frugalista. Being all of a sudden economical is *actually* addictive.'

'There's a time and place for it, is all I'm saying.'

'Have you heard, Marks & Spencer are selling, like, jam sandwiches now?'

'Yeah, the old dear's having kittens over it.'

'Oh my God, no way! I think it's an amazing throwback to the olden days. My Gran remembers a time when bread and jam was considered a treat.'

'Well, it sounds to me like we're headed back there again.'

'You're right, though. Let's ban recession talk from this table. This night is supposed to be a celebration.'

I tell her it's cool – apology accepted and blah blah blah. I mean, the current economic climate is all you ever hear about every time you turn on the focking TV these days. It'd have to affect you. Unless you just watched boxsets.

'So how are you?' she goes. 'Are you seeing anyone?'

See, with Sorcha, they're always the same questions.

I'm like, 'Oh, I'm still making the bedsprings creak, if that's what you're getting at. In a major way. I've been with, like, four girls in the last three weeks – no names, no pack-drill – including this top-heavy little minx who works in the bank and who I'm kind of, like, stringing along, basically for the crack of it.'

She sort of, like, throws her eyes skyward.

I laugh. 'Whoa, what's this, jealousy?'

She laughs then. 'It's hordly jealousy, Ross. I just think it's a bit, I don't know, sad.'

'Sad, as in?'

'Sad, as in you're thirty years of age now and you're still behaving like a – oh my God – teenager? Do you want to end up like Johnny Ronan?'

There's no two ways of answering that. 'Of course I focking do!'

'You don't, Ross. You couldn't.'

'That's exactly who I want to end up like. Sorcha, he's, what, fifty-focking-whatever. And he's still out there, loving it, loving it, loving it. Even though he looks like he got run over by a focking pitch-morker.'

'So that's how you see your future?'

'Pretty much, yeah.'

'Well, I'm not being a bitch, Ross, but a lot of people, including our friends, are wondering when you're going to stort acting your age.'

'Maybe never,' I go. 'Someone's obviously been talking to Erika, though.'

'It's not just Erika. It also happens to be *my* observation? Look around you, Ross. Everyone else is, like, moving on with their lives. Take a look at Christian.'

'Be hard to – he's in the States.'

'But look at everything he's got going for him. Wife. Little boy. Amazing job. Lauren said in her Facebook status the other day that they were trying for another baby.'

'Fair focks – I'd be the first one to say it.'

'He's your best friend, Ross. Do you never wake up in the night and think, oh my God, I could have had everything that he has, except I wasn't mature enough to recognize happiness when I had it.'

'This is a bit heavy, Babes. I could say in my defence that I've enjoyed my life.'

'I mean, you're actually losing your looks, did you know that?'

'Well, a lot of people would disagree with that particular assessment. I've actually got this weird feeling that my thirties are going to be my best decade in terms of birds.'

'Birds like Chloe and Sophie?' she goes. Then she just, like, shakes her head, like it doesn't bother her, even though it clearly does. 'How's Ronan?' she goes then, not-so-subtly changing the subject.

'He's fine,' I go. 'As it just so happens, he's having a bit of girl trouble himself at the moment.'

'Oh my God, is he *back* with Blathin?'

'God, no. The opposite, if anything. She's put the word around Mount Anville that he's, like, a bastard to women?'

'Oh my God, that is going to be *such* an amazing thing for him.'

'I know.'

'Every girl is going to want to be with him, Ross.'

'I know.'

'That's a huge turn-on for a Mount Anville girl.'

'Who are you telling? Yeah, no, I had a word with him. I mean, he's only, what, twelve, going on thirteen – I don't think he really understood what it meant.'

'That is, like, so exciting for him. And your poor dad – how is he since the op?'

'He's fine. They're actually dischorging him tomorrow. Still needs to watch himself, though – and blahdy blahdy blah.'

She nods. 'I must call out to see him. I downloaded loads of stuff off the internet for him about the kind of things he should be eating from now on.'

'I think the, er, hospital might already have that covered.'

'Well, I'll bring it out to him anyway. Skinless chicken is one of the major things. And white fish, obviously. Do you know if he and Helen own a juicer?'

'Er, I don't actually know.'

'My dad says they really miss him in Shanahan's, by the way – especially on Friday nights.'

I laugh. 'He was practically port of the furniture in there. Jesus, do you remember the amount of blood there used to be on his plate? His dinner always looked like a focking crime scene.'

She laughs. She's always loved my humour. 'He'll be back there, Ross. When he's better. I'm sure of it. It's not only steak they do, you know.'

'I know.'

'They have, like, a vegetarian option? My mum sometimes gets it, even though she's not a vegetarian.'

'Not sure I can picture him eating, I don't know, mushroom risotto, can you?'

She suddenly flashes a smile at me. 'Helen said you were a real hero, Ross.'

'What?'

'When he was in the hospital in France. She said she went to pieces. Being in a foreign country and everything. She said you took – oh my God – total charge.'

I just shrug. 'He's my dad, Sorcha.'

'Well, maybe some people didn't think you had it in you. She said you were a rock. You were the one who did all the talking to the doctors. You arranged the air ambulance to bring him home. I think a lot of people, when they heard about everything you did, were thinking the exact same thing. Which was, oh my God.'

'Like I said, Sorcha, he's my old man. Whatever differences we've had in the past. I mean, if anything ever happened to him, I'd . . .'

I can feel myself, roysh, suddenly filling up, so I quickly go, 'So how's Honor?'

And Sorcha just rolls her eyes. 'Oh, we're still at war.'

'What?'

'She still won't eat anything that's own brand.'

'And do you still have her on twenty euros phone credit a week?'

'I know you think I'm being hard on her, Ross . . .'

'I actually don't.'

'But she's got to learn. She's turned this thing into a battle of wills with me and I'm not going to give in.'

I laugh. See, she didn't exactly lick it up off the warm maple hordwood.

'It's not funny, Ross. She's so cheeky to me.'

'I'm sorry.'

'And it's such a struggle to get her to do anything. This morning it took me twenty minutes just to get her to make her bed.'

'Make her bed? Jesus, what about that Vietnamese bird you have in, supposedly cleaning? Why can't she do it?'

'Oh my God, that's exactly what Honor said.'

'Well, maybe she has a point.'

'Linh is not there to act as her personal maid, Ross.'

I shrug. 'Maybe *I* should be the judge of that. I'm the one who's, like, *paying* her?'

'Ross, you've got to stop indulging her. It's important for children to have structure and responsibility in their lives. Suri has to do chores, just as an example.'

'Who?'

'*Hello?* I'm talking about Tom and Katie's baby?'

In other words, Cruise and Holmes. I laugh. She talks about famous people like she meets them every Sunday morning for salmon focking kedgeree.

'It shouldn't be a burden to her, Ross. All I ask her to do is make her bed, take her dishes to the dishwasher after she's used them and put her dirty clothes in the laundry.'

I still think that's work Linh should be doing, although I know Sorcha well enough at this stage not to push it. Instead, roysh, I ask her how *she's* doing. I'm like, 'Have you decided what you're going to do yet, as in work-wise?' because it's, like, six months since that boutique of hers went tits-up.

She just, like, shakes her head. 'I suppose I'm still taking time out to connect with my grief. You know my friend Giovanna – she used to work in that herbal tea shop I liked in the George's Street Orcade?'

I actually laugh out loud. There's a name from the past. 'Of course I remember Giovanna. The bird who used to do the doggie yoga?'

'Don't give me that, Ross. It happens to be called doga.'

'Well, either way, it was yoga for focking dogs – is she still doing it, by the way?'

'Actually, no.'

'Of course she's not. I'd imagine there's less call for it now – people aren't being as stupid with their money anymore.'

Giovanna always hated me, mainly because I used to rip the piss out of her, right to her face.

'Yeah,' Sorcha goes, 'I'm actually trying to tell you something really amazing here, Ross.'

'Sorry. Shoot.'

'Well, Giovanna has an actual degree in psychology and she says that what I'm going through is *possibly* like a bereavement?'

'That's fantastic. Hey, where's her degree from – did she ever mention?'

'What?'

'I'm just asking, is it, like, Dumb Blonde School or any of those?'

'Sorry, Ross, how does that affect the basic point she's trying to make?'

'It doesn't, I suppose. Okay, continue.'

She just, like, stares me out of it for a few seconds – to let me know she doesn't *need* my permission? – then she goes, 'Anyway, that was what she said, that all these people out there who, like me, have lost their businesses, their jobs and whatever else, they're all going through grief of one kind or another. And unless people connect with that grief – reach an accommodation with it, if you like – it'll come back and basically bite them. Can you imagine what that's going to mean for, like, Irish society, Ross?'

Yeah, it's definitely DBS. I've ridden enough of the alumni to recognize the spiel.

'That all sounds like good shit,' I go, helping myself to the last pork rillette.

She's like, 'There's no doubt, Ross, that when my boutique closed, I definitely went through something.'

'Yeah,' I go, 'the front doors of Brown Thomas in an Opel focking Astra, wasn't it?'

She gives me what I think is called a *withering* look? It's the same look you give as you're passing some old biddy who's doing, like, thirty in the fast lane of the Stillorgan dualler because she plans to turn right at some point in the next half an hour. What can I say? I've always been a slave to the one-liner.

'*Anywaaay*,' she just goes, 'all I'm saying is – I know you've never given her a chance, Ross – but Giovanna is, oh my God, *so* an amazing person. She's not only a psychologist, she's also a Buddhist. And, well, two or three other things as well. She's read, like, the Koran, just as an example – four times or something? Literally from cover to cover. This is what she does, see. She takes, like, little bits from everything. The good bits obviously. As a matter of fact, I was actually thinking of joining her Healing Through Tai Chi class.'

She sips her Coteaux du Languedoc 2006 and looks at me over the top of her glass for a reaction.

I'm just there, 'Great.'

'Do you accept the point she's trying to make, Ross – that the upside of the whole mass unemployment thing is that it leaves more time for personal and emotional development?'

'Er, yeah – I think I said coola boola, Babes.'

'She does it in, like, the circus field in Booterstown. Half-seven every weekday morning. Oh my God, it's nearly all, like, out-of-work people and people who've lost their businesses.'

'Again, you'd *have* to say fair focks.'

'But it'd mean *you'd* have to bring Honor to Montessori every morning. Would you mind?'

I actually *laugh* at that. 'Would I mind? What, getting an extra hour of bonus time with my daughter every morning? Er, have you any idea how much that's going to make my actual day?'

She smiles. It's obvious that whatever she once felt for me is still definitely there. 'Well, thank you, Ross.'

'Look, Sorcha, I accept now that I wasn't much of a husband to you. Fast hands – a blessing *and* a curse. But I promised you – didn't I? – that the one thing I would always be is an amazing, amazing, amazing father.'

She puts her hand down on top of mine, leans across the table and plants *the* most, I suppose, tender kiss on my cheek. She's wearing her Clarins *Eau Ensoleillante*, which has always done it for me. The old swelling in the pants, in other words.

'We're *always* going to have a connection,' she goes.

I just shrug – easy breezy – and go, 'Like high-speed broadband, Babes. Like high-speed focking broadband.'

As she's sitting down, roysh, I catch her looking at something over my shoulder. It's like she's suddenly *seen* someone?

I'm there, 'What's wrong?' half looking behind me.

She goes, 'No, nothing,' then she sort of, like, stands up. 'I just need to go to the ladies, okay?' and I suddenly cop it. She's obviously arranged a cake for me, for the old birthday and blahdy blahdy blah.

So I end up playing the total innocent, roysh, cracking on not to know, determined not to spoil the romantic moment. I'm like, 'You do what you have to do, Babes. I've got the focking meat sweats here myself. I feel like I could shit two waist sizes.'

She sort of, like, half smiles at me, then focks off, I'm presuming to talk to the *maître d'* or head waiter or whatever about candles and blah blah blah. So I'm just sitting there, chasing a piece of Wavreumont around the plate with a cheese fork, when all of a sudden a man's voice behind me goes, 'Ross O'Carroll-Kelly?' and I swear to God, roysh, I turn around, expecting to see him holding an enormous Death By Chocolate and striking up a chorus of Happy actual Birthday.

I'm there, 'The one and only – accept no substitutes,' then I notice, roysh, that it's actually – *weirdly?* – just some focking skinny dude in, like, a suit, holding what would have to be described as a sheaf of papers. I don't even manage to get a word in edgeways. 'Ross O'Carroll-Kelly,' he just goes, 'this is a Family Law Civil Bill, an Affidavit of Means and an Affidavit of Welfare . . .'

I'm like, 'Whoa, whoa, whoa – what are you even talking about?'

'I'm serving you with divorce papers,' he goes, 'on behalf of your wife, Mrs Sorcha O'Carroll-Kelly (*née* Lalor). Can I consider them served?'

I'm, like, too in shock to even *answer*? People at other tables are having a good focking goo, of course. This must be the kind of shit that passes for, like, entertainment these days.

'Can I consider these papers served?' he again goes.

'Er, pretty much,' I somehow manage to, like, blurt out. Then off he focks.

Ten seconds later, roysh, Sorcha's back – she actually *was* in the Josh

Ritter. She cops the – again, if it's a word – *sheaf* of papers in my hand and goes, 'I thought it was the best way to do it, Ross. Through, like, a third party? We said – didn't we? – that we'd avoid, in so far as we can, handling this divorce in an adversarial way. It's going to be long and painful enough road as it is. I just thought, we'd have a nice meal, a lovely chat – which is what we've had – and then at the end . . .'

I'm there, 'Er, yeah, cool,' still in total shock, if the truth be told.

'Giovanna especially agreed that it was an amazing way to handle it.'

'Oh, did she?'

'Yeah. Adult, I suppose. She was the one who in fact *suggested* it?'

I sit there, roysh, just staring at this, like, stack of paper, at the word divorce specifically, there in capital letters. It suddenly seems so, I don't know, final. Like a wrung neck.

She asks me if I'm having dessert and I just shake my head. The thing is, I feel like I've just been served it.

2. Pack of bankers

'Who are you texting, Honor?' I just happen to go – this is when we're, like, pulled up at the lights at the Four Seasons in the old Shred Focking Everything van – and she goes, 'Er, *Malorie*?'

She's pretty snippy with me as well, the way she says it – like it should have been somehow *obvious* to me?

I'm like, 'Who's Malorie?' because they say – don't they? – that parents should make it their business to know who their children's friends are. 'What part of Dublin is she from?'

Without even looking up, she's there, 'Highfield Road.'

'Highfield Road,' I go, instantly relaxing. 'I think I can work with that.'

She goes, '*All* my friends are from, like, RaRaRa?'

I'm like, 'Where?'

She throws her eyes in the air and goes, 'You own an iPhone – look it up.'

'Well, I possibly shouldn't while I'm driving, Honor. Could you maybe just tell me?'

'Oh my God!' she goes, like I've really pissed her off now. 'RaRaRa – it's, like, Ranelagh-Rathmines-Rathgor?'

'Sorry, Honor. It's just I've never heard it called that before.'

'Yeah, whatevs! What even *year* are you living in?'

This possibly *is* me showing my age, but I remember a time when kids only spoke to adults like that on the *Late Late Toy Show*. You'd see some little kid getting snippy with Pat Kenny, and the entire audience would laugh, and you'd laugh at home, and you know that everyone you met for the next week would be laughing as well – but at the same time you were secretly thinking, if she was mine, I'd dangle her by the focking ankles from the top of the Stephen's Green Shopping Centre until she apologized.

Nowadays, as far as I can see, all kids talk to their rents like that – like they think adults are pretty much *stupid*? There's nothing we can do about it, of course. All we can do is accept it.

Her phone beeps and off she goes again, texting like her life depends on it, smoke practically coming out of the phone.

'Malorie's wearing her chestnut Uggs as well,' she eventually goes. Which is hilarious, roysh, because this is exactly what Sorcha and Erika have been doing since they were, like, thirteen – consulting each other first thing in the morning before deciding on their outfits for the day.

'So this Malorie,' I go as we're driving across *actual* Ballsbridge, 'is she, like, your best friend?'

She's there, 'Er, *yeah*? Oh my God, she's, like, *so* book.' This is without even looking at me. 'Especially when she's slagging off povs.'

I laugh so hord, I end up nearly wrapping the cor around a lamppost outside Roly's. Because it's a word I've been known to use myself. I just didn't expect to hear it from her mouth – at least until she was in, like, Mount Anville.

I'm there, 'I take it you mean poor people?'

'Er, *duh*!? Yes, I mean poor people. Malorie's always laughing at Anita and Sian – their dad's basically *unemployed*?'

'Actually,' I go, 'there's a lot of that about, Honor – without wanting to bore you about, I don't know, global affairs and shit? There's a lot of people suddenly on the dole. I was actually talking to your grand-mother about it recently. Good people, as well as the usual kind.'

She's there, 'Oh my God, Mom's *always* saying that – it's like whatevs!' and then she suddenly stops, roysh, and looks up at me with her big cocker spaniel eyes. 'You won't tell her I said povs, will you?'

I laugh. This kid can wrap me around her little finger. I'm there, 'Of course I won't.'

'She's already cut my phone credit.'

'I heard.'

'I shouldn't even be *on* pay-as-you-go. All my friends are on, like, *bill pay*?'

There's, like, silence between us then. Some dude on the radio says that we may never know the true cost of NAMA. In fact, our children's children's children might not even know.

'Well, either way,' I go, 'I won't tell her you said povs. Although, in fairness, it's a word I've often used – never had a major issue with it, to be fair.'

'Oh, *Mom* thinks that no one in this world is entitled to look down on anyone else.'

I again laugh. I *have* to.

'That woman and her madcap ideas,' I go, just shaking my head.

'It's not even *her* idea? It's, like, Giovanna's? She's always going "Giovanna said this" and "Giovanna said that". She's – oh my God – *such* a sap.'

'Well,' I go, 'this is the same Giovanna who told your old dear it'd be a good idea to serve me with my divorce papers while we were in a restaurant. Focking Dax as well. Not that I'm asking you to choose sides in this whole thing. You're free to make up your own mind.'

My phone rings. I check the screen and it's, like, Aithne – as in Aithne from the bank, so I end up just switching it to silent, then letting it ring out.

I take the left turn at Merrion Square and that's when Honor, out of the blue, goes, 'Park here?'

I'm like, 'Here?' because Little Roedean's is actually on the *other* side of the Square? 'Why do you want me to pork here, Babes?' and it's only as I'm saying it that I realize the obvious answer to the question. She doesn't want her friends to see her pull up in a – let's be honest here – van. Which I totally understand, by the way. With what we're shelling out in fees to this place, I'd be seriously worried if she *was* comfortable with it?

She's like, 'Vans are, like, so not book. Malorie says they're for skanks.'

'Oh, does she?'

'And pay-as-you-go phones are for, like, drug-dealers.'

'Okay, look, no offence taken. I'll throw it in here and we'll, like, walk around.'

I grab her schoolbag and her little straw boater off the middle seat and hand them to her.

I'm like, 'Just to point out, though, that I won't *always* be driving this thing? No, the plan is to basically build the business up, then hire a pack of Johnny Punchclocks in to do the *actual* work. Or preferably flog it for a fat wedge.'

She's there, 'Yeah, whatevs.'

We toddle around to the school, me holding her hand, so honestly proud. I'm thinking, *this* is what being a father is all about. We tip down the steps into the basement. On the way into the classroom, we end up running into another little girl, who I immediately presume to be Malorie.

It's possibly the chestnut Uggs.

Honor – this is unbelievable – goes, 'Hi, Babes!' Then Malorie gives it the same, 'Hi, Babes!' and they just, like, air-kiss each other, we're talking both cheeks.

I end up just watching this scene – you can imagine – with my mouth open, totally mesmerized.

'They're like teenagers the day they're born,' I hear this voice behind me go. I whip around and there's this, like, woman stood there. If I had to compare her to someone, it'd be Kate Garraway, and of course there's no shame in that.

'I'm Una,' she goes, offering me her hand. 'Malorie's mum.'

'Hello there,' I go, laying it down like a Fiddy track. Er, sorry, *what* was that Sorcha was saying about me being too old for this game? 'I'm actually Ross – as in Honor's old man?'

'It's lovely to finally meet you. Honor talks about you all the time.'

I can't tell you what an amazing thing that is to hear.

The two of us end up standing there for the next ten minutes having this incredible, I suppose you could say, *philosophical* discussion about children of today – all Malorie will eat, she says, is tofu – while I drop in one or two subtle questions, trying to find out, slyly, what her marital situation is – 'What does Malorie's old man think of the whole tofu situ?' – at the same time trying to cop a look at her attention-getters through the gap in her shirt buttons.

'John and I are separated,' she goes.

And I'm like, 'Oh, that's a bummer – that's a serious bummer,' and you can see me, I'm sure, big sincere face on me. Jesus, it would take a bloody good fire crew half a day to cut me out of her. 'I'm actually in the same boat myself,' I go. 'Except we're going down the whole divorce road. I will say this, though – I hope you're back in the game in terms of meeting people and blah blah blah.'

'Well, it's only been three months, as it happens.'

'Doesn't matter. My advice would be that it's never too early.'

I'm actually about to put the squeeze on her for her digits when I'm suddenly distracted by something out of the corner of my eye – and I think you'll understand when I tell you what it is. On the wall next to us, roysh, there's a poster, with the words 'Sports Day' in, like, huge block capitals on it, then underneath happens to be the date, which is April something-or-other.

'I'm sorry,' I end up having to go, laughing, 'I was thrown off my stroke there by that, er, poster. See, sport would be one of the things I'd be *most* famous for myself?'

She's there, 'Oh, really?' obviously not a rugby fan.

I'm like, 'Big-time,' and then I nod in Honor's general direction. 'I suppose this is a chance to find out if the old winning mentality runs in the genes.'

'Except,' Una suddenly goes, pointing out the smallprint at the bottom of the poster, 'it says here that the races are all non-competitive.'

Now, I'm not even a hundred percent certain that that's even a proper word, but I know instantly what they're *trying* to say? And you can understand, I'm sure, my reaction.

'Er, are they talking about races in which no one actually tries?'

Una laughs. 'No, I read about this in the school newsletter. They're saying that the emphasis isn't *on* winning.'

'Er, then they're not races.'

'They are – they're just races in which everyone who takes part gets a medal.'

'But obviously not the same medal?'

'Yes, *exactly* the same medal.'

'But . . . what's the point of that?'

'I think the idea behind it is that we shouldn't – *as* a society – celebrate one individual's dominance over others.'

'Jesus, it's egg-and-focking-spoon.'

She laughs. I think she's genuinely attracted to me. 'I did hear somewhere – it might have been on GMTV – that competitiveness can be very destructive for young people's minds. Which, as you know, isn't in keeping with the spirit of Montessori.'

I just, like, shake my head and continue staring at the poster.

'Anyway,' she goes, 'it was lovely to finally meet Honor's dad.'

I'm there, 'Er, cool.'

'Hopefully, I'll see you again. Maybe we'll get a coffee one of the mornings.'

'Er, yeah, whatever.'

And I let her just walk away – that's how caught up I am in staring at the words 'Non-competitive' and wondering what kind of world I've brought my daughter into.

Ronan's pretty handy with a shovel, it has to be said. I actually compliment him on it. He says that his old pal Buckets of Blood told him once that if you knew how to dig a hole, quickly and cleanly, there'd always be work for you in gangland.

'How *is* young Buckets of Blood?' the old man goes.

See, I sometimes forget that they shared a landing for a few months.

'Ah, still keeping he's snout clean,' Ronan gives it. 'Still doing he's painting and he's decorating – and the *odd* birra debt collection, you know yisserself.'

'Well, we all must do what we can – especially in the current economic what's-it – eh, Ross?'

I'm like, 'Yeah, I suppose. Ro, that might be enough trenches.'

This is, like, the three of us, by the way, in Helen's back gorden on Ailesbury Road, putting down a, basically, *vegetable* patch?

Fionn, who was here about an hour ago collecting more of Erika's stuff, said he read somewhere that in times of economic hordship, humans instinctively return to the land. Allotments are very much back in fashion, he said, though this is more about the old man finding – what was it his cardiologist said? – gentler pursuits.

'The foolish man seeks happiness in the distance,' he suddenly goes. 'The wise man grows it under his feet.'

I just nod, showing an interest. I'm like, 'Okay, whose quote is that?'

'Oh, someone or other,' he goes. 'It was scratched onto the wall of the cell where I spent most of my time – quote-unquote – *inside*. Probably been there for years. I thought, what a wonderful sentiment. Committed it to memory – not that I properly understood it, until, well . . .'

'Okay,' I go, quickly changing the subject, 'potatoes, there, there and there. Cabbages, what, there and there? Rutabaga – that's swede to you, Ro – there. French beans, courgettes . . .'

The old man looks back at the gaff. 'Let's make that last trench a little herb garden, shall we?'

Ronan leans on his shovel with, like, a big leery smile on his face. 'What kind of heerbs are we talking, Grandda?'

The old man cracks his hole laughing. 'Good lord, not that kind! Cannabis, hasheesh and what-not! No, I was thinking more your standard parsley, chives, lemon mint – that type of affair.'

'Pity that,' Ronan goes. 'I know a couple of feddas would pay good bread for the utter kind.'

He finds this hilarious as well. 'I expect you do, Ronan. No, I was thinking, you know, just a little something for Helen. Might cheer her up – been a bit down in herself, you see.'

I'm there, 'What's wrong with her?' because, like I said, I'm a huge, huge fan. 'It could be just delayed shock – after, well, everything.'

The old man pulls a face. 'No, it'll be a touch of the old empty nest syndrome, I shouldn't wonder. Erika flying the coop.'

I laugh.

'Tell her not to sweat it, then. She'll be home before the clocks go forward. Or back. Whatever they're doing in a few weeks' time.'

'I think not,' the old man tries to go. 'No, she and young Fionn seem to be terribly happy together. You know, she confided in her mother the other night that she couldn't believe the one for her was right in front of her eyes this whole time.'

And what can I do except roll my eyes and shake my head.

'Sounds like a focking romcom trailer. Something with Katherine Heigl in it. And maybe Paul Rudd . . .'

I suddenly stop, roysh, because the old man's breathing sounds all of a sudden funny. Actually, I think the word is, like, *laboured*?

I'm instantly wiping down the gorden bench with my hand, going, 'Dad, quick, you need to sit down.'

He's there, 'No, no, I'm quite all right, Ross.'

I'm like, 'Dad, please!'

'Ross, I'm really fine. Just a little shortness of breath, that's all. Comes and goes. Think I'll pop inside, though, and see how Helen's getting on. She's preparing *lunch* for us, don't you know!'

I watch him walk slowly back to the house, expecting him to fall with every step.

'He's grand, Rosser,' Ronan goes.

I sit down on the bench myself. Ronan sticks his shovel into the mud, then ends up sitting down beside me.

'He's grand,' he goes again. 'That's what he's breathing always goes like.'

I'm there, 'I know. It just takes a bit of getting used to, that's all. I keep thinking . . .'

'Don't be talken like that. Thee wouldn't have let him ourra the hospital if he wadn't alreet.'

'Yeah, that's true. Anyway, how are the rehearsals going?'

He knows, roysh, that I'm deliberately changing the subject, but he still rolls with it.

He's like, 'Er, moostard,' taking a sudden interest in a blister on the palm of his hand, yet at the same time *smiling*?

I'm just there, 'Hey, come on. Don't get focking coy on me, kid. Spill.'

'You were reet, is all.'

'Okay, that's nice to hear. About what?'

'About, you know, all the geerls thinking Ine a bastord to women. I needn't have woodied.'

'Continue.'

'Well, alls Ine saying is, I'd be feerly popular, is all.'

I feel the corners of my mouth curling up into an actual smile. 'Okay, define fairly popular for me.'

He laughs, still a bit embarrassed. 'They're *all* into me, Rosser . . .'

I laugh then.

'So Blathin's plan basically backfired like I said it would.'

'Well, thee do be practically fighting wit one anutter to talk to me and that.'

I just clench my fist. 'Put that in your wheelchair and, I don't know, push it around the place! You see, Ro? This is possibly the only thing in the world that I'm capable of teaching you as your father.'

'Well, you were reet, is all Ine saying.'

'Yes! But what about you, Ro? Do *you* like *them*? As in, like, girls in general?'

His face just lights up. 'I love them, Rosser.'

I'm like, 'Really?'

'You bethor fooken believe it.'

'More than you love, say, gangland crime?'

'I suppose so, yeah.'

I can't tell you what a relief it is for the father of a soon-to-be thirteen-year-old northside kid to hear that.

'So,' he goes then, 'what do I do, Rosser?'

I'm literally flabbergasted. 'What do you do? Jesus, Ro, you've got off with girls before, haven't you? I've seen you with hickeys all over that neck of yours. Fock, the first time I met you I thought you'd been baton-chorged.'

'No, I mean, which of the geerls do I go for? See, it's like I've got too many fooken choices.'

I resist the urge to shake my head, because I need to be more patient. See, I'm not used to being in the role of, like, *teacher*? Even though I *am* revelling in it now.

'Ronan,' I go, 'do you remember a couple of years ago – I think it was for your, like, *tenth* birthday? – I took you to Pizza Hut in Blanchardstown Shopping Centre.'

'Yeah, what about it?'

'Do you remember you couldn't decide between the Hawaiian and the Four Cheeses?'

'Yeah.'

'And I said you didn't have to, because it was, like, an all-you-can-eat buffet?'

'Yeah.'

'Well, that's pretty much what the game of love is like. You can try a little bit of everything. It's like I said to you when I explained the rules of the Ten Euro Bargain Bonanza – fill your boots, son.'

He nods his little head and I don't think I could explain in words how, I suppose, *fulfilled* I suddenly feel?

I'm in, like, Kielys with the goys, enjoying a few scooparooneys while filling them in on what's been happening in my basically life. It's great to be all back together again like this – all we need now is Christian and it'd be just like old times.

They're all backing me up, it has to be said, on the whole Little Roedean's Sports Day thing.

'Non-competitive races?' Oisinn, for example, goes. 'Fionn, isn't that one of those – what's the word for it again?'

Fionn's there, 'An oxymoron,' absolutely delighted to be showing off his, I suppose, intelligence.

I'm wondering how often him and Erika are doing it now that they're actually living together. Of course, you *can* get sick of it, especially if it's with the same woman, day in, day out.

'You *would* have to wonder,' he goes, 'what will be the long-term effects of indoctrinating children into believing that winning is unimportant once no one's feelings get hurt. What it's going to do – I think – is turn out a generation of young people with fragile egos, who can't make decisions and who are unable to cope with disappointment and failure.'

'And how's that going to help our competitiveness,' JP goes, 'as a nation – I hate to use the phrase – but *going forward*?'

I'm there, 'The other thing to remember is that it's the family reputation that's on the line here. What, Ross O'Carroll-Kelly, who did all the things he did on the rugby field, is supposed to teach his daughter that the right thing to do is to *not try*? In an actual *sporting* event? I'm telling you now, it's not going to happen.'

Oisinn gets the round in and you'd have to say fair focks. Seventy-something million in the shit, back living with his old pair, yet he's still not afraid to stick his hand in his skyrocket.

'So,' JP goes to him, 'I hear Hennessy's arranged a date.'

'What's this?' I go, realizing that I'm in the dork once again.

Oisinn's there, 'Oh, it's just this meeting with my creditors,' like it's no major deal. 'I mentioned it before.'

'When is it?'

'What?'

'When is it, Dude?'

'It's, like, next Monday week?'

'Okay, where?'

'Well, Hennessy's office.'

I rub my hands together and have a bit of a chuckle to myself. 'Bring it on!' I go. 'That'd be very much my attitude. There's a lot of shit I want to get off my chest.'

This seems to somehow *surprise* Oisinn? He's like, 'What are you talking about, Ross?'

I laugh. 'Dude, I'm not letting you face the firing squad on your own.'

He looks at the other two. 'But I won't *be* on my own. I've got Hennessy representing me.'

'Well, you've also got me – whether you like it or not. I've decided to, like, testify on your behalf.'

'Testify? Dude, it's not a court case.'

I laugh. 'Oh, isn't it?'

'Well, no. I'm just putting a solvency plan to them, to try to save myself from bankruptcy.'

'Okay, then. But, look, I was the one who persuaded you to come home, wasn't I?'

'Well, yeah, but . . .'

'No buts, Oisinn. I told you in, wherever, Monte focking Corlo – didn't I? I said that whatever shit-storm you were facing, you weren't going to have to face it alone.'

JP's head suddenly pops up. 'Hey,' he goes, 'here's Danuta!'

I turn around, roysh, and it *is* actually her. My hort instantly sinks. I don't know how Fionn and Oisinn feel about it, but personally I think JP's bang out of order inviting her to crash what's *supposed* to be a goys' night out? And I'm not just saying that because the girl hates the focking sight of me. Anyway, roysh, even allowing for all of that, I still make the effort.

'Heeey!' I even go. '*Look*-ing good!'

She's like, 'What?' one of those girls who's always on the immediate defensive.

I'm like, 'Hey, it's a compliment. I've always thought you looked like Maria Kirilenko and I've said that from day one. Ask your boyfriend there.'

'And thees ees supposed to mek me heppy?' she just goes, 'that you theenk I em attractive woman. You are fugging eediot peerson.'

I laugh, trying to make a joke out of it. See, I don't think she's the full bag of clubs.

'Well,' I go, 'my advice would be to just go with it. She's actually the best-looking of all the Russian tennis players, if you want my opinion.'

She turns to JP and goes, 'How can you be ferrents with thees stoopeed, stoopeed man?' and not one of the others, by the way, makes an effort to even back me up. They're all taking a sudden interest in the Munster versus Edinburgh match, which Kielys, for whatever focking reason, have decided to show.

'Ah, that's just Ross,' JP goes, actually *apologizing* for me? 'It could be just a cultural thing, Danni. I think a lot of what he says gets possibly lost in translation. Hey, why don't you tell everyone about your new business venture?' but she continues just staring at me, roysh, until *he* ends up having to go, 'Danni's thinking about setting up one of these cash for gold places.'

Oisinn's like, 'Cash for gold? Well, it certainly seems to be where the money is these days.'

She nods, all delighted with herself. 'Eez many stoopeed people in thees country, do crezzy theeng, now haff no money, now loowis everything. Boo fugging hoo, yes? So I say to them, but you haff gold! You have reeng you can sell – for wedding, for engagement, for whatever. I giff gute price. Then melt eet down. Fugg eet!'

I just think, what a focking headbanger – albeit a cracking-looking one with unbelievable nips.

Suddenly, roysh, I cop Fionn getting up to go to the jacks. I give him a second or two, then follow him in. He's standing at the trough, performing the old urinal splits to prevent splashback.

'So,' I just go, 'this is where all the big knobs hang out.'

See, that'd be a line I'm, like, *famous* for?

He barely looks over his shoulder at me, just goes, 'Oh, hi, Ross.'

I open up the old fly and step up next to him. I'm like, 'So, er, how are things?'

He's there, 'Great. Lot of work on at the moment. I'd never have believed that teaching in the Institute would be so much harder than teaching in Castlerock. It's almost university standard.'

'Yeah, thanks for that, Fionn. I actually meant how are things with you and my sister?'

He laughs. 'They're great, Ross.'

'Because all I'm saying is that living with a bird – it's true – is a lot different to, I don't know, having sex with one on a regular basis.'

'Thanks, Ross.'

'Hey, I'm just trying to give you the benefit of my vast experience.'

I give the old hose a shake and put it away.

'I mean, long term, you two might decide that you work better as basically friends.'

I'm about to remind him, roysh – another famous line of mine – that more than four shakes is considered a wank, when he goes, 'Or, Ross,' and this, bear in mind, is with a big smile on his face, 'you might have to get used to the idea of me one day being your brother-in-law.'

* * *

46

'Can I say something,' Sorcha goes, 'even though it might sound a bit, I don't know, *sappy?*'

I go, 'Yeah, shoot for the stors, Babes,' at the same time making a conscious decision not to laugh in her actual face. See, she's forever stealing lines from songs and movies to use in conversation – she told me once, in the middle of a borney, that in the twist of separation I excelled at being free.

'Giovanna's right – you might not have been a good husband . . .'

'Giovanna doesn't even know me.'

'But one thing you *are* is a really good father.'

'I wondered was there going to be a compliment at the end of it. Well, thanks.'

She hands me my coffee – in her favourite *Sex and the City* mug, I can't help but notice, the one she bought in the Warner Brothers studio gift shop in LA with 'Shopping is My Cardio' on it. I'm only making the point because I definitely think she still feels something for me, despite wanting to push ahead with the whole divorce.

She's like, 'That's why I'm so happy that we're handling our break-up in an adult way. Giovanna would probably go mad at me for saying this, but I think Honor *needs* a strong male figure in her life.'

'Some would say her mother does, too.'

She ends up just smiling at me. 'Nice try, Ross.'

I shrug, as if to say, hey, if you don't ask, you don't get.

This is us, by the way, in the kitchen in Newtownpork Avenue. I called around to, like, dismantle Honor's old cot, which I'd been promising to do for ages. Sorcha's talking about converting the old nursery into a – get this – reflection space. We're talking scented candles, we're talking Paulo Coelho books, we're talking – I would *imagine* – her Bedouin Café Arabic Chillout CDs?

'Yeah, no,' I go, 'just going back to what you were saying there about me being unbelievable with my kids, the whole fatherhood thing is something I've definitely got a handle on. I'm dishing out advice left, right and centre to Ro, by the way. I have to admit, I'm actually on fire at the moment.'

As we're talking, I'm flicking through this scrapbook about Paris that Honor's been keeping for, like, months now. It's stuffed to the gills with pictures of, I don't know, all the major buildings, then photographs she's cut from all Sorcha's magazines, of all the fashion shows and blahdy blah. She's become all of a sudden obsessed with the place. According to Sorcha, it's because Malorie got to go when *her* mum and dad got separated.

I stop at a picture of the Eiffel Tower, which I always recognize.

Sorcha's like, 'Oh my God, she *so* wants to go.'

I'm there, 'Why don't you take her, then?'

'Maybe one day.'

'Why not now?'

'Oh my God, Ross, you sound just *like* her? I'm trying to teach her that we don't live in a world of instant gratification. That's all gone.'

'Come on, how much would two flights to Paris cost? Although if she won't eat own-brand food, she'll hordly fly Ryanair. You'd have to focking Taser her to get her on board.'

'That's my exact point, Ross. I really *am* beginning to think we've spoiled her. She's never grateful for anything she's given.'

'Kids never are – that comes hopefully later.'

'I don't agree. She's a little madam, Ross. She needs to learn that treats have to be earned. It's a lesson we should have all learned as, like, a people.'

'Well,' I go, 'speaking of lessons, do you mind me mentioning that I'm actually worried about what they're teaching her in that Montessori?'

'Worried?' she goes. 'What are you talking about?'

'What am I talking about? I take it you haven't heard about this so-called sports day they're organizing.'

'The non-competitive one?'

I actually laugh – and not in a good way. 'You *knew* about this?'

'What's wrong with it?'

'You knew about this and you didn't think to tell me.'

She's busted in a big-time way. 'Oh my God,' she tries to go, 'are you going to tell me what the big deal is?'

'The big deal is that our daughter is being told that winning doesn't matter. This is something she's learning in a supposed school.'

'The lesson she's learning, Ross, is that we are – all of us – good at something. But those skills don't necessarily make us superior to anyone else.'

'What kind of horseshit is that to fill a child's head with?'

'Ross, do you know what *word* our daughter actually used recently?'

48

'No, what?'

'Pov.'

'Pov?'

'Yes, Ross, it's short for poverty victim. She said it about the twins who she *used* to be friends with.'

'Well, I've never heard her say it.'

'Oh, don't worry, Ross – I know who she picked it up from.'

'My guess would be one or two of the kids she's hanging out with in Imaginosity. We might have to stop bringing here there.'

'She got it from you! And there's no excuse for talking about other basically human beings like that. Our daughter needs to learn that – oh my God – no one in this world is better than anyone else.'

I end up just shaking my head. 'Look,' I go, 'I'm far from an economist. All I'm saying is, if *that's* what we're going to stort teaching kids, this country really *is* as focked as everyone's saying.'

Sorcha puts the chocolate HobNobs away before I can grab another, a sure sign that I've touched a nerve.

'Well,' she tries to go, 'Giovanna said at Healing Through Tai Chi yesterday that this is one of the lessons we need to learn from the whole Celtic Tiger experience. While we were all striving for what we *thought* was prosperity, we lost sight of the importance of pretty much *spiritual* things?'

I sort of, like, roll my eyes.

'You can do that all you want, Ross. What I'm saying is right. We *all* got caught up in this thing – this, like, contest to always have the best kitchen, the best . . . whatever else.'

'Okay, *you've* got the best focking kitchen on Newtownpork Avenue – which means you're one to talk. And secondly, why does everyone have to keep slagging off the Celtic Tiger? I seem to be one of the few people in this country who remembers how amazing it was while it lasted.'

'Because, Ross, it was only ever a lifestyle dream that was sold to us by banks and major corporations. This is what Giovanna's trying to get us all to see. And, yes, I accept your point about this kitchen. I got sucked in, the same as everyone else, mistook material goods for happiness. But we *weren't* happy, Ross.'

'*I focking was.*'

'I'm talking as, like, a *society*? Why do you think there was so much aggression out there?'

'Aggression? What the fock are you talking about?'

'Look at our roads, Ross. What do people do as soon as they see a cor trying to merge ahead of them? Or even change lane? They put their foot on the accelerator.'

'*You* do that all the time.'

'And it doesn't matter how fast they're driving, the important thing is to get in front of the car that's ahead of you. No one even looks to see what speed they're doing anymore.'

'You certainly don't. You're always too busy texting.'

'Fock you!' she goes, suddenly losing it with me. 'Just fock you, Ross!' and I immediately know that I've pushed her too far.

'Okay, I'm sorry,' I go, hopping off the high stool and trying to put my orms around her. 'Hey, I was only joking. I was playing devil's . . . something, something.'

She stops struggling and just looks at me. She never could resist my hugs.

'Come on,' I just go, 'one size fits all!' and she just shakes her head, then literally melts into my chest. I just, like, stroke her hair and I can tell she feels instantly safe in there.

The next thing, roysh, she pulls away and looks at me. 'Ross,' she goes, 'please take this seriously. I'm trying to help our daughter to adjust to the new economic paradigm.'

'Okay,' I go, somehow managing to keep a straight face.

Then she has a quick look over my shoulder at the clock. 'Anyway,' she goes, 'I'm sure you've better things to be doing on a Saturday night.'

I just nod. The weird thing is, roysh, I actually have no concrete plans, although obviously there *are* girls I could ring at just the drop of a hat.

'Just don't be too hungover tomorrow,' she goes, walking me out to the door, 'and I'm only saying that thinking of Honor.'

Sunday, see, is my day to spend some quality – unsupervised access – time with her.

I'm like, 'Cool. So, er, what are you doing tonight yourself?'

She just shrugs. 'Probably just a Chinese, then curl up on the sofa for *Dancing On Ice*.'

It's a focked-up thing to say but that actually sounds great. She always has the gaff lovely and toasty.

'Actually,' I go, 'do you, er, fancy a bit of company?'

She's there, 'I don't really think that's a good idea, do you?' and before I have a chance to think of an amazing comeback, she gently shuts the door in my face.

Jesus. I'm finally getting to see what Sorcha meant about Honor and her shit-fits. She wants me to bring her to Dundrum Town Centre, which is where we end up going every focking Sunday. All *I'm* saying is that it's good to try out new places – like Herbert Pork for a change. But *she's* practically screaming the roof off the cor, telling me that the pork is – oh my God – *so* lame and she wants a strawberry fro-yo.

This is on Clyde Lane in the middle of, like, Ballsbridge.

'We'll get you one after,' I try to go. 'All I'm saying is that a bit of exercise might do you the world of good, Babes. Especially with this supposed sports day coming up – in, what, six weeks' time?'

But on and on the hissy fit goes. She even, like, swears at me. 'Bring me to focking Dundrum!' she goes. 'I don't want to go to the focking pork!'

And bear in mind, roysh, she's not five until, like, November.

Now, in the normal run of things, I wouldn't agree with, like, bribing kids, but in this case – I have to hold my hands up here – I end up going, 'How would you like me to take you to Paris?'

That stops the tears pretty much immediately. She sort of, like, huffs. 'Mom said I have to wait until I'm old enough to, like, *appreciate* it?' she goes, her poor little eyes all red and puffy, her bottom lip stuck out.

Even though she's a little bitch, she'd melt your actual hort.

'Like I keep telling you,' I go, 'I wouldn't always listen to your mother.'

She looks at me, sat there in the passenger seat, waiting to hear my words of wisdom. 'What if *I* told you that you didn't have to wait? What if I told you that *I'll* bring you this summer?'

Her little face just lights up. 'Really?'

'Abs-and-pecsolutey! Disneyland, the whole focking bit.'

'Disneyland's lame. I want to go for, like, Paris Fashion Week.'

I laugh. She's definitely her mother's daughter. 'Paris Fashion Week it is, then. I'll bring you for Paris Fashion Week.'

'Oh! *My* God!'

'Hey, it's not a major deal. There's still money out there, despite what everyone's saying. But you know that thing that Mommy's always telling you – about how rewards have to be basically earned?'

'I *make* my own bed. *And* put my dishes in the dishwasher.'

'No one's arguing with that.'

'Linh does nothing. Oh my God, she is, like, *such* a lazy bitch!'

'And I'm watching her like a hawk, Honor. I'm watching her like a hawk. But, look, I'll tell you what it is. I'm going to be honest with you – and I'm possibly guilty here of trying to live out my dreams of sporting glory through you – but I'd really like you to win the twenty-five-metre sprint in this sports day you've got coming up.'

'*Win* it?'

'Exactly.'

She looks confused. 'But Ms Mhic Mathúna says there *are* no winners. She says that the real victory is in taking part.'

Mhic Ma-focking-thúna. The damage these so-called teachers can do to children's minds.

'Let me show you something,' I suddenly go, then I climb out of the van.

Honor undoes her own seat-belt and gets out as well, then follows me around to the back. I open the back door, roysh, and whip out the StairMaster that Sorcha bought a few years ago, after I passed what was *intended* as an innocent comment about her orse while she was putting the Christmas decorations back up in the attic.

'That's Mom's StairMaster,' Honor goes, instantly recognizing it. See what I mean? Sport is definitely in the genes. 'She's been looking for that.'

I'm there, 'Well, don't you focking tell her I took it. I covered up for you about the whole pov thing, didn't I?'

She just nods.

'Honestly, Honor, she wouldn't actually understand, even though we believe in basically the same thing, which is that you have to work hord in this life if you want to get the rewards. Okay, I'm going to spell it out for you. If you want me to bring you to Paris, you're going to have to win this race. And if you want to win the race, you're going to have to basically train.'

She's like, 'Train?' turning her tiny little nose up at me. I might as well have asked her to wear shoes from Zerep.

I'm like, 'It's an unfortunate fact of life, Honor, that if you want success, you have to first put in the hord yords. Look at my rugby career
as evidence of that.'

She still doesn't seem impressed, even though she's watched the
DVD of the 1999 Leinster Schools Senior Cup final with me maybe,
like, a dozen times.

I'm like, 'Paris, Honor – just think.'

'Malorie's already been.'

'I bet Malorie didn't get to stay in a five-stor hotel, though, did she?'

'No, it was, like, an Ibis?'

'Well, it won't be an Ibis for you, if you win this race. It'll be focking
luxury all the way, that much I can promise you.'

'Okay,' she just goes, suddenly full of, I'm going to call it, resolve.

I'm there, 'Now, I'm not talking about anything mental, Honor. All
I'm saying is we might stop off here on the way to school every day, do
a few minutes on this thing. Then I could time you running laps – storting from, say, Roly's Bistro, then running once or twice around the
block. There's an actual stopwatch on my iPhone.'

She smiles at me, her tantrum totally forgotten. She's a total daddy's
girl.

'Fine,' she just goes, her game-face suddenly on.

So I grab her by the hand and we head into the pork, over towards
the tennis courts, her yabbering the whole way about the *Carrousel du
Louvre* and loads of other shit that goes in one ear and out the other.

I put the old StairMaster down on the grass and switch the gradient
from light – Sorcha bought it for her conscience more than her orse –
to medium. Honor steps onto it and suddenly, roysh, off she goes,
working away like you wouldn't believe, while I try to undo some of
the brainwashing that the crowd in Little Roedean's have been expos-
ing her to, giving her one or two of my own personal sayings, mostly
motivational quotes that helped me back in my rugby-playing days.

It's all, 'Remember, no one *wins* silver, Honor – they *lose* gold,' or
it's, 'Second is the loneliest word in the English language,' or even, 'It's
not enough that I should be on the green – every other focker must be
in the bunker.'

Unbelievably, she ends up doing, like, a quarter of an hour on the
thing, breaking her mother's record – I *could* point out, if I was a nasty
person – by a full three minutes. That's how much she wants to see

Paris. I tell her that's enough, let's keep something in the tank for tomorrow. And it's at that exact point that I hear the old man's voice come crashing through the air like the fall of Baghdad.

'Hello there, Ross! And Honor – hello, Darling!'

I end up having to remind her about our deal out of the corner of my mouth.

'Don't say a word about training,' I go. 'Remember, if people get wind that you want to actually *win* this race, they're going to disqualify you – and that'll mean we won't be going anywhere.'

She just nods, I suppose, sadly.

It turns out to be not only my old man, roysh, but Helen and Erika as well and the two women are, like, linking him, one either side. I actually forgot that he lives so near here now. I'm definitely going to have to be more careful.

He goes, 'I was just telling Helen and your sister how I used to take *you* to Herbert Park when you weren't much older than Honor there. We used to fling the old Gilbert around . . .'

His train of thought is all of a sudden interrupted by the sight of the StairMaster. 'Hello, what's all this how-do-you-do? Isn't that Sorcha's what's-this-you-call-it?'

But Honor, roysh, just throws her orms around his leg and goes, 'Granddad!' and of course then *he's* suddenly off in another world, giving it, 'Hello there, little one,' and all the rest of it. 'Shall we go look at the squirrels?'

Honor seems really excited about that – she obviously wants something from him – and it's Helen who bends down to pick her up, presumably because *he* doesn't have the strength yet.

'We've just had your mother for Sunday lunch,' he goes. 'She's finished writing this famous misery lit novel of hers, you know.'

I laugh. It never ceases to weird me out how they've all stayed friends.

He's like, 'Sent it off to the publishers yesterday. *Mom, They Said They'd Never Heard of Sundried Tomatoes*! Where does she come up with them?'

'Why would be more my question.'

Then they walk off – him and Helen, carrying Honor – in the direction of the trees, leaving me standing there with Erika and the StairMaster.

In the distance, I hear Honor go, 'Granddad, will you buy me some mobile phone credit?'

That's when Helen stops, turns back to me and goes, 'Has she been running, Ross?'

I'm like, 'Sorry?'

'She's sweating. Look, she's wet right through.'

I end up pulling one of those, I suppose, confused faces that have become, like, a *trademork* of mine? One thing I've learned in life is that if you never give a straight answer, no one can accuse you of lying later on.

I look at Erika. Usually, she'd be on it like a bonnet. 'Strangely,' she just goes, 'I don't even want to know what you're up to this time.'

I pick up the StairMaster. 'How's Fionn?' I just happen to go – see, I can be nice. 'Has he realized how out of his actual depth he is yet?'

She tells me I'm, like, pathetic, then follows the others over to see the squirrels.

'What's this shit I'm hearing?'

Hennessy is hilarious. Never even says who it is who's ringing. Just gets straight down to business.

'Hearing?' I go. 'I don't know, what *are* you hearing?'

'I'm hearing that Charlie Kelly's fucking idiot son is talking about showing up at this meeting with Oisinn's creditors.'

'Well,' I go, 'you've heard right. Can you fit me in, maybe somewhere towards the end? The big finale.'

'Fit you in?'

'Yeah. Bear in mind now that I'm standing in the queue in Donnybrook Fair here – it's difficult for me to talk. But yeah, no, I'm pretty determined to go along and say my piece.'

'Say your piece?' he goes. 'What the fuck do you think this is?'

'Dude, I'm the one who persuaded him to come back to Ireland to face the music, remember? Means I feel kind of responsible?'

'You stay the fuck away.'

'Plus I'm one of his oldest friends.'

'You will fuck this up . . .'

'I also played rugby with him.'

'. . . like you fuck up everything.'

'Dude, they're going to want to hear from the likes of me – in other words, people who can go into a bit of a spiel about his character and blah blah blah.'

'You show your face at this meeting and I will, personally, beat the fucking piss out of you.'

'Well, that's an opinion. I'm sorry you feel that way.'

'Yeah, you show up, then. You just fucking try me.'

'I will.'

'You won't.'

'I'm going to.'

'I swear to fuck, if you come within a hundred fucking feet of my office . . .'

'Let's just agree to differ.'

'No, let's agree that you stay the fuck away.'

'I have to go here – this bird's finished ringing up my lunch.'

'I don't want to see your ugly fucking face Monday morning.'

'Like I said, that's a difference of opinion.'

'Stay the fuck away.'

'I'll see you there.'

Ronan's watching a *soccer* match – Manchester Something against, I don't know, one of the others – and he's making pretty light work, it has to be said, of that porkie bag and cuddy chips. I'd never say it to his face but the kid has been piling on the old poundage since he gave up the cigarettes and it's no surprise, eating like a focking plane crash survivor.

Then again, it does *suit* him?

I can't even begin to tell you, by the way, how much I hate soccer. But it's like that thing you always hear people say, isn't it? In other words, you'd do anything to support your kids, doesn't matter what they're mixed up in.

For me, that's meant finally coming to terms with the fact that Ronan possibly isn't going to wear the number ten jersey of Ireland one day. There's no even rugby *in* Castlerock anymore, which is focking Tom McGahy's doing – and all because I made his life hell back when he was a teacher.

So Ronan's back watching soccer again. I keep telling myself there's no actual shame in it. Blackrock College are supposed to have a pretty decent soccer team, even though it's kept mostly under wraps. But if this is what he considers sport, then I'm just going to have to come to terms with it.

'Are you bored?' Ronan suddenly goes.

We're in his gaff in Finglas, by the way.

I'm like, 'No.'

'It's just you keep fooken sighing.'

'Sighing?'

'And tutting.'

'Oh, sorry, it's possibly, like, a *subconscious* thing?'

'Do you want me to turden it off?'

'No, no, keep watching.'

'Are you shewer?'

'Yeah, no, I was just thinking there in my, I don't know, mind – and this isn't having a go at soccer players – but *what* is the Jack with all the tats? I haven't seen that much prison ink since your focking granddad was in Mountjoy.'

He actually laughs at that. See, he's a chip off the old block when it comes to, well, enjoying my sense of humour.

'Oh, by the way,' I suddenly go, '*Seven Brides for Seven Brothers*. Give me an update.'

'An update?'

'Yeah, an update.'

'Yeah, no,' he goes, 'Ine enjoying it,' and then he turns back to the TV, with a big red face on him.

'I focking bet you are!' I instantly go. 'Come on, give me the skinny. How many of the brides have you got off with so far? I'd say Bla's bulling as well, is she?'

'Leave it, Rosser.'

But I don't. I'm like a dog with a bone here. 'Hey, come on. I want the info. Even just give it to me ballpork.'

'Alreet,' he goes, just turning to me. 'One.'

I'm like, 'One?' trying my best to hide my disappointment?

'Yeah. Yasmin.'

'She's called Yasmin – well, that's something at least.'

'She's playing Milly.'

'Okay. But what's the deal, Ro? I thought you said they were *all* seriously into you?'

He just shrugs, like he doesn't want to actually *say* the words? It's called modesty. He'll hopefully grow out of it.

'Thee are.'

'Of course they are! Because that's what women are basically like, Ro. They want what they're told they can't have. Why do you think Visa and Mastercord are forever focking plastic at them?'

'I suppose.'

'No suppose about it,' I go, then I take one of his chips. 'Okay, so who's next?'

'What?'

'On the hitlist. Who else do you like? Or I'll phrase that another way – who's the best of the rest, in terms of looks?'

He looks like he hasn't even *considered* it? 'Er, I suppose Filipa Lowndes.'

'Okay.'

'She's playing Dorcas.'

'Dorcas! Jesus, even the names take me back. Is there anyone famous that she actually looks like?'

'What?'

'Okay, doesn't matter. The more important question,' I go, giving him the guns, 'is when are you going to make your move?'

'Me move?'

'Ro, when you're hot, you're hot. That's what you have to accept. Why don't you ask her out?'

'No need. *She* already ast *me*, Rosser.'

'What?'

'To Eddie Rocket's.'

'Empty focking Pockets! That's where me and actual Sorcha first got together. Which one?'

'Donnybrook. She says she wants to go over lines.'

I laugh. 'Oh, I bet she does. That's a line in itself.'

'I said no, but.'

'You said no? Why?'

'Why do you tink? Cos of Yasmin.'

'Whoa, whoa, whoa, you're not going *out* with this Yasmin, are you? As in, like, boyfriend-girlfriend?'

'No. Well, I never ast her, in anyhow.'

'You only, like, kissed the girl, yeah?'

'Yeah.'

'Well, then. What's the biggie? Er, you're a free *agent*?'

He looks, I don't know, down in the dumps about something. I instantly understand when I hear what he says next. 'But see, Rosser, she *thinks* she's me geerl friend.'

'But she's not.'

'I know. But how do I *tell* her that? She keeps texting me, man.' He waves his phone at me. 'Keeps buying me fooken credit.'

'She *buys* you credit?'

'To make sure I can always text her back.'

I can't tell you how suddenly angry that makes me. They're un-focking-believable – at any age.

I'm like, 'Look, Ro, I've been around the track a time or two. I know you've heard a lot of the stories and I can vouch for the fact that most of them are true. Either way, believe me when I tell you, women have a million ways of getting what they want. And that's why *we've* got to be cleverer than them.'

'Reet.'

'Honestly, you smile at a girl the wrong way, the next thing she's picking out focking songs for a mix tape. Okay, I accept there's no such thing as tapes anymore, but from the sounds of it, it hasn't made life any easier.'

'Er, okay.'

'I'm presuming, with all this attention you're suddenly getting, that the last thing you want is a serious girlfriend.'

'Yeah.'

'So tell her that.'

'It's heerd, but.'

See, he's too focking soft. I saw that with the trouble he had breaking up with Bla.

'It shouldn't *be* hord,' I make sure to go. 'Bear in mind, Ro, that down the line, she's probably going to dump you anyway – especially with no rugby,' and then I flick my thumb at the old plasma on the wall. 'Can you honestly see three or four hundred Mounties turning up to watch you play *that* shit?' and he nods, roysh, like he knows I have a point.

'But *how* do I say it, Rosser? What woords?'

I'm like, 'It's like tackling someone in rugby, Ro. It's got to be firm and it's got to be fair. Actually, it doesn't necessarily have to be fair now that I think about. I'll tell you what,' then I stand up, roysh, and whip my phone out of my pocket.

'Watch and learn from the master.'

I get Aithne's number up, then I hit dial. I hold the phone up to my ear and tell Ro, 'This is what's called putting the gorbage out.'

She answers on, like, the second ring. Way too keen. But I'm straight on the offensive anyway. '*Seven* missed calls in, what, two weeks? What are you, some kind of stalker?'

I wink at Ro. I suppose it's like one of those nature programmes you sometimes see, where the adult animal teaches its, I don't know, offspring, by basically example.

She immediately storts muttering and stuttering. 'Excuse me?' she goes. 'We arranged to meet – that Friday night? In Bleu? I sat there for a focking hour.'

Shit! I genuinely forgot about that.

'So pardon me,' she goes, 'for trying to find out was there a genuine reason or was I just stood up.'

'Whoa, whoa, whoa,' I go, 'you've no right to stort cross-examining me.'

I give Ro another wink, then I put the call on speakerphone for him to appreciate the full affect of the master at work.

She's like, 'What?'

'As in, coming the heavy with the questions. We were only with each other once, bear in mind. I didn't tell you to stort picking out church music.'

'Church music? What are you talking about?'

'I'm saying it was a use and abuse situation. It sounds to me like you need to get over that basic fact.'

'That's not what you said the night we were together. You were the one who mentioned the relationship word.' I make the old yabber-mouth sign with my free hand and roll my eyes. Ronan smiles. He's genuinely impressed. 'You were the one who said you wanted to finally settle down.'

'Hey, you heard what you wanted to hear. Look, you're no different to any other girl – you saw something real pretty and you went for it. Good luck to you.'

'You focking . . . bastard.'

'Hey, we can all say bad words, Baby.'

'Wanker.'

'That's another one.'

'Focking asshole.'

'Oh, they're *all* good. Personally, I think you'd be better off just accepting it. You'll always have the memory.'

That's really twisting the knife. But Ro's looking at me in, honestly, total awe.

'Memory?' *she* has to go then. 'You think it was something I'd want to remember? *Your* tiny penis? Ross, it was like having a focking wardrobe fall on top of you with the key still in the door . . .'

I suddenly kill the call.

I'm like, 'That's another lesson for you down the line, Ro. Always hang up before they stort with the really personal shit.'

Okay, it's confession time.

One of the things I've actually kept from you over the years is my – let's just call them – nocturnal activities in the hog pens of Temple Bor. I've never told you, for instance, that the bouncers in the old cultural quarter – from Buskers to Club M – have nicknamed me The Fox, for my ability to steal in, in the middle of the night, and pick off vulnerable hens.

There are literally hundreds of married women in this town – as well as the major cities of northern England – who can claim that Ross O'Carroll-Kelly was their final fling. And that's not a bad consolation for anyone about to embark on long-term marriage.

Now, I know exactly how some people – my detractors mainly – are going to respond to this. They're going to say, er, the dude can have literally any woman in the world he wants – why does he need to go hogging? So I'm going to tell you. Going to let you in on a little trade secret. Sex with a bird who's about to walk up the aisle – doesn't matter what shape she's in – is some of *the* best sex you are ever likely to have. Why? Because it's her last real shot at it. We're pretty much talking death-row sex and she wants to make it count.

Anyway, I'm telling you all of this as, like, a *preamble* – if that's a word – to the story of what happened after I left Ronan's that night.

Okay, so it's, like, half nine – this is, like, a Sunday night, remember – and, it has to be said, I'm feeling pretty good about myself. And I *think* understandably? Having worshipped gangland scum for most of his thirteen years, my son has finally found a reason to idolize *me* and it's an amazing, I suppose, sensation.

So I'm driving through the old Shitty Centre and I just think, fock it, I'm going grab a focking Bucky's on the strength of this. So I pull the van in, there opposite the old Bank of Ireland on College Green, where I end up having to give the finger to this taxi driver who tries to tell me that where I've porked is actually port of the rank?

I tip across the road, roysh, and I'm just pulling the door of the place, wondering are they still doing the Christmas drinks – February, focking doubtful – when my eyes are suddenly drawn to this, I suppose you could say, *gaggle* of women standing around outside Londis, wearing half-nothing, smoking themselves hoarse and swearing like a focking truck-stop.

They've got all the – okay, big word coming up – but *paraphernalia*, we're talking, like, angel wings and devil horns and magic wands that are shaped like mickeys at the top. Smack bang in the middle of them is the half-cut bride-to-be – one thing you have to say about me is that I'm always on the mooch – wearing a bridal veil that, by itself, accounts for about eighty percent of the material covering her body.

'Don't do it!' I shout in her general postcode. 'Be the biggest mistake of your life. And *I* should know!' and the next thing, roysh, all fourteen or fifteen birds on the hen night are looking in my direction, squinting their eyes, trying to make me out.

'Oh-aye,' one of them goes, 'what's *he* pfookin saying?' and I immediately recognize the accent as being the accent of the city of Liverpool.

'Arrr-eh,' it's the bride-to-be who suddenly goes, dropping her cigarette on the ground and grinding it under a mirrored heel, 'he's pfookin gorchiss – look arrum!' and then they all stort going, 'Come over ere, eh? Come over ere!'

So I end up just tipping over.

It has to be said – in case you think I'm just bigging myself up here – that it's one of the ugliest focking hen-nights I've ever seen. Straight out of M. Night Shyamalan's imagination.

'Ahm Denise,' the bride goes. The one getting married always has first dibs. The rule's as old as, I don't know, God.

'I'm Ross,' I go, smooth as eggs, 'and the pleasure – believe me – is all mine.'

'Ooze *e* pfookin think he is?' one of the other zombies goes. 'James pfookin Bond? Ahm gonna pfookin beerst him.'

It's an unfortunate fact of life, roysh, that at least thirty percent of English birds who are on a night out would prefer a fight to a ride. Happily, roysh, Denise isn't one of them. She's, like, totally chormed by me.

'Arrr-eh,' she goes, 'the way he shpeaks is luffly, innit, eh? So where you goin, eh? Yowt for the night?'

She's horrendous, I'm going to admit it – and a real focking bed-breaker. If I had to describe her as looking like anyone, it'd be Johnny Vegas in a focking bikini.

I'm there, 'I *was* just going to grab a coffee. But it looks to me like the evening's just taken a turn – a very much unexpected one.'

'He's thawken pfookin shite,' one of the friends goes, then announces that she's going to put her cigarette out on my face.

So I just ramp up the chorm, of course. 'I'm actually being serious. You girls have suddenly got me rethinking my plans for the evening.'

'Why don't you come wirrus for a bevy, eh?' Denise goes. Oh, she's calling shotgun alright. '*You* can be me pfookin hag, eh?'

I laugh and think, yeah, why the fock not? I'm pretty much guaranteed my bit here at the end of the night and what's the actual alternative? A vanilla latte, then home for twelve rounds with the age-ing, one-eyed champ. Fock that.

'Sweet as!' I just go. 'Lead the way.'

Anyway, it turns out they're headed for Club M. They generally are. So in we focking trot.

The place, it has to be said, is far from rammers. When the night-clubs are only half full on a Sunday night, that's when you know the country's in serious shit.

Recession or no recession, though, I can't resist playing Jack the Lad. We're only in the door two minutes and I've suddenly whipped out my wad and ordered, like, four bottles of sporkling wine.

Obviously champagne would be wasted on these people – you might as well pour it onto the pavement outside Iskander's now.

Anyway, once they've all got a drink in their hands, the hostility that I *was* feeling from one or two of them begins to melt away and they're suddenly all loving me.

'Arrr-eh, isn't he gareat?' they're all going and I even hear one or two of them go, 'He's gorra fantastuck body on um, asn't he, eh?' which is an amazing thing to hear, even coming from mongs.

Even though they're tanning the drink, *I* end up taking it easy, because – I haven't forgotten – I've got Oisinn's creditors meeting at, like, eleven o'clock tomorrow morning and I still fully intend saying my actual piece.

But even relatively sober, I'm still amazing company, in fairness to me, dishing out compliments to all the birds – lies, basically – and even demonstrating one or two of my dance moves for them.

Anyway, to cut a long story short, I eventually manage to isolate Denise from the herd and we end up sitting in, like, a booth, just the two of us, shooting the shit, me with a pint of Ken in front of me, her with some kind of cocktail that looks like it should be eaten with a focking spoon. And it ends up being pretty deep, what we talk about.

'I meant what I said,' I go. '*Don't* do it.'

She laughs. 'You're norra believer in maddidge then, no?'

I laugh then.

'See, if you'd asked me that, like, five or six years ago, I might have had a different answer. But no, not really.'

I'm suddenly getting this, I don't know, whiff of something. It smells like focking Deep Heat and it instantly brings me back to my rugby days.

'So worr *ave* you gorr against maddidge, then?'

'That's a good question. I *could* answer it by saying personal experience. Didn't work for me. Didn't work for my old pair either.'

'Arrr-eh, you're difforced, then, are ya, eh?'

'Soon to be. Separated at the moment but we're about to go down that particular road, yeah.'

'Arrr-eh, soddy to hear that.'

'Don't be. I was a dirty dog, in fairness to me. The thing is, I'm not really sure that I believe in – what's that thing where you *don't* sleep with other people?'

'Ahm not shewer – er, monogamy, is it?'

'That's the one. See, I'm not sure I believe it exists. Or should be even allowed to.'

'Ah do,' she goes. 'See when ah get maddied? Ahm not gonna be doin' this anymore.'

This meaning, presumably, what we're going to do later. She's, like, presuming an awful lot, when you think about it, especially for a shmug.

'There's a lot of people who make that promise,' I go.

'*Ah* mean it, like.'

'Oh, a lot of people *mean* it as well. Do you mind me asking, how even old are you?'

'Ahm twenty-fav.'

I laugh.

'Twenty-five? Well, all I can I say is that you've a lot to learn,' and then – nice and sleazy, this – I put my hand on her thigh, which is all fat and goosepimply, like a Manor Form chicken, and I give it a bit of a tweak. 'And, luckily for you, I just love to teach.'

She laughs – drunkenly – then goes, 'Do you not get tarred of it, though, eh?'

'Tired of it?'

'Yeah. Casual sex, like.'

I *really* laugh then. 'Er, no. I can't say I ever do.'

'Arrr-eh, no offence, right, but when ahm your age, ah want to be keerled up on the shofa with the man ah luff and a pfookin Chanese, watching *Thex Facti* or *Dancing on* pfookin *Ice* . . .'

I don't even let her finish the thought. I put my hand around the back of her neck and pull her towards me, throwing the lips on her. We spend, like, twenty or thirty seconds like that, just sucking face and she actually loves it – not being nasty here – like Kerry Katona loves chips. Then I get that hum again, except this time it's pretty much *overpowering*? I pull away.

'Have you been eating Fisherman's Friends?' I go.

'Eh?'

'I'm talking about the Johnny Bell,' I go, wiggling my nose. 'What is it?'

'Arrr-eh, no, it's wintigreen, that.'

'Wintergreen?'

'Yehrr, it's oil. To keep the heat in. Pfookin freezing out there, case yer aven't noticed.'

I laugh. I suddenly remember JP and Fionn coating themselves in Vicks VapoRub before they did their focking streak at the Heineken Cup final.

'Would you not think of wearing more clothes?' I go, not unreasonably, I would have thought.

'No way,' she goes. 'It's like me mam says, if you've pfookin gorrit, you've gorra pfookin flaunt it.'

She doesn't even seem to be joking either.

It turns out, anyway, that they're actually *staying* in Blooms?

Within an hour of meeting me, she's decided that she can't hold out any longer and she has to have me up in the room now. In the lift, she's all over me like a focking freed hostage. And of course I'm giving as good I'm getting – chewing the lips off her – and I'm suddenly horder than Schalk focking Burger.

We practically crash through the door of her room, then collapse onto the bed, pulling and tearing at each other. The next thing I know, roysh, she slaps me lightly across the cheek, then jabs a finger in my face and goes, 'You're me pfookin last, right?'

I'm there, 'Er, okay.'

'Me faanal fling.'

'Coola boola.'

'Well, make it one to pfookin remember – do yer ear me, eh?'

What she means, I can tell you from past experience, is that she's going to want foreplay.

'No better focking buachaill,' I go, then I end up giving her a good twenty minutes of preliminaries, including kissing every flab and fold on her body, before finally setting the dogs on her.

It ends up being one to remember alright. Not being big-headed but I end up romping her bow-legged.

'Arrr-eh,' she goes when it's all over, trying to get her breath back, 'that was pfookin garreat, that was. No pfookin complaints from me.'

'Complaints?' I go. 'I don't entertain them.'

She laughs.

'What's that thing they always say?' I go. 'No correspondence will be entered into,' then I roll out of the bed and go off to drown the fish.

It's while I'm there, stood over the bowl, that I cop the sudden weird *taste* in my mouth? It's not just a taste either – it's, like, a sensation? It's, like, dry and whatever else. It actually feels like I've been licking Shake 'n' Vac up off the focking floor, then I instantly realize that it's from that, I don't know, whatever-the-fock-it's-called oil that she had all over her body.

I wander over to the mirror. My lips are, like, tingling as well. I drink a glass of water, then another and it seems to do the trick.

I go back out to Denise.

'No offence,' I go, 'but that shit on your body is focking lethal.'

That's when I realize that she's actually fast asleep.

I end up having an un-focking-believable sleep myself. But then I wake with a sudden fright because it feels like it's about, I don't know, three o'clock in the afternoon and I'm totally convinced that I've slept through Oisinn's big day.

So I grab my phone, roysh, and check the time. It turns out it's only, like, half nine, which still gives me, like, an hour and a half.

I get up and find my clothes, some of which, by the way, are in pretty much flitters. I don't bother waking Denise. Or maybe she *is* awake and she's pretending not to be. See, that's another great thing about receipting and filing a bird on her hen-night. You don't have to go through the whole awkward ballet of trying to pull your chinos on without handing over your contact details. They generally want you already gone by the time they open their eyes.

Which, in this case, I am.

Five minutes later, I'm doing the old Walk of Shame through reception and out onto whatever the fock that street is called. It's only as I'm turning the corner that I remember I've been basically illegally porked all night and, yeah, even from fifty yords away I can straight away see that the cor has been, like, clamped.

Which isn't a major deal to me in the normal run of things. Happens to me so often that I've got those parasite fockers on speed-dial. In fact, the receptionist usually knows my voice before I've even mentioned my name.

I say *usually*.

Except not this time. Because when I dial the number and she answers, I realize that there's something suddenly not quite right with my mouth.

I'm late. Which I definitely didn't want to be. I'm also still in the threads I was wearing last night. And even though it *is* beige chinos and a light blue Ralph, there's no getting away from the fact that I reek of tequila, *Coleen X Summer* and what Oisinn – who knows a thing or six about smells – straight away recognizes as methyl salicylate.

Every head turns when I step into the boardroom, we're talking thirteen or fourteen men, then one or two women, all dressed in suits. Big focking serious faces on them as well. A few of them are checking me out as if to say, who's this dude suddenly arriving?

Oisinn and Hennessy are sitting together at the top of the board-room table and Hennessy, it has to be said, doesn't look a happy rabbit to see me. He turns to Oisinn and I'm pretty sure I hear him go, 'The fuck is *he* doing here?' so I just hold my hand up, roysh, as if to say, er, no one mind me, then I plonk myself down in one of the chairs lined up against the wall and stort concentrating really hord to try to catch up on what I've missed here.

'This meeting,' one of the suits at the table goes, 'is supposed to be in camera – only *interested* parties?' and everyone is suddenly staring in my general locale.

Oisinn – fair focks – goes, 'This is my, em, accountant,' and honestly, roysh, all their focking eyes go wide. I'm wondering why is that so focking hord to believe? One of the few things I *was* actually good at in school was – I don't know – sums.

'My client's postition,' Hennessy goes, suddenly grabbing their attention back, '*is* as I've outlined it. His net worth has been wiped out by, I think we'd all agree, the very much unforeseen global economic meltdown. He has liabilities totalling €79.8 million. He has assets of €18 million . . .'

This dude with, like, grey hair suddenly cuts him off. 'I think there's a serious question mark against that figure of €18 million, based, as I *suspect* it is, on an overvaluation of his property portfolio.'

This woman sitting beside him – nothing to see, please disperse – storts flicking through her notes, going, 'How many rental properties does your client own?'

'Seventy-three,' it's Oisinn who straight away goes.

'And they're, what, mainly apartments?'

'Mostly. I've got, like, fifteen houses and, yeah, fifty-eight apart-ments.'

'And you have mortgages outstanding on all of these properties?'

'Some of them.'

'*Most* of them?'

Oisinn nods. You can tell this bird isn't *used* to being shitted? 'Most of them, yeah.'

'The vast majority of them?'

'Yeah.'

'And how many of them are occupied at present?'

Oisinn suddenly turns and looks at Hennessy for obvious back-up.

'Sorry,' Hennessy goes, 'is this leading somewhere?'

The woman actually laughs. She has legs like focking banana trees, I notice. Jesus, I wouldn't touch her with rubber gloves on.

'Yes,' she goes, 'I'm trying to establish how much income these properties are generating and what percentage of his monthly mortgate liabilities does it constitute.'

Hennessy doesn't even get a chance to answer. The dude who asked the original question – he's got one of those faces you'd never get tired of slapping – goes, 'With respect, I think that's irrelevant. We're way past that point. Look, some of these properties haven't even been built yet. We obtained an order six months ago to repossess, what, three apartments I think it was, in Carrickmines, after he defaulted on the loans. The sherriff turned up at the address – it was still a field!'

I actually laugh out loud at that. I mean, talk about stories that capture the spirit of the times.

That's when Hennessy seems to suddenly lose it. 'And who presided over a system that allowed that to happen?' he practically roars at the dude. 'You people!'

'No one forced your client to take out these loans.'

'All I'm saying is, *he* didn't know it was all going to turn to shit overnight. In case you haven't noticed, my friend, these are un-fucking-precedented times. For everyone. May I remind you, a few months back, your entire fucking bank was only worth a hundred and twenty million? Two years ago you couldn't have bought three houses on Shrewsbury Road for that. But, unlike my client here, you bastards are immune to the laws of action and consequence. Because the Government pillaged the National Pension Reserve Fund to save your incompetent fucking asses.'

I give Oisinn the old thumbs-up. Hennessy seems to be really sticking it to them. Let's see how they come back from this.

One of the other dudes at the table – a square-headed focker with Gok Wan glasses – clears his throat, then goes, 'Can I just remind you, Mr Coghlan-O'Hara, that none of us *needs* to be here today. Speaking for my own institution, we're *quite* prepared to pursue your client through the courts for what we're owed. *I* came here today because I was under the impression that there was some kind of solvency plan that we were going to be asked to consider. I can't speak for any of the other creditors here, but frankly, I couldn't care less what you think of the bank recapitalization.'

That seems to soften Hennessy's cough, roysh, because he's instantly all apologetic. 'Okay, I'm sorry,' he just goes. 'I shouldn't have lost my temper. All I'm asking is that my client be offered the same leeway in sorting out his financial affairs as you people were in sorting out yours, taking into account, like I said – unprecedented times and everything.'

The woman gets back on her high horse then. I swear to God, I'd nearly be tempted to say something if I understood a focking word of what was being said. 'Your client has no money,' she goes.

Hennessy looks at Oisinn. 'That's correct. Right now he's living on the charity of his parents.'

'And no income.'

He's just there, 'My client is a designer of ladies' fragrances,' which actually gets a few sniggers. My fists suddenly tighten. I feel like actually decking someone in this room. 'He *has* indicated to me his desire to return to that profession . . .'

'In the event of him *not* earning seventy-whatever-it-is million from this in the short term,' the dude with the glasses goes, with a big focking smirk on his face, 'what other plans does he have to meet these . . . *considerable* liabilities?'

'Well, as the Government said recently, the property market may have already bottomed out. This property portfolio of his, it's only going to increase in value.'

There's, like, a sudden burst of laughter in response to that. I have to say, if the Government really *did* say that, I actually think these people are bang out of order.

'In addition,' Hennessy tries to go, 'my client is a shareholder in an oil exploration project off the coast of, I think I'm right in saying, Mauritania.'

Oisinn nods.

'Oh, we're praying for an oil strike now,' the woman goes, at the same time picking up her briefcase. '*I've* definitely heard enough,' and she flicks it open and storts putting all her, like, notes and shit away?

The rest of them stay seated.

Hennessy goes, 'All I'm asking is that you wait six months. Come on, give a break to a guy who's been a good customer . . .'

'To a guy who's already fled the jurisdiction once,' the dude with the glasses suddenly goes. 'And how do we know he won't do it again?'

Another dude, who's been quiet up until now, goes, 'A guy who has admitted that at least some of his financial problems came as a result of a gambling addiction . . .'

I'm suddenly at, like, boiling point.

'Hey,' Hennessy goes, banging the table with his fist, 'I offered you that information in mitigation, not to be used against my client.'

'Internet poker, isn't that what you said?'

That's when I decide that I can't listen to anymore. I'm not having one of my best friends in the actual world dissed from a height like that.

I jump to my feet. Then I hear myself go, 'Thuck you, you thucking thathole!'

Every pair of eyes in the room, roysh, is suddenly looking at me. To be fair, I'm possibly more surprised by what came out of my mouth than *they* are?

'*What* was that?' the focker with the glasses has to go.

The woman – *so-called* – is like, 'I didn't catch it either. But I'd be very interested in what he has to say, especially about these accounts.'

It's weird but it feels like my tongue is, I don't know, *paralysed*?

'He hathens thoo thee a thriend thoth thine,' I hear myself go. 'How thucking thare hou theak athout thim thike that. He thayed thugby! Thugby! Thand you theat him thike a thommon thiminal?'

I look down the table, roysh, and Oisinn and Hennessy are just, like, staring at me in total shock. And we *are* talking total.

I think everyone, you'd have to say, is in pretty much the same *boat*?

My mouth is pretty much focked from the gallon of wintergreen I licked off that skank's body.

The woman sort of, like, flicks her thumb at me and goes, '*This* . . . is your *accountant*?'

Neither of them answers. Hennessy actually has his head in his hands, while Oisinn is wearing a look of what I'd probably have to describe as resignation.

I'm like, 'Thorry Hothinn. They her houth of horther. Hang hout of horther.'

'I'm sorry,' *she* goes, 'I'm not sure what the politically correct phrase is, but with fourteen million euros of our money at stake, I feel I'm almost duty-bound to ask – is he mentally . . . *all there?*'

'No,' Hennessy instantly goes and he's honestly as mad as I've ever seen him. 'He's fucking not.'

The next thing I hear, roysh, is the sound of chair legs scraping off the floor. They're all suddenly bailing and of course I know instantly that *I've* actually focked this up – and in a major way. They all just file out of the room. One of them – it's actually the dude with the glasses – pats me on the back and then, as if he's talking to a three-year-old, goes, 'I'm really sorry you had to be put through this.'

And then the room is suddenly empty except for the three of *us*.

'I ought to fucking kill you with my bare hands,' Hennessy goes.

'I'm thorry,' I go. 'I hoth hup hall nighth hicking thum thkank's vothy.'

'I told you to stay away, didn't I? You knew better, though. You know what you are? You're a useless fuck.'

'Hey, thath outh oth orther.'

'I said it to your father when he told me he was signing over the shredding business to you. I said, this is a company that could be worth ten, twenty million by the time this financial crisis is behind us. And you're going to hand it over to that dumb fuck of a son of yours?'

'Hath unthair.'

'It ain't unfair. It's true. I told him. Give him a year. Not even a year. Give him six months – and he'll have run that business into the fuckng ground.'

Oisinn just stands in between us, possibly saving my life. 'Come on,' he goes, 'I could use a drink. Let's go toast my bankruptcy.'

3. Are you trying to seduce me, Mrs Rathfriland?

It's, like, Paddy's Day and I'm in Dundrum, back doing the whole Daddy Daycare bit. We're sitting in Bucky's, the three of us, Honor munching away happily on a fruit cup and Ronan sitting there with the sleeve of his Shamrock Rovers jersey rolled up to the shoulder, staring angrily at the nicotine patch at the top of his orm, wondering presumably why it's doing fock-all to take the edge off his cravings. He even slaps it a couple of times, like you would a focked TV.

'Take my advice,' he looks across the table at his sister and goes, 'don't ever smoke. See, if was diffordent for us. We never knew any of the dangers when we steerted. In ear day, we werdunt toalt. Now there's no excuse, but. Thee know now that they're bad for you.'

He's a comedian – always was.

'Listen to your brother,' I go, even though she doesn't *need* to be told? She hangs on his every focking word.

'The only reason I *would* smoke,' she goes, 'is to, like, keep my weight down when I get older? But even though I hate to say it, I actually agree with Mom – it's, like, *so* a disgusting habit.'

I'm thinking, Yeah, this coming from the woman who lived on fock-all in college except Marlboro Lights and celery. Except I don't *actually* say it? Because they reckon – don't they? – that parents who are getting divorced shouldn't, like, diss each other in front of their actual kids, because, long term, it *can* be bad for them.

So instead, all I go is, 'I wouldn't take everything that girl says as Gospel, Honor. I'd be reluctant to use the word hypocrite, but a lot of the time, it has to be said, she's making it up as she goes along.'

I take a sip of my caramel macchiato.

'Well,' Honor goes, 'she's being a complete tord at the moment anyway.'

I end up having to laugh, even though I know it's possibly wrong. 'What's a tord, Honor?'

'You own an iPhone – look it up.'

That's become her answer to everything, by the way.

'I presume it's short for, like, retord, is it?'

'Er, *yeeeah?*'

'Okay. And how's she being one? And bear in mind that I'm not defending her.'

'Er, she's making a holy focking show of herself, that's how. Every morning in the circus field in Booterstown.'

She gets up off the chair, roysh, and she's suddenly stood on one leg with her two hands stretched out in front of her – a posture I instantly recognize as Repulse Monkey from the illustrated guide that's stuck to the door of Sorcha's fridge.

'*This recession cannot hurt me,*' she goes. '*Money is temporal and not of the spirit.*'

I'm nearly on the floor laughing, of course, because it's a spot-on impression. But then I catch Ronan looking at me and I sense disapproval. I think *he* thinks I let her get away with too much sometimes?

'Possibly don't rip the piss out of your mother,' I go. 'Blah blah blah.'

Ronan puts it a little bit better. 'She's doing her best, Honor. She's troying to come to teerms wit losing her shop, so she is.'

Honor's like, 'Yeah, whatevs! This morning? I found her – oh! my God! – pouring water into an empty bottle of, like, Molton Brown shower gel, to try to get the last few suds out. I was like, "Oh! My God!" and she was like, "Honor, you wouldn't believe how much money we can save – *as* consumers – by cutting out waste."'

I'm suddenly busy checking out this bird who's in the queue – think Diora Baird and you're in the right postcode – trying to get a good scope of her orse around a sandwich board advertising the Storbucks Ethos Water Fund.

Honor goes, 'And have you any idea what my *actual* life will be like if anyone in Montessori finds out what Mom is *doing* every morning? Especially – oh my God – Malorie! My life would be basically *over?* We're talking toats.'

I can see it now. She's wearing a pair of low-slung skinny jeans, with an inch of crack showing. The old half-moon over Rock and Republic.

'Ine only saying,' Ro goes. 'Should maybe give her a break.'

Honor's like, 'Like, everything out of her mouth these days is Giovanna said this and Giovanna said that.'

I laugh. 'She has an actual point there, Ro. I've known this bird she's talking about since back in the day. She's full of shit. I was telling Honor before, she's the one who told Sorcha to bring me out for dinner, then serve me with my divorce papers.'

'*Giovanna said that good Prosecco is actually better than champagne,*' Honor goes. '*Giovanna said that it's a time not for anger but for serenity and oneness . . .*'

I just laugh. I can't help it.

'It's certainly not a time for serenity,' I go. 'And I doubt if it's a time for oneness either – whatever the fock it even is. It's a time – like I was telling you when you were training this morning, Honor – for being ruthless, even if that means screwing over everyone else.'

'Bollocks,' Ronan goes.

I'm like, 'Hey, I've never been afraid to call it, Ro. That's one of the things that even my fiercest critics have to admit about me.'

'No,' he goes, suddenly putting his head down, 'that boord who's arthur walking in.'

He has my instant attention, of course. I'm like, 'Bird?' and I take a subtle look over the old left hammer. There's, like, three young girls, all Drummies, standing in the queue now – we're talking Uggs, bed-head hair, the whole bit – and I know instantly what he's talking about. I was a teenager once, remember. I've been that soldier.

I'm like, 'Go on, which one?'

'The blondie one,' he goes.

I laugh. Probably because she's the best of the three. I'm like, 'Is she in the play?'

He nods.

'Which one is she?'

'Milly.'

'Ah, *that's* the famous Yasmin?'

'Yeah.'

I cop another look. 'Fantastic.'

Honor instantly hates her, for some reason. 'Er, *sack* the stylist?' she goes, which is a line I've heard her old dear say more than once. 'Girls with swimmer's shoulders shouldn't wear racer-back tops.'

Ronan, I notice, has suddenly got his hand up, shielding his actual face.

I'm like, 'Whoa, what's the deal, Ro? What's wrong?'

'I got off with Filipa, Rosser.'

'Oh, so you went to Eddie Rocket's after all?'

'Yeah.'

I laugh. 'This was the girl who supposedly wanted to go over lines with you? I knew that was horseshit. Fan-focking-tastic! That's two stamps on the old dance cord – five to go. Okay, I'm trying to remember who else is in it. Is there a Martha? Or am I thinking of *West Side Story*?'

'Rosser, I still haven't broken it off with Yasmin.'

I'm there, 'But you were never going out with the girl – we've been through this, Ro.'

'But I never put her straight. I mean, what if she knows the score – about me and Filipa?'

'You mean Dorcas.'

'It's the same fooken peerson, Rosser.'

'Oh, yeah. It's just there's a lot of names, isn't there?'

'I don't want to see her,' he goes, suddenly standing up.

I laugh. I'm there, 'You can't escape, Ro. You'd have to walk past the queue. She'll see you.'

He stares at the exit, roysh, like it's an – I don't know – raging river he's been told to jump.

Honor is just, like, staring at the girl's legs, going, 'Er, D.V.B. jeans? Oh, my God, Victoria Beckham doesn't even wear them anymore. Er, *lmao*?'

'Ro, why don't you just face her?' I go. 'The worst you're going to get is a slap across the chops.'

He just shakes his head. He's like, 'No – no, I can't, Rosser. Ine going to the jacks. Bang on the door when she's gone, will you?'

So that's exactly what happens. He ends up locking himself into the old council gritter. And it's obvious, roysh, that he's going to be stuck in there a while, because the birds have bought their coffees *for here* – and *hers* is, like, a *venti*?

Honor, under her breath, goes, 'Whatever she's drinking, it better be, like, a *skinny* one.'

I just shake my head – yeah, I'm going to admit it, feeling a bit let down by Ro. I turn around to Honor and I'm like, 'I've got the Stair-Master in the boot. Will we hit the corpork – do five or ten minutes on it?'

She's like, 'What about Ronan?'

Like I said, she actually *idolizes* him?

I'm there, 'Let him stew in there for a while. He could actually do with toughening up.'

They're sat in that little restaurant in the Merrion Shopping Centre, the two of them, thick as focking thieves. Which pisses me off beyond belief, I'm going to be honest with you. I think because it's where he used to invite *me* to meet him for coffee? And, yeah, I always told him to go fock himself. But now he's here with *him* and it just bothers me, that's all.

'They've got a Basil Blackshaw,' the old man goes over the top of his *Irish Times*. 'It's of . . . well, a turkey or somesuch.'

Fionn says he's long been an admirer of Blackshaw's gestural style and his adherence to traditional Irish tropes.

The old man's in his element, of course – someone actually listening to him. 'Well, they've also got a Camille Souter,' he goes, proving the point I always made, that once you show any interest in what he has to say, he ends up losing the run of himself. 'I'm told on very good authority that it's an extraordinary piece. Buy it, was the advice I received, sight unseen.'

'That better be decaf,' I go, pointing to his cup, then the two of them look up, suddenly snared.

'Hello there, Kicker!' the old man goes, trying to cover his tracks.

Except I just stare Fionn out of it. 'Because he has, like, a hort condition?'

Fionn's like, 'I know that,' getting suddenly all pissy with me.

'Not that your conversation is going to set his pulse racing.'

He just rolls his eyes and goes, 'Ross, why don't you pull up a chair?'

I'm like, 'Er, I don't *need* an invitation from you.'

I sit down, then stort trying to catch the waitress's eye.

'Fionn and I have just been discussing ort,' the old man goes. 'Don't know if you knew this, Fionn, but young Ross here was quite the painter as a child.'

This, I have to tell you, is an out and out lie. I only ever remember one painting I did, when I was, like, twelve? It was of this little boy – he was working class, I'm going to admit it – and he was staring into the window of BTs on Christmas Eve with, like, tears just rolling down his face.

Ms Nelson – as in, my ort teacher? – described it as a 'searing indictment of inequality and social exclusion'. The old man – see, he pretends to forget – described it as 'seditious' and burned it in the fireplace, while the old dear wanted to send me to a child psychiatrist.

I laugh. I'm like, 'What do you all of a sudden know about ort?'

The old man folds over his newspaper and puts it down on the table. 'Just that Bank of Ireland is selling off its collection,' he goes. 'Well, it's going for a proverbial song.'

Fionn's there, 'It's good PR for them, what with the bail-out and the recapitalization and everything.'

It's actually on the tip of my tongue to go, he's not *your* dad, Fionn – he's actually *mine*?

'The only question,' the old man goes, 'is do I buy now or do I wait to see will AIB follow suit? *They've* got a Jack B. Yeats, I happen to know. *And* a Roderic O'Connor.'

I change the subject. 'What are you two even doing here?' I go. 'And, bear in mind, I don't mean that in, like, a jealous way?'

The old man's there, 'Our good ladies are in the shop,' by which he obviously means the cheesemongers. 'Packing up the last of the stock.'

Fionn tries to get in then. 'Must be something of an emotional heave for you, Charles – saying goodbye to the business.'

'Not at all,' the old man goes. 'No, I had my time, Fionn. Enjoyed every day of it. Captain of industry and so forth. Now it's time for me to hand over the flame to the next generation of entrepreneurs. People such as young Ross here . . .'

I flash Fionn one of my serious fock-you smiles.

'Yes, indeed. I sneaked a look at the books this morning. Happened to be in the accountants' office – hope you don't mind, Ross. Well, one thing I certainly know is how to read a spreadsheet. And it's obvious to me, Ross, that even in the few weeks since I handed it over to you, Shred Focking Everything is going from strength to proverbial strength.'

I just shrug. 'Well, it *is* the end of the Celtic Tiger. And, to quote you, there's a lot of people out there who don't want the public knowing shit. It's no wonder I'm creaming it in.'

'You and your famous humility,' he goes. 'No, no, Ross – I know how intense the competition is, out there in the document disposal game. But you're running circles around the opposition – of course, you're no stranger to that!'

Fionn, it's no surprise to see, is a bit put out by all this attention I'm suddenly getting. He picks up the old man's paper, throws his eyes over it, then mentions that the Chairman of the Bundesbank is warning about the potential for moral hazard if countries like Ireland keep bailing out their banks with public money. I roll my eyes, as if to say, yeah, that might pass for interesting conversation in the staffroom of the Institute, but you're in the real world now.

He looks up then, grinning like a shot fox, and I realize that Erika and her old dear have just walked in.

'Hello, Ross,' Helen goes, because, like I'm always saying, she has a major soft spot for me. 'Well, that was a day and a half's work we got through.'

She kisses the old man and says she hopes that's decaf he's drinking and I feel good, roysh, because I was the one who said it originally.

Fionn doesn't even notice, of course. Him and Erika are too busy being all over each other. They're, like, giving each other little pecks on the lips, then whispering shit in each other's ears, which I think is rude, personally, although I decide not to make an issue out of it.

'Ross,' the old man goes, 'what about that game of pitch and putt we've been promising ourselves? Is there any danger you could tear yourself away from the coalface of the economic recovery for an afternoon?'

Except I don't answer, roysh, because my eyes are drawn to Fionn and Erika's hands. I'm just, like, staring at their fingers, all – I don't know – *intertwined*?

'Jaysus fooken Caroyst,' Larry goes, leaning against the wall of the lift, his hand over his hort, 'you frightened the fooken loif ourra rus, Rosser.'

'*I* frightened the life out of *you*?' I go. 'I'm going to have to go back to my aportment now and change my focking boxers. Why did you have to shout, "Shoot him! Shoot the bastard!"'

'Ah, we thought you were the loar,' it's Terry who goes. 'Thee catch us with this lot and we're looken arra ten-stretch.'

I look down, roysh, and they've got, like, five or six Aldi bags at their feet, stuffed to the guts with bundles of, like, fifty yoyo notes. Maybe I'm, like, jumping to conclusions here but I presume they're some of the ones that Aithne was banging on about in the bank that day.

There's that expression, isn't there? Fences make great neighbours. In my case, you could say that neighbours make great fences.

'Come on, let's geroura this lift,' Terry goes and I sort of, like, hold the doors back while they struggle out onto the landing with the bags. It's only then, roysh, that I notice the bird who's with them.

You know me. I instantly turn on the chorm. I can't actually help it. It's one of those things that just happens – it's pretty much *automatic*? 'And who,' I go, 'is this . . . creature?'

I say this even though she's actually disgraceful looking – a real focking mess. She's the identikit skobie bird you see on Mary Street, swearing at her kids, or pissing it out of Penneys with thirty pairs of shit jeans stuffed into a holdall and a security gord giving chase. She's got all the usual – the velour tracksuit, the platinum blonde hair, the ink spot on the cheek and a pair of earrings that look like the kind of things that dolphins jump through to please their focking trainers.

'This is Saoirse,' Larry goes, as happy as a man with tits in his pockets.

I take her hand – hey, it's what I do.

'Saoirse,' I go, except I actually pronounce it '*Say-har-sha*', trying to make it sound, I don't know, mystical – less like the name of a baby delivered in the exercise yord of Mountjoy Women's Jail. I'm like, '*Say-har-sha!*' then I hold her hand up to my mouth and kiss her fingers. I give it, 'Chormed.'

Of course I might as well be feeding strawberries to a donkey. 'Are you on fooken drugs?' she goes, then she turns to Larry. 'The way he fooken talks, Laddy – fooken snoppy bastoord.'

I just drop her hand. I'm there, 'Er, just cos I, like, speak properly, that doesn't make me a snob. Okay, as it just so happens, I *am* one? But I was actually just being nice. I didn't go hurting your feelings, did I? Even though there's a lot I *could* have said.'

She looks at me, roysh, like I'm a No Win scratchcord she's just picked up off the floor of the focking 78A. We're talking pure focking hatred. Then she turns to Larry. 'Gimme some money, will ye?'

'For what?'

'Ine getting me hayor done, I told ye.'

'Again?'

'I helped ye caddy all these fooken bags up, didn't I? Ye fooken doort boord.'

Larry's smile would honestly melt a clamper's hort.

'And I don't want fooken funny money eeder,' she goes. 'The fooken girdle noticed it the last toyum. Nearly called the fooken Geerds, she did.'

Larry reaches into the pocket of his tracksuit bottoms and hands her, like, a wad of notes – real ones, I'm presuming. She smiles – a horrible focking sight – then literally storts getting off with him in front of me and Terry.

I end up just standing there, checking out her grillwork – they're a bit on the small side – though mostly out of habit. Then she hops back in the lift.

The next thing I know, Larry has me in a headlock. 'I fooken saw that,' he's going, except he's actually laughing, 'you doorty fooken adimal, checking her out. You keep your eyes and your bleaten hands offa hor, do you hear me?'

Of course I'm there struggling for breath and at the same time thinking, er, you *actually* have no idea how little focking threat I pose.

''Mon in,' it's Terry who goes, slipping the key into the door. It's never an invite when he says that as much as a summons. Not that I mind. They might be two of most feared men in, like, gangland, but they're actually cool as neighbours go. We've even become, not exactly friends, but sort of, like, *friendlyish*?

Larry goes, 'I mean it, but,' more serious this time, 'you steer the fook clear of her. I know what you're like. You'd gerrup on a crack of thunder, you doorty fooken pox.'

We all laugh, even though it's a bit uncomfortable. If I rode her in a dream, I'd knock on his door the next morning to apologize.

'Sure we mirras well lire up a joint so,' Terry goes, when he's shoved the counterfeit money into the hot press. 'It's fooken Sarradee night, wha?'

I'm like, 'Er, not for me actually. Might just have a beer if you've got one.'

I sit down on the sofa and a can is put in front of me. Galahad Premium. Jesus Christ.

'So,' Larry goes, plonking himself down beside me, 'what do you think?'

I'm like, 'Sorry?' stalling for time, because I've a vague idea where this conversation is possibly headed.

Terry's forting around with the remote. He eventually finds Sky Sports News. Danny Woolen says he's settling in well after his move from Greenock Morton to Gateshead on a free transfer, if that means anything to anyone.

'Saoirse,' Larry goes. 'What do you think – as a fedda who loves he's boords, like.'

I'm like, 'What do I *think*?' and I stort pulling all these – I suppose – *non-committal* faces, like you do in school when a teacher asks you what the, I don't know, *theme* of some focking poem is. 'I'm not even sure the word has been invented yet.'

'Nice?' he goes.

I have to just nod and go, 'Very.'

I mean, what else am I going to say? She wouldn't get a dart in Pearse Street Station?

'Laddy's in luff,' Terry goes.

Larry laughs, roysh, but at the same time he doesn't, like, *deny* it? Then he storts rolling a joint.

I can hear Rooney, their Rottweiller – slash, tiger – borking like focking mental out on the balcony, wanting to get in, probably to ride me. I don't know if I said it before but he has, like, a thing for me.

'So,' I go, 'whatever happened to your rule? As in, no girlfriends? Too much aggravation, can't be carrying around baggage in your world, blah blah blah?'

'Ah,' Larry goes, licking the edge of the cigarette paper, 'that was before I met Saoirse.' He has, like, a sly look up at his brother. Then he goes, 'Ine getting out, Rosser.'

'Out?'

'Ourra the gayum. That's what that money in the hot press is fower.'

'What is it – like, your pension?'

He laughs. 'Could say that. And by the way, if you know anyone's looking for cheap gowult . . .'

'Cheap . . .'

'Gowult, Rosser. Rings. Chains. Athin like that.'

Danuta immediately pops into my head. I *could* send them her way. But then I think, fock it, why would I do anything to help that mental-case, albeit an amazing-looking one.

I just go, 'Course. I'll, er, let you know.'

'Make shewer you do. Everyting must go – know what Ine sayin?'

84

I actually end up laughing at that. 'Here, I thought you goys never retired? I thought you were making so much moo that you stayed in until someone, I don't know, *popped a cap in you* or whatever the *actual* slang is?'

Larry laughs. It probably *is* funny the way I say it.

'Well,' he goes, 'maybe Ine gonna be the foorst who knew when the toyum was reet. Nah, between isser selves, Rosser, the eerse is arthur falling ourra the auld cocaine meerket. Know worra mean?'

'This focking recession. Jesus, is there anyone it's *not* affecting?'

'Well, I just have a feeden things is gonna get real fooken nasty – if you know worrum saying.'

'Well, it sounds like you've really thought this out. Good luck to you. I should also say fair focks. Where are you retiring to, by the way? I'm presuming Alicante.'

He gets suddenly serious with me again. 'Why do you always presume it's Ali-fooken-cante?' he goes and for a second he looks like he could *actually* tear my focking head off. You never really know where you stand with these two. Then he suddenly smiles. 'Ah, no, Ine only pulling your fooken woyer, Rosser. It *is* Alicante. Gonna buy a bar over there.'

I look at Terry. I'm like, 'Are you going as well?'

He nods. 'Twenty-five,' he goes, 'and gone ourra the gayum.'

I'm there, 'I'll tell you something for nothing – Rosa Porks isn't going to be the same without you.'

In other words, we might have a chance of selling our focking gaffs now.

The two of them look at each other and smile. I can say in all honesty that I've never seen them happier.

Oisinn says that if I apologize one more time, he's going to put the focking phone down on me.

'Look, that's a good thing for me to hear,' I go, 'but I still feel bad. If I'd known my tongue was going to end up pretty much paralysed, I honestly wouldn't have stayed up half the night licking that skeezer's body.'

He says he really appreciates me saying it and I tell him that I actually mean it – every word.

'But what happens now?' I make sure to go. 'What you said that day about voluntary bankruptcy and blahdy blahdy blah – you can't actually mean it.'

He's there, 'I do. Matter of fact, Hennessy's already filed the petition. It's listed for the High Court next week.'

I end up nearly fanging the red light coming up to the D4 Hotel. That's how in shock I am.

I'm like, 'What?' suddenly stamping on the brake. There's, like, a screech of tyres, the whole bit.

'Yeah. That'll be it, Ross. All over.'

See, I honestly didn't think it was going to *happen* that quickly?

'But what if you come up with, like, a seriously rocking business idea between now and then?' I go. 'I'm presuming we could make this whole thing just go away.'

He just laughs. 'You always believed in miracles.'

I'm there, 'Er, Clongowes Wood, second round of the Junior Cup, many focking moons ago. What were we, thirty-something points down? We won it, Ois,' and I give Honor a little nudge in the seat beside me. 'We won it in actual gorbage time.'

She looks up from her phone, rolls her eyes and goes, 'Yeah, whatevs!'

'Look, I smell what you're stepping in,' Oisinn goes. 'I mean, Hennessy's trying to get me to go to England.'

'England?'

'More lenient laws. That's why bankruptcy holidays are becoming the big thing.'

'Why don't you go on one of them, then? Jesus, I'd come with you.'

'Because I'm tired of running away. Look, bankruptcy isn't a punishment, Ross. It's to discharge people of their debts so they can get on with their lives. And that's what I want to do. Get my life back again.'

The light turns green and I take off again. I shake my head. 'Look, I'd stand up in that courtroom and speak on your behalf if you thought it'd do any good. And, look, I'd do it properly this time – keep the boys in the barracks the night before.'

'Nah, it won't even last that long. Hennessy said it won't take more than a few minutes.'

'So what exactly is going to happen?'

'The court will appoint an official assignee to discharge my assets for the benefit of my creditors.'

'Flog everything you own, in other words.'

'Yeah.'

'This *focking* recession!'

'Then they'll decide how much money I get to live on.'

'Well,' I go, 'all I can say is that it better be a decent wedge,' honestly not knowing what else to say to him. I mean, I was the one who told him that everything would be fine if he just came home. As long as you have your mates around you and blah blah blah. Little did I know.

I turn around to Honor again. 'Hey, don't drink too much water,' I go. 'There's such a thing as over-hydration – weird as it sounds.'

She's just like, 'Okay, you're being *lame* now?' and she goes back to her phone.

Oisinn seems happy with the sudden change of subject, though. 'Hey, how's the training going, by the way? Is she another world beater, like her old man?'

That's an unbelievable boost for me.

'Yeah, no,' I go, 'she's just put in an incredible session. And if she wins this race, her daddy's taking her to Paris – isn't that right, Honor?'

She doesn't even look up. She's like, 'There's no if. I'm *going* to win. We're talking Toats McGoats.'

I laugh. 'Did you hear that, Oisinn? She's definitely got my confidence and killer instinct.'

He laughs as well.

I ask him then if he's seen JP, because it suddenly occurs to me that the dude's been keeping his head down recently. The last I heard, Danuta's old pair were over from Russia, pretty much *visiting*?

'Yeah,' Oisinn goes, 'they're here for, like, two months.'

'Two months?'

'Yeah, see her old man's helping her set up this cash for gold place she's talking about. He's, like, bankrolling her. Supposed to be her twenty-first birthday present.'

Weird present. But then it doesn't exactly surprise me.

I'm there, 'Well, you know how I feel about the girl. She's not the full set of Callaways. I said it from day one. Even though I'd be in there like swimwear if I thought there was an even sniff of it.'

'Cash for gold, though. God, there's always money to be made from misery, isn't there? From drug-dealers to priests to personal injury solicitors – they all understand that rule. Did you hear what she's calling it?'

'What?'

'End of the Rainbow.'

I laugh. It actually fits perfectly.

'I know JP was pretty nervous about meeting the rents,' I go. 'Two focking months, though. Although you know J-Dog when he switches on the old aunt-seducer chorm.'

'True. By the way, I saw Fionn and Erika yesterday.'

'Oh, yeah?'

'Yeah, they were walking around Bulloch Harbour. Hand in hand.'

'I wouldn't read anything into that. Look, she's panicked and grabbed the nearest goy to her. They say thirty is the tipping point for birds in terms of settling.'

'I actually think you're wrong, Ross. I mean, yeah, I couldn't believe it myself when I came home and heard they were together. I mean, Fionn and Erika? But now, I don't know. I think they're genuinely in love.'

I crack on that the signal is suddenly bad and I tell him I'll have to bell him back later. Then I hang up.

Honor's still texting away merrily, by the way. I go, 'Actually who are you on to there? Malorie?'

She doesn't answer.

I'm like, 'Who are you texting, Honor?'

She looks up again. 'I *said* yes when you asked me was it Malorie. Are you, like, deaf or something?'

'Sorry, Babes, I mustn't have heard you.'

'Try cleaning your ears out, then.'

'I might just do that.'

She just, like, shakes her head. 'You are, like, *so* retorded.'

There's, like, silence in the van then. She continues staring at her little screen, her thumb still doing ninety. There's a sudden burst of laughter from her as we're crossing the canal. 'Oh my God,' she goes, 'that's lollers. That is, like, *so* lollers.'

I'm there, 'Okay. And am I allowed to ask what you're laughing at?'

'A girl in my class,' she goes. 'Sara Somers. She's got, like, split-ends. Her parents are, like, *so* poor – even though she *pretends* to be rich? Malorie is being – oh my God – *such* a bitch about her.'

I'm like, 'That *is* funny, I suppose. Is this Malorie one running in the same race as you, by the way?'

'Oh my God, you *are* deaf. I already told you that she was.'

'Did you?'

'Er, like, a *week* ago?'

I let it just wash over me.

I pull into Merrion Square, roysh, then we hop out of the van and stort making our way around to the school. Totally out of the blue, I go, 'Do you really think you can trust her?'

'Oh my God! Who are you even talking about?'

'Malorie.'

Actually, it isn't totally out of the blue. I know exactly what I'm doing here. Malorie has an obvious ruthless streak in her and I need Honor to stort thinking about her as the opposition – even the enemy.

'Oh my God,' she goes, 'you are such a . . .'

'I'm just saying, Honor, don't be taken in by her. For instance, how do you know *she's* not training for this race?'

'She's not.'

'You don't know that. She could be out running laps of Brighton Square every morning. Or even the St Mary's pitch.'

'She's, like, my best friend? I think I'd *know*?'

'Oh, would you? Your best friend, is she?'

'Er, *yeah*?'

'Okay, how come I heard her slagging you off the other morning?'

She's like, 'What?' and she looks really, genuinely hurt. I hate myself, by the way. But it still has to be done.

'Oh, yeah. Well, more slagging your mother off really. Saying all sorts about her.'

'Like what?'

'Like, she's making a tit of herself in Booterstown every morning.'

'Are you saying she knows about the tai chi?'

'She certainly seems to. Because she was saying it to – yeah, in fact – that girl you were both slagging off, with the split-ends.'

'Sara Somers? Oh my God, she *hates* Sara Somers. She says her dad's, like, a dole scrounger.'

'Does she hate her, though? That's my point. Or does she really hate you? Because she was also saying something to her about – yeah, about how Honor O'Carroll-Kelly eats own-brand food.'

'Oh my God, that's a total lie.'

'She called you an Own Brandy. She mentioned something about, I don't know, fish cakes?'

'I didn't eat them. Even though Mom ended up cutting my phone credit to, like, twenty euros a week.'

'Look, that's the story that *she's* putting around, Honor. I mean, I didn't want to tell you any of this but you sort of, like, twisted my orm. All I'm saying is that this is the girl who's standing between you and a trip to Paris – and just be wary of her.'

We're nearly at the school, roysh, when I notice Honor's eyes suddenly narrow and her lips push out. I'd recognize that look anywhere – she's got a lot of her mother in her, see. I look, roysh, and Malorie's about twenty yords in front of us, climbing out of her old dear's Selfish Urban Vanity.

She waves at us, as does her old dear – like I said, Kate Garraway.

'Don't wave back,' I go, out of the corner of my mouth.

Honor goes, 'I'm not going to. Oh my God, what a bitch,' which are the exact words I want to hear.

As it happens, I've got a couple of hours to kill before my first pick-up of the day, so I stay porked in Merrion Square, studying Honor's – I suppose you could call them – *lap* times?

I wasn't exaggerating when I told Oisinn that the training session she put in this morning was incredible. In the space of basically a week, she's managed to shave a full seven seconds off her personal best time for the two-hundred-metre sprint around Ballsbridge Terrace. That's an amazing improvement in anyone's language.

And what was even more encouraging from my point of view – *as* her coach – was that when she came haring around the corner from Kites, puffing and sweating like a focking migrant worker picking mussels, she was actually disappointed to find out that it wasn't more.

'Can I go again?' she went, to which I had to say no, then I ended up having to warn her about the dangers of, like, burnout, while she did ten minutes on the StairMaster, focusing mostly on her quads, glutes and calves.

She's in unbelievable shape, physically. A major port of sport, though, is obviously mental. I still feel a little bit bad for turning her against Malorie. But then I remember how Father Fehily used to put photographs of Willie Duggan and Neil Francis on the wall of the dressing-room to get us to hate Blackrock. And pictures of Terry Wogan and Henry Kelly to get us to hate Belvo.

It's called motivation. And it's just as I'm thinking that that my phone storts vibrating in my hand. I answer it. It's, like, a woman's voice?

'Is that Shrod Focken Avrything?' she goes. 'Did *ay* rang the rait nommer?'

She's obviously from the North. Mature, definitely. Sexy would also be my guess.

I'm just there, 'It most certainly is,' nice and focking sleazy. 'What can I do you for?'

She's like, 'Ayv got some robbish here wanting shrodden – can ye come and teek it?'

I'm there, 'Oh, I think I can manage that small thing,' flirting my hole off now. 'I'm going to have to take down your particulars, though.'

She's like, 'Sorray?'

I'm there, 'Er, your *details*?'

'Och, aye,' she goes, suddenly all aflutter and when she finally pulls herself together, she gives me her address, which ends up being in, like, Malahide.

To cut a long story short, I get on the old coast road and I'm there in, like, half an hour. The gaff ends up being this humungous place – not unlike ours in, like, Foxrock? – set behind this six-foot-high wall and these black wrought-iron gates. I get out of the van and have, like, a mooch around. There's, like, an intercom set into the wall and a nameplate beside it that says Venezia, which means it's definitely the place.

She must be watching me, because her voice suddenly crackles through the little, I suppose, grille. 'Just drave op to the hyse,' she goes and the next thing, roysh, the big gates automatically open, then I hop back into the van and drive it up to the front door.

Of course, you can imagine what's going through my head – utter filthbag that I am, I'm wondering is she as hot as she sounds. Although if there's one thing I've learned in the document-shredding business, it's that quite often they're not – especially the nordies, who can come across as, like, sexy on the Wolfe, then you meet them face-to-face and they end up being raddled.

I press the doorbell, then do my usual, which is stand there with my hands by my sides flexing my actual abs, because the way this boiler-suit is cut *is* pretty flattering, it has to be said.

Through the frosted glass, I can see a figure making its way up the hallway to the door and – though it possibly makes me sound like a bit of a perv – as she reaches for the handle, I stort to feel – as they say – an uprising brewing south of the Rio Grande.

The next thing, roysh, the door slowly inches open and we're sud-denly staring into each other's eyes and I instantly realize, with a fright that almost stops my focking hort, that I know her.

She just smiles. 'Well,' she just goes, as if nothing ever happened, 'what abycha?'

It's Regina Rathfriland.

I go to say something, roysh, except I'm so in shock that no actual *words* come out?

She goes, 'Are ye gonnay just stond thur or are ye gonnay come un?'

Of course I don't even budge. I'm like, 'Sorry, what do you even want?'

'Did *aye* nat tell ye on the phawn?' she tries to go. 'Ayv got dacu-ments want shrodden – all Toddy's old stoff.'

I'm just like, 'Don't give me that. There's any number of companies you could have rung who are doing the exact same thing as me. Get Rid Quick. Slash & Byrne . . .'

'Well,' she goes, sort of, like, averting her eyes, 'ay also wanted tee apalajays.'

'It's not you who should be apologizing . . .'

'Well, *aye* feel bawd abite ut.'

'It's whoever knocked me into that actual grave.'

'Och, that was Toddy's brother.'

'Toddy's brother?'

'Aye, Sommy. Wouldn't hold yer broth, bay the wee. You'll get nath-ing from hom.'

I end up just shaking my head. 'Focking members only jackets. They didn't even look good the first time they were in.'

She actually laughs at that. Sense of humour – again, one of my favourite qualities about myself.

'So, are ye coming un?' she goes, holding the door open wide for me and of course you know me – I'm a people-pleaser.

I follow her into the hallway.

It's only once I've calmed down that I stort to take – okay, you decide if it's a word – but an *objective* look at her? She's wearing, first of all, a tight pink Benetton aertex and she has amazing honkers for a woman of, what, sixty? She's also wearing this white, like, tennis skirt, except shorter, then gordening gloves and – give me the benefit of the doubt on this one – MBTs, which in normal circumstances *are* an instant mickey repellent, except I've discovered that they don't look as bad on the end of a nice set of pins. Sorcha's old dear *also* wears them while she's pottering in the gorden and she's got legs like the focking Taney Bridge. But Regina's are all, I don't know, toned and tanned and what-ever else.

Halfway down the hall, she suddenly stops and turns to me. 'Ye con untherstond – can't ye? – why everyone was so ongry when *she* torned up. Your soster.'

'Half-sister.'

'Wee scrobber wracked may morge.'

'Well, from what I hear, it wasn't in great shape either way.'

She doesn't react to this, roysh, just stares at me for a few seconds with literally no expression on her face, then nods at the door behind me and goes, 'They're all in thur – all bagged-op. Ay'll be in the gorten . . . if you want may.'

My eyes follow her orse all the way down the hallway – I can't help it, even though she's ancient – then I push the door of what turns out to be the study, where there's, like, twelve or thirteen black sacks bursting at the, literally, seams with all these, I don't know, reams and reams of paper. I stort carrying them, in twos, outside to the van, then I crank up the machine and stort feeding the pages into it.

While I'm doing it, I'm wondering what it would be like, as in sex with a woman of, like, sixty? Oisinn was with a fifty-two-year-old once and he said she'd flaps like Craig Doyle's passport. But then *she'd* had five kids, whereas Regina – from what Erika said – only had the one. *And* she didn't have her until she was in her basically forties.

Anyway, I'm suddenly interrupted from my – I'm going to *call* them musings? – by a sudden rap on the side of the van, then I hear Regina say that there's some fresh lemonade inside if I'm thirsting for something. So I finish up – I only have, like, two bags left at that point anyway – then I head back into the gaff, then down the hall to the kitchen.

There's something in the air. A dude with my kind of experience instantly knows.

She's got Bublé on – a song I straight away recognize as 'Baby (You've Got What It Takes)'. Oh, there's a glass of lemonade on the table alright, but the thing that my eyes are instantly drawn to is *her*, sitting in one of the chairs, holding her leg in the air and sort of, like, running her gloved hand along her thigh and over her knee.

'Och,' she goes, 'them thorns have may legs destroyed, so they hov.'

It suddenly all kicks off again down in El Paso.

'My old dear's a major Bublé fan,' I go.

My voice sounds weak and, like, *trembly*?

She's there, 'Is thot rait?'

I'm like, 'Big-time. She's got pretty much everything he's ever put out.'

'That's *vary* onthresting, so it is.'

She wets her lips. I knock back the lemonade in pretty much one gulp, then – possibly just to break the tension – I wander over to the sink and stort rinsing out the glass.

Except I can *feel* her eyes on me, checking me out in a big-time way. I'd say she could tell you how much change I've got in my back focking pocket.

'Ay thonk you *lake* may legs,' she goes.

That instantly throws me. I'm the one who usually makes all the running. See, I'm old-fashioned like that. You could even call me a traditionalist.

I'm there, 'Excuse me?'

'You've been storing at thum since ye walked three thot door.'

I just shrug. 'They're nice, there's no denying. They supposedly tighten everything up, do they, the old MBTs?'

She doesn't give me an answer. I suppose I'm not really looking for one. She just puts her leg down, then stands up and moves over to me. 'What else do you lake to dee,' she goes, 'apart from look, thot uz?'

She's standing, like, two inches away from me, looking straight into my eyes, roysh, then her stare suddenly drops to my mouth and I can't say officially *who* makes the first move, just that we're suddenly sucking the lips off each other and her hands are all over my pecs like the winning lottery numbers are written on them in Braille.

Her lips are actually surprisingly hord. And rough – like a focking Brillo Pad.

There's, like, no stopping us, though. It's pure animal lust.

She unzips the front of my – you'd have to say – boiler-suit, then yanks the entire thing down to my waist, while I whip out the old tools for the job.

'Upstairs?' I go, knowing that birds usually like the whole bed aspect to the sex thing.

'Catch yerself awn,' she goes, between gasps. 'Ay can't weet that lawng,' and the next thing I know she's pretty much tackled me to the ground. I'm suddenly on, like, the flat of my back and she sits – I think the word is – *astride* me?

Anyway, look, I'll spare you the juicy details – never been the type to kiss and tell – other than to say that she ends up being a blasphemer, screaming, 'Jesus! Och, Jesus!' at the top of her voice, while galloping herself cross-eyed and wiping the floor with me like Mr focking Sheen.

It's actually over unbelievably quickly. You could throw a bucket of ice water over us and still not hold back the inevitable. It's like, boom! Then it's finished.

After the fireworks, she continues sitting on me for maybe a minute, obviously waiting for her breath to return and her vision to clear. Then she climbs shakily to her feet. I reckon it's a long time since anyone's rattled her scaffolding like that.

She throws me a tea towel, then staggers out of the kitchen, her knees knocking together like a new-born foal. The next thing I hear is the shower running and I'm already patting my pockets for the keys to the van.

Sorcha asks me – oh my God – *what* is going on with Honor. Of course it's difficult to tell on the phone if she's angry or if it's an actual genuine question. My first thought is that I've pushed the kid too far in terms of the whole motivation thing and she's ended up ripping Malorie's hair out by the roots.

Then I remember the old rule. Don't admit or deny anything until you've actually been accused. Then deny it and keep *on* focking deny-ing it.

I'm like, 'What do you mean, Babes?' all innocence. 'Is she being a total bitch again?'

'She's losing weight,' she goes. 'I put her on the scales yesterday, Ross, and she's lost – oh my God – six pounds in, like, two weeks.'

I laugh. 'Is that jealousy I can hear in your voice? The old green-eyed monster and blahdy blahdy blah?'

She's not laughing, though. 'I'm worried, Ross. I'm wondering should I take her to the doctor.'

I actually don't need this. I'm in bed with a serious bangover from yesterday's antics in Malahide.

I'm there, 'The doctor? I, er, don't think that's a great idea, Babes.'

'I'm wondering is it anxiety-related.'

'Anxiety? She's, like, not even five.'

'She might be secretly worried about her parents getting divorced. It might also explain why she's been behaving like a little madam.'

'Look,' I go, 'I honestly think you're overreacting. She's probably just shedding her puppy fat. Happens to a lot of kids. I mean, I've seen *your* baby photos, remember. Jesus, you were a focking ballooba.'

'Ross!'

'Hey, that's a compliment. What I'm saying is, you lost the weight, didn't you? So it's possibly just natural.'

'Well,' she goes, softening a bit, 'her muscles *are* defining.'

'There you are, then.'

'She has quadriceps that I would – oh my God – *die* for?'

I'm tempted to say the obvious – *you'd* have them as well if you hadn't focked the StairMaster in the attic after, like, two goes on it.

'She's also eating very healthily,' she goes.

I'm like, 'That's a good thing, isn't it?'

'Well, I have to admit I was little bit suspicious at first.'

'Suspicious?'

'Ross, you remember the struggle I used to have to get her to eat, like, fruit and vegetables. Now it's pretty much all she'll eat. I won-dered at first was it her way of, like, rebelling?'

'Rebelling?'

'Against me giving her own-brand food. Is she doing it to spite me?'

'I would have thought a girl of four and a half eating fruit and vegetables was an actual good thing. They say you should have, like, five a day, don't they? Although, personally, I don't know where the fock I'd find the time.'

'Then I wondered was she orthorexic?'

'Orthorexic? Jesus, Sorcha, I don't even know what that is. Come on, I thought this Healing Through Tai Chi crack was supposedly chilling you out. Honor is a happy, healthy, athletic young girl – and for that we should just be grateful.'

'I suppose. Did I tell you the other thing about her?'

Oh, for fock's sake.

'No, Babes, what?'

'She's fallen out with Malorie.'

I play dumb. 'Malorie? Which one's she again?'

'Malorie,' she goes. 'As in, like, her best friend?'

'Kids that age have so many friends, don't they? Sometimes it's hord to keep track.'

'I met her mum this morning coming out of Wilde & Green. She said Honor suddenly doesn't want anything to do with her daughter.'

'Ah, that's a shame. I'm still trying to picture this kid. For some reason I'm drawing a blank.'

'Well, her mum seems to be a big fan of yours, whatever lines you were using on her.'

'Well, you know me, Babes, I like to get with everyone.'

'You must know her. She looks a bit like Kate Garraway.'

'Oh, her! Yeah, she *is* a fan actually. Yeah, I know her daughter now. Like I said, Sorcha, kids of that age. You're best friends today – tomorrow you're strangers. I honestly think you're worrying with no actual reason.'

'Maybe you're right.'

I'm like, 'Course I'm right. Where are you, by the way?' because I can hear, like, banging going on in the background.

Wait'll you hear what she says.

'I'm in the cobblers, Ross.'

Like you, I laugh.

'The cobblers? They don't really exist, do they?'

'What do you mean they don't really exist? Of course they exist.'

'Yeah, but only in, like, children's books.'

'Er, *no* – also in the real world, Ross.'

'Jesus. Well, what are you doing in there?'

'I'm getting two pairs of shoes re-heeled.'

'Re-heeled? This isn't you ripping the piss, is it?'

'Ross, you can get new heels put on shoes. It's actually becoming really popular again . . .'

The old dear's right. It's back to the focking caves we're headed.

'As a matter of fact, I'm also getting two pairs of Honor's shoes *resoled.*'

I'm like, '*Resoled?*' and then I laugh. 'How do you think she's going to take that?'

'I don't really care how she's going to take it. She's going to have to adjust to her reduced material circumstances like millions of others. Giovanna was saying this morning that it'd be good for the universe's collective soul if we *all* rediscovered the forgotten art of make-do and mend.'

'Sorry, I'm still trying to get my head around the fact that this country has a cobblers.'

'Okay, I'm hanging up on you, Ross. I can't talk to you when you're being like this.'

A hundred and forty-eight euros.

At first, roysh, I think I must have misheard him. It's the only explanation. 'I actually thought you said *one* hundred and forty-eight euros,' I even go.

Oisinn just runs his thumb over the Heineken logo on his glass and says fock all and I end up nearly falling off my stool.

'You *did* say one hundred, didn't you?'

All he does is laugh.

I'm like, 'Tell me that's per day?'

'Per week.'

'To *live* on?'

'Yeah.'

I end up literally thumping the bor with my fist, going, '*Someone* should have to resign over this focking recession. And I mean that. It's actually gone *beyond* a joke at this stage?'

He shakes his head.

'Ross,' he goes, 'try to see it in relative terms. I'm only bankrupt. That still makes me richer than about eighty percent of people in this country.'

I'm there, 'Even so – a hundred and forty-eight yoyos? Fock, we used to spend that on a bottle of champagne back in the day. And not even drink it either. Send it over to Rosanna or whoever else's Diana Vickers we were trying to get into.'

'And what happiness did it bring me, Ross?'

'Dude, I hope you're not about to stort dissing the Celtic Tiger. I seem to be the only one actually defending it these days. And it's getting horder and horder, believe me.'

'But the question still stands. If I was happy, why was I hoovering up lines of coke?'

'Loads of people were doing that.'

'Why was I gambling?'

'It was internet poker, Oisinn. Jesus. We know dudes with actual degrees who gave up their jobs to do that full time. Again, they were just the times – everything seemed possible.'

This is us in the old Merrion Inn, by the way.

'But why couldn't I have been happy just being a designer of fragrances? I mean, I could have lived very comfortably on the money I made from *Eau d'Affluence* and my range of scented holy waters. It just wasn't enough for me.'

'Well, the old man says the only reason we had a Celtic Tiger in the first place was because of people who refused to admit that they had enough. You were one of the people who helped bring it about. You'll always be able to say that.'

'I mistook prosperity for happiness, Ross. Like a lot of people did. Because it *never* made me happy. I'm focking serious about that, by the way. Not for one day. When I made a killing on shares or, I don't know, some property deal or other, the thrill never lasted more than an hour or two. I mean, the next day, it was like it had never even happened and I'd have to do it all over again. Until I turned one hundred million euros into a seventy-five-million-euro loss.'

He drains the last of his pint and I ask the lounge girl for two more.

'So you lost a hundred million euros,' I go, 'then another seventy-five on top of that – I'm not even going to attempt to do the maths. What I *do* know is that you shouldn't have to live out the rest of your days as a basic pauper. I'm going to put you on the payroll for Shred Focking Everything.'

'Ross, I'm not even allowed to have a bank account.'

'So I'll pay you in cash. I'm coining it in at the moment. And don't worry, you won't have to *do* any actual work.'

He just smiles at me and goes, 'It's very kind of you, Ross, but no thanks. Look, I'm going to have to just accept that the world has changed for me, like it's changed for hundreds of thousands of other people out there.'

I actually laugh. 'You're beginning to sound like Sorcha,' I go. 'I think I mentioned to you, she's going through another one of her phases – life is a meandering stream and all that horseshit. She's doing tai chi every morning, in the circus field in Booterstown.'

He just nods. 'I *thought* it was her. I saw her the other morning from the top of the bus.'

The bus? Jesus, I could focking cry for him.

He ignores the – it may or may not be a word – but *pitying* look on my face?

'Is there any hope for you two?' he just goes.

I just shake my head. 'Nah, that boat sailed a long time ago, Dude. She's determined to go ahead with the whole divorce thing. Served me the papers – in a focking restaurant and everything.'

He shrugs, like it's *not* a major deal? 'But divorce takes years in this country. You could be, like, thirty-five years old before it's final. What I'm saying is, there's still time for you to win her back – *if* that's what you want.'

I'm there, 'Nah. To be honest, it's very much a case of onwards and upwards for me now. Actually, speaking of which . . .'

I give him a big filthy wink and his face suddenly lights up. He loves my stories, see – especially the ones where I've been a dirty focking dog.

'I was with this bird the other day. Although *woman* is possibly more the word.'

'Woman?'

'Oh, big time.'

He's suddenly grinning at me like a focking axe killer.

'Don't give me that,' I instantly go. 'You were with one once – remember that hog you pulled out of Leggs that time? Jesus, she looked like she'd been beaten into her fifties with a focking tyre iron.'

He holds up his two hands, all innocence. 'Hey, why are you being so defensive? I never said a word.'

'Because I know what you're thinking?'

'Go on,' he goes, still smiling. 'How old?'

I just shrug. 'Okay, I'm going to say it. Sixty.'

He's like, 'Sixty?' except he practically *shouts* it?

I'm like, 'Yeah, sixty,' trying to make it sound like it's no major deal.

He laughs. 'Shit! The bed! That is one ripe mango, Dude.'

'Yeah, but she's actually a *young* sixty?'

'There's no such thing as a young sixty, Ross. Sixty is sixty.'

'Well, what I mean is that she's not one of the fat ones. More meat on a focking breadstick, in fact. Yeah, no, she really looks after her bod. She obviously works out. MBTs and blah blah blah. And the boat race isn't bad either.'

'Is there anyone she actually looks like?'

'If I *had* to say someone? I'd say Catherine Deneuve.'

'Catherine Deneuve?'

'Big-time.'

'Well, whatever sugars your waffle. Where did you meet her, by the way? I'm presuming Howl of the Moon or one of those?'

'You're presuming wrong. Yeah, no, I actually met her on my rounds.'

'What?'

'Yeah, she rang up, had a shitload of documents she wanted shredded . . .'

He laughs. 'Jesus, it's like something off You Porn.'

'Well,' I go, 'it deserves to *be* on You Porn, the workout I put her through.' I knock back a good lungful of the old Happy H, then I decide to give him the full SP.

'Okay, I'm going to level with you here – it was actually . . . do you know Regina Rathfriland?'

He knows her alright. I can tell from the sudden delight on his face. 'The one whose husband . . .'

'Topped himself, yeah.'

'I was going say was riding your sister,' he goes. 'You two sure are going through that family,' and he's genuinely cracking his hole laughing as he's saying it.

This is going to sound maybe big-headed but it's pretty obvious that one of the things he really missed about Ireland was me.

He's suddenly serious then. 'Here,' he goes, 'she *does* look like Catherine Deneuve.'

'I told you.'

'I saw a photograph of her – think it was in the *Indo*. She couldn't be sixty.'

'Well, like I said, she's *in* good nick. I mean, sex with a sixty-year-old woman – I honestly thought it was going to be like sticking my dick in a fire bucket.'

'She's a genuine looker.'

'Well, she knows a few tricks as well. It was honestly some of the best Ant and Decs I've ever had. And I didn't hear any complaints from her either, before you say it.'

He laughs.

'By the way,' I go, 'keep this strictly between us, will you?'

'Okay.'

'I don't want Fionn having the goods on me – especially because I'm hammering him over the whole Erika situation.'

Oisinn smiles at me then and shakes his head. 'So are you going back for more?'

'Nah. It was a definite once-off thing for me. I mean, I shredded pretty much every piece of paper *in* the gaff.'

'Dude,' he goes, 'you're kidding yourself. A rich woman rings you and ends up – from what you're telling me – basically hopping you? She's a focking cougar, Ross. And you're going to be her new plaything.'

'Let me see if I can remember this joke,' the old man goes, 'the way your godfather tells it . . .'

This is us, by the way, stood at the fifth tee box of the pitch and putt course in Glencullen.

'Okay, there was God and there was – oh, who was it? – it was Saint Peter, yes, and they were playing golf, naturally enough. First hole is, I think, a par three. So Saint Peter steps up, hits a, oh, wonderful shot. I mean, straight onto the green. God says, "Terrific shot, Pete." You can imagine Hennessy telling this same joke, of course – does the voices and everything. So then God steps up himself. *Slices* the bloody ball. It clears the fence and it bounces out onto Nutley Lane. I mean, have you ever heard the likes of it, Ross? So the ball sits there, dead, for maybe ten seconds. Next thing, a bloody articulated lorry comes along – wheel clips the side of the thing, sending it shooting, like a bullet, in the air, back over the fence, onto the course but into the water. So – what was it next? – oh, yes, a frog of all things catches it. So he's sat there on a lily pad – lovely little chap – with the thing in his mouth when all of a sudden, without a by-your-leave, a bloody great eagle swoops out of the skies and pulls him out of the water. The next thing – yes – the eagle's flying over the green when the frog croaks and drops the ball. So it hits the ground and bounces straight into the hole. And that's when Saint Peter, he turns to God and he says . . .'

Are you going to play golf or are you going to just rip the piss? See, I was there when Hennessy told him the joke, in St Vincent's Hospital, the day after the op. He's just forgotten. I don't bother bursting his bubble, though.

'What was it that Saint Peter said to God? Something – oh – terribly, terribly funny. Oh, me and my memory. Your godfather tells it much better than I do.'

'I disagree,' I hear myself go. 'I thought you told it really well.'

He smiles. 'Do you mean that, Ross?'

I'd forgotten, roysh, how a simple compliment can make his focking day.

'I do, yeah.'

'Well, that's a wonderful thing to hear,' he goes, squinting across the seventy or eighty metres to the hole. He puts his tee down, then plops his ball on top of it. 'Do you know what I'd love to do, Ross?'

'What?'

'Open up and bloody well drive this thing.'

'Dad . . .'

'See how far I could hit it. Maybe as far as that little farmhouse over there.'

'You heard what the cordiologist said. Chipping and putting. They had your actual chest open, you know? If you did an actual swing, you could rip – I don't know – *something?*'

He nods sadly. 'I know you're right, of course. It's just, well, getting the head of that driver behind the ball and sending it a hundred, a hundred and fifty yards into the yonder, it's the best way I know to work out my anxiety and frustration. I expect you saw the news last night. Well, of course you did. You barely said a word in the car – lost in thought.'

I was actually wondering what the fock Una Healy sees in Ben Foden.

'What, er, news are you talking about specifically,' I go.

He's like, 'Sean FitzPatrick, of course – taken in for questioning, Ross, like a common bloody criminal. And of all the places they could have taken him, they took him to Bray. Oh, the indignity of it.'

I give him a look of, like, sympathy. 'Yeah, no, I knew you two were big golfing buddies.'

'Has nothing to do with golf, Ross. You don't have to tramp the Green Monkey with a chap to feel empathy with him in his hour of suffering. *They* disgraced themselves as well, don't you know. The – inverted commas – fourth estate. Waiting like bloody ghouls outside the station. Sanctimonious bloody whatnots. Already forgotten, of course, the days when their newspapers were pretty well *bursting* at the seams with advertising. Well, let me tell you this, without Seanie – and about ten others like him – there would have *been* no boom . . .'

The thing about the old man is that he *can* be very interesting. He can make you actually *think*?

'I mean, *I* wanted to drive out there last night – Bray, Ross! The very notion! – and make that self-same point. To the photographers with their lenses and the reporters with their bloody questions. This is the man who put me and thousands of entrepreneurs like me on the road to success. We should be honouring the chap, not coursing him like a terrified animal. Couldn't swing it with Helen, unfortunately. She said, "Charlie, you can't afford to get all worked up," and so forth. I said, "Well, what if I just popped out there with a few things for him – he'll need clean clothes and we're about the same size. Or I could hang around, see does he need a lift home or a sympathetic ear." Alas, Helen wouldn't hear of it.'

'Maybe she had a point, though. The doctor said you also have to watch your basically *stress* levels?'

'Well,' he goes, 'I can tell you, it does my stress levels no good whatsoever what I read in yesterday's *Times*. They're saying if he is eventually declared bankrupt, he might only be allowed to keep goods to the value of €3,500. The poor chap's got ties that are worth that, I'm sure.'

He stands next to his ball and takes a couple of practice chips.

'Yeah, no,' I go, 'that whole bankruptcy thing *is* a disgrace. I suppose you heard about Oisinn. I won't even tell you what they're expecting him to live on a week. You wouldn't feed a focking dog on it.'

He nods. 'Hennessy tells me you said your piece at the creditors meeting, Ross. But alas your words fell on deaf ears . . .'

I haven't a clue, of course, whether Hennessy told him what actually happened and this is just the spin the old man's choosing to put on it. See, that's the other thing about him – he's only ever been able to see the good in me.

'Well, you tried,' he goes. 'At the very least, you did that.'

All of a sudden there's, like, voices behind us. 'Sorry, fellas, would you mind if we played through?'

I turn around, roysh, and there's, like, three men – I'd say in, like, their thirties – standing there waiting.

I'm like, 'Play through?' on the immediate defensive.

'Yeah,' one of the fockers goes. 'You guys are chatting.'

'*And* you're dragging those big golf trolleys around with you,' one of the others just gives it. 'We'll have this hole played in no time.'

The old man's like, 'Well, of course!' bending down to pick up his ball and tee. 'Come on, Ross, ours is more of a leisurely game.'

I stare at the three of them – taxi drivers, definitely. I'm like, 'Sorry if we're not fast enough for you. *He's* recovering from focking hort surgery, you know.'

'Ross!' the old man goes. He's moved over to this bench, maybe ten *yords* away? 'Come and sit, Kicker. *We've* got all day.'

So I tip over and join him.

'Looks to me,' he goes, 'like I'm not the only one who has to watch his stress levels.'

I'm like, 'People sometimes piss me off. You're okay, though, are you? As in, like, generally?'

'Fit as the proverbial what's-it.'

'But you're doing all the shit they told you to in the hospital, are you? Exercise, eating healthy . . .'

'Fifteen to thirty minutes of walking every day. White fish, vegetables, whole-wheat pasta. Yes, I'm a changed man. Watching my blood pressure as well, of course. Oh, a year ago, Ross, I'd have been back at those chaps just like you. Play *through*? Quote-*unquote*? The bloody nerve!'

'I actually felt like decking one of them.'

'Do you no good in the long run. That anger.' He takes a breath, then goes, 'You know, what happened to me, Ross – the ticker and so forth – it had nothing to do with the cigars. Or the XO, for that matter. Or good old John Shanahan's certified Irish Angus.'

'Well, the doctors seem to disagree.'

'No doctor knows my body better than me, Ross.'

'So, like, what gave you the hort attack, then?'

'Not *what*? Who.'

'Okay – who, then?'

'That bloody woman.'

'The old dear? Jesus. I accept she's a focking whelk but I thought you two had ended up being mates.'

He shakes his head. 'Not your mother. No, I'm talking about that wretched Rathfriland woman.'

I feel my face just drop. I'm like, 'What?'

'Yes, that Toddy Rathfriland's wife. The grieving widow. What's this she calls herself?'

'Er, Regina. Something like that.'

'That's right. Regina. I should *know* her name. It's hewn on my bloody heart.'

'So, like, how did she end up giving you a hort attack?'

'How do you think? All that bloody stress she put me under, threatening to drag your sister's name through the mud.'

'Well, all she did – and this isn't, like, defending her – is name her in her divorce proceedings as basically the other woman.'

'Precisely,' the old man goes, pulling a cigor the size of a baby's orm out of his inside pocket and popping it, unlit, into his Von Trapp. 'I mean, bad enough that her husband took advantage of an impressionable and sweet-natured girl . . .'

'I'm not sure you know her as well as you think you do. But continue.'

'But then that woman – a real piece of work, by the way – threatens to put her through the ordeal of being publicly named and shamed. And all to extort one point seven million euros from me. That's what did it, Ross . . .'

'Yeah, no, but I'm sure the old steaks wouldn't have helped either. Blue rare – fock.'

'It was the look on her face when I agreed to hand over that money.

She grinned, if you can believe that. Well, Hennessy wanted to take her on, don't you know. Let's put her on the stand herself – see how she likes the heat. I couldn't do it to poor Erika, though. She'd be a girl forever branded. And that bloody woman knew that. The most conniving, manipulative woman it's even been my displeasure to meet. Oh, she screwed me, Kicker. She screwed me royally.'

You're not the only one. I can't help but think about her, sitting on top of me, riding me like a focking toboggan around the parquet floor. I don't need to tell you how suddenly bad I feel.

The old man's eyes suddenly come alive. 'Hello,' he goes, 'looks like our friends have finished,' and he stands up. 'Let's see can we get our heads around this famous fifth, shall we?'

He says he's soddy.

I don't give him any response, which is easier to do over the phone, because he can't see my hort basically breaking for him here.

Then he says it again.

'Ro,' I go, 'you don't have *be* sorry. I just don't get it, that's all. I mean, you're probably the toughest kid I've ever met. You used to go and visit your granddad in Mountjoy, remember, and not a bother on you. The things you used to shout at the wardens . . .'

'Doorty screw bastards.'

'Exactly. You're possibly the most intelligent kid I've ever met as well. What did you get in your Christmas exams again?'

'All Aıs.'

'All Aıs. Jesus. And yet, with all that going for you, you're not capable of giving the flick to a girl who's terminally hord of accepting.'

'I don't like hoorting people, Rosser,' he goes. 'Especially geerls.'

I end up nearly dropping the sack of documents I'm carrying – that's how actually loud I laugh. 'Ro, don't believe all that 'As Only a Woman's Hort Can Be' horseshit – that's just a song for birds to have their periods to.'

The woman sitting behind the reception desk of the company I'm collecting from gives me an out-and-out filthy.

'Believe me when I tell you, Ro, that women are every bit as ruthless as men in these situations.'

'Are thee, Rosser?'

'Yes. They're no different, see. Married, engaged, living with someone – they're always looking for opportunities to trade up, just like us. Look, you just happen to be hot at the moment. I hope it stays well for you. I genuinely do. But next week, it could be some other kid, from – yeah – Blackrock, who just so happens to be an even bigger bastard than you. And believe me, Ro, in that case, you won't see these girls for dust.'

'Alreet,' he goes. 'Look, Ine on me way into rehearsals now. Yasmin's already gone in.'

'Okay, so how are you going to handle it?'

'I don't know. What am I going to say to her, Rosser?'

I think for a minute.

'Okay, one that always worked for me was, you wait until everyone is standing around and then you go, at the top of your voice, 'Okay, hands up everyone in the room who's going out with someone at the moment?' and then when Yasmin goes to put her hand up, you go, 'Yeah, you can keep *yours* down!' I suppose the beauty of it is that it's funny *and* to the point? Then tell her in front of everyone that you did the dirt on her.'

'A bit heersh, but, isn't it, Rosser?'

'Yeah, but remember, Ro, these girls love you *because* you're a bastard. As Blathin found out – to her actual disgust.'

'Okay. What'll Yasmin do, but?'

'Look, worst-case scenario, Ro, you're going to have a sore face and a headache for the rest of the afternoon. But then you're free of her and your stock has all of a sudden risen higher.'

'Reet.'

'So go on. Make me proud. And make sure that Filipa knows that *she's* no claims on you either.'

I finish work early, basically figuring that – recession or no recession – there's no point in running myself into the actual ground. I mean, I've shredded documents for, like, three different companies already this morning and I think I've earned the right to spend an afternoon in bed calling for mayo.

So I drive back to, like, Ticknock.

I'm walking through the corpork, trying to remember does Siún Nic Gearailt ever read the lunchtime news, when, from twenty yords away, I notice the roof of Larry's Daihatsu Charade going up and down like

108

I don't even know what. It's only when I get closer and cop the two sets of feet sticking out of the back door, wearing his and hers Nike Air Max runners – *hers* pointing at the corpork ceiling, *his* pointing at the corpork floor – that I realize it's Larry and Saoirse, going at it like focking porn stors.

I try to, like, tiptoe by them. Except Larry, being an *actual* gangland criminal, has ears like a focking gazelle, having spent most of his adult life expecting to catch a bullet at any minute. So he ends up looking over his shoulder, just as I'm creeping past, and I hear him go, 'Ah sure it's only Rosser, so it is!'

Then she – Jesus, she has a face like a focking fish kill – *she* goes, 'Ast him, Laddy! Go on, ast him!' and he jumps up off her, then he walks over to me, which is no mean feat in itself. I can see from his tracky bottoms that he's horder than Os du Randt.

'Have you any joddies?' he just goes.

I'm like, 'What?' although it's not that I didn't hear him. It's more a case that I can't believe my actual ears.

'Rubber fooken joddies,' he goes again. 'Huddy up as well – don't want me disappointing the lady now, do ye?'

I'm there, 'Er, okay,' and I, like, pat the pockets of my jumpsuit. The thing is, roysh, I always carry two or three with me. You know *my* little fellas in top hats and tails. I've had to learn the hord way.

I hand him one and he barely even says thanks. It's as I go to walk away that he suddenly remembers something. 'Hee-er,' he goes, over his shoulder, 'there was a lethor arrived for ya – tis mornen. Postman musta stuck it in ear box be mistake.'

I'm like, 'Okay, cool.'

'It's on the table in the kitchen.'

'*Your* kitchen?'

'No, yooers.'

'Mine?'

'Yeah, I let meself in.'

'You let yourself in? Are you telling me you've an actual key to my aportment?'

'I ceertainly fooken do. It's veddy noice, by the way.'

'My aportment?'

'No – what's in the envelope.'

'You opened it?'

'I did. It's a bleaten cheque.'

'A cheque.'

'I won't tell ye how much it's fower, but.'

'That's, er, very nice of you, Larry.'

That's when *she* lets a focking roar out of her. 'Will ye huddy up, Laddy? Talken to dat fooken faggi!' which is lovely, of course.

He pulls a face, roysh, as if to say sorry about *her*, then he goes back to giving her the old shipping news.

I head up to the aportment and let myself in, thinking, I'm going to have to change all the focking locks now.

He was right, though, there *is* an envelope on the table – already opened, just as he said.

I look inside and there it is, roysh, a Jeff Beck. And it's for, like, five hundred snots. But who's it from? I can't read the signature on it. There is, though, a note – a tiny little slip of paper, folded in four, so small that you'd nearly miss it, tucked away in the corner of the envelope.

I open it out and I read it with a sense of what would have to be described as definite shock.

'For services rendered,' it just says. 'Regina, x.'

4. Darkness falls over Ticknock

So I'm in the sack, spitting zeds, dreaming happy thoughts, when all of a sudden I'm listening to the theme from *Hawaii Five-O* and I find myself reaching for my phone while still waiting for the old brain to engage.

It turns out to be some dude, roysh, with *way* too much personality for whatever focking time it is on a weekday morning. He's all, 'Hello,' full of the focking joys, 'I'm looking to speak with Ross O'Carroll-Kelly.'

I rub my face, trying to get my act together. 'Whoever you are, you better have a good focking reason for waking me up.'

He actually laughs. 'This is Nick Swanpoel from Ephesus Property Management.'

Ephesus? They're the crowd that are supposedly running Rosa Parks these days.

I'm like, 'Okay, the floor is yours – be quick.'

'Well, we're just ringing around to inform all of our residents – we'll be doing it formally, by letter, as well – that demolition will begin soon on the three unfinished blocks.'

I actually sit up in the bed. 'Demolition?'

'Yes, they're actually going to do it by controlled explosion. That's why we're suggesting you keep all your windows closed. I expect there's going to be a lot of dust.'

I'm like, 'Whoa, horsey. I'm still back at demolition here. What are you even talking about?'

He's there, 'The unfinished blocks. The builder's decided to tear them down. The place is going to be a bit of a moonscape, I'm afraid.'

'Do you mind me asking why?'

The focker tries to be a bit clever with me then. 'How long have you been sleeping there?'

He even laughs.

I'm like, 'Excuse me?'

He goes, 'I'm sorry – my little joke. I'm talking about the collapse of the country's economy.'

'Yeah, I know all about it, thanks very much. My point is, those blocks are nearly finished.'

'Well, unfortunately, the builder doesn't have the money to complete the work. He's as good as bankrupt,' he goes, and then he does his funny little laugh again. 'Just like the country.'

I'm there, 'There must be someone who'd be prepared to finish them. These are actually amazing aportments, you know. And you said it yourselves on that big banner you hung between two of the blocks – fifteen percent already occupied!'

He finds this, for some reason, hilarious as well. 'That's called seeing the glass as half full,' he goes. 'Or fifteen percent full, in this case.'

I'm there, 'Can I just say, this isn't the dream we were sold when we bought our gaffs here. What would *actual* Rosa Parks say about this if she was alive today? Has the builder even thought about that?'

'I don't imagine so. He lives in Portugal now. Or so it said in the *Irish Mail on Sunday*. Anyway, like I said, there's also a letter on its way to you. The demolition is happening on Friday week, the 23rd of April. There'll be noise. And don't forget, the windows.'

Then he hangs up.

I'm left lying there wondering what time it even *is* and whether I should think about maybe getting up for work. That's when I suddenly remember the cheque on the bedside locker.

I reach for it, roysh, and I end up just staring at it. My issue is that five hundred snots is, like, *way* over the odds for the work I did. I mean, I was only going invoice her for, like, *half* of that? But now I'm thinking about those words she used – services rendered – and you can imagine what's going through my head. Is she paying me for the shredding or for the sex? Because if it's for the sex, that'd make me a . . .

Well, let's just say it'd make me feel weird – flattered, yes, but at the same time weird.

I think about maybe ringing Regina. I even dial her number, then I change my mind before it even rings, because how do you even ask someone a question like that? But then I change my mind again and this time I go through with it. She answers pretty much straight away.

She's like, 'Helloy?'

See, I normally *hate* the Northern accent – *may fawther dayed in a*

Brotush prosun for somethun he dadn't doy – but on her it's *actually*, believe it or not, *sexy*?

'Hey,' I just go, trying not to give off too much of a vibe, wanting to keep it professional, 'it's Ross.'

She's like, 'Hoy?'

I'm there, 'Er, *Ross*? As in Ross O'Carroll-Kelly? The shredding goy who you, er . . .'

'Och, aye – what abite ye?'

See, I never really *know* how to answer that question? So I end up just going, 'I'm ringing just to say, er, pretty much thanks for the cheque.'

'Och, noy problem. Thonks for all your hord work – yee really put your bock intay ut.'

I'm thinking, is that one of those, like, *double entendres*?

'Okay,' I go, 'that's exactly what I'm ringing to ask you. Was that cheque payment for the shredding or for, well, the *other* thing? Or is it even half and half?'

She seems a bit taken aback by that. 'Are *yee* asking me am ay peeing yee for sax?'

'Well, pretty much, yeah. But only because the accountant is going to ask me the same basic question – as in, how does he enter it into the books?'

She goes, 'Well, only one of those thangs is consadered taxable income. If *ay* said it was for the sax, yee wouldn't hov tee declore it, would yee?'

Now, I've been with a lot of women during the course of my life – it would be impossible to even *attempt* to hang a number on it – but this is the first time, I have to admit, that one has left me genuinely speechless.

She suddenly laughs – she has a very sexy laugh. 'Will yee catch yerself awn,' she goes. 'It was for the shrodding, of course.'

I laugh then, relieved, although it would have been – like I said – a major boost for the old ego to think that someone *would* pay me for it.

'*Ay* kind of hoped *ay* wasn't the only one whoy enjoyed the sax, though.'

I'm like, 'Yeah, no, I *did* enjoy it.'

'Thot's good. And anyway, if ay *hod* been paying for it, ay'd have demonded batter service.'

I'm thinking, Jesus, to service her any better than I did, I'd have to take on staff. .

'Well,' I just go, 'if it was for just the shredding – like you claim – you've actually overpaid me.'

'Hov ay?'

'Yeah, it should only be, like, two-fifty? Do you want to maybe write me another cheque – I'll rip this one up.'

'Why don't yee just keep it and it'll cover naxt taim?'

'Next time?'

'Aye, when can yee come ite here again?'

I'm suddenly thinking about the old man and what he said. This woman was the reason he ended up nearly dying. Except I'm suddenly back to being a fifteen-year-old virgin again.

I'm there, 'Er, are you saying you've more documents there that need shredding?'

She laughs, except in an, I don't know, *exasperated* way?

'If it'll meek yee feel botter, ay can fill a fyee sacks op and leave them in the stody. If yee want tee pretand that's way you're comen horr.'

'Yeah, maybe,' I go. 'Might make it seem less, I don't know, like something off the internet.'

She laughs. 'Okay, whatever works for ye, Ross. What dee can ay expact yee?'

I know it's wrong. But then the sex was incredible – so what I do, roysh, is I leave it open.

'I, er, might have a window Thursday lunchtime,' I go. 'Although I have to emphasize that that's a might.'

And they have these giant teacups, I'm telling her, that you can actually sit in and they, like, spin around. And if you could see her little face. Excited doesn't describe it.

Actually, it literally doesn't describe it, because what she looks is bored shitless.

I'm trying to interest her in the Disneyland Paris brochure, giving it, 'You remember we watched *Alice in Wonderland*, don't you? The Mad Hatter and blah, blah, blah.'

'Oh my God – *so* lame.'

'You're not into that, no. Well, turn over to the next page, Honor –

that's Sleeping Beauty's *actual* castle there. And they have – are you ready for this? – a fireworks display every night?'

She goes, 'Yeah, psoc, Dad.'

'Psoc?'

'Pretending to smile out of *courtesy*?'

Jesus Christ, she's hord work.

I'm there, 'Look, I'm just trying to come up with an added incentive for you to win this race next week.'

'I'm *going* to win the race.'

'Okay, that's what I like to hear. Confidence was always one of my major strengths as well.'

'Only because I want to see, like, the *Champs Elysées*?'

I just shake my head. 'The *Champs Elysées*! Listen to you! Okay, what even is it?'

'You have an iPhone . . .'

'Maybe just tell me, Honor. Might be quicker all round.'

'Oh my God, it's, like, this toats famous street? All the major fashion houses are there. Louis Vuitton. Guerlain. Charles Jourdan . . .'

She's her mother's daughter – ain't no bout-adoubt it. 'Hey, whatever bloats your goat, Baby. Anywhere you want to go. And it'll be Paris Fashion Week as well. I promised you that, didn't I?'

'Oh! My God!'

That's when I decide that it's maybe time to get her mind focused again. 'I hate to remind you,' I go, 'but there's another seven days of training ahead of you and you've got a major amount of work still to do.'

I reach into the old glovebox and pull out a few sheets of A4 paper. One of the things that Father Fehily was big on back in the day was visualization techniques – in other words, roysh, imagining the moment of actual victory. How does it look? How does it sounds? How does it, I suppose, smell? He was actually years ahead of other rugby coaches in his thinking.

There's no doubt that all that shit helped me. Which is why I got on the old worldwide yesterday and printed off a shitload of photographs of people who I'd personally consider winners.

You could even call them heroes of mine.

I put the first one in front of Honor. 'Er, *who* is that?' she instantly goes.

See, that's the amazing thing about kids. They're, like, constantly hungry for information.

'That,' I go, 'is a goy called Johnny Sexton, kicking a penalty against Munster in the Heineken Cup semi-final last year. Do you know how old he was?'

'Er, *no?*'

'Actually, I don't either. Something stupid, though. I mean, look at him, he's still a focking kid. Felipe Contepomi, who you've heard me mention a million times, had to go off injured and this goy here ended up being thrown in at the deep end. The point is, Honor, he wasn't afraid. He just put his focking game face on, went out there and nailed it. A hero. End of.'

'Yeah, whatevs.'

I show her the next one. 'This,' I go, 'is a goy called Shane Horgan, who's another personal hero of mine and – I'd like to think – friend. In fact, he'd have been your godfather if *I'd* had my way. This is a try he scored against England, the first time the Irish rugby team ever played in – okay, you're going to have to hear it from someone – Croke Pork. Rog hung it up in the air for him and *he* leapt about six feet off the ground to catch it. I actually think the two of them were secretly ripping the piss out of Gaelic football. But they all count, Honor. They all count. And I'd actually regard it as one of *the* best moments of the entire Celtic Tiger.'

'Yeah, falling asleep now.'

I turn to the next page. I'm like, 'And this dude here is . . .'

She straight away cuts in. 'Brian O'Driscoll.'

I laugh. I'm forgetting, of course, that him and Amy were never *out* of Sorcha's shop.

'Well, I probably don't *need* to say anymore,' I go. 'But this is *him* in Edinburgh, having won, first, the Grand Slam, then the Heineken Cup, all in a matter of weeks. A lot of people were kind enough to say to me at the time that it could and should have been me out there. I sometimes feel that Drico ended up living the life that was meant for *me*? It's like that movie, *Sliding* focking *Doors*. But he has it, Honor. Just like I had it. You can see it in his eyes. And in Shaggy's eyes. And in Johnny's there. They're winners, Honor . . .'

I'm actually feeling a little bit emotional here. That's how much I love my sport.

But *she* just rolls her eyes, then goes back to texting whoever she's been texting from Newtownpork Avenue to Ballsbridge.

I end up being a bit hurt, to be honest. I've gone to a lot of trouble here.

'Who are you even texting?' I go. 'And I have to ask that, as your father.'

She's there, 'It's, like, Sunny?'

I'm like, 'Who's Sunny?'

'She's this, like, Chinese girl in my class? She's, like, *so* book.'

'Oh,' I go, even though I haven't a clue who she's talking about, '*her*?'

'You don't even know her. Oh my God, you're *so* lame.'

'I do know her.'

'How?'

'Okay, again, I wasn't going to say anything but I heard her saying shit to Malorie.'

'Malorie? Malorie's a bitch.'

'Well, she's not the only one. This Chinese one was saying that Honor can't afford new shoes. She has to get her old ones repaired in a, I don't know, cobblers?'

Fock. She looks like she's about to burst into tears. Which wasn't my intention. What I wanted was to give her something to think about when the race storts getting tough after ten, maybe fifteen metres – an added incentive to break through the famous wall.

'I'll put you on bill-pay,' I suddenly hear myself go.

She looks at me, her mouth wide open. 'What?'

She's *actually* the cutest little girl in the world, even though I'd be obviously biased.

'Oh, you heard me right,' I go. 'No more pay-as-you-go for you. You'll be on bill-pay – like normal girls of your age.'

'But Mom said . . .'

'Your mother's irrelevant. Where is she this morning, can I just ask? Standing on one leg in a field in Booterstown listening to some focking chancer spout shit for an hour and a half.'

She laughs. She's like, 'Oh! My God! Lmao, Daddy! Lmao!'

I'm there, 'Lmao is right. I couldn't have put it better myself. Your mother's out of this particular equation. So listen to me instead. What I'm telling you is – if you win this race, as well as bringing you to Paris,

I'm going to get you set up on, like, a proper network. And I'll pay all the bills. We're talking free, unlimited texts.'

Her face finally lights up. See, that's the ability that sport has to inspire.

I reach across her and open the passenger door of the van, then watch her step down onto Pembroke Road. 'Okay,' I go. 'Now, let's see how fast you can run from the American Embassy to the Audi Centre.'

I can't believe that Sister Ildephonsus is still playing the piano in all the school musicals. After the trauma that we put her through, I thought she'd have earned an honourable focking dischorge by now. But no – there she *still* is, sat at the old Steinhoven upright in the Mount Anville concert hall, hammering out the opening bars to 'Bless Your Beautiful Hide', with what would have to be described as a *contented* smile on her face?

The next thing – the worst possible timing – she happens to look up just as I'm taking my seat in the front row and she hits an immediate bum note, after which her playing falls to literally pieces. You can see all the kids on the stage, roysh, scratching their beards, wondering, er, what *is* the Jack here?

Of course I'm as entitled to sit in on rehearsals as any of the other parents here. Except poor Sister Ildephonsus is obviously having flashbacks to fourteen or fifteen years ago, when I was stood up there, where Ronan's stood now.

He's a little pro, by the way. He ignores the honky notes she's playing and just gets on with the opening scene. He's in the General Grocery, except they've actually made it an Aldi, just to give it that whole Ireland-in-the-current-economic-blahdy-blah vibe.

He goes, 'Hee-er, you wootunt happen to have an aul woife under yisser checkout there, would ye?' because, as you know, he's playing Adam.

Of course, *I'm* straight away laughing at the top of my voice. I can feel all the other parents giving me serious daggers as well but I don't actually *care*? I love the kid. I'm biased. Build a bridge and get over it.

Possibly the main reason I'm so excited, though, is that literally every girl who's involved in the production – we're talking the chorus, we're talking the kinfolk, we're talking Milly and the other six brides – is clearly in love with him. And I'm saying that as someone who has long experience of having girls staring at him in the exact same way. Their eyes are full of – being honest – *longing*?

And I suppose what's made me so suddenly proud to be his father is that he's finally aware of it – as in, there's a sudden swagger about him. For the first time ever – and I can't tell you how proud I am to be able to say this – he actually reminds me of me.

The bird on the till storts giving out yords to him, going, 'You theenk you can come into shop and buy wife like she eez box of Corn Flecks?' See, they've actually made her Polish, which is also a nice touch. Shows they've got their finger on the definite pulse. 'Theez you must know – there eez ten men for effery woman in theez place.'

'Sounds like Club 92 back in the day,' I happen to go to the woman sitting beside me. She's not *that* unlike Karen Allen, in fairness to her. 'Of course *I* was never put off by the odds.'

She shushes me, which is actually rude, although I let it go and just turn back to the stage, where Ro – shoulders back, chin in the air – is going, 'Ine maddying no one until I check out every geerl who's out there.'

'And scene!' I hear someone shout and I'm the only one who ends up actually clapping.

'Brilliant!' I shout. 'Focking brilliant!'

It would not be an exaggeration to say that the girls are suddenly swarming around him, all fighting for his attention. The other six brothers are just standing around – like Rog watching Johnny Sexton weave his magic.

I shake my head in literally awe. Because despite all my fears, he's turned out to be every bit the ladies man that I was – and still am, I like to think.

'He's turned into quite the little Don Juan,' I hear this little voice suddenly go.

I turn my head, roysh, and who's suddenly sat there in front of me – with her face all sour, like she's spent the last hour supping brake fluid – only Blathin herself. I'm ready for her, of course. 'I don't even know what a Don Juan is,' I go, 'although I'm presuming it's Spanish for something.'

'It's Spanish for male slut,' she straight away goes.

See, they're taught to debate in Mount Anville before they learn to even tie their Dubes.

I stick out my bottom lip, as if I'm considering this. 'Well,' I eventually go, 'you turned him into one, by putting the word around the school that he was a bastard to women?'

The thing is, roysh, that Blathin's still hurting, so she's obviously determined to ignore any of the genuinely *good* points I have to make?

'Of course,' she ends up going, 'it shouldn't come as any surprise, having *you* as a role model.'

Now, there are two areas, as far as I'm concerned, where my record should never be open to question. The first – the main one – is obviously as a points-kicker. The second is as a father. Which is why I end up going, 'Er, *excuse* me?'

She just smiles at me – not a nice smile either. 'He's like a Mini Me version of you,' she goes. 'Oh, I know you think it's hilarious. But I'm the one, remember – *as* director – who's having to pick up the pieces.'

'Yeah, whatever.'

'Yasmin keeps bursting into tears, mid-scene. Filipa's mother wants to take her out of the play. The poor girl can't eat, can't sleep . . .'

'We've all been there, Bla – even, I dare say, you.'

'He *told* her that he loved her.'

I end up laughing in her face. It's just that he's *such* a chip off the old block.

'Look, everyone *knows* that's just a line,' I try to go. 'You're not in love with anyone at thirteen.'

She just goes, 'You're a total orsehole,' except she practically *roars* it? I'm thinking, *she's* not going to be winning many debates if she ends up having knicker-fits like that.

Most of the other parents in the hall are, like, staring at me as Blathin wheels herself away, then looks over her shoulder one more time to go, 'Total!'

It's at that exact moment, roysh, surrounded by adoring girls, that Ronan looks down from the stage and gives me a big dirty wink. And I have to tell you – because it's the basic truth – that I've never felt prouder.

Sorcha gave the old man a juicer. And it's not just *a* juicer – it's *our* juicer, the one that Simon and Guy Easterby bought us when they crashed our wedding. Something tells me that giving away wedding gifts is another one of Giovanna's big ideas.

The old man is stood over it, going, 'How does celery, carrots, alfafa sprouts, apples and ginger sound to you?'

I'm there, 'Revolting, if I'm being honest.'

'Well,' he goes, suddenly firing up the machine, 'prepare yourself to be amazed, Ross, because, while it *is* awful, it's not half as awful as it sounds.'

I watch him, like, feeding the ingredients down the tube, then this pale green liquid – okay, I'm going to say the word – pretty much *ejaculates* out of the little tap and into the clear plastic jug? He's just, like, shaking his head, roysh, like he can't believe someone could have invented such a thing.

He stirs what's in the jug, then goes, 'I expect you've been reading all about Greece being bailed out. Of course you have – in business, the global is local and the local is global. Seems *our* contribution to it is to be something in the region of one point three billion.'

'One point three billion?' I go. 'I thought we were, like, broke?'

'I'm glad you said that. Because if a young financial whizzkid like you doesn't understand it, then what hope is there for the rest of us, eh? Still, I have faith in Brian Lenihan, just as I have faith in you.'

He pours the juice into a glass, then puts it down in front of me with a real – I don't know – *flourish*? 'Taste that,' he goes, 'and tell me what you think.'

It's the colour of – my guess is – chemical weapons.

I sniff it, then I take, like, a sip. It *is* revolting. I'm like, 'I can't drink that.'

'Contains four fifths of your recommended fruit and vegetable intake for the day. Have one of these when you get up in the morning – you're nearly on par, Ross, and it's not even bloody lunchtime.'

'But then you're shitting baby food all afternoon,' I go. 'Dude, I literally can't drink that.'

Helen arrives into the kitchen, smiling. She rubs his back, as if to say – I don't know – nice try, then goes, 'Ross, I'll make you some coffee.'

I tell her thanks, because she always has good beans, in fairness to her.

Then I watch the old man wander over to the sink, run the hot tap

121

and stort taking the machine aport. There's some amount of cleaning in it, which is why we hordly ever used the focking thing.

I get the impression, though, that his feelings are hurt – something I never would have noticed before.

And that's when Regina pops back into my head. Imagine what it would do to him if he ever found out. Probably put him right back in the hospital.

Then I think about the sex – it *was* incredible.

But then I think, no. I couldn't actually bring myself to do it.

The chorus from 'Crazy Love' comes, I don't know, wafting up from the kitchen, and that's when the Shiva Rose storts automatically twitching.

The old hum of breakfast. Without even opening my eyes, I reach out with my foot and explore the bed. There's, like, no one else in it.

This is going to come across as possibly sexist but there is no better feeling in the world than knowing that the woman you've spent the night making amazing, amazing love to is downstairs cooking for you with a big satisfied smile on her face.

'It's roddy!' she suddenly shouts up the stairs, which must mean we're not eating it here in the bedroom.

I hop out and consider getting dressed, except my clothes are, like, strewn all over the gaff. Some in here. Some on the landing. Some in the – believe it or not – gorden.

So in the end I just open the sliderobe, whip out a random bathrobe and throw it on me. It has, like, a logo on the breast pocket, I notice, for the Bel Eire Health and Wellness Spa – the famous destination hotel that she and her husband owned next to the Topaz filling station on the way into Urlingford.

Although it's supposedly focked now.

The material is, like, unbelievably soft. It *actually* feels like a hug? I tie the little belt at the front, then I think about maybe going through Regina's knicker drawer and stuffing a couple of pairs into the pocket of my chinos. Except in the end I don't. Which is possibly a sign that I'm finally maturing.

I tip down to the kitchen. Regina is stood with her back to me, plunging the coffee, wearing a caviar-black body wrap with black leggings and white slipper socks. I can see her yoga mat laid out in the sunroom. She's obviously been up for a while.

Eleven o'clock in the morning and I've got an instant trombone on me. By rights, I should be, like, totally sexed out.

'Bublé again?' I go, just for openers.

See, I usually hate that morning-after awkwardness, which is the reason I usually leave through a focking window.

She turns around, but she doesn't answer, just stares at me like she's seeing an actual ghost.

'I'm only joking,' I go. 'I actually don't mind him.'

Again, nothing.

In the end, I find myself having to go, 'Is everything okay?'

'That's *Toddy's* robe,' she just goes.

Of course there's no coming back from a line like that. I'm thinking, you've just slept with a dead man's wife – now you're wearing his clothes.

I'm there, 'I, er, just grabbed it from the wardrobe. I think you might have actually ripped my pink Hollister T-shirt last night.'

She suddenly snaps out of it – whatever *it* is. 'Och, it's okee,' she goes. 'Ay just got a frait, that's all, when ay saw yee stood in the door thurr.'

'I can take it off if you want.'

'Och, no – sit and hov your brackfist.'

I pour my own coffee while she bends down to grab two plates out of the cupboard. She has the flexibility of a focking Chinese gymnast, which is an amazing advertisement for the whole yoga thing.

The sex, by the way, was again amazing – for both of us, I hasten to add. Reluctant as I am to write my own raves, you can't fake the kind of noises that she was making yesterday afternoon – and twice last night.

'What's that thang,' she goes, out of the blue goes, 'that thang yee keep whuspering in may ear when we're, yee know, meeking love?'

I'm there, 'Are you talking about, "Ham and eggs, Baby! Ham and eggs!"'

She nods. 'Aye, thot's ut – can you nat dee thot naxt taim?'

Next time? She's taking a hell of a lot for granted there.

Still, I go, 'Are you sure? And I only ask because a lot of girls really love it.'

She looks at me like I'm as mad as focking cheese. 'Hov any geerls *told* yee they love it?'

'Er, not specifically,' I go, sitting down at the table, 'but I'd consider myself a pretty good judge. Although I *will* stop saying it – if you feel it's definitely not doing anything for you.'

'Thot'd be greet.'

I take a sip of my coffee.

'Because they say that,' I go, 'don't they – certainly any of the women's magazines I've flicked through while I've been in the dentists – the key to good sex is, like, communication? More of this. Less of that. Faster. Slower. Strap this on . . .'

'Here,' she goes, 'dee something useful with your mithe and eat op,' and she puts my breakfast down in front of me. It has to be said, it looks *and* smells amazing.

'What even is it?' I go, except already horsing it into me.

'It's a pormesan amlette,' she goes, 'with sugared beacon.'

Ham and eggs. I stop myself from saying it.

I'm there, 'I could even just say it *less* often? See does that work for you.'

'*Ay* already told yee,' she goes, all serious, 'ay don't want yee saying it at all.'

'Coola boola,' I go, holding my two hands up. 'Coola boola.'

She puts her plate on the table, then sits down opposite me. This is some nosebag, I don't mind saying it.

See, usually when I wake up with a bird, I make do with the old Munster supporter's breakfast – a mouthful of water straight from the faucet and a scratch of my balls.

She's an unbelievable cook, in all fairness. I'd put her on the same level as my old dear. Then I remember that she and her husband were both originally chefs. It's possibly how they even met.

After, like, a short silence, she goes, 'Ay'm sorray – ay can be a wee bit norkee in the mornens.'

'So I notice. I thought yoga was supposed to help with that kind of thing.'

'Well, anywee, ay jost want tay see, ay really enjoyed last nait.'

'You certainly seemed to,' I go. 'Jesus, the focking squeals out of you.'

She laughs at that. A lot of people have commented on the fact that I have a way of putting others in instantly good form.

I end up totally cleaning my plate, roysh, then she happens to look at me just as my eyes are straying towards the door.

'Yee can leave if yee want,' she goes.

I'm like, 'Sorry – force of habit. Continue. You were saying you really enjoyed the sex.'

'*Ay'm* nat keeping you hurr,' she goes. 'You can leave noy – *ay'm* serious.'

I'm like, 'No, it's cool, honestly. This is what normal people do, isn't it? Sit around the next day and have the post-match chat.'

She puts her knife and fork on her plate, like she's finished eating – even though she's got half her focking breakfast still left. 'Look,' she goes, '*ay'm* nat looking for a reletionshup horr. Ay'm nat looking for some beg, camplicated thang . . .'

'That's, er, cool.'

'Ay'm well awur of the age gop here.'

'Yeah, you're literally twice my age – and that's not me being a bastard.'

'So nayther of us is thanking abite thus in the lawng term, am I rait?'

'Definitely not.'

'We're jost tee people hoy hoppen to enjoy each other's cormpany.'

'Again, I agree.'

'But *yee* don't want ut devaloping intee something?'

'No.'

'Look, *ay* don't ayther. So let's jost go on deeing thus. And let's nat put a neem on ut. Or a leebel. Let's nat meek any pramises tee each other – other thon tee enjoy the moment. Nee demonds. Nee quastions. Nee, "Why dadn't yee rang may?" We'll jost dee thos – whenever it's convenient.'

I actually laugh, except in, like, an *admiring* way?

'Can *I* just say,' I go, 'if only all women thought like you, then every man in the world would end up happily married to the first bird he ever met – that'd be my prediction. But look, I'm going to level with you. What you're offering. The sex. The breakfast – unbelievable, by the way. The whole no-questions-asked thing. It's all muesli to my ears. The only reason I'm going to have to possibly say no is – being honest? – my old man.'

'Yeer what?'

'My dad.'

'What abite hum?'

125

'He's recovering from an actual hort attack.'

'Ay'm sorray. Och, ay dudn't know.'

'Well, he blames you for giving it to him.'

'What? Hoy?'

'Er, you took him for one point seven mills. He wasn't a happy bunny either.'

'Hoy do yee thank *ay* felt? Walking intee *may* own badroom and fainding *may* hosband hoving sax with thot wee whore?'

'Look, there's none of us are angels here. My point is why did *he* have to pay the price?'

'Because *he* chose tay. *Ay* wasn't traying tee gat at *hum* – or *her*, for thot motter. Ay *hod* vary good grinds for davorce – what was *ay* supposed to dee, pretand lake ay never saw onythang.'

'I suppose not.'

'And onywee, what's any of thot got tee dee with yee and may?'

'Nothing, I suppose. It's just if the old man found out . . .'

'Hoy's he *gonna* find ite?'

'Good question.'

'Do *yee* tall hum abite every gorl yee sleep wuth?'

I laugh. 'I'd be never *off* the phone to him if I did.'

'Well, then.'

I notice she has the sleeves of her black body wrap pulled down over her hands – like you do when you're grabbing something out of the oven and you're too lazy to take out the oven gloves.

'I suppose the other thing,' I go, 'is that it feels a little bit, I don't know, morbid?'

'What are yee talking abite?'

'As in, your husband's barely dead in the ground. I mean, we met at his actual funeral.'

'Look, *ay* wasn't thor looking tee meet someone. Jesus, give may some cradit. Ay called yee ite to the hyse thot dee tee apologaze – nathin more. *Ay* dadn't in may waildest dreams expact what hoppened tee hoppen. But ay don't thank either of us could holp oursalves.'

This, I can tell you for a fact, is horseshit. She went all out that day to try to be with me. Couldn't believe her luck.

I'm there, 'But what about, well, the way you looked at me when I walked into the kitchen just then wearing Toddy's robe. The dude's only dead, what, four months?'

'Look, Toddy and ay were over a lawng taim ago. If it hodn't been your soster, it would have been some other wee scrobber. No offence, lake.'

'None taken. You should see the goy she's ended up with, by the way.' I laugh. 'I mean, he's one of my best friends – focking unbelievable rugby player back in the day, though I'd never tell him that to his face. She can do way, way better, though. Maybe *he's* her punishment for what happened.'

I go to touch her hand but she pulls it away quickly, like she's been, I don't know, burned or some shit?

I'm there, 'Are you okay?'

She's like, 'Och, aye,' and she stands up, then picks up our plates and takes them over to the sink.

I'm going to say it again, that was some pretty amazing nosebag.

'Ay thank if there's a lassen tee learn from Toddy's dath,' she goes, staring out the window of the kitchen, 'it's tee enjoy whatever taim we hov, whale we con.'

It's the same lesson, you could say, from my old man's hort attack.

When she's rinsed down the plates, then stacked them in the dishwasher, she turns around and gives me what would have to be described as a look – at the same time licking her lips like a storving dog.

Then, roysh, slowly – I'm also going to use the word *seductively*? – without even breaking eye contact with me, she moves over to the table where I'm sitting.

'What are your plons for the dee?' she goes.

'I'm, er, supposedly collecting a rake of documents from a place on Baggot Street.'

She reaches down, grabs the belt of my robe and just pulls the knot loose. The thing just flops opens and she drops to her knees.

'Oh noy you're nat!' she goes. 'Oh noy you're nat!'

Tina rings me and she's got a serious focking strop on – to the point where I'm actually wondering is it Shark Week for her.

'I come home from a torteen-hour shift in Beaumont,' she goes, 'to find a woman at me doe-ur.'

'Jesus Christ,' I go, 'would it kill you to even *try* to pronounce it as door?'

'At me doe-ur,' she goes, 'giving ourra bout Ronan.'

I'm like, 'Ronan?' on the immediate defensive. 'Who actually was she?'

'One of the udder mudders. Her young wan's in dis play he's doin.'

'It's *actually* a musical?'

'Whatever it is. What's dis de young wan was called?'

'Yasmin?'

'No.'

'Filipa.'

'Fiddipa – dat was it.'

'Cool. She actually plays Dorcas. So what did she actually say, this woman?'

I still can't believe the mother of an actual Mountie drove out to Finglas. She *must* have been upset.

'She says Ronan broke the young wan's heert.'

I laugh. 'I heard something about that alright – from Blathin. There's a name from the past, huh? So what's Ronan's defence?'

She's like, 'He's not saying athin. He won't even talk to me abourrit.'

'Well,' I go, 'he's a teenager now, Tina. Get used to that.'

She totally loses it with me then.

'Are you fooken giving him advoice about geerls?'

I'm like, '*Excuse* me? Why would you even think that?'

'Because,' she goes, 'de tings he said to dis young wan coulda come straight ourra your mout.'

Yeah, *I'm* busted. Not that I *give* a fock.

'Look,' I go, 'what's this woman's actual beef? Is she honestly saying that *her* daughter's never going to play someone like a basset horn? It's Mount focking Anville. Do you know what those girls grow up to be? Bitches, Tina. Out and out . . . I'm just trying to think is there an equivalent school on your side of the city that I could give you as an example, maybe in Sutton or Howth.'

'Stop fillin he's head with all dat rubbish.'

'All I'm saying is that you have no idea what these girls are like.'

'I know what me *son* is like!' she practically roars down the phone at me. She could sell sports socks and Cheeky Chorlies on Henry Street with that focking voice of hers. 'He's a *nice* kid, so he is.'

'Well, some might say too nice.'

'And de last ting he needs is lessons from *you* in how to treat people.'

★   ★   ★

The day of the Little Roedean's Sports Day finally arrives and we're all stood around in Merrion Square while the Principal – it's Doireann or Dearbhail or one of those – announces the names of the ten runners for the twenty-five-metre dash.

There's a lot of, I don't know, oohing and aahing from all the other parents, it has to be said, because the actual storting line looks like a shot from one of those Anne Geddes calendars that Sorcha loves, we're talking kids of all shapes and colours, we're talking Indian, we're talking Chinese, we're talking – and this *is* racist, even though I still have to say the word for the purposes of the story – black.

A lot of, like, foreign embassy staff have their kids in Little Roedean's. In fact, multiculturalism is one of the main reasons that Sorcha wanted Honor to go there.

I spot Malorie's old dear and I give her a little wave – she's gagging for me in a serious way – which, of course, doesn't escape Sorcha's attention. She gets in an instant snot with me. 'You're unbelievable,' she just goes.

I'm there, 'People person – like I told you. Hey, you're the one who wants to push ahead with the whole divorce thing.'

She's like, 'Oh, don't kid yourself that it would *even* bother me, Ross.'

Dearbhail – I'm ninety percent sure it *is* Dearbhail – is having a hord time getting all the runners under, I suppose, storters orders. Most of them, I can't help but notice as a former sportsman who did it at the highest level, aren't even *focusing* on the race? They're, like, looking around them or they're yabbering away among themselves.

Honor, I'm proud to say, is stood in lane three with her big-time game face on, staring straight ahead at the twenty-five yords between her and glory. Her mother storts calling her name, roysh, and waving to her and I have to tell her not to break her focus, which Sorcha definitely doesn't appreciate.

'Look, take it from someone who's been there and done it,' I try to go, 'a major port of it is about concentration.'

She, I don't know, *scowls* at me? 'Filling her head this morning with all that motivational rubbish,' she goes.

'What?'

'Oh, I heard you in the kitchen, Ross, when I popped outside to put something in the recycling bin. *Fall seven times, stand up eight . . .*'

'That's hordly rubbish. It's one of Fehily's old lines.'

'She's not even five years old, Ross!'

'Well, I *could* mention how old Tiger Woods was when he hit his first hundred-yord drive. I won't, though.'

'Hello? It's *supposed* to be non-competitive?'

No such thing in this world, I think to myself. No such focking thing.

'On your marks . . .' this Dearbhail one suddenly goes.

And they're all finally ready.

Sorcha shouts, 'Good luck, Honor! Remember, just be the best that you can be,' which makes me snort so loudly that actual snot comes out of my nose.

But Honor, I'm happy to say, doesn't even flinch.

'Set . . .'

I go, 'Remember what's at stake here, Honor! Win at all costs!' which seems to shock one or two of the other parents.

'Go!'

Honor's off like a bullet from a gun. In fact, it's immediately obvious that there's only, like, three kids in the race who can live with her sudden turn of pace from a standing stort – her ex friend Malorie, Sunny, the Chinese girl who she also fell out with, then a little Indian boy called Faarooq – and they're all *still* a good metre behind her.

Sorcha's there giving it, 'That's it, do your best, Honor! Keep going! Just do your best!'

Honor's *actually* flying, roysh, but then suddenly, somewhere around the mid-point in the race, she hits the famous barrier where the legs stort to weaken. This is where something like creatine would actually do a lot of good, though obviously I'd never give something like that to my daughter. Not until she's sixteen anyway.

What happens is that Faarooq comes back at her on the inside and he's suddenly running neck-and-neck with her. Sunny's been dropped but Malorie still has a bit of fight in her and is also matching the two of them stride for pretty much stride.

'Just remember,' Malorie's old dear goes, 'your father and I will love you no matter what, Darling!' which also causes me to *actually* laugh out loud.

Faarooq's old dear is shouting something in, I'm presuming, Indian. Whatever it is, the kid comes on strong and steals that little bit ahead.

That's when I suddenly come to life as a coach. 'Come on,' I shout at Honor, 'find that extra gear that we talked about in training.'

Sorcha looks at me – six or seven of the other parents look at me as well. 'Training?' she goes.

I'm too busy concentrating on the race, though, to even entertain it.

Honor kicks and closes the distance, then eases a little bit in front.

'Come on,' I'm going, 'focking burn them off. Malorie *and* the other one.'

'Stop it!' Malorie's old dear shouts at me. 'They used to be friends.'

'There's no such thing as friends in sport!' I remind Honor, just in case she overheard it. 'Only winners and losers! Which one are you going to be? Which one are you going to be?'

Malorie comes back strong on one side of her, then Faarooq on the other. Five yords from the line, roysh, the three of them are running pretty much level.

I'm there practically screaming, 'Bill-pay, Honor! Bill-pay!'

Faarooq, I swear to fock, is just about to dip over the line, while Malorie is maybe half-a-step in front of Honor. That's when suddenly, without any warning, Honor's two orms suddenly shoot out. She grabs Malorie by the hair and Faarooq by the scruff of the neck, and then, with what Ryle Nugent would possibly describe as 'wonderful economy of movement', she pulls them both backwards, in the process thrusting herself over the finishing line, needless to say, first.

In all the excitement, I end up just waving my fist at Faarooq's old dear. 'Yes!' I go. 'In your focking face!' which *is* a bit horsh, I'm prepared to admit, but then these *are* the precious moments as a parent – if you can't enjoy them without rubbing everyone else's nose in it, you'd have to ask yourself what kind of a world are we suddenly living in?

Unfortunately, the result – or, to be more exact, the manner of it – doesn't go down at all well with the other rents. It goes without saying that I don't speak any other languages, though it doesn't take much brainpower to work out that they're screaming pretty much blue murder and it's mostly directed at me.

Sorcha's suddenly raced the length of the, I suppose, track and has scooped Honor up in her orms, blocking her ears, I suppose to protect her from some of the more ugly comments that are now being shouted.

Sunny's old man certainly knows the word 'cheat' because he practically spits it at me, roysh, and I've no choice except to keep going, 'That's not what the record books going to say!' over and over again, right in his face.

All the parents go to grab their kids, most of whom are crying, I should point out.

Faarooq's old man's English is pretty good, I soon discover, because he's suddenly threatening all sorts, including the cessation of diplomatic relations between Ireland and India, which sounds pretty heavy, it has to be said, while Malorie's old dear – a huge fan of mine before – is suddenly demanding that the race result be declared null and void.

'Er,' I end up having to point out, 'you were the one saying it didn't actually *matter* who won? All of you said it. So what's suddenly changed?'

She's holding Malorie in her orms and the kid has turned on the major waterworks. 'She pulled my hair!' she keeps going. 'Oh! My God! She pulled my actual hair.'

'Your daughter cheat!' Sunny's old man shouts at Sorcha.

I wouldn't mind but *his* precious daughter didn't even place, despite her very good stort.

I look at Honor, sat in Sorcha's orms, and she seems a bit overwhelmed, it has to be said, by the reaction she's getting.

'Rise above it,' I make sure to tell her, 'like *I* did back in the day. Ask Rog, Johnny, any of the goys – learning to live with the boo-boys is all port of the game.'

But that's when I suddenly notice Sorcha's tears. 'Part of the game?' she just goes. 'Ross, I can't *believe* what I just watched our daughter do!'

The other parents seem to be enjoying the fact that I'm suddenly getting heat here.

I'm there, 'You watched her win, Sorcha.'

I look at Honor sitting in her orms and I give her a big wink. 'Well done, Kid.'

Malorie's old dear decides to get in on the act then. I'm glad I never told her that she looks like Kate Garraway. 'Is that what you call winning?' she goes. 'You think the way to get ahead is to cheat and lie your way through life?'

I look around at all the faces just staring at me.

I'm like, 'Jesus Christ, two years ago, everyone thought that. Why am I suddenly a bad person? What's happening to this supposed country?'

Dearbhail steps forward then, writing something on her little clipboard. When she's finished, she looks up and goes, 'Now, we'll proceed with the medal ceremony. I'll ask all of the young people – and their parents – to go to the table over there, where they will be presented with their medals . . .'

I smile at Honor. I'm like, 'Yours is the only one that means a thing, Babes.'

'Everyone except Honor O'Carroll-Kelly, who has been disqualified for cheating.'

I don't know why he insists on putting himself through it. Putting *me* through it as well. The plan was to go to Bellamy's to watch Munster get their orses handed to them by Northampton, except when I picked him up from his old pair's, he said he wanted to come here, presumably to see *this* instead. Although I don't bother arguing. It's Oisinn. How long have we been mates?

'Here,' I go, squinting my eyes, 'that's that painting you bought that time. What was that dude called who did it?'

He's like, 'John Kingerlee,' and he doesn't say it in, like, a *defensive* way?

I end up just shaking my head. 'I'm going to be a hundred percent honest with you, Ois, I never knew what it was actually *of*?'

'Of?'

'Well, obviously a painting's got be *of* something. Either a cow or a house or a – I don't know – *waterfall*? Especially one that costs – how much was it again?'

'Fifty Ks.'

'I mean, fifty focking Ks. I used to stare at it sometimes – you know, when you'd throw one of your famous porties – and I'd think, maybe those white blobs there are actual clouds. Or sheep even. But that was with, like, six or seven cans inside me.'

Oisinn is, like, cracking his hole laughing, which is nice to see. He goes, 'It's a grid composition, Ross,' like that's any excuse.

I'm like, 'Dude, no offence, but when you first showed it to me, that was the one time I did wonder whether the whole Celtic Tiger thing had maybe gone a little bit too far. Pictures that aren't actually *of* anything.'

This is us, by the way, staring through the railings of his old gaff on Shrewsbury Road, while a team of, I suppose, removers strip the place basically bare.

'Do you want to know the hilarious thing?' he goes. 'I bought it without even seeing it.'

I laugh.

'I wouldn't beat yourself up over that,' I go. 'That just was the way it was back then. I bought two aportments, remember, in Bulgaria. I mean, who'd ever focking heard of the place?'

I watch two men carry out a nineteenth-century mourning bed, then just fock it down, like it came from, I don't know, Jim Langan Furniture. I watch Oisinn's face for a reaction, except there's none.

'So,' I go, 'what's going to, like, happen to all this shit?'

'It'll be auctioned off,' he goes, easy breezy about the whole thing, 'and the proceeds divided among my creditors.'

'This focking recession!' I go, actually kicking the railing – I don't *know* why? Possibly just to offer him a few words of support.

He laughs, then just puts his orm around my shoulder. 'Ross, I'm telling you, I'm okay with this.'

'What, with everything you own in the world being sold to . . . Jesus, who even *knows* who? My old man might even stick in a bid for your paintings. He's talking about buying one or two off the banks.'

He looks back at the gaff. 'I don't care who ends up getting them. I'm being serious. I don't care about this gaff.'

I'm like, 'Er, you *must* do? I mean, why else are we here?'

He shakes his head. 'I just wanted to see would I feel something – you know, if I saw it happening with my own eyes.'

'And you're saying you don't.'

'I *actually* don't.'

'Even though that's an actual Comtoise longcase that they're just focking in the back of that truck there?'

'I have no attachment to it, Ross. I've no attachment to any of this stuff. Most of it, I didn't even buy myself. I hired somebody to buy it for me. I mean, I won't *miss* any of it.'

'Even that writing bureau? Like, that was from, I don't know, some other century – literally ages ago.'

'I couldn't even tell you what room it was in, Ross.'

'It was in the vestibule.'

'The vestibule,' he goes, suddenly turning his back on me. 'Whatever.'

He stares up the road, like he's taking it in for the last time. I suppose in a way he is.

'Hord to believe,' I go, 'that this was, like, *the* most expensive road in the world to buy a house.'

He's there, 'It was actually the sixth most expensive,' trying to put a positive spin on things.

'Well,' I go, 'the old man reckons they're all going to be moving out. Sean Dunne. Paddy Kelly. Derek Quinlan. This road might end up being like one of those actual ghost estates. Who would have ever seen that coming?'

He turns and storts walking back to the cor. He climbs into the front passenger seat and I get in beside him.

'By the way,' he goes, obviously wanting to talk about something happier, 'how did the sports day go?'

I just roll my eyes. 'Don't ask.'

He's there, 'Did she win?'

'That depends,' I go. 'Are you asking me morally?'

'What?'

'Long story, Ois. I'm going to give Sorcha a few days to calm down, is all I'll say on the matter. Let's just hit the battle cruiser, will we?'

Except he pulls a face. He's there, 'I, er, might just go home.'

Meaning back to his old pair's. He has no home anymore.

'Dude,' I go, 'it's, like, the quarter-final of the Heineken Cup. Come on, Bellamy's is going to be full of muckers.'

'I don't know.'

'Here, open the old glovebox there and see what I've brought.'

He does exactly what I say and I watch this smile suddenly – I don't know – *erupt* across his face. Because he recognizes my old universal TV remote.

'I'll stick it up my sleeve,' I go, 'just like the old days. And every time those fockers look like scoring a try, I'll switch the focking channel.'

He laughs. He actually *cracks* his hole laughing. I genuinely think

I'm one of the main reasons he's coping so well with the shit-storm that's blowing through his life right now.

'Okay,' he just goes, 'let's do it.'

'How's dat young lad of yoo-ers?' he goes.

It's weird, roysh, but if you'd told me before this whole current economic climate storted that I'd end up being bezzy mates with an actual Dublin gangland criminal, I'd have said you were off your meds. But here we are, me and the infamous Larry Tuhill, sitting on my balcony, knocking back a couple of sundowners, as dorkness falls over Ticknock.

'Ronan?' I go. 'Yeah, he's great.'

'Has he given up the idea of going into croyim.'

'I hope so. It's a constant worry, of course. Finglas and blah blah blah. For the moment, though, I'm happy to say that he's discovered girls.'

Larry takes the cigarette out of his mouth and blows four smoke rings in the air. 'I said dat to Tetty,' he goes. 'Dat young fedda, he'll discover boords and dat'll purrim on de oul straight and naddow. Ah, feer play.'

'Well, that's my exact attitude. See, he finished it with that girl he was going out with. Did you ever meet Blathin?'

'Little boord in de wheelcheer?'

'Exactly. Anyway, broke it off with her. Next thing he knows, he's got a reputation for being a bastard.'

'I can wonderstand dat – de pewer geerl.'

'Poor girl nothing. She's dissed him all over the southside. Of course what he's since discovered is the exact same lesson that *I* learned back in the day – there's nothing a bird likes more than a bastard.'

'Well,' he goes, 'Ine going to have to take your woord for dat, you being a man of expeerdience.'

I'm there, 'Are you saying you're not?'

'Not reedy, no.'

'But Saoirse, she's not your first girlfriend, is she?'

'She's me foorst love, Rosser. I mean, I've been wit boords – fooken lowids. But I never really felt athin – apeert from the obvious.'

'God, I love the obvious.'

'Wit Saoirse it was love at foorst sight. For me, in anyhow. Foorst two or tree toyums I was wit her, she kept saying, "Are ya shewer you're not an unthercover cop?" She can be a bit padanoid, see.'

'I did pick up on that.'

'But what can I say? It's arthur growing from theer.'

'And now you're off to Spain.'

'Dat's reet. One or two little bits and pieces to look arthur. Den we're ourra hee-er. Going straight – de boat of us. Hee-er, she wants to ast ya something, boy de way.'

'Ask me something? As in?'

'A favour. Ine gonna leave it to her – she's gonna pop in.'

'In here?'

'Doatunt look so woodied, Rosser.'

'I'm not worried. I just know she hates me.'

'She dudn't hate ya. Fact, she said something veddy noice about ya de udder neet. Well, she was saying ye were a doorty fooken pox who always had he's nose in de eer . . .'

'Lovely.'

'But den she said you were a good-looken fedda, but.'

'I have to admit, that's a nice thing to hear.'

'Wadn't for me. Says I, a good-looken fedda, is he? I could sort dat out wit a fooken Stanley knife in five fooken minutes. Slash he's fooken face.'

I laugh. The problem with Larry and his brother is that you never know when they're joking and when they're serious. Means you're always on edge.

'You tink Ine laughing,' he goes, while *actually* laughing. 'I was veddy jeadous when she said it, but. For abour an hour, reet, I tink I'd have been capable of athin.'

Fock's sake.

We sit there in silence for a couple of minutes then, me quietly shitting myself. I finish one can and crack open another.

After a while, he goes, 'Ye heerd about de udder blocks being demodished, did ye?'

I'm there, 'I did, yeah.'

'Ah,' he goes, 'I tink we're getting ourrat de reet toyum. You'd wonther what's gonna happen to Rosa Peerks, wouldn't ye? I'd haten to see it go downhill.'

Yeah, that focking ship sailed the day the Deportment of Social Welfare stuck you and your brother next door, I think to myself.

The next thing I hear is the patio door sliding open. Saoirse is suddenly stood there. I actually forgot that they have a key to my place.

She doesn't even look at me – just looks straight at Larry. She's like, 'Did ye ast um?'

'Ast um yisser self,' he goes.

'Ine not fooken astin um – he's a fooken faggi.'

This conversation goes back and forth for a bit.

'He's not a faggi. I toalt ye, dat's joost de way he talks.'

'Walking arowunt wit he's nose in de eer.'

'Like I said, he's a nice fedda. He caddent help where he was borden, Saoirse.'

I go, 'Yeah, goys, I'm actually still sitting here, you know.'

Soairse – again, without looking at me – goes, 'Fooken ast um, Laddy, will ye?'

Larry rolls his eyes, turns to me and goes, 'Rosser, is your piss clean?'

What a focking question. I'm like, 'I'm pretty sure, yeah.'

'Can Saoirse have a cup of it, can she?'

Jesus Christ. With most neighbours, it's a cup of sugar.

Saoirse looks at me for the first time. 'It's for me probation officer,' she goes.

I'm like, 'Er, yeah, no problem.'

Larry's there, 'See? A lovely fedda.'

'Where are you?' I go.

He's like, 'Milltown,' except he says it in, like, a near-whisper?

He's with a bird. There's no *doubt* he's with a bird. Take it from me – I know the M.O.

'Go on, who is it?' I go and then there's, like, a moment's silence while he moves presumably out of earshot of her.

'Grainne,' he goes.

It sounds like he's stepped out into the gorden.

I laugh. I'm sure he knows how instantly proud of him I am, even down the phone line.

I'm like, 'Is that her real name, Ro, or her stage name?'

'Real,' he goes. 'She plays Ruth.'

'Ruth? Brilliant! And you're in her actual gaff?'

'Yeah, her ma's arthur making me tea and everyting.'

'Tea? Bla's gonna have a major Swiss-hissy when she finds that out. How many's that, Ro – three?'

He's there, 'Fower.'

I'm like, 'Four?'

His voice goes even lower then. 'Yeah. I've been wit her cousint as well. Jenny. Plays Martha . . .'

'Ro, you remind me so much of myself I could nearly cry here.'

'It's fooken gas, Rosser. Even though they're related to each utter, they're rippin the fooken back ourrof each other.'

'That's what they're like, Ro. You're learning – that much is obvious.'

'I was with Jenny arthur rehearsals and she was all, *"Grainne's, like, obviously my cousin and also my best friend in the world, but I wouldn't trust her as far as I could throw her?"* And Grainne's just arthur sayin the same thing to me bout Jenny.'

I'm like, 'Girls are bitches, Ro. That's just what they do. You try explaining that to your mother, though.'

'I know.'

'See, people think that shit storts in Junior Wez. But they're at it in the focking pram . . .'

'Ine finding that out for meself, man.'

'Now, here's another thing you need to learn, Ro – a major port of getting birds to really, really like you is to constantly undermine their confidence.'

'Unthermine it?'

'Basically, yeah.'

'What, by telling them they're fat?'

I laugh.

'Jesus, no. I mean, yeah, *I've* done that once or twice myself, usually with models – or girls who *claim* to be models. But you don't have to come out and say it like that. Just comment on other girls. I mean, you've got the perfect set-up with the two cousins. So you say to Grainne, just slip it into conversation, "God, that Jenny's really, really good-looking, isn't she?" and then, next time you see Jenny, say pretty much the same thing to her. You go, "By the way, has Grainne ever done any modelling? Because she actually *should*?" Stops them getting too big for their boots. Girls with low self-esteem will always want you.'

'Here, tanks, Rosser.'

'Hey, don't thank me. I'm actually tempted to tell you not to change a thing in terms of your gameplan. I mean, four out of the seven – and it's only, what, the end of April? You're nailing it, Ro – you're nailing it in a big-time way.'

He's delighted, of course, to get the recognition. His voice goes all, I think the word is, like, *conspiratorial* then? 'Here, will I give you a fooken laugh, Rosser?'

I'm like, 'Go on – I bet this is going to be good.'

'I was having an oul mooch around in the gaff here – old habits doy heerd – and I spies this photo, reet, that thee have on the mantelpiece. *Old* fooker. Thought I recognized him. So I says to Grainne, "Who's this sham?" Says she, *"Oh my God, that's my granddad!"* Know who he was, Rosser?'

'No, who?'

'I'll tell you who he was – the fooken judge what sent me grandda to prison.'

I laugh so hord that everyone in Kielys ends up just staring me out of it.

'Scoring girls,' I go, 'is so much more enjoyable when there's an element of payback involved.'

He's like, 'You bethor fooken believe it, Rosser,' and then I hear someone call his name.

'On the way, Mrs Maverly,' he goes. 'Two sugars, yeah.'

I'm like, *'Mrs Maverly?* You're some focking operator, Ro.'

He's like, 'I bethor go in anyhow. By the way, you'd want to give Sorcha a bell.'

'What?'

'She's not happy wit you bout sometin.'

'Er, did she go into specifics?'

'No, I called out to the gaff arthur rehearsals last night. See me sister. When I said your name, Sorcha boorst into tears.'

'I'll, er, maybe go and see her in the morning.'

He's like, 'Women, wha!'

And what can I do except laugh and go, 'Yeah. Women!'

Sorcha asks me if I'm satisfied. This is in the middle of the circus field as well – in front of, like, two hundred and fifty basically unemployed people doing Snake Creeps Through The Grass.

All I'm saying is there's a time and a place for a stand-up row and this is definitely not it.

'Are you satisfied?' she just goes, repeating herself now. And anyway, it's one of those questions to which there *is* no real answer.

'Look,' I try to go, 'I think the whole thing has been possibly blown out of all proportion?'

'Oh, do you?' she just goes.

All two hundred and fifty of them are listening to this, by the way. Then again, they've no actual choice. She's roaring at me at, like, the *top* of her voice? And the sound is really carrying as well.

Might be the sea air.

'Well, how about this for proportion,' she goes. 'They're not going to let Honor graduate.'

I actually laugh at that. 'You don't graduate from Montessori, Sorcha. You just, I don't know, leave.'

I try to catch one or two people's eyes – see is there anyone who could potentially be on *my* side? – but they're obviously a tough audience. It seems to me that the healing through tai chi crowd stick very much to their own.

Sorcha goes, 'There's an actual graduation ceremony, if you must know, Ross, at the end of May. And thanks to you, Honor is not going to be part of it.'

That's when Giovanna comes over and puts her orm around Sorcha's shoulder. *She* hasn't changed a bit, by the way. Nose ring, dreads, big peasant blouse. She *could* look like Kaya Scodelario if she made the effort. But she doesn't.

'Remember the breathing exercises,' she tells Sorcha.

Oh, she's waited for this moment, ever since the night I met her when I was hammered outside Bruxelles and I called her a focking con ortist.

I decide to just blank her out.

I'm there, 'Sorry, Sorcha, I'm still trying to get my head around this. Are we talking an *actual* graduation here – with, like, gowns and those, I don't know, basically hats?'

'They're *called* mortarboards,' Sorcha goes, with *real* hatred in her voice.

'Breathe!' Giovanna goes, massaging her shoulders. 'Breathe!'

I'm like, 'Well, I myself personally think it's a bit OTT for, like,

143

Montessori. I mean, she's, like, not even five – what could she have even learned?'

'Oh, she's learned how to cheat.'

'Bear in mind, Sorcha, that there's, like, other people listening to this conversation.'

'And how to – oh my God – lie to her mother.'

'I'd hordly say she lied.'

'You were training her, Ross. Every morning. Oh, I know *all* about it. You two had your little secret, didn't you?'

'I just don't see what the biggie is – a lot of kids train, Sorcha.'

'It certainly clears up the mystery of where my StairMaster disappeared to.'

'Well, pordon me for wanting my daughter to grow up with the killer instinct,' I just go. 'She's going to need it out there, Sorcha. Because let me tell you, it's a focking brutal world we're suddenly living in.'

I look at the rest of the group. 'I'd expect you lot to understand that. Look at the focking state of you – do you honestly believe this is a time to be calm?'

Of course, not one of them shouts, 'You have a point, fair focks.'

'It's a focking jungle out there,' I go, staring deep into Sorcha's eyes. 'And you've got to be tough to survive.'

Giovanna looks around the rest of the group. 'That's just what the capitalist machine wants us to believe,' she goes. 'If the spirit is nourished, you have all you need to survive.'

Sorcha looks at me, as if to say, what's your answer to that, Ross?

'Okay, I didn't want to be the one to break this news,' I go, 'but have you heard that Laura Ashley's supposedly in trouble.'

Oh, *that* hits home. I watch the, first, shock register on her face – she was never focking out of there – and then the shock turn into actual anger. I can see it. But that's when Giovanna decides to stick her hooter in again.

'Let's return to our positions,' she goes, trying to steer Sorcha back to the class. 'Carry The Tiger Over The Mountain, then Repulse The Monkey – three, no, let's say, *four* times.'

I'm just there, 'You keep your big focking honker out of it, by the way!' because she *does* have some beak on her. I always said that about her.

She goes, 'How dare you!'

So I'm like, 'How dare *you*! I'm trying to have a conversation with my technically still wife here. Two years ago, let me remind you, you were doing yoga for focking Alsatians.'

That's softened her focking cough. Oh, there's a few interested looks suddenly being exchanged in the class now.

'Oh, yeah,' I go, looking around the group. 'Doggy focking yoga. In fact, if anyone was guilty of ripping the piss during the whole Celtic Tiger thing, it was her.'

I turn back to Sorcha. I'm like, 'Babes, please!' but there's no actually talking to her.

'You've put me in an – oh my God – horrible position,' she goes.

I'm like, 'Tell that so-called school to shove their graduation up their orses. The amount of money I'm paying them in fees. In fact, *I'll* tell them.'

'I'm talking about Paris, Ross.'

'What?'

'Oh, I know what you promised Honor as an incentive to cheat.'

I just shake my head, disappointed more than anything. 'The kid seems to have been doing a lot of blabbing all of a sudden.'

'Paris?' she goes. 'A bill-pay phone?'

I'm there, 'You know she's still calling the poor kids in her class povs?'

'And she told me how you turned her against her little friends. And now the dilemma for me is, I don't know whether to bring her to Paris, thus validating the lesson you've taught her that it's okay to cheat and to lie, or do I refuse to bring her and risk further fracturing her trust in adult authority figures?'

'The universe will provide the answer,' Giovanna tries to go.

I'm like, 'I thought I told *you* to shut the fock up,' and then I turn back to Sorcha. 'Okay, which of the two are you veering towards, do you think?'

That's when she ends up totally losing it with me. 'What I'm *veering* towards,' she goes, 'is what I should have done years ago. I'm cutting off your access.'

I'm like, 'What?' because it actually feels like I've been kicked in the balls.

She goes, 'I'm not letting you see Honor anymore.'

I'm just there, 'You . . . You can't do that, Sorcha. I have actual rights.'

'Well,' she goes 'you've actually, like, *invalidated* them?'

She has a quick look over her shoulder at Giovanna and it's instantly obvious where she got that line from.

'Don't listen to *her*,' I go. 'Sorcha, you can't just decide that I'm not allowed to see my daughter anymore. We'll see what the courts have to say about it.'

She flashes a smile at me then. She seems for some reason suddenly pleased with herself. 'Okay, let's have it out in court,' she goes. 'And all those parents who saw what happened at the sports day . . .'

'Hey, she won.'

'Malorie's mum. Sunny's dad. They can all have their say on what kind of a father you are.'

She turns to Giovanna then. 'See, he forgets that my father is one of the country's leading experts in the area of, like, family law?' and Giovanna looks absolutely delighted to hear it, of course. 'He's been collecting material on him for years. He has a file, like, *this* thick!'

I'm like, 'Babes, you're upset.'

She goes, 'He could get a barring order put on you today, Ross – all I have to do is say the actual word.'

'Look,' I try to go, 'this will all seem different in a few weeks' time.'

But she tells me to just stay away from them – 'I *so* mean it' – or, oh my God, she *will* get the Gords involved. Then she goes back to the class.

I drive home from Booterstown in a, literally, daze. I'm thinking, she can't mean it. She *can't*. How many times has she said shit like that over the years and I've always been able to, like, sweet-talk her round.

But deep down – maybe it's the shit that Giovanna's putting in her head – I suspect that this time she actually means it.

I don't remember a single thing about driving home. All I remember is being suddenly stood outside my door with the key in my hand. And that's when I hear it.

What I mean by *it*, roysh, is this, like, sobbing? It's a girl, bawling her basic eyes out, and it's coming from, like, the stairwell?

At thirty years of age, I should know by now when to leave well enough alone. But maybe there *is* good in me after all. Or, then again, maybe crying speaks to that little part of my, I suppose, hort that thinks, 'Tears equals vulnerability equals opportunity.'

Either way, I push the door and stick my head out into the stairwell. And there, sitting on the stairs, yeah, bawling her eyes out, with her platinum blonde lion's mane in her hands and her muffin top spilling out over the band of her turqoise Love P&G sweatpants, is Saoirse.

'What's the story?' I go, not that I even care, especially now that I *know* I've no interest.

'Fook off,' she goes, without even looking up at me, 'you snoppy bastoord.'

So I just nod. I'm like, 'Fair enough. It was only intended as a figure of speech anyway,' and then I go to, like, turn away.

'It's Laddy,' she goes, suddenly looking at me over her shoulder. Her make-up looks like two focking crows splattered on a windscreen. 'He's a fooken loyer, so he is.'

Er, he's also one of the country's leading dealers in coke and illegal firearms, I'm thinking – who the fock told you he was a catch?

'A liar?' I go, even though I still don't know why I'm even bothering.

'Said he was gerring out, so he did – ourra de drugs and evyting. Fooken pox bottle is all he is. A doorty fooken pox.'

That interests me. If him and Terry are suddenly *not* moving out, I doubt if I'll be getting out of Rosa Parks in *this* focking lifetime. That's why I end up just sitting down on the step beside her.

'Maybe you're being a bit horsh,' I try to go. 'I'm sure if you two sat down, you could . . .'

She goes, 'What de fook do *you* know about athin?'

She has a mouth on her like a focked fanbelt.

I laugh. 'Well, on this kind of shit – relationships, blah, blah, blah – I'm actually a bit of an expert. I know enough to see that Larry's madly in love with you. And that you should definitely go to Alicante to live – all of you. Soon.'

Jesus, she could be the Lord Mayor of Dublin with the amount of gold hanging around her neck.

'And live wi a fooken loyer?' she goes. 'Is that what ye tink?'

God, she's focking horrendous-looking.

I'm there, 'Okay, let me hear it – what actual lie did he tell?'

She wipes her eyes with the back of her hand. 'He said he was arthur sellin de last of de coke and he said he wadn't gettin any mower in. He toalt me he'd sell de last of it and den we were gone.'

'And?'

'He's arthur gettin in a load mower. And he tried to bleaten hide it from me, so he did.'

I nod, roysh, in what would have to be described as a really *understanding* way? Then I go, 'Okay, think it through. The orse has supposedly fallen out of the cocaine morket.'

'What?'

'That's what they're saying. He told me that himself. This recession's affecting everyone, don't forget. It's not *just* estate agents and architects anymore. It's going right the way down the food chain. Maybe – yeah, this is it – maybe he's worried that he won't have enough money to keep you in the, I suppose, style to which you're accustomed. Have you thought about that?'

'You're only sayin dat cos he's a mate of yewers.'

She could go out with Shirley and Heather from *EastEnders* and still not be the looker of the group.

'Well, he is and he isn't. All I'm trying to get you to see, Saoirse, is that all this extra, I suppose, drug-trafficking that he's doing on the QT, he's doing it for you. To make sure you're set up properly when you finally move to – I don't know, whatever country Alicante is even in.'

'Spayen,' she goes, definitely softening.

I'm like, 'Spain, then.'

There's, like, silence between us then. I look down. Jesus, trackie bottoms tucked into socks with, like, white plimsolls – she's like a focking Eurovision entrant from before I was born.

'Ine soddy,' she goes, 'you've probley fooken bethor tings to be doin dan dis.'

I shake my head. 'Nah,' I go, 'I was only going to watch TV. I've got six or seven *Xposés* Sky Plussed.'

She suddenly screws up her face. 'I fooken hate dat Galenda Giddleson.'

I shoot her a look. 'Okay, go easy now – you're talking to someone who has a serious thing for her.'

'*Her?* The fooken eyebrows on her.'

Even I have to laugh at that, though. 'One of the things I love about her is that it doesn't matter what you buy her for Christmas, she always looks surprised. And don't think I'm dissing her. I've said that to her actual face. She's as much in love with me as I am with her.'

I'm suddenly aware of the fact that Saoirse is, like, staring at me –

we're talking *intensely*? I don't even need to look at her to know there's an immediate sexual tension between us.

I've been in this position a thousand times before and the worst thing is that I know I've got actual options here. I can get the fock out of here, for example. I know from, like, first-hand experience how fertile birds like her are. *Or* I can do what I actually end up doing, which is turn and look at her, her face a mess of mascara and pan stick.

Her hand reaches around the back of my neck and she pulls my head towards hers.

Not that there's any resistance from me, I'm admitting.

We end up just kissing at first. She's incredibly good. I don't *know* why that surprises me? She's probably been around the track more times than an electric hare.

Then one thing leads inevitably to the next and, before either of us has stopped to consider what we're doing, she's undoing the zip on my Shred Focking Everything boilersuit and I'm pulling the ripcord on her trackie bottoms, there on the actual steps.

Our groans and grunts echo around the stairwell.

In I go and it's, like, happy days. I'm just beginning to find my stroke when all of a sudden I hear this enormous explosion – the building literally shakes – followed by a sort of, like, fizzing noise.

It's like, *Ker-boooooooom! Ffffffffffff!*

I'm like, 'What the fock was that?'

Maybe I'm suddenly realizing the danger of what I'm actually doing here. Saoirse just wraps her legs around my bare orse. 'Keep fooken goin,' she goes.

I'm like, 'But it sounded like an actual earthquake.'

Then it happens again. *Ker-booooooom! Ffffffffffff!*

I'm like, 'Jesus!' and I honestly don't know *how* I maintain.

'Der teardin dowin dee utter apeertments,' she goes. 'Dee rang to say.'

I'm like, 'Shit, I remember now . . .'

'Don't fooken stop,' she goes. 'Ine nearly dare!'

So what else am I going to do except I bring it home.

Ker-booooooom! Ffffffffffff!

Ten seconds after it's all over, we're both fixing ourselves up, there in the stairwell, agreeing that it's possibly best all round if this stays strictly between us.

'Are ye mad?' Saoirse even goes. 'Laddy'd moorder ye if he fowint out. Maybe even moorder de boat of us. *Ine* not goin to say a woord.'

I can't say that I relax when she says that. I can't even say that I breathe a sigh of relief? Somehow, I instantly know that this is something I'm going to end up regretting for what remains of my basic life.

5. Goin' courtin'

Fionn says they drove past one of these ghost estates the other day. It was in, like, Mullinavat. He looks at Erika, who's got a bottle of Nando's peri-peri in either hand, trying to work out which is hot and which is, like, extra hot.

He goes, 'What did the sign say again, Darling?'

Er, *darling*? I'm in serious danger here of ruining the old man's traditional May Day borbecue brunch by spewing all over it.

Erika decides on the extra hot, then smiles and goes, 'Oh, yes, it said, twenty percent already occupied!' like she's delighted to hear it. See, even when she's talking about the economy she can be a bitch.

'That's right,' Fionn goes, 'with an exclamation mark at the end – like it was an actual selling point that one out of every five houses had somebody living in it! It's another mark, I suppose, of how far we've fallen.'

I'm wondering, of course, is it a dig at me.

He's, like, turning the sausages while he's saying all of this. Flipping the burgers. Turning the steaks. This might come across as childish but doing the actual borbecuing was always, like, *my* job? He's even wearing the novelty apron with the French maid's outfit painted on the front that I bought for the old man three or four Father's Days ago.

But of course I *say* fock-all to him. Don't want him to know that it actually bothers me.

'Come, come,' the old man goes, helping himself to a roasted green pepper to go with his skinless chicken breast, 'there's to be no recession talk at the table. Helen and I are banning it altogether, aren't we?'

Helen just smiles.

'We shan't even be discussing,' he goes, 'NAMA's application for an eighty-seven percent – what's this they're calling it? – yes, *haircut* – inverted-commas, indeed – to the loan for the IGB site. Much as I'd love to, it's all off the agenda.'

I look at Fionn – I'm not even sure if that chicken's properly cooked – and I can't resist going, 'Did you hear that, Fionn? No talking about the current economic blahdy blah. Then again you've never been to one of the old man's borbies before, so you probably wouldn't really *know* the rules? Even though you've got your feet pretty firmly under the table there, using the borbecue tool set that *I* shelled out a hundred and fifty snots for.'

She jumps straight to his defence, of course – and I'm talking about Erika.

'How did Honor do in the Sports Day?' she goes, even though Sorcha's almost certainly already told her.

I mean, they tell each other focking everything.

'First over the line,' is all *I* go, still trying to, like, *bluff* it?

Erika smiles, like she's genuinely delighted – it's just a thing she does. 'That's amazing,' she goes, 'because Sorcha told me that she was disqualified for cheating. And that she's not going to be allowed to attend her graduation. It's really interesting – isn't it? – how two people can come away from the same event with two totally different perspectives?'

I cop a sly look at the old man, except he doesn't seem to care one way or the other. I decide to turn up the heat on Fionn then – serves him focking right as well, letting his girlfriend fight his battles for him.

'What were you even *doing* in Mullinavat?' I go.

See, I vaguely remember selling gaffs there during my days as an estate agent and the job we had – even when the Celtic Tiger was still on – of persuading people that it was a commutable distance from Dublin.

'Oh,' Helen goes, perking up, 'did you find a site?'

Erika's there, 'Two or three, potentially,' and I'm suddenly looking from her to Fionn, then to Helen, then to the old man, going, 'Er, is *anyone* going to loop me in here?'

Fionn lays a plate of chicken down in the middle of the table and everyone says how delicious it looks. The French maid look does nothing for him, by the way – and I'm not just saying that out of jealousy.

'It's my new business idea,' he goes – *full* of it.

I actually laugh. I'm like, 'Business idea? Yeah, can I just remind you that you're, like, a *school*teacher?'

He doesn't even react to that. Too scared of letting himself down in front of his girlfriend and her old pair. Instead, he goes, 'Yeah, that's actually where the idea came from, Ross. Battle re-enactments!'

I'm like, 'Battle re-enactments?'

'Exactly. For students studying History for the Junior and Leaving Certificates. Eight or ten Saturdays of the year, they can gather in a field and actually participate in historically correct re-creations of the major battles they're learning about in school, everything from the Siege of Leningrad to the Battle of Clontarf to the Battle of Arklow. It's a way of gaining a better understanding of the main military flash-points they're learning about but doing it in a way that's engaging and – dare I say it – fun.'

I just roll my eyes. It's a focking incredible idea. I'm not going to let *him* know that, though.

Erika helps herself to a piece of chicken.

'One thing,' she goes, 'that's certainly not in short supply in this country at the moment is fields. There's a lot of developers out there who paid ridiculous money for land that's never going to be built on. A lot of them are happy to lease it – well, they're obviously desperate to get *something* back.'

I go, 'You two seem to have really thought this through.'

Fionn takes it as an actual compliment. He even smiles at *her*. 'Erika's done up a whole business plan,' he goes, the two of them suddenly lost in each other's eyes. 'I mean, she's spoken to all the main schools and there's genuine enthusiasm for the idea. We think we could have as many as two thousand people for the first one.'

I'm like, 'Two *thousand*?'

I cop a sly look at the old man and it's a long time since I've seen him looking so proud. Erika's always had an unbelievable head for business, of course. I'm actually remembering the Divorce Fair that she and Oisinn organized in the RDS.

I'm like, 'Two thousand people! Okay, paying how much each?'

Of course he's too focking cool to even tell me. 'Well, we haven't worked out a figure yet.'

'Probably fifty snots, I'd say – yes or no?'

He doesn't answer either way. He just returns to his steaks, then goes, 'What we *are* determined to do is to make sure that they're faithful re-creations of actual events. Which means, everyone will be in costume obviously and, well, I want to make sure we re-stage each battle exactly as it happened.'

'You see?' the old man suddenly goes. 'This economy won't stay down for long, not with the likes of you two, as well as Ross there, stoking the embers. Proving something that became a maxim of mine during the last so-called recession – empty pockets never held any man back, only empty hearts and empty minds.'

'Well,' Fionn goes, 'I'm genuinely excited about the idea of giving young people, who are interested in history, a genuine appreciation for what I like to call the corporeality of warfare.'

Of course what can I say to that? 'This focking chicken better be cooked.'

He looks at me, pissed off at me for having put a halt to his gallop. 'It should be fine,' he tries to go.

'All I'm saying is, I don't want to wake up tomorrow with a focking orse like a bullet wound.'

'I checked it with the thermometer, Ross.'

See, he has an answer for everything, the four-eyed fock. 'A thermometer?'

He holds it up. Must have brought it himself. 'One hundred and seventy four degrees Fahrenheit,' he goes.

Then Erika backs him up again by going, 'I'm just thinking, Fionn, do you know where you could re-enact the Battle of Dresden? In that apartment development where Ross is living!'

Of course, Fionn reacts like this is the funniest thing he's ever heard – laughs so hord, in fact, that he ends up nearly dropping a plate of sausages. He puts them down in front of us. They're mostly perfect, I'm prepared to admit, although one or two of them *are* actually *overdone?*

'Yes,' the old man goes, suddenly all interested, 'what on earth happened, Ross? Helen and I drove through Ticknock the other day. Place looks like a proverbial bomb hit it.'

I bite into the chicken, at the same time just shaking my head, like even *answering* that question would be beneath me. 'They demolished the unfinished blocks,' I go. 'No biggie. In fact, when you think about it, it makes Rosa Parks an even more exclusive development – now that there's, like, fewer aportments. At least they can say now that they're, like, one hundred percent occupied.'

'Yeah,' Erika goes, 'by social housing types. We've *met* your neighbours, remember.'

I'm suddenly thinking about Saoirse – or, more specifically, galloping the girl bandy in the stairwell last week – and my mood, it has to be said, just plummets.

My mind drifts back to, like, the morning *after* it happened, when I woke up literally screaming from a nightmare. I was walking along a road – it actually *looked* like South William Street? – and I was passing, for the sake of argument, Dakota, when this Daihatsu Charade started coming towards me. Pimped to within an inch of its life, of course – we're talking tailfin, blue neon underlighting, classic Jay-Z on the stereo practically setting off earth tremors. I was enjoying the song – it was actually 'Brooklyn's Finest'? – when, all of a sudden, the front passenger window rolled down and a hand stuck out of it holding what looked very much to me – a man who's always loved his rap and hip-hop videos – like an *actual* Glock. I didn't even get the chance to run. I just heard, like, five or six loud bangs, then I suddenly woke up, drenched in literally sweat.

The thing is, roysh, it felt so real that, even after I woke, I ended up lying there for, like, five minutes, convinced that I *had* been shot?

Then I got up and wandered through the aportment and out onto the balcony. I literally couldn't believe my eyes. I felt like I was standing on the surface of the moon. It was just – as the old man said – mountains of grey rubble, as far as the eye could see. Which wasn't *very* far, as it happens, because after five or ten seconds, I storted to get all this, I suppose, brick dust in my eyes and my throat and I had to go back inside.

I cracked open a can of Heineken, sat down and tried to get my head around it all, my eyes, every few seconds, drawn to the window, staring out at this sort of, like, grey dust blowing around in a basic swirl. It might sound like an exaggeration but the world seemed suddenly different, like it was the day after some terrible disaster.

Which, in a way, I suppose it was.

I told myself what I've been trying to tell myself ever since. She might not tell Larry. I mean, *she's* possibly as scared of him as *I* am. Plus – I think *she'd* even agree – that she was more gagging for me than I was gagging for her.

But then I keep coming back to that basic question. This is a *woman* we're talking about – where does logic come into it?

No, she'll tell him. That's as sure as Ronan O'Gara looks shit in red and fantastic in green. I just don't know how or when.

Might be in a fit of temper during an actual row. Maybe in a moment of honesty while they're making up. Maybe she'll use it as a chip to renegotiate the terms of the Alicante deal. But she'll tell him. I know the species only too well.

'Ross!' I hear the old man go. I suddenly snap out of it. 'Aren't you going to say congratulations to your mother?'

Fock. I'd no idea that she was even coming. No idea what I should be congratulating her on either.

I turn around and she's stood practically on top of me, wearing a Hervé Léger bandage dress, that, I'm going to be honest, is *far* too figure-hugging and reveals *way* too much skin.

'Jesus Christ,' I go, 'you look like a focking scarecrow wrapped in *papier mâché*.'

This she decides to ignore. Instead, she just hands me a book and, as I'm taking it from her, I notice that all the others – we're talking Fionn, we're talking Erika, we're talking Helen, we're talking the old man – are each all holding one as well.

It's this new misery lit novel of hers. I can't believe someone actually went ahead and published it.

I check out the cover. It has a picture of a little girl on it – not much older than Honor, I'd say – and she's staring at the camera with, like, tears rolling down her face, then underneath it's like, *Mom, They Said They'd Never Heard of Sundried Tomatoes*, which is obviously the title, then underneath that, it's like, 'The heartbreaking story of a happy childhood turned suddenly deprived!'

'Fresh from the printers,' she tries to go.

Notice how she *always* has to be the centre of attention?

I turn to Fionn. 'I'll tell you something,' I go. 'If I *do* end up shitting through the eye of a needle tomorrow from that focking chicken, at least I'll have something to wipe my hole with now. I'm actually going to stick it in the freezer the second I go home.'

There's, like, immediate silence. I've never been afraid to call it, see – no matter what the reaction.

Then the rest of them stort giving her what she basically wants – in other words, *praise*? Helen, being nice, says it's a wonderful achievement. Erika says it's a totally new departure for her. And the old man goes, 'Fionnuala O'Carroll-Kelly is back! Exclamation mark! No, no – three exclamation marks!!!'

None of them having even opened it, by the way.

Fionn – he's a *total* focking crawler – storts reading from the back cover.

He's like, '*Zara Mesbur is a well-adjusted, happy-go-lucky seven-year-old girl, growing up in Foxrock, her life circumscribed by the general round of South Dublin life – gymkhanas, the school orchestra and playdates with her friends, Louisa and Eily. But little does she know that an unexpected downturn in Ireland's economic fortunes is about to turn her normal life upside down. Suddenly, she finds herself cast into a new and darker world, where simply spending money is considered an act worthy of shame and where basic gourmet food items, such as Lomo Iberico and truffle butter, are regarded – rather like opium – as part of some disgraceful, decadent past. Zara, though, refuses to allow her spirit to be broken and never stops dreaming of escaping from a world in which Michelin Star restaurants are forced to offer "reasonably priced" set menus and shoppers trudge up and down Grafton Street, in desperate huddles, dead-eyed and unsmiling, in search of "bargains". "Mom, They Said They'd Never Heard of Sundried Tomatoes" is a heart-rending story of one girl's attempt to keep her sanity in a world gone suddenly mad.*'

I stand up. I've heard enough and I suddenly feel the urge to get the fock out of here.

'Where are you going?' the old man goes. 'You've barely eaten a thing!'

I know exactly where I'm going. Somewhere, of course, that *he* can never know.

Regina's playing with my hair. For as long as I can remember, I've always loved birds playing with my hair. I find it very, I don't know, soothing. We're lying on her bed, on top of the covers, and I realize that I must have fallen asleep after I gave her the malt.

I open my eyes. It's bright. It's obviously still the afternoon. 'You aweek?' she goes.

She's, like, spooning me. I'm there, 'Just about. How long was I out?'

'Abite an orr,' she goes.

An hour? It definitely felt like longer. I've got that sudden feeling you sometimes get, that there's something I'm supposed to be *doing* today? I let it go, though.

I'm just like, 'I love birds playing with my hair.'

She's there, '*Ay'm* a bord noy, am ay?'

I laugh. 'I hadn't thought about it like that. I suppose you are, in a way.'

'Yee've gat one or tee gree ones here, yee know thot?'

I quickly sit up. I'm like, 'As in, like, grey hairs?'

Now it's *her* turn to laugh? 'Calm dine,' she goes. 'Ay said it's only one or tee.'

I lie back down. 'Pordon me,' I go, 'for not wanting to end up grey at, like, thirty.'

'You're voray veen, aren't yee?'

I'm like, 'It's not vain to want to keep your good looks.'

Then I spot an opportunity to give her a compliment. Hey, there's a reason I'm popular.

'Speaking of which,' I go, 'you're pretty well preserved yourself. You're actually a good ad for yoga.'

'Aye,' she goes. '*And* plostic sorgeray.'

I'm like, 'What?'

She laughs. '*Ay've* hod averythang done.'

'Seriously?'

'May nose. May lups. May chun. May forehead. Even may urrs. And lanes remeeved from averywhere.'

'Jesus, that's another thing you have in common with my old dear. Although your surgeon's obviously better qualified than hers. She's ended up with a face like a bucket of chum.'

'Well, *ay* jost believe in looking after yeerself. If you're hoppy on the iteside, you're hoppy on the anside.'

'Good point.'

'So, are yee gonna stort daying it?'

I'm like, 'I'm not dying my focking hair.'

She laughs, then gets suddenly quiet and goes, 'Toddy went gree at thortay.'

The mention of her dead husband's name brings me suddenly back to earth again. How do I respond to that?

I go, 'Did he? I mean, I knew he dyed his hair. You could see it in

158

photographs. Anytime he was ever in the *Sunday Indo*, I used to say, Jesus, it doesn't even match his eyebrows. Sorry, I didn't mean to . . .'

'Ay'm lorning,' she goes, 'nat to teek offence every taim you open your mithe.'

I'm like, 'That's a good thing. That's actually a very good thing . . . So why *did* he go grey, then?'

She shakes her head, then she's there, 'Strass, ay suppose. We were traying to get our forst restaurant op and ronnen at the taim. We'd just moved dine from Balfawst – there was a war on, as you prabably know.'

I nod and try to look, I don't know, *knowledgeable*? 'I presume we're talking about Hitler and all those goys.'

'Hatler?' she goes – *not* a happy rabbit. This is after saying she *wasn't* going to take offence every time I opened my mouth? 'Ay'm saxty, Ross, not nanety! Ay'm talking abite the Troubles.'

'Oh, *that* war!' I go, still none the focking wiser.

'We came dine here in soventy – soventy-one. Toddy wanted tee sat up a restaurant and, well, obviously that wasn't gonnay hoppen in Balfawst. So we meeved tee Doblin.'

'Well,' I go, 'you ended up doing pretty well for yourselves. That'd *have* to be said,' because as well as this gaff – which has, like, eight bedrooms, by the way – she still owns, like, seven or eight restaurants *and* that destination spa hotel that I might have already mentioned. 'Until, of course, the economy went basically tits up.'

She laughs, then goes, 'See, that's somethang that really bathered me – see all the thangs that were written abite Toddy after he dayed? Said it was a tapical teel of the taims – a mon who overreached, trayed to gat rich tee quack. Tee quack? *We* were at it twenty-fave, thortay years before we saw *any* mawny. In the soventies, eighties, we'd *one* restaurant – the one in Howth . . .'

'Are we talking The Gorden of Eatin?'

'Well, it was jost called Toddy's in those dees. Thray or four naits a week, you'd coint the teekings and it wasn't even worth your wail openin. That's hoy it was.'

'Yeah,' I go, 'the old pair are always banging on about the seventies and eighties. They seem to have been shit.'

She nods. 'Well,' she goes, 'you can jodge for yourself – looks lake we're goin back thor, noy.'

She suddenly sits up. She's like, 'Will ay swutch on the tally for yee?'

I'm like, 'The *tally*? As in, the TV?'

'Aye – isn't your team pleen today?'

That's what it was! It's focking Leinster against Toulouse in the semi-final of the Heineken Cup. I can't believe I had to be reminded. 'Er, cool,' I go.

She switches it on. It's a good-size screen as well. The teams are just walking out. Leinster are wearing *light* blue? Which I actually hate. I'm there, 'We destroyed these fockers three or four years ago. Probably one of my all-time favourite matches. Denis Hickie! Jesus!'

Regina gets up off the bed. 'Ay mait go fax us something to eat.'

I'm there, 'Are you not going to watch this?' secretly focking delighted, of course. See, I hate watching matches with birds slash women. Sorcha used to always insist on sitting next to me, offering me her expert analysis on which players she considered – oh my God – really, really good-looking.

'Do yee foncy aggs Banadict?' she goes. She's suddenly sat at the dressing table, putting clips in her hair.

I'm there going, 'Eggs Benedict? I focking *love* eggs Benedict.'

'Well,' she goes, 'hoy lawng is each hawf?'

See, I *prefer* women with no actual interest in the game? I go, 'Forty minutes.'

'Okay, that's just enough taim. And when the rogbay's over, *ay'm* throwing yee ite.'

Sex. Rugby. Breakfast. The road. Suits me. But I still go, 'Why?'

'Because ay'm hoving a me-deet.'

'A me-date?'

'Aye – a deet with maysalf.'

'What does that involve?'

'Anythang *ay* lake. Mait go shapping for ontiques. Mait gat a coffay somewhere and read the peepers. Mait sut arinde all dee in may drassing-gine lastening tee Motzort's *Raquiem* or Ravel's *Bolero*.'

Suddenly the ball is in the air and I let an instant roar out of me. It's portly down to Leinster being involved in yet another European Cup semi-final but also portly down to having found a strong, independent, no-questions-asked woman, with her own life, interests and – let's be honest – money, who not only rides like she owns the focking patent on it, but who's actually *happy* to cook for me while I lie in bed watching Drico and the boys do their stuff.

'Yeeesss!' is what I *actually* say, clapping my two hands together.

Regina smiles and shakes her head as she steps into her slippers. Then she leans over me – blocking the TV, although I resist the temptation to say it – and she gives me a kiss.

It's as she's leaning in for seconds that I suddenly hear it. Someone banging on the bedroom door. Then a girl's voice goes, 'You bitch! You focking disgusting bitch!'

I end up nearly focking levitating. I'm like, 'Who the fock is that?'

Regina just rolls her eyes. 'Och, it's only Hedda,' she goes.

I'm there, 'Who?'

'Hedda. You *know* ay hov a daughter – yee mat her at the funeral.'

I'm like, 'Er, yeah, but I didn't know she actually *lived* with you?'

She bangs on the door again – six or seven knocks this time – then goes, 'I know what you're doing – and you're a total focking scuzz-bucket.'

Of course you can picture me. I'm there, 'Errr, I might actually split, Regina. I'm actually Sky Plussing this thing anyway?'

'Stee where yee are!' she goes. 'Agnore her. She's a wee batch.'

I'm there, 'You're calling your actual daughter a bitch?'

'She bleems *me* for Toddy's dath,' she goes. 'Och, she was always her doddy's wee gorl, see,' and then turns her head, roysh, and just, like, shouts at the door, 'Yee live *your* lafe, Hedda, and ay'll live *mane*. Just lake we said we'd doy.'

David Skrela puts one between the Leinster posts, then Hedda's voice comes through the door again. 'Oh my God, he's only been dead, like, *four* actual months? I'm just saying, I think you're disgusting. You're *focking* disgusting!'

'I suppose you saw that Leinster lost.'

Sorcha doesn't say anything – probably speechless that I'd use *that* as an opening line, especially after what happened. The thing is, roysh, I'm just trying to get things back to *normal*?

'Although,' I go, 'Munster got their orses handed to them the following day – focking Biarritz – which has definitely cheered me up, I can tell you that for nothing.'

'Ross,' she just goes, 'what do you even want?' like her every instinct is telling her to basically hang up on me.

I go, 'I thought I'd give you a week or so to calm down.'

'Calm *down*?'

'Yeah, the shit you said that day in the actual circus field – you can't have meant it.'

She just goes, 'Oh, *I* meant it, Ross.'

I'm there, 'But I miss her, Sorcha.'

'I don't actually *care*? I'm not prepared to risk you damaging her any more than you already have.'

'*Damaging* her?'

She laughs. 'Ross, *you* might be in denial? *I'm* actually not? Our daughter has turned into a horrible little girl . . .'

'Whoa!'

'Despite all my best efforts . . .'

'I'm not having that.'

'Despite all the books I read on parenting. Look at her.'

'Er, what am I looking at exactly?'

'She's completely materialistic . . .'

'Jesus, which one of us wasn't at four-going-on-five?'

'She's self-centred. She's cheeky. She has no respect for anyone.'

'All kids are like that these days . . .'

'All kids are *not* like that.'

'It's TV.'

'It's not TV either. It's you.'

'Me?'

'You're full of bad energy, Ross. *I'm* not the only one who's picked up on it either.'

'Oh, let me guess who else might have. Giovanna, by any chance? She's only bulling because I told her she was full of shit in front of the rest of the Karate Kids.'

'No, she's been saying it about you for years, Ross – from the very first time I introduced you, that day in the George's Street Orcade.'

'Er, she wished me a happy autumnal equinox and I laughed in her focking face. *You* laughed about it later, if I remember correctly. Although you seem to have lost your sense of humour about her. It's like you've joined an actual cult.'

She goes, 'Just stay away from us, Ross.'

And I'm like, 'What, forever? Honor's my daughter, Sorcha. *She's* going to want to see *me* – have you thought about that?'

It sounds to me like she has, roysh, because she goes, 'When the divorce is finalized, my dad says we'll agree to one day per month – of *supervised* access.'

'Supervised? What, all because she cheated in some stupid focking race?'

She goes, 'And if you ring again, Ross, I *will* get that barring order.'

Then she just puts the phone down on me.

I end up just sitting there in the van for, like, ten minutes, staring into space, listening to some dude on the radio saying that Quinn Insurance is seeking three hundred and one redundancies and another dude saying that if the Government doesn't implement the cuts rec-ommended by tough-talking Dublin economist Colm McCorthy and An Bord Snip – and soon – then we can say goodbye to our sovereignty, because the IMF, believe me, are following events in Ireland very, very closely.

I'm thinking, one day per month of supervised access? She can't mean it. Maybe if I'd opened with an actual apology. Maybe I'll try that tack the next time I ring. Or maybe *I* should just get lawyered-up as well.

I'm porked on, like, Mespil Road. I've got a collection to make at, like, half two and it's only just gone five past. In other words, I've sud-denly got way too much time on my hands to think.

It's only, like, two weeks since I last saw Honor, but I already miss her like you wouldn't believe. And I'm talking everything about her. The way she gives filthies to girls she doesn't even know at the juice bor in Dundrum. The way she goes, 'Er, *lame*?' whenever I put a song on in the van that isn't Lady Gaga, Kesha or Katy Perry. The way she puts her hand in front of my face and goes, 'What-ever!' whenever she asks me to buy her some piece of clothing that *I* think makes her look like one of those prostitots they're always writing about in Sorcha's magazines.

I miss her so much, I can feel myself on the point of actual tears here.

That's when Ronan rings and I'm suddenly reminded that I've actu-ally got *two* saucepans – and right now this one needs me. Which means it's no time for me to be selfish.

His opening line is, 'Rosser, you bender!' and I can't help but laugh. He'd put you in good form straight away.

I'm like, 'Hey, Ro, what's happening?'

'Need a woord from the woyiz,' he goes.

I end up just shaking my head. 'Look, Ro, I'm not a hundred percent sure anymore that *I'm* the person you should even be asking.'

He's surprised by that, in fairness to him. In fact, he cracks on not to have even *heard* it?

'I'm actually serious,' I go. 'A couple of things have happened that have me all of a sudden asking myself what kind of role model I even *am* to people – and my own kids are included in that.'

'Will you give your fooken eerse a rest and just listen. Alreet, there's this boord, Pippa . . .'

I laugh. I'm like, 'Pippa?' at the same time thinking, yeah, who am I even kidding? I can't *help* but get involved. 'Okay, is she one of the seven, Ro?'

'Yeah, she plays Liza. In anyhow, Ine talking to her the utter day, reet? Using one or two lines you gave me. I swear to fook, Rosser, I was thinking, Ine in here, because she's giving me all the signs you told me to be watching out for – the full eye contact, hit me a couple of slaps as well . . .'

'*Playful* slaps?'

'Playful, yeah. In anyhow, I asts her out but she says she's already seeing someone . . .'

'Well, *seeing* someone, Ro, is a lot different to going out with someone. In fact, I always took it as a green light. Who is this tosser she's supposedly seeing?'

'He's name's Johnny Marcus.'

'Johnny Marcus. Sounds like a bit of a sap – although that might be me just taking your side. What school's he in?'

He goes, 'Clongowes,' and I end up laughing so hord that I think I'm going to cough up an actual organ.

'I'm sorry,' I go, 'it's just a me-and-Clongowes thing. Hey, me and Rob Kearney came to practically blows at the Nespresso concession stand in BTs two Christmas Eves ago. Although there's no hord feelings. All it shows is how seriously we both take our rugby.'

'Well, in anyhow, Pippa's seeing this Johnny Marcus sham – and she's arthur telling me that she likes me, but alls she wants to be is friends.'

'Birds use that line all the time, Ro. It can be translated in a hundred different ways.'

'But then she says it's her beertday this Sunday and she's going out to dinner – wirra few friends.'

'Friends? Okay, I'm presuming Eddie Rocket's.'

'No, Yo Sushi.'

I'm like, 'Yo Sushi?' See, I keep forgetting it's Mount Anville. 'So what's the Jack, are you going to go put this Johnny Marcus joker under pressure?'

'Well, I made a few inquiries, Rosser, to find out was there any utter feddas in the frame.'

'Clever.'

'It turdens out that two of the utter brutters have ast her out as well – Benjamin and Caleb – and she's invired them boat to her peerty as well . . .'

'She's a player,' I straight away go. I just, like, blurt it out. It's amazing, roysh, because this kind of shit comes just *so* naturally to me. 'An out and out player, Ro. She loves the attention.'

'So I shouldn't go, then?'

'What and line up with all the other *X Factor* finalists? Fock that. She's doing it for her ego, Ro. Gather you all around – all her focking suitors. They're un-focking-believable, aren't they?'

'Well, what'll I do, so?'

See, this is me, of course, in my element. I'm like, 'Here's what you do. Who else in the cast have you *not* got off with yet?'

'Melissa and Anna.'

'In other words?'

'Well, thee play Sarah and Alice.'

'Okay, who'd be the uglier of the two?'

'What?'

'Who's the ugliest? Come on, you must be able to judge.'

'Er, Melissa, I'd probley say. She has a turden in her eye.'

'A *turden?*'

'Yeah. You never know if she's checking you out or if she's waiting on a Luas.'

'Well, fantastic. She's hordly likely to knock you back, then. Okay, what you've got to do is, you've got to get off with her this Sunday.'

'Sunday?'

'At the exact same time that this Pippa is having her focking, I don't know, sushi porty. I still can't believe the focking cheek of the girl.'

'So why am I doing that, Rosser?'

'Because the first thing that Pippa's going to notice is that you're the only one of her, I suppose, fan club who hasn't turned up. And she'll think, er, what's the deal there? What makes this goy so special? See, birds have this thing about dignity and self-respect in men – they like to try to take it away.'

'So then what?'

'So then, you go into rehearsals on Monday as usual and you tell her you're sorry you missed her porty. But call her by the wrong name. Do that as a general rule, by the way, with any girl you like. Call her Pamela or some shit. See, they take it as an instant challenge. So she's suddenly thinking, er, *he* just got my name wrong – *why* isn't this dude into me all of a sudden? Then the word gets back to her – because it will, believe me – that you were with the other one with the wonky eye.'

'But would she not be laughing at me for that, Rosser?'

'The *last* thing she's going to find it is funny, Ro. If anything, she's going to be humiliated. She's obviously going to be thinking, *hello*? He blew me off for *that* freak of nature? And she's going to have to try to be with you, Ro, if only for her own pride.'

Ronan just laughs. 'Rosser,' he goes, 'you're the fooken man, so you are.'

I honestly can't tell you – after two weeks of pretty much killing myself with questions about whether I *am* actually a good father? – how great it feels to suddenly get that recognition.

I'm falling out of love with Sharon Ní Bheoláin. This fact suddenly occurs to me while I'm standing in Kielys watching *Six One*. See, there's only so much bad news I can hear from a woman – even one with a mouth as pretty as that.

'You know,' I turn around to JP and go, 'I think the last time I saw that girl smile was in the blood bank, about two weeks before this whole current economic thing storted, when I pulled up my top and asked her did she want to feel my abs.'

He barely acknowledges it, by the way, even though he seemed to think it was hilarious at the time. He's barely touched his second pint either, while I'm already half wankered.

Something's obviously eating him.

The thing is, roysh, with J-Town you always have to be careful. He has this whole, I don't know, sensitive side – he was a priest before he was ever a repo man, remember – and there's no telling what effect seizing people's TVs and X5s all day is having on his, I don't know, *soul*?

The point I'm trying to make is that you have to, like, tread lightly around him.

'What's the Jack?' I go. 'I've seen mortuary slabs with more life about them than you today.'

'I'm fine,' he tries to go. 'In fact I'm better than fine.'

'Better than fine? Who are you trying to kid? Dude, we played rugby together, remember?'

Which means I know him nearly as well as he knows himself. That's why he ends up just staring into the, I suppose, *distance*?

'Is it the suddenly recession?' I go, nodding at the TV. Bryan Dobson's saying that the National Treasury Management Agency has floated the idea of cancelling its monthly bond auctions due to the market turmoil caused by the Greek crisis. And he says it like it's a bad thing. 'Is it getting to you?'

'No.'

'Because you know Renords is reopening? They might even be getting me to do the honours, by the way. Well, that's if Jamie Heaslip knocks it back. Robbie Fox is supposed to have something new in the pipeline as well. I mean, surely that's a sign that we're possibly through the worst of this thing.'

'It's not that,' he goes, then he pulls various faces before deciding to eventually tell me. 'It's Danni.'

Focking Danuta.

I laugh, roysh, because I was the first one to say it. She's stunning – no complaints on that score – but she's as mad as focking toast.

I'm like, 'Look, Dude, I'm not the kind to say I told you so – which is lucky for you.'

He goes, 'Well, it's not so much Danni. It's more . . .' and then he has a sudden look over both shoulders. 'It's more her old man.'

I mentioned, I'm pretty sure, that her old pair are over at the moment from basically Russia.

I'm like, 'Don't tell me they're as bananas as she is. I'm sorry, Dude, I shouldn't be dissing your girlfriend. But let's be totally honest here, she's never exactly warmed to me.'

'Yeah,' he just goes. 'There's just something about you, Ross, that rubs her up the wrong way.'

I laugh.

'Well, thanks for the support,' I go. 'I think she's possibly got that thing – what was it that Declan Kidney said he had when he didn't pick me on the team for the IRB U-19 World Championship in 1998?'

'A low tolerance threshold for bullshit.'

'Exactly. *She* seems to have a very similar attitude to Declan Kidney. Whether that's a good or bad thing, it's up to history to decide. But anyway, what's the deal with her old pair?'

Again, he has another look behind him. Fock, he's even making *me* nervous at this stage?

He's there, 'The funny thing is, Ross, I never really thought about it – as in, I didn't put two and two together. Even when she mentioned that her old man was in the old repossessions game himself back in Novosibirsk. Even when she told me that she was going into the old cash for gold business and that *he* was giving her the money to set herself up.'

I'm like, 'Dude, you've lost me.'

He goes, 'Think about it, Ross. What do girls in this part of the world usually get for their twenty-firsts?'

I'm there, 'Mini Cooper Ones, obviously. What's your actual point?'

'Well, *he* gives his daughter the seed money to set up a high street, mail-in, gold-melting company in one of the Western world's fastest shrinking economies. Now do you understand what I'm saying?'

'Still no, to be honest. But then you know how slow *I* am.'

'Ross,' he actually shouts, 'I think my girlfriend's father is a member of the Russian mafia!'

Of course that pretty much silences the early evening crowd in Kielys. Recession or not, this is still actual Donnybrook, remember.

I'm there going, 'What?' suddenly remembering all the – you'll have to check if this is a word yourselves – but *derogatory* things I've said about her? Being honest, I'm about to say something else when JP instantly shushes me and I can tell from the look of sudden fear on his face that the dude – Danuta's old man – is standing right behind me.

I whip around, roysh, expecting to see – and this is a sign that I watch possibly too much TV – Tony Soprano in a furry hat. But he's actually a skinny little focker in a black leather jacket with a comb-over and a humungous hooked nose. I'd say The Beatles were still all mates the last time the focker smiled as well.

'Igor!' JP goes, obviously crapping himself. 'You found the place!'

Igor – the name is, like, oh my God by itself – looks at him like he's been accused of beasting a donkey. 'Yes!' he goes and not in a happy way. 'You tell me where eez and I find. What eez problem?'

'Er, no problem. What'll you have to drink?'

'Orange juice,' he goes, at the same time staring at me, I suppose, *suspiciously*? 'And who eez theez person?'

'I'm Ross,' I go, sticking out the old hand. It's nice to be nice – I've always been a big believer in that motto.

'Rozz?' he goes, except he sort of, like, rolls the R, and it's obvious from the way he refuses my hand, and from the way he looks at me – from head to toe, roysh, with pure contempt – that his daughter's given him a little flavour of what I'm like. 'You are eediot that eez friend of JP, yes?'

I'm there, 'Well, if that's what you want to believe, then yeah.'

He suddenly decides that I'm no longer worth talking to then. He takes the glass of orange juice from JP and goes, 'Danuta tells me that your father eez een – how to say – real estate?'

JP's there, 'Er, he *used* to be? Yeah, no, he ran Hook, Lyon and Sinker for, like, twenty-something years. But it actually closed with the whole property crash and everything.'

'I weesh to speak weeth heem – theez eez possible?'

'Er, I don't see why not.'

'He eez expert on property market, no? He can tell me which eez gute site to open goalt shop. Where to put eet, so to – how to say – maximize potential, yes?'

Jesus – and I thought *my* in-laws were a tough crowd.

JP's there going, 'Er, yeah, sure.'

I whip my pint off the bor and knock back a mouthful, just for something to be doing.

There's a definite tension, see.

That's when I notice Danuta all of a sudden appear through the doors, with this woman, who I straight away take to be her old dear. Not that there's any resemblance. I don't know who the fock Danuta takes after but it's obviously not this woman, who looks like the wooden Indian outside that cigor shop on Grafton Street, except dipped in glue, then kicked through Sydney Vard.

Danuta says something to her old man, which I don't quite catch – my Russian's rusty – then they stare at me, roysh, like I'm something that just won't flush away.

Of course you *know* me and one of the many things I was famous for back in the day was my ability to win over a hostile crowd.

So I decide to switch on the famous Rossmeister chorm and concentrate it on the old dear.

I go, 'Hello there! And let me say from the word go that I can see where Danuta gets her good looks,' trying my best not to sound sarcastic. 'I'm Ross. Forget what you might have heard . . .'

Then I grab her hand – she has hands like a focking dockworker, by the way – and I move in to, like, air-kiss her. My timing, as it happens, couldn't *actually* be worse. At the exact point, roysh, that my lips are reaching their destination, she just happens to turn her head, presumably to ask Danuta for a translation of what I'm saying, and – well, I'm not proud of it – but I end up kissing the focking troll full on the mouth.

All of a sudden, roysh, it's like all of the air has suddenly been sucked out of Kielys. There's, like, total silence, except for the sound of Danuta and her old pair all shouting at the same time in Russian.

'What eez theez,' Danuta's old man eventually goes to me. 'You keez my wife like theez! Like sex meniac!'

See, this is possibly going to *sound* bad? But I'm pretty sure our tongues touched as well.

'Hey, it was an accident,' I try to go. And then, acting out of pretty much fear, I end up doing something stupid.

I go, 'Eeeuwww! Yuck! Yuck!' and then – this is the *really* stupid bit? – I make a big show of basically spitting on the floor, just to show them, I suppose, that I didn't get anything out of it, as in my jollies.

Danuta's old man's eyes go wide, while the old dear just storts shouting – again, in Russian.

He goes, 'You disrespect my wife like theez?'

I hold my hands up. 'Igor, I'm just trying to get you to see that I've no actual interest in her.'

'You put tongue in my wife's mouth. Then you do theez – hock-speet! – like you vont to be seek?'

'I'm not saying I want to be sick. What I'm saying, if anything, is that, well, she wouldn't be *my* cup of tea.'

'Cup of . . .'

'It's another way of saying that I don't find her in any way attractive.'

Danuta is very helpfully translating this entire exchange for her old dear.

Igor goes, 'You are saying she eez ugly woman?'

'Dude, I'm not saying she's ugly. I'm just saying – okay, I'm trying to come up with an, I don't know, *diplomatic* way of saying this? – that when *you* look at her, well, *you're* obviously not seeing what *I'm* seeing. Otherwise, I think it's fair to say, you would never have married her. I mean, a lot of people would say that's the miracle of love.'

JP decides to throw his two yoyos in then.

'Ross,' he goes, taking my pint glass out of my actual hand, 'you need to walk out of here – very, very quickly.'

It's an unbelievably busy day. I'm hord at it. Four hours over the shredder and I'm sweating like a northsider in Argos waiting for his number to come up.

That's when I get a text that puts an instant smile on my face. It's from Regina and it's like, 'U need 2 come 2 malahide right now, iv got itches in places that noi but u can reach! I'm serious btw.'

She's mad for me. And the hilarious thing is that it's only, like, two o'clock in the afternoon.

The amount of money I've stuck in Wes Quirke's old man's pocket over the years. Still, once Ronan's happy. Which, it has to be said, he certainly seems to be – loosing off his Glock so that the cop cor that's been, like, pursuing him ends up totally full of holes.

I check the score and it's already a new record, although there's no way of knowing whether that's even genuine. He's always pulling the plug on the machines, see, to clear the entire history and make sure *he* ends up on top of the pile?

They're forever warning him about it.

'You're unbelievably good at this,' I *still* go, because kids respond well to what Sorcha always calls positive reinforcement. 'A head shot, Ro – the focker's wearing a vest! Whoa, did you see his brain exploding?!'

While he's waging his one-man war against the Baltimore police, by the way, he's also singing 'Goin' Courtin''.

I end up just smiling at him. I can't help it. I'm there, 'Am I to take it from your happy mood today that I was right about Pippa?'

'You certainly were,' he goes, literally blowing this one cop away – double tap to centre mass. 'She rang up the utter night.'

'And?'

'She obviously heerd about me getting off with Melissa.'

'You little focking dirtbag! I told you. See, that shit always gets back to them.'

'She ast me did I want to go bowlin wit her.'

I'm like, 'Bowling?' and I end up having a little chuckle to myself. 'It sounds to me like someone's getting desperate. So what did you tell her?'

'Toalt her I'd tink abourrit.'

I just laugh. What would any parent do? I'm like, 'Ro, I hope this doesn't come across as, like, patronizing, but I am so focking proud of you at this moment in time.'

He's there, 'Tanks, Rosser,' as he takes down an actual helicopter for a 30,000-point bonus.

I'm there, 'I'd say Blathin must be having knicker-fits on a pretty much hourly basis.'

I don't know why, roysh – might be her comment about me as an actual father – but that girl has gotten under my serious skin.

He laughs. 'She's going fooken mental, Rosser. See, Ine listening to her the whole time and she's saying to them, "Can't you see what he's doing? He's, like, playing you off one another?"'

It's a good impression of her actually. I just shake my head. 'They won't listen, Ro, if that's what you're worried about. All it's going to do is, like, intensify the competition.'

'I know.'

I go, 'Watch her, though.'

'What?'

'They're focking schemers, Ro. Just make sure she hasn't got something up her sleeve.'

'What like?'

'I don't know. But always bear in mind – hell hath no fury and blahdy blahdy blah.'

'Reet.'

'But anyway, back to Pippa – when are you planning to be with her?'

'I was tinking of maybe leaving it till the night befower the show.'

'Brilliant. Let her sweat. Let her sweat like a petting zoo. Here, isn't there one other?'

'Yeah. Anna.'

'Anna. Brilliant! How close are you there, do you mind me asking?'

'Already in hand, Rosser. She's Melissa's best mate, see.'

'Just trying to keep track here – Melissa's the one whose eyes are focked, yeah?'

'Exactly. So what I did, reet, was I brings Melissa to the pitchers.'

'What film, just for the record?'

'*The* fooken *Back-Up Plan*.'

'Jennifer Lopez and Alex O'Loughlin – slick. Continue.'

'Alreet, so ten minutes into it, I steerts getting off with her. Fooken amazing kisser, Rosser.'

'The ugly ones often are, Ro. When you think about it, they *have* to be?'

'So halfway troo, I pretends to get all upset. Cracking on to be crying. She's all, "What's wrong, Ro?" Then I tells her, "Look, Ine soddy, but it's yisser friend Anna that Ine really interested in. I feel teddible but I was only using you to get to her."'

'You came up with that yourself?'

'I did, yeah.'

'Focking fantastic. I presume you got a slap across the chops.'

'I did. She called me a bastoord . . .'

'Again, I hope you took that as an actual compliment.'

'Then she walked out.'

'Don't worry, *I* can tell you what happened at the end of the movie, if you're interested . . . I'm also presuming that Melissa then *told* Anna what you said.'

'She did.'

'And let me guess – Anna's been standoffish with you ever since. But at the same time, she's definitely – okay, you'd know better than me whether this is a word – but *intrigued*?'

'Bang on, Rosser. I keep catching her looking at me. So I says to her

173

at rehearsals yesterday, "Look, I feel bad stringing your mate along like that. But keerds on the table – I've feelings for you. I just couldn't think of any utter way of getting closer to you."'

I laugh. 'You know what, Ro – you are *definitely* my son. I actually feel bad about asking your mother for that DNA test now. So what, may I ask, is the current state of play?'

'She says she really, really likes me, reet, but she won't *be* with me because of her friendship with Melissa.'

'That's almost certainly horseshit, by the way. It's just something they say.'

'I know. Because she ast me if I wanted to go to her recital tomod-dow night.'

'Recital?'

'She's in the Rathgeer Junior Orchestra.'

'Playing? Let me guess, the violin?'

'The contrabass.'

'And she wants *you* to see her in action?' I laugh. 'You're *in* there, Ro – I hope you know that. She doesn't give a fock about her mate. That's, like, an act.'

'I know.'

'That's what they're like, see.'

'I know . . . I love them, but.'

'Oh, we *all* love them, Ro. We all *love* them. But it's like I was saying to you there about Blathin. Women are like dangerous animals – they have to be handled right.'

He nods. He really values my advice.

He goes, 'Anna's not great, but.'

I'm like, 'No? Meaning looks-wise?'

'Fooken red hair. *And* she has a sticky-out ear.'

'Jesus, what is going *on* with that school? Although, I have to admit, even in my day, they did produce the occasional bad vintage.'

'Still,' he goes, diving clear just as the Feds open up on him, redu-cing the door that he just walked through to literally splinters, 'thee all count, Rosser.'

'Hee-er,' a voice behind me goes, 'I've a fooken bone to pick wit you!'

I just freeze – there in the hallway.

It's Larry.

I could just ignore him – go into the aportment and slam the door, maybe even barricade myself in. But my hand is shaking like you wouldn't believe and I couldn't trust myself to get the key in the actual lock.

So instead, roysh, I end up just turning around.

He's standing at the other end of the corridor – with Saoirse beside him – having obviously just stepped out of the lift. They're, like, holding hands, so I presume they've done the whole making-up thing.

'Ine not angry,' he goes, although his body language would actually contradict him. He's suddenly let go of her hand and he's, like, walking in my direction at high focking speed. 'Ine just saying, an apodogy would be nice.'

I'm like, 'An apology?'

He's there, 'Do you not tink you fooken owe me one?'

He's suddenly stood right in front of me.

I just hold my two hands up, deciding that the best course of action here is to basically plead for mercy. 'Look,' I go, 'all I would say, in my defence, is that it takes two to tango.'

I look over his shoulder and watch the shock register, through an inch of panstick, on Saoirse's face.

Fock, I think. Maybe she *hasn't* told him.

He looks over his own shoulder then, following my line of vision. 'Two to tango?' he goes. 'What the fook's he on about?'

She goes, 'I don't know. Fooken dope.'

Larry turns back to me. 'Are you out of your fooken element? Ine talken about the Champions Leeig final.'

'The what?'

'Inthor against Bayeern – last neet. You were apposed to come and watch it in eers.'

I suddenly remember the note that was shoved under the door, written on the back of a bookies docket, pretty much summoning me. 'I, er, was actually working late,' I go.

Which is total horseshit, of course. Three in the afternoon is working late for me.

He's there, 'Tetty and me got fooken cans in for you and evyting. What's that piss you drink again?'

I'm like, 'Er, *Heineken?*'

He laughs – the same man who wouldn't let anything that costs more than a yoyo per can pass his lips.

'Er, *Hoy-niken*?' he goes, doing an impression of me as well, which Saoirse seems to find hilarious – or at least she pretends to. 'Eight fooken cans. And there we were, waitin in for ye?'

'Like I said, I'm sorry.'

'Well, you won't be ast again.'

I'm like, 'Er, okay.'

'Ah, Ine only messin – the Wurdled Cup's steertin in anutter few weeks. Tree matches a day. I says to Tetty, suren we'll be practically livin in his when dat steerts.'

I'm there, 'I, er, wouldn't be a hundred percent sure about that, Larry. Like I'm always telling you – I wouldn't be, like, a *major* soccer fan?'

He just, like, stares me out of it. 'I said, we'll be practically livin in yoo-ers when it steerts.'

And I'm there, 'Er, yeah, cool, whatever.'

Saoirse puts her key in their door then. 'I'd bethor hang dat washin out on de balcony, Laddy.'

Washing on the balcony. Is it any focking wonder that it's only me and ninety social welfare recipients living in this shithole?

'Look at him steerding at your eerse!' Larry suddenly goes. 'Watch what you're puttin out deer, Seersh! This fedda be robbin yisser fooken knickers, so he would . . .'

Saoirse and I exchange a look.

'Be sniffin dum,' *he* goes, 'de filty fook!'

Saoirse opens the door and disappears inside.

Larry sort of, like, punches me in the orm and goes, 'You know Ine only pullin your woyer, doatunt ye?'

I'm like, 'Yeah, I suppose we've *always* had the crack, in fairness.'

'Well, Ine wantin to say sometin to ye, Rosser, and I mean dis veddy gen-uine-ly. I heerd you'd a woord wit Seersh de utter week. I heerd you put her straight . . .'

I put her over the jumps is what I did.

I'm like, 'Look, forget it even happened.'

He's there, 'No, no, no – in all feerdness to you, Rosser, I heerd you said a lot of veddy nice tings about me to her . . .'

'Well, a lot of them I would have meant.'

'I says to Tetty, *we're* veddy lucky to have a fedda like him livin next doh-er. You do hear teddible stories about some people's neighbours.'

I'm thinking, yeah, put a glass up to your wall and you'll hear one or two from me.

'Well,' I go, 'I'm definitely going to miss you when you *do* eventually move out,' hoping that he's going to mention an actual date.

'In anyhow,' he just goes, suddenly sticking out his hand, 'Ine just wantin to say tanks, reet?'

So I shake his hand, roysh, and I'm going, 'It's cool,' except he storts getting a bit, I suppose, *emotional* then? He grips my hand tightly and pulls me close to him and storts whispering, 'I luff her, man. I fooken luff her,' in my ear, *while* actually hugging me?

I'm there going, 'Well, my basic attitude would be, get her over to Alicante, then. Stort enjoying your retirement. Forget all about Ireland, the past and whatever else.'

'I never felt dis way befower,' he goes, this is pretty much sobbing, 'not abourra boord,' and then he suddenly pulls back and sort of, like, holds me at orm's length and goes, 'If she ever did the doort on me, Rosser, I'd fooken moorther the fedda.'

Oh, fan-focking-tastic.

'Why are you even *thinking* like that?' I go, at the same time trying *not* to look scared?

Which I am, by the way. I couldn't be more scared if Sione Lauaki came home from work and caught me shitting in his sink.

'I'm just sayin what I'd do, Rosser. I'd happily do fooken life for addyone what tried to take away what we have thegedder.'

I end up saying the first thing that comes into my head, roysh, to try to get him *off* the actual subject? I'm like, 'Are you still looking for someone, by the way, to take that gold off your hands?'

'Goalt?'

'Yeah, remember you mentioned it?'

'I do, yeah. There's a fooken lot of it, but. It's mostly chayins, know whorra mean?'

'Look, I don't know anyone who even *wears* chains. But I do know a bird – she's Bagh-focking-dad, by the way – who's going into the old cash for gold business.'

'Much is she payin?'

'Sorry?'

'For twenty-two caddots. What's she offerdin – peer gram?'

'I've no idea. All *I'm* offering to do is make the actual connection.'

He nods, I suppose you could argue, *thoughtfully*?

'Alreet, do it. Hee-er, there bethor not be any loar involved.'

I laugh. I'm like, 'Er, *that's* unlikely. Considering her family seem to be connected somehow to the Russian mafia.'

His face is suddenly lit up like Vegas. 'The Rushidden mafia. Make shurden give dem me number.'

As I turn to walk away, he suddenly remembers something else. 'Hee-er,' he goes, 'there was mower post arrived for you tis mornen. It's on de table in de kitchen.'

I'm there, 'I'm presuming *my* kitchen?'

'Yooers, yeah. It's a peercel dis toyum. Postman couldn't firrit in your box. It's a good job I was hee-er.'

'Thanks, Larry.'

'Ine always tinking about ye, Rosser. Dat's what mates do, am I reet?'

'I suppose.'

'It's veddy nice, by the way.'

'What is?'

'What's insoyid.'

Jesus focking Christ. 'You opened it, did you?'

'Hee-er, stop being a fooken oul wan, will ye? I'm not going to ruin the suproyiz for ye.'

'Thanks for that, Larry.'

'Don't fooken mention it.'

There *is* a package on the table when I walk in. It's, like, a small, cube-shaped box and it's covered in, like, brown wrapping paper, which Larry, this time, has at least attempted to stick back the way it was.

I pick it up. There's a fair bit of weight in it as well, whatever the fock's in it

I tear off the paper and – it's exactly like I thought – there's a square box inside, we're talking black, with the words 'Patek Philippe, Geneve' written on it in, like, embossed silver lettering. I'm thinking, the only Patek Philippe I know is the crowd that make . . . When I open the lid, I immediately stop – frozen in literally shock. There's, like, a watch inside. Not an ordinary watch, either. It's a limited edition, platinum, split-seconds, single push-piece chronograph, manually crafted and worth – this would be, like, a ballpork guess? – but somewhere in the region of thirty Ks.

I take it out of the box – you wouldn't believe the actual weight of the thing – and I stare at it, all shiny and new, in my hand. I feel the strap between my forefinger and my thumb – we're talking hand-stitched, brown-lacquered alligator leather.

I don't even need to look at the little cord that's with it to know who it's from. But I do anyway.

It's just like, 'Love, Regina, x.'

The old dear's on *The Late Late Show*, plugging her so-called book.

I'll say one thing for the scabrous wound, at least she's honest. She's on a panel with this other woman – the wife of some senior counsel – who's spouting the usual shit about how, as a nation, we all have to share the pain. And you know just looking at this woman that if she was asked to share her *pain au chocolat*, she'd be in the focking High Court in the morning.

Like I said, the old dear, at least, calls it like she sees it. She cuts across her, her voice all thin and screechy, going, 'I *beg* your pardon, I don't see why people like me should have to share *anyone's* pain . . .'

'I'm talking *as* a society,' the other one tries to go, looking at Tubs.

The old dear's not having any of it, though. 'I'm sorry, I can't listen to this rubbish. It was people on low and middle incomes who lost the run of themselves during the Celtic Tiger years that caused this mess – nothing else. And now it's people like me, who could afford to pay for their extravagances with money, Ryan – not credit cards, not bank loans, not hire purchase, but money! – who are being asked to foot the bill for everyone else. And we're being asked to look bloody contrite while we're doing it . . .'

She's had more work done as well. There's at least another pound of orse fat in that face.

The other one tries to get back in there, except the old dear's on a roll now.

'I didn't interrupt you,' she goes, 'when you were mouthing your platitudes.

'At the moment, I'm having to go to London and New York to shop because of the bloody paparazzi, guilt-tripping me for spending money that's mine and well earned. And no one's talking about what caused this entire global financial crisis – giving mortgages to the unemployed and the poor.'

Even though it *is* hilarious, I decide to hit the sack. Massive day tomorrow. Meeting the goys for a pint – JP's the latest to join the three-oh club – then it's the musical. Ronan's big night.

Which is what reminds me. Isn't tonight the night he was going sup-posedly bowling with Pippa?

I check the time. It's, like, half eleven and still no word, so I end up ringing him myself.

He answers pretty much straight away.

I'm like, 'Well?' because I can't actually *contain* my excitement?

He goes, 'Ah, there you are, Rosser. Soddy, Ine just home – I was going to ring you.'

I'm just there, 'Bowling, Ro – what happened?'

'Well, we went to Stillorgan. Ah, she's from Dunthrum, Rosser. I couldn't expect the geerl to travel out to this side of things . . .'

I'm like, 'Er, will you stop playing it cool for even ten seconds. Did you get off with her?'

At first, roysh, he doesn't say anything, but I can pretty much *hear* him smiling down the phone. Then he goes, 'You bethor fooken believe I got off with her.'

I just, like, clench my fist and go, 'Yeesss!!!'

'That's the seven of them,' he goes.

I'm like, 'The full cord. There's possibly only a handful of people who've ever done it, Ro. And I'd say we're definitely the first father and son duo to both do it.'

He's delighted to hear that, of course. It's, like, a port of history.

'Anyhow,' he goes, 'I'd bethor get the head down. Tomoddow's the big neet.'

I'm just like, 'I'll see you there. And, Ro, I possibly don't tell you this enough, but I'm actually proud of you tonight.'

I text Honor. I know Sorcha would commit possibly murder if she knew, but the point still stands that she's my basic daughter. And I miss her. I'm going to admit that.

So I go, 'Hey Hon, sorry bout d sports day, mite hav gone a bit ott about u winnin! : (How r u?'

She's straight back to me with, 'SOK. Omg malorie is such a crybaby. She's also retarded.'

And it's, like, so amazing to hear from her – even if it is just texting back and forth.

'4 wot its worth,' I go, 'u were d only 1 who showed dey had d big match temperament on d day. Only 1 winner 4 me – an it was u!' and then I add a smiley face to the end, just for the good of it.

She goes, 'Soz, wot is malories even problem? NEway, lollers, shes not going 2b goin 2 mt anvil next yr cos they cant afford it. Guess where shes goin 2b goin?'

I'm like, 'Dunno.'

She's there, 'Loreto on d green!'

I go, ':)'

And she's like, 'Such a sad bitch.'

I go, 'Mayb dont tell ur old dear dat we're textin btw, she'd go ape.'

She's like, 'I cant believe u say dat instead of that. Only knackers say dat.'

I laugh. See, this is what I missed.

'Sorry i meant that not dat. Either way it still applies. Dont tell her cos she'd flip.'

Then I don't hear anything from her for, like, an hour. But she must be reading one of Sorcha's magazines, roysh, because when she texts me back again, she goes, 'Omg, reese witherspoon is SUCH a stick insect.'

'This woman, I met her in Leggs, okay? Oh, she's a cracking little troublemaker. Face is a fucking mess but she's got a pair of baby-feeders on her to die for – to fucking die for . . .'

This is JP's old man – in case you hadn't already guessed, holding court in his usual Slatterys on Grand Canal Street.

'I pour her a glass of wine and I says, "What kind of shit are you into?" She says, "Everything." I says to her, "Are you into S&M?" She says, "I said everything, didn't I?" Five minutes later we're checking into the very first hotel we see . . .'

I always wonder what it must be like for JP to hear his old man tell these stories – especially given that he's still married to JP's old dear. Now that I think about it, the dude usually goes into a kind of trance until they're over.

'So we go up to the room – sixty fucking euros, I'm spoiling this bitch – and I'm in the toilet. Like to crack one out before I get started, so's it's not a fucking skeet shoot. I shouts out through the door, "You sure you're into S&M?" No answer. So I says it again. "You sure you're into S&M?" Still nothing. I go back into the bedroom. She's out to the fucking world. And I think, yeah, that's S&M Irish-style – she *sleeps* while I *masturbate*.'

We all laugh. You'd nearly have to with the form he's in. He's celebrating, see, having found the site for Danuta's new cash for gold business. Her old man's supposed to have paid him, like, twenty Ks for the job as well. Which is, like, shrapnel compared to what he's earning in the old repossessions business. But it's a well-known fact that property is where his hort still lies and this is the first actual money he's made from it since Hook, Lyon and Sinker went tits up and taking on water.

JP goes to get the round in but he won't let him. He hands him a fifty and goes, 'Hey, it's *your* birthday! Same again – for everyone,' which is basically the three of us plus Oisinn.

I'm still only halfway through my *last* pint.

'Any sign of Sorcha coming around?' Oisinn just happens to go.

I'm like, 'No, she seems pretty immune to my sweet-talking powers this time. There's talk of, like, barring orders,' and, as I say the words, I can feel myself suddenly filling up, and Oisinn – being a genuine mate – changes the subject.

'Are you still plugging that old woman?' he goes, checking first of all that JP's old man's not listening. *He's* got a mouth on him like the port tunnel, see – luckily, he's storted chatting to some randomer he just met.

I'm there, 'I've swung in once or twice, yeah, when I've been passing,' trying to sound all – I suppose – *blasé* about it? 'She's a woman who knows how to show her appreciation as well. She bought me a watch. Not an ordinary watch either. I'm talking about a Patek Philippe.'

'What?' he goes, his jaw practically on the floor. 'That's, like . . .'

'Thirty Ks' worth. I must be good, huh?'

He laughs. 'Obviously. Dude, you know what this means? You are now, officially, a gigolo.'

Of course *I* end up having to laugh then. 'I suppose I am. Dude, I'm telling you, I should have gone for an older woman years ago. She's mature, confident, independent – which means there's, like, no jealousy issues. She never asks me where I've been or who else I'm seeing. She just texts me whenever she's horny and says, by the way, if you happen to be passing . . .'

'And then she buys you a watch worth thirty Ks.'

'Ideal focking set-up.'

Oisinn laughs, but then he gets suddenly serious. 'Just make sure she doesn't develop feelings.'

'She won't.'

'I'm sure you know what you're doing. Could get messy, is all I'm saying.'

I hear JP's old man go, 'Did I tell you I spent fifteen grand on a suit last week? Yeah, it was a sexual harassment suit,' and the dude he's been talking to just cracks his hole laughing.

JP arrives over with the drinks and puts them down in front of us. 'Oh,' he goes, suddenly remembering something, 'Danuta spoke to your neighbours.'

I'm like, 'Terry and Larry?'

'Yeah, they've got two hundred pound in weight of good-quality gold that they want to get rid off and they're prepared to let her have it for well below its normal melt value. So, anyway, thanks.'

I'm there, 'Is that you or Danuta saying that?'

'Well . . . both.'

'Did she actually say anything – as in, anything positive about me?'

JP's old man rejoins the conversation then. 'Hey, what do you expect?' he goes. 'You stuck your tongue down her mother's throat. That might be a tradition where you're from, you sick fuck. But the Russians, they don't go in for it so much.'

They all laugh, of course.

I'm just like, 'Yeah, whatever. By the way, where's this cash for gold place going to be opening?'

JP and his old man, at the same time, go, 'Foxrock.'

You can imagine my reaction, I'm sure. I'm like, 'What?'

'Yeah, in the village,' JP's old man goes. 'A few doors down from Thomas's.'

I end up just laughing.

I'm there, 'Yeah, good luck getting the rezzies to accept that!'

And one rezzy in particular.

Opera glasses. She *always* has to be the centre of attention.

'It's not *The Phantom of the* focking *Opera*,' I go, out of the corner of my mouth. 'It's an actual school musical.'

This she decides to ignore – wouldn't give me the pleasure of seeing her upset, see – then the old man and Helen suddenly arrive to rescue her.

'Fionnuala!' *he* goes. 'We both finished it last night,' meaning, presumably, her book.

It's hugs and kisses all round by the way.

'Oh, it had me in floods,' Helen goes, obviously being nice.

The old man's there, '*Tell* me we haven't heard the last of little Zara Mesbur! *Tell* me the property market recovers and her father returns to quantity surveying and she finally gets that pony she's always dreamed of owning.'

'Charles,' *she* goes, touching his cheek, you *could* say tenderly, 'you'll have to wait.'

His eyes light up. 'So you're saying there *will* be a sequel!'

'Already started work on it,' she goes, clearly loving it. '*Mom, This Guacamole Tastes Like Mushy Peas*?'

This is all while barely even acknowledging my presence, by the way. I feel about as wanted as a teenage pregnancy.

And, speaking of which, I spot Tina over by the refreshment bor, focking chatting away to McGahy, Ronan's school principal – the man, remember, who got me stripped of my Leinster Schools Senior Cup medal – as if nothing ever happened.

I stand up and stort tipping over to them, with the intention of reminding her where her loyalties are *supposed* to lie?

I'm trying to come up with something really funny and original to say about that focking skip on wheels that McGahy's *still* driving, when all of a sudden, roysh, I feel this crunching pain in my left foot and I hear what *sounds* like a bone *actually* snap.

I'm obviously there, 'Aaarrrrgggghhh!!!'

And it's only when I open my eyes that I realize that Blathin has run over my foot with her wheelchair.

I take off my Dube and I clutch my foot, which is throbbing, just to point out. In fact, it's actually a surprise to discover that there aren't two or three bones loose in my sock.

I'm like, 'Jesus! You did that on purpose – don't even try to deny it. Fock!'

She looks at me like I'm an All Day Breakfast in a focking tin.

'So,' she goes, 'Ronan's been with – as in *with* with? – all seven brides. That must make you proud, does it?'

Jesus, I'm in actual agony here.

I'm there, 'I think you might have damaged my medial plantar, by the way – the same one I severed against Gonzaga back in the day.'

She just smiles at that. She literally doesn't care. There's badness in her – see, people crack on not to see it just because she can't walk, but *it's* there.

'Ronan's going to find out,' she goes, 'that he can't treat girls like that without there being consequences.'

I'm like, '*Consequences?* Do you know who you're beginning to sound like now? Kathy Bates out of *Misery,* that's who! The focking *mad* bint, just in case you haven't seen the movie.'

Then it finally hits me, like a delayed reaction, what she just said.

I'm there, 'What do you mean, by the way, that he's *going* to find out?'

I don't actually *get* an answer? Because I suddenly hear this voice behind me go, 'Ah, howiya, Bla-hee-in,' and it's focking Tina, obviously letting me down again. 'How *are* ye, luff?'

I feel like going, 'Tina, would you not even *try* to tailor your accent? You're in Mount Anville, not Mount Sackville.'

Bla goes, 'Oh, hello, Ms Masters,' all sweetness, of course, and expensive orthodontics. 'I'm fine, thank you. I hope you enjoy the show tonight. Ronan is – oh my God – *so* amazing in it. He's going to be very much the centre of attention tonight.'

Tina sort of, like, cocks her head to one side and goes, 'Ine soddy it didn't woork out wit youse two.'

'That's okay,' Blathin goes, smiling, all easy breezy, 'what's for you won't pass you,' and I'm thinking, yeah, if that's your *actual* attitude, why did you put the word around that he was a bastard? 'Anyway, I'd better get backstage. The show's about to start.'

Then she wheels herself off.

I shoot Tina one of my seriously disappointed looks. 'Fraternizing with the enemy, huh?' which is a line we used to use back in the day if someone on the S was friends with someone from Blackrock, Michael's, Terenure – anywhere other than Castlerock actually.

She's like, 'Grow up, Ross,' trying to make out that *I'm* the one being childish?

But I just hammer the point home. 'Oh, of course, you saved McGahy's mother's life – that's the connection.'

'I'm a noorse, Ross.'

'You're also a snake.'

'What would you I'd radder done, put a pillow over her face?'

'No. Save her life, by all means – *if* that's what the job entails. Just don't look so focking pleased with yourself for doing it.'

She shakes her head, roysh, like I'm a child she can no longer be bothered *orguing* with?

We go back to our seats, me focking hobbling, by the way. I'm definitely going to need an X-ray.

'Is Ross limping?' I hear the old man go. 'Are you limping, Ross?'

As it happens, roysh, I don't even get a chance to answer, because no sooner have I taken my seat in the front row – the proud dad – than my phone all of a sudden rings. It turns out it's the man himself and it's immediately obvious from the tone of his voice that he's, like, stressed about something.

'Nerves are normal,' I try to go.

He's like, 'It's not neerves, Rosser. It's Bla. She's up to something.'

'Ladies and gentlemen,' a voice goes over the PA, 'please take your seats, as the performance is about to commence.'

I'm like, 'Up to something? They're *all* up to something, Ro. The trick is to figure out what.'

'I can't, but. She called a production meetin half an hour ago – except it was for just the geerls.'

'The brides in other words?'

'Yeah. Thee come out, reet, and they're all of a sutton givin me the cowult shoulder. What are thee up to, Rosser?'

I wish I had an answer for him. That's what being a father is supposedly about. If I had a few minutes to think, I might come up with one. But the next thing I know, Sister Ildephonsus is clanking out the opening bors of 'Bless Your Beautiful Hide' and Ronan's going, 'Bollocks, I'm up. I'll see you, Rosser,' and literally five seconds later he steps out onto the stage in his riding britches and his knee-high boots and his big blowsy shirt, singing, 'Bless your beautiful hide,' with the worry obvious on his face, even *with* the red beard.

He wanders into the – like I told you before – Aldi, then says his famous line, asking the checkout bird whether she has any wives on special this week. Of course it brings the actual house down. I look around and everyone's cracking up, then they're, like, turning to each other and saying shit like, 'Oh, he's a real Dub, isn't he? How fun!'

I seem to be the only one who can tell that he's, for some reason, stressed.

'Ine not leavin here,' he goes, 'until I find me a woman what I can maddy.'

The next thing, roysh, in walk six of the seven brides, all carrying their Bags for Life. I mean, the whole thing's very clever, whoever came up with it. He looks the six of them up and down and goes, 'What about these? Are any of these going speer?' except I can see from his body language that he's not as cocksure of himself as he originally was. In other words, the swagger is gone.

He wanders into the little coffee shop next door to the Aldi, which of course ends up being a Storbucks. 'Gimme a grande, skinny, double-shot frappalapo to go,' he goes. Then Yasmin – who plays Milly, the barrista – ends up dropping the stainless-steel foam jug on the ground, the idea being that it's, like, love at first sight between them?

Anyway, everyone knows the Jack. They get married, then he takes her off to the backwoods, which in this case is Lucan. That's when she ends up meeting the brothers and Ronan goes, 'Happy days, feddas – least we're gonna steert getting a bit of decent nosebag around here!'

Again, the laughter.

'Isn't he wonderful?' I hear the old man go. 'Of course, lest we forget, his father was an entertainer too, albeit in the art of egg-chucking,' which is a nice thing for me to hear.

Milly cooks the dinner, using Rachel Allen's *Home Cooking* – another nice touch – then Ro and the other six goys sit down and stort horsing into it. Milly has a total conniption, calls them – oh my God! – animals and ends up tipping over the actual table.

Then off she focking storms. End of Scene One. Everyone's loving it.

Except Ro still looks worried, like he knows that something's cooking

– and I'm not talking about Rachel's delicious gnocchi with Gorgonzola.

And, of course, he's right.

Scene Two kicks off, with Milly sitting in her bedroom, not a happy bunny.

It's a nice bedroom actually. I noticed Ikea got a serious big-up in the programme.

Ro has to knock on the door.

'Who is it?' *she* goes.

Ro's like, 'It's Adam. Your husband.'

In he steps. The audience genuinely loves him. That's when Milly, of course, storts giving him an earful.

'You don't want a wife,' she goes. 'You want a cook, a cleaner, a washerwoman. Oh! My God! Someone to, like, slave for you?'

I'm sitting there thinking how this could be based on *my* actual marriage, when all of a sudden I notice a change come over Milly's face. It's very, I don't know, subtle, but she seems to be basically smiling. No, not smiling – actually *sneering*?

'Plus,' she all of a sudden goes, 'I've been, like, *hearing* things about you?'

Ro's there, 'Errr,' because it's immediately obvious that what she said isn't in the original script.

'You've been, like, *cheating* on me?'

Ro's, like, totally speechless. All he can think to say is, 'I haven't, Middy – I swayer.'

'Oh my God,' Milly goes, 'you're an *actual* liar, Adam. I *know* you've been with Dorcas – in, like, Eddie Rocket's in Donnybrook? And I know you were in Ruth's house for tea – *and* you got off with Martha the same day after rehearsals . . .'

Ro tries to, like, regain control of the scene. 'I waddunt,' he goes, utter pro that he is. 'I didn't. I don't know where you're getting yisser information.'

The old dear takes her opera glasses away from her face and turns to me. 'Is this *in* the original musical?' she goes.

It must be what everyone is suddenly wondering, roysh, because there's, like, an instant tension in the room. No one's laughing anymore. In fact, they're just, like, looking at each other, bewildered would possibly be the word.

'You were with Alice – as in *with* with? – after the Rathgor Junior

Orchestra recital in, like, Stratford College,' Milly goes. 'You brought Sarah to see *The Back-Up Plan* in Dundrum *and* you were with Liza last night, down the back of the 116 on the way home from – oh my God – bowling?'

Ro's like, 'Ah, you're bleaten padanoid, you are. Come on, let's just get some kip.'

'In fact,' Milly goes, saying the words like she's turning over a winning flush, 'you've probably got someone hidden in that PAX oak-effect wardrobe with sliding doors.'

Ronan turns and stares at the wardrobe. And even though Ikea will be obviously delighted with the mench, you can see the actual fear on the kid's face, like he knows deep down that he's pretty much powerless to stop whatever's about to basically go down here.

'Like I said,' he tries to go, 'padanoid. Maybe we need a break.'

Milly's there, 'Why don't you open the door, then, Ronan,' because she's not even, like, *pretending* to follow the script now? 'If you think I'm paranoid – open it.'

He stares hord at the wardrobe.

'Open it!' some focking busybody in the audience shouts – as you possibly know, I've never been a fan of Mount Anville parents.

Ro looks down at me for the first time, I'm presuming for, like, *guidance*? But, for once, I have no words of wisdom for him and – I'm deeply ashamed of this, I'm prepared to admit – I end up just looking away.

Then the entire audience gets going. They're like, 'Open it! Open it! Open it!'

Ro looks, it has to be said, totally resigned to whatever's about to happen. He just walks slowly over to the wardrobe and slides the door to one side.

Of course the six of them are in there – we're talking Dorcas, Ruth, Liza, Martha, Sarah and Alice – and there's, like, a collective gasp from the audience, then a burst of what would have to be described as, like, *nervous* laughter?

The next thing I hear is the sound of Blathin's wheels, which could do with a blast of WD-40, as it happens. I don't know about the rest of you but I've always associated squeaky wheelchairs with, like, *evil*?

I watch her sort of, like, wheel herself to the back of the hall, where the controls for the lighting are?

Then, all at once, roysh, the girls, including Milly, make a grab for Ro. It's at that exact moment that the stage lights go off and the entire hall is cast into pretty much dorkness.

'What on earth is going on?' I hear the old man go.

A lot of people are asking the exact same question.

The next thing anyone hears is the sound of, like, cloth ripping, then Ronan struggling, then at the same time issuing threats. 'Get off me,' he screams, 'yiz doorty-looken bitches,' except his words fall on, like, deaf ears.

The tearing just continues.

I'm just sat there with my stupid mouth open, like a focking grouper.

I should at least shout something. For instance, 'Leave him alone. He didn't do anything the rest of you won't be doing – believe me – once you discover rugby players.'

Except I don't. I just sit there in, like, silent shock.

'Dis is fooken *you!*' I hear Tina go and, even though it's dork, I automatically know that it's directed at me. 'I toalt ye. Fillin he's head wirrall dat rubbish.'

'Okay, Blathin,' a voice goes up from the stage. I could be wrong but I think it's, like, Dorcas. 'Now!'

Somewhere a switch is flicked and a single spotlight is suddenly shining on the stage from overhead. There's, like, a collective gasp from the audience. There, caught in the blue beam – stork Vegas naked, with his clothes in literally flitters at his feet – using his red beard to hide his manhood from the crowd, stands my son.

He looks totally – in a word – humiliated.

'Do you know somethin,' I hear Tina, beside me, go. 'He's never going to forgive you for dis, Ross. Never.'

6. Dead man walken

'It's called *what*?'

Regina seems pretty shocked. If it's true that she really *did* live through a war, I think her reaction, personally, is a little bit OTT.

'It's called going through the cord,' I go. 'And it's not a major deal.'

She's like, 'Yee? His fawther? Told hum to tray to gat off with seven gorls?'

And of *course* it's going to sound bad if *that's* how you phrase it?

I'm there, 'Yeah, I did. Get it while you're hot – that's always been a basic philosophy of mine. So he broke one or two horts along the way. I don't see what the big deal is? Have you any idea what teenage girls can be like?'

I'm preaching to the converted, of course. She *has* one. 'Aye,' she goes, 'they *con* be little coys, so they con.'

I'm like, 'Thank you. At last. Back-up from *someone*. As proven by the fact that they stripped him basically naked in front of, like, two or three hundred parents. See, people think Mount Anville is all conversational Japanese and furniture restoration classes. But there's a focking edge to those birds. Take it from someone who married one.'

I roll over in the bed, with the intention of grabbing one of the strawberries that we were eating last night. Except the old Green & Black's that she melted has, like, hordened in the bowl and the strawberries – being honest – look a bit skanky from lying there all night in the heat of the room.

'So, what,' she goes, 'first you're not allied to see your wee gorl – and noy you're not allied to see your wee falla?'

'It's not that I'm now *allowed* to see Ro?' I go, trying to put a positive spin on it. 'It's just that his old dear reckons *he's* not going to want to see *me*, mainly down to the humiliation he suffered. I thought I'd give him maybe a little bit of space. We're actually the best of mates.'

She gives me this, I suppose, *understanding* look? 'It's nat easy, is ut? Being a porunt?'

'You can say that again. It's a constant battle to try to do the right thing. And, as I've discovered to my cost, the right thing isn't always the *obvious* thing? Jesus, even thinking about it makes me want to go back to sleep here.'

'*She's* still nat talking to may.'

I'm like, 'Who? Hedda?'

She nods. 'It's, what, tee weeks noy? Giving me the salent treatment. *Ay* says to her the other dee, "No one's meeking yee stee here. Yee're fanished college noy for the year – why don't yee thank abite moving ite? If you heet me that moch." I mean, ay'd give her the monay to move ite. Forther, the batter.'

'You can't actually mean that?'

'At the moment, ay *doy* mean it. It's hord to lav with someone who despases yee.'

I'm lying there, roysh, suddenly wondering did *my* old dear ever think the same thing about *me*?

It's then that I decide to bring up the subject of the watch. See, the plan *had* been to mention it when I arrived. Except Regina opened the door with a face on her like Amy Winehouse let loose in Boots. She actually grabbed me by the crotch of my chinos and dragged me up the stairs, going, '*Yee* were supposed to be here an orr ago – *ay* nearly hod tee stort withite yee.'

There was very little talking done after that, aport from the usual swearing and taking the Lord's name and – I'm happy to say – one or two complimentary remorks about my performance, which are always gratefully received, no matter how many times you hear them.

'Regina,' I go, 'can I just say something about the watch you sent me?'

'Do yee lake it?'

'Like it? Of course I like it – it's, like, thirty Ks' worth.'

'Good.'

'It's just, look, I've got tonnes of presents from birds before – except it'd usually be, I don't know, CDs or after-shave or even the odd shirt. No one's ever spent that amount of money on me.'

She gets up on one elbow. 'So why hov yee gat thot feece on yee, then?'

'Okay,' I go, 'at the risk of possibly offending you a second time, was it meant as some kind of payment?'

She just stares me out of it. I'm thinking, uh-oh! She's like, 'Pee-ment? Ay ought tee slop your feece for yee.'

I'm there, 'I'm sorry, it's just . . . Look, that chat we had a few weeks back. We agreed that we were two people who enjoyed just having sex.'

'Whoy enjoyed each other's cormpany, is what we said.'

'Each other's company, then. A bit of fun. No questions. No demands. Swing in when you're horny. Then I come home one day and find a watch worth, what, thirty Ks on the kitchen table? Anyone would ask the same question – as in, does it come with strings?'

She just nods, roysh, like she can suddenly see *my* angle? Which is another good advertisement for older women.

'Look, ay'm sawry,' she goes. 'Ay didn't even thank. Look, ay jost saw it in the wandow of Weir's – *ay'm* spontaneous lake thot. Always hov been. Espacially when it comes to mornay. Ay'v always hod thot ottitude – mornay's for meeking yee hoppy. If it doesn't, then you mait as well be purr.'

'Well, I've always made that exact point to my wife – that money and happiness are pretty much the same thing. If they weren't, then explain to me why there's so much misery around the place right now.'

'Look,' she goes, 'ay can brang it bock if it meeks yee feel oncomfortable.'

I'm like, 'No! That's the last thing I want. I love it. I just wanted to check . . .'

'Thot there's no strangs?'

'Exactly.'

'There's *no* strangs – okee?'

I'm like, 'Cool.'

'And noy,' she goes, '*ay'm* going to have to throw you ite.'

I laugh. It suits me. I was terrified she was going to ask me to have sex with her again. The truth is that I'm in no fit state. One or two of the positions she had me in last night, I think, might have aggravated my rhomboideus major injury from years back and I've a dick on me like a Vileda super mop – and I don't mean the handle end.

'What are you doing for the day?' I go, not that I even care.

'Ay'm meeting Levinus and Debra for lonch. They're may and Toddy's oldest frands. Och, we go wee back.'

I suddenly feel like the luckiest goy in the world. We're talking not only gymnastic sex with a guilt-free dismount. But she's just brought up the subject of her friends without once suggesting that I might like to meet them. She has zero interest in showing me off. I don't know why I didn't go for an older woman years ago.

'Ay'm gonna hov a shorr,' she goes. 'You meek yoursolf useful – go dine stors and meek some caffay.'

I give her the guns, then tip downtairs to the kitchen, in just my boxers and my Jackman! T-shirt with the Batman crest on it, except with a bald head and two big ears, and I lash on the kettle. While I'm waiting for it to boil, I'm checking out my reflection in the glass countertop of the breakfast bor.

One thing I have to admit is that I'm looking really well since I turned thirty.

'Nice watch,' are the words I suddenly hear, except said in a voice that obviously doesn't *mean* it? I turn around, roysh, and I have to admit, I end up getting a bit of a shock.

The only time I've ever laid actual eyes on Hedda was at her old man's funeral, when she was the one screaming the odds at me and my sister. But she was dressed that day for, well, a funeral, and what I hadn't realized, until this very moment, is that she's one of those, like, emos?

I'll describe exactly what she looks like and you can picture it if you can. She's wearing a black and pink, horizontally striped, long-sleeved top with, like, skinny, black, three-quarter-length trousers – with a totally unnecessary black mini skirt over them – and black and pink chequered Vans. Oh, and a white tie – for what reason, only she focking knows. Her hair is, like, dyed black with, like, different coloured streaks, then combed forward and to the side, so that it covers one eye. She's got, like, a ring in her bottom lip and one in her nose and her make-up looks like it was shot onto her face from fifty yords away with a focking paintball gun.

I have to admit, that whole Avril Lavigne thing has never done much for me.

'It's Saturday,' I go, because – like I said – she's giving *me* serious tude herself, 'should you not being hanging around outside the Central Bank looking unhappy?'

She doesn't take the bait. Instead, she goes, 'Did *she* buy you that?' referring, of course, to the watch.

I'm there, 'What do you care? I thought you actually hated her.'

All she does is look me up and down, then go, 'There's a name for people like you.'

I'm there, 'Hey, don't worry, I've been called them all.'

She's like, 'Male prostitute.'

I laugh – can't help it. 'Actually,' I go, 'that *is* a new one,' and then I go back to making the coffee.

Regina has that Lavazza shit, which I really love.

Hedda walks around the central island as if to get a better look at me. 'Oh my God,' she suddenly goes, after studying my face for a few seconds, 'I've just realized who you are.'

I'm genuinely there, 'Really? You wouldn't have struck me as a rugby fan.'

She goes, 'You're *her* brother,' and you can hear the delight in her voice, 'that fucking slut who slept with my dad. I remember you from the funeral.'

I just pour the water into the pot and try not to say anything I'll regret.

'So,' she goes, unwilling to just leave it, 'what's your angle? What are you after?'

Again, I refuse to get sucked in.

She laughs then, like she's had another sudden realization. 'How much did your dad have to pay my mum again?'

'Excuse me?'

'To keep your sister's name out of the divorce. Oh, don't worry, I have ears, you know. Was it, like, a million or something?'

'It was one point seven, in fairness to it.'

She nods. 'One point seven. And you're sleeping with my mother, what, to try to con that money back from her.'

I'm actually plunging the coffee when she says this and I stop, mid-push, and fix her with a look. I know I shouldn't, but I'm having to defend my – okay, this is pushing it – but *honour* here? 'I'm sleeping with your mother,' I go, 'because she rides like she actually discovered it.'

She sort of, like, wheels away from me. 'You're disgusting.'

'I'm actually serious. It's some of the best sex I've ever had. And I think she'd say pretty much the same thing if it came to it.'

I make a big show then of looking at the watch, even though I've no even interest in the time. 'And, hey, if she wants to show me her grati-tude for making her toes curl two or three times a night, who are we to say it's wrong?'

She looks like she wants to dig those black painted nails of hers into my face. Except, as far as I know, emos are, like, *non*-violent? 'I just think you're sad,' she instead goes, before turning her back and walk-ing out of the room, 'if my mum is the best you can do.'

Wee coys. I have to say it – Regina wasn't wrong.

I leave Ronan a message, just going, 'Hey, Ro, it's your, er, old man. In other words, Ross. Rosser . . . Er, yeah, un-focking-believable what hap-pened that night, wasn't it? Jesus . . . I, er, hope you're okay. I suppose, if anything, it proves what I was saying. In other words, that crowd aren't the sweet little innocents they crack on to be when they're playing their – I can't remember if you said it was a viola or a contrabass. Either way, maybe give me shout back. Or even just text me . . . Are we still meet-ing in Quirkey's this week?'

An hour later, roysh, he still hasn't returned my call, so I ring him a second time – and again, roysh, it rings and rings, then ends up going through to his voicemail. 'Yeah,' I go, 'look, your old dear said you might possibly be upset with me. Look, I know this maybe *seems* bad at the moment? I've ruined your life and blah blah blah. But you'll bounce back from this, Ro. You will. Take it from someone who lived through a thousand similar, I suppose, humiliations. Well, none *that* bad, but you take my point. And anyway, Mount Anville's only, like, *one* school? There's the Loretos – Dalkey, Foxrock, the Green. You haven't even storted on them. Then there's Holy Child Killiney – even though they're a bit, you know . . . And Muckross. I mean, don't knock Muckross. A lot do, but I *never* did. Anyway, maybe give me a ring.'

Half an hour later, still nothing, so I ring one last time and leave a message going, 'And don't forget, Ro, who's *actually* to blame for this – in other words Bla? Oh, she's a sly one. You'd never think it, of course, sitting in her little wheelchair. But Jesus, you definitely dodged a bullet there. Anyway, I'll talk to you hopefully later. Again, it's *her* fault, when you think about it.'

I've never ridden a bird on an airplane. Mad as that sounds. This thought occurs to me while I'm lying in bed one afternoon, making a mental checklist of all the – I suppose you could call them *ambitions*? – that I have and haven't achieved.

I suppose thirty *is* a time for taking stock.

I'm wondering how do I do it – become a member of that very respected club. Mile High or whatever it's called. It'd mean obviously having to fly somewhere. And somewhere pretty far away as well – as in France, or any of those – as it'd mean obviously having to chat up a bird on the flight, then persuade her that it was a good idea. Unless I just took one of my regulars – Chloe or Sophie – on a Ryanair flight to, say, Liverpool. Although where's the thrill in that? Ryanair would probably let you do it. Matter of fact, they've almost certainly got a rate for it. It'll be on the onboard menu, in between the Boxerchips and the Bullseye Baggies.

This is me just thinking aloud, by the way, something I've been known to occasionally do. And it's while I'm doing this that it suddenly comes on the TV – an ad for the Wheel of Dublin, this new Ferris wheel which is supposedly *our* answer to the London Eye?

'*An unforgettable experience,*' the dude on the ad goes, '*offering a three-hundred-and-sixty-degree, panoramic view of Dublin.*'

I'm thinking how relieved the old dear's going to be that they've stuck it in the North Docks. You know her view – the northside is the place for that kind of carry-on.

And you can possibly guess what occurs to me then. Er, who says it has to even *be* on an airplane? I mean, millions – possibly billions – of people have already done that. But doing the nasty in one of those Ferris wheel pods, the night the thing opens, would be a far more major deal. Because I'd be the actual first. I doubt if I'll be the last, of course – especially given how close to Gardiner Street and Ballybough they've put it. The locals are going to be breeding on that thing like focking germs on a toilet bowl. But to do it before anyone else has even *thought* about it – well, you know how much I love a challenge.

But who with? That's the next question. I think, okay, what about Regina? Then I think, come on, Ross, you can do better than that. Think of this as, like, a belated thirtieth birthday present to yourself.

Then a name pops into my head – Orna, well, something or other.

The name's not important. She's, like, a bird from Cork who I chatted up one night in the Bailey two or three months back. If you put a gun to my head, roysh, and told me I had to describe her as looking like someone, I'd end up having to say, honestly, Frankie Sandford. The only drawback with Orna is that she's a pain in the hole. She never stops banging on about, firstly, how proud she is to come from Munster – even though Rog and Paul O'Connell are the only actual players she can name – and secondly, how she went to, like, the best college in Ireland.

'You can't spell success without UCC,' is one of her, like catchphrases.

On the balance side, though, she's as gamey as Gordon Ramsay's rabbit and venison pie, which is the reason *she's* the one who ends up getting the call.

'Who is this?' she goes, after I give her one or two filthy comments by way of introduction.

'It's Ross,' I go. 'As in, Ross O'Carroll-Kelly?'

She cracks on *not* to be impressed? She's like, 'What do *you* want?'

Like I said, it *has* been a few months.

'Wondered what you were up to on Friday night. How do you fancy a date with a difference?'

She laughs, except in, like, a sarcastic way. 'I can't believe the gall of you. That'd be typical UCD, now.'

Jesus, let it go. It was, like, years ago. And I didn't go to a single focking lecture.

I'm there, 'You're pissed off that I haven't been in touch, aren't you?'

She's like, 'Don't flatter yourself.'

I'm there, 'And yet at the same time you have to admit that you really enjoyed yourself that night. I know *I* did. I could barely walk the next day.'

'Well,' she goes, 'you found your legs eventually, because you were gone out the door by the time I woke up.'

Girls don't love that, no matter where they're from.

'Okay,' I go, 'honesty time . . .'

'I don't know why I'm even listening to this.'

'No, you're right – I owe you an actual explanation. The truth is that – okay, I'm not proud of myself – but I was actually seeing someone else at the time.'

'That doesn't surprise me. I said that to Muireann when you didn't call.'

'Seeing several birds, in fact. But I thought, oh no you don't, Ross.

200

This particular girl is special. She's not to be messed around – way too good for that. So before anything serious happens here – before you go down that road where you definitely know you want to go – you've got to clear out your in-tray. Which is what I've done. And here I am.'

There's, like, silence on the other end of the phone. Birds love that kind of talk, see. 'You're full of S, H, one, T,' she goes, except I can tell she doesn't mean it. She's, like, loving me again – that much is pretty obvious.

I'm there, 'So Friday . . .'

'What is this date with a difference?'

'Okay, have you seen that new Wheel of Dublin? It's supposedly, like, *our* London Eye.'

'I have. I saw an ad for it on the television. I was thinking how Cork needs something like that.'

Jesus Christ.

'Well, do you fancy it, then? I was thinking we could go up in it – whatever happens and blah, blah, blah – then maybe get a drink afterwards.'

'I must be mental . . .'

'But you're going to say yes.'

'Like I said, I *must* be mental.'

'Hey, you won't regret this, Orna.'

'Orla.'

'What?'

'My name is Orla.'

'Are you sure? It's just I have you in my phone as Orna.'

'I think I know my own name, Ross.'

'Hey, it's cool. I must have just hit the wrong button when I was key-ing in your digits. Do *you* find your thumbs are too fat for the iPhone?'

'I'll see you on Friday,' she just goes. 'Oh, the lads are going to think I've lost the plot.'

So Friday comes around, as it eventually always does. I meet Orna slash Orla in town and we get an Andy McNab down to the O2. We can see the wheel in the distance the whole way down, all lit up and blahdy blah. It's seriously impressive, it has to be said.

So we get down there and join the queue. There must be, like, five or six hundred people ahead of us and the estimated waiting time is, like, an hour. Which is cool. I stand there, roysh, listening to her crapping on about her job, pretending to be interested – all tactics, of course – and nodding occasionally to make it seem like I'm sympathetic.

'I always said I'd never leave my job,' she's going. 'I love working in the VHI. But the money that Quinn are offering *is* much better. But then with everything that's gone on with the Quinn Group, you'd wonder how secure it'd be.'

We reach the top of the queue just as I'm storting to give up the focking will to live. A dude in a fluorescent yellow bib opens the door of the pod and in we go and sit down on the two little benches, opposite each other. Then the dude goes to put another couple in with us.

I go, 'We'd, er, prefer *not* to share, if it's all the same to you.'

He's like, 'Soddy, there's a massive queue back theer, so there is. The only way we're gonna get through it is . . .'

My quick thinking again saves the day. I check that Orna-Orla-what-ever isn't paying attention, then I look at the dude, touch the ring finger on my left hand and mouth the words, 'I'm going to propose!'

His face is suddenly lit up like a runway. He puts his orm in front of the other couple, blocking their way, then goes, 'Wait for the next one,' before whispering, 'The fedda's gonna propose.'

Oh, I'm going to propose alright. I didn't say what, though!

The wheel storts moving. A man's voice comes through the little speaker, welcoming us to this new and exciting attraction that offers a unique view of Dublin's skyline. He says it takes seven minutes to do a complete rotation.

Seven minutes, I think. That's just about enough time. Who am I even kidding? For me, that's enough time to do it twice.

Then we stort moving. The second we're airborne, I move across to where she's sitting.

She's going, 'The other reason I don't want to leave the VHI – and you might think this is a stupid reason to stay in a job – but I'm on the ladies football team and I think we've a really good chance of winning the Insurance Federation of Ireland Night Owls Championship this year.'

I put my hand on her knee. She turns and sees me giving her one of my famous it's-*all*-good looks.

'What are you doing?' she goes.

She's, like, smiling as she says this, letting me know that my advances aren't exactly unwanted. That's the thing I remembered about this bird – she's hord work but she's open-minded.

I'm like, 'I thought it might be fun to do it, you know, up in the air.'

She laughs. 'You must be joking.'

I move my hand further up her thigh and give it a bit of a squeeze. 'Does it feel like I'm joking?'

She laughs again. 'You don't half have tickets on yourself, do you? Look, I'd love to – but I can't. The thing is, I've got my . . .'

You've got to be kidding me. 'Your what?'

'My . . .'

'Your period?'

'Yes.'

'Oh, for fock's sake.'

'Yeah, it's not something I can help, Ross.'

She could have focking told me, though. I mean, who goes on a date without declaring that? Jesus, I could throw her off the focking top of this thing.

It's a good job I don't say what I'm thinking, though. Because she suddenly looks at me, with a dirty big grin on her boat, then goes, 'Maybe I can still do something for you?'

She's talking about a blowie. She's definitely talking about a blowie and it straight away cheers me up, it has to be said. I mean, the amount of shit I've listened to her talk since I met her tonight.

'What do you have in mind?' I go.

She's like, 'Oh, I'm sure I can think of something,' and she suddenly drops to her knees – like something off the, honestly, internet – and storts – if you can believe this – unbuttoning my chinos. I'm thinking, happy focking days, then I sit back and just, well, enjoy the view, so to speak.

I'm not the only one either. What I suddenly realize, as the wheel moves anti-clockwise to the two o'clock position, is that the people in the three or four pods above us can see exactly what's going on. Their eyes are out on literally stalks, their mouths slung open like the focking Aillwee Caves.

Orna or Orla knows nothing about this, of course. She's too busy about her work. But I'm loving the, I suppose, *notoriety*? I thinking, okay, if you want a show, I'll give you a show and I stort pulling these, like, porn stor faces at them. They're disgusted – you can see it. But not disgusted enough to turn away. Although they do lose sight of us as they each drop below twelve o'clock. Then it's the turn of the people behind us to suddenly get a good eyeful. Same thing. Horror, but at the same *fascination*?

The girl's working like an emigrant down there, it has to be said, and I'm thinking, okay, I'd want to stort thinking about bringing it home at this stage. Because we'll be back on *terra* whatever-the-word-is in, like, three or four minutes and there's a fair chance someone is going to call the Gords. It's then, roysh, just as we reach the midnight point ourselves, that Orna or Orla stops performing her magic and goes, 'Oh, shit!'

This is with her head still down, by the way.

I'm like, 'What's wrong?'

She goes, 'I think I'm stuck.'

'Stuck? What do you mean stuck?'

Her voice is, like, muffled, by the way. Of course it is – she's talking into my practically crotch.

'I think . . . I've got you . . . stuck in my braces.'

'Braces? You don't wear braces.'

'Hold on. I'll see can I . . .'

My body, roysh, is suddenly gripped by a pain I've never focking known. I hear myself go 'Aaarrrggghhh!' except it doesn't sound even human. It's the kind of sound I'd imagine you'd hear if you shoved a freshly boiled baby potato up a cat's orse.

It's my pubes – it feels like they're being ripped out by the actual roots.

I'm like, 'What the fock!'

'I told you, you're caught in my braces.'

'I didn't notice you were wearing . . .'

'It's an Invisalign.'

'A what?'

'It's one of those invisible braces.'

'Well, I've never heard of them.'

'It's, like, a see-through plastic covering that goes over the teeth.'

'Another focking secret you kept from me. Aaaarrrggghhhh! Orna . . .'

'Orla.'

'Orla, then. Please, stop trying to jerk your head free.'

'I have to. Ross, I can't stay like this. We're going to be back on the ground in a couple of minutes.'

As if to prove her point, the pod suddenly lurches, then storts moving again, our time at the top over. The people in the other pods are still, like, agog, except I'm not showboating anymore. I'm focking kacking it. *And* I'm in pure agony.

'Do you have, like, a nail scissors?' I go.

'A nail scissors?'

'Yeah.'

'I think there might be one in my handbag.'

'Okay, don't you move. I'll see can I get it.'

I reach out my leg, roysh, and I manage to hook the handle of her fake Miu Miu with my foot, then drag it towards me. We're coming down, it seems to me, a lot faster than it took us to get up there. We're suddenly at nine o'clock and I realize I'm going to have to be quick here.

'Ross,' she goes, 'I'm just going to pull my head. It'll be like ripping off a plaster. It'll hurt for a second but then . . .'

I'm like, 'Please, in the name of all that is holy, don't focking do it,' and as I'm saying this, roysh, I'm rooting through her bag, tipping make-up and nail files and emergency tampies all over the floor, in my desperate search for this famous scissors.

We're somewhere between the seven and eight o'clock positions now when *she* moves again. 'One quick pull,' she goes, clutching my two thighs and shaping up to do it.

I go, 'No! Please, no! Look, I've got the scissors in my actual hand. Just let me . . .'

The pod lurches again and the focking thing slips from my fingers and skids across the floor. *She* hears it, of course.

'What was that?'

'Fock. I dropped the focking scissors.'

'That's it!'

'No, wait. If I take off one of my Dubes, I might be able to hook it with my toe.'

'Ross!'

'Seriously, hang on – I'm going to try and get my sock off here . . .'

'Ross, I'm just going to have to . . .'

'Aaaaarrrrgggghhhh!!!!'

She does it. She goes and focking does it. She pulls her head back violently, giving me a pretty much Brazilian in the process. I have never felt pain like it – and I've tackled Denis Leamy, remember.

'Jesus, Orna!'

'Orla.'

'*Whatever.*'

I realize – we both do – that we're all of a sudden back on the ground again. And you can imagine the sight that greets the four or five hundred people standing in the queue – me sitting there with my chinos around my ankles and a face as red as Thomond Pork, *her* on her knees trying to pick what was once *my* hair out of her invisible dental brace.

The dude in the fluorescent yellow bib has a big shit-eating smile on his face. He looks at me and goes, 'I take it she said yes.'

I text Honor. I'm, like, *entitled* to? I know Sorcha's angry but she can't keep me away from my actual daughter. I go, 'Hey Hon, hows life?'

She's straight back with, 'Er pardon my french but that woman ur married to is f*ing delusional.'

I actually laugh. Delusional? I wouldn't have known how to spell that word at her age. Wouldn't be a hundred percent sure of it even now. It's predictive text, you see. Who says all this new technology is actually bad for kids?

'Why do u say shes delusional?' I go.

She's like, 'We wer in starbucks and i wanted a muffin. She was like, iv an even better idea, lets buy sum cake mix in tesco n make our own!'

'Jesus. That's not d same ting.'

'I kno! I was like, er, soz? I want a skiny peach n rasbry 1 – not 1 made from a packet. She was like, theyr 2 dear honor. 2 dear? Er, soz, since when is €3.80 2 dear for NEthing?'

'I wudnt have Ne probs paying it. Never hav.'

'Well she was like, the 1s you make urself taste nearly d same – and its more fun.'

'They dont taste d same – that's an actual fact. Wotever about d fun.'

'Toats!' she goes. 'She's being such a knob at d moment. Everything is giovanna said this and giovanna said that.'

And I'm like, 'Giovanna? Now theres sum1 who needs 2b taken down a peg r2.'

The old man is well out of the woods – at least that's what they're saying in the hospital.

'I'm happy to report that I have the robust good health of a man, oh, ten years his junior,' he goes, slapping the left breast of his Cole Haan camel-hair coat.

He's sat in the passenger seat beside me, even though it's his Merc I'm driving.

'Oh, we went through all the rigmarole. Joel – well, he positively *insists* I call him that – he sat there, behind his desk, with his clipboard and his questionnaire. Have you drunk any alcohol? Not a drop. Have you smoked? Cigars have gone the same way as the brandy and the red wine, am happy to report. What about your diet? You're not still eating cheese, are you, Charles? Only if it's the cottage variety, says I. And no red meat either. What about exercise? Lots of lovely long walks with my wonderful partner in life, with whom I've been given a second chance!'

My eyes immediately drift to the rear-view mirror, I suppose to get Helen's response. She's delighted obviously.

I pull out onto the Merrion Road.

'My cholesterol,' he goes, 'is already down to the lower end of the borderline high range. If that's not a cause for celebration, I don't know what is! Did you phone Erika, Darling?'

Helen goes, 'Yes, I texted her. She's very happy.'

I just roll my eyes. I'm thinking, yeah, what kind of daughter goes away on the day of her old man's six-month check-up?

Fionn took her to Milan to celebrate their – get this – ten-month anniversary.

Who even *celebrates* ten months? Someone who's clinging on by his focking fingertips, is the answer, and counting every focking day as a blessing.

Helen's there, 'They went to see *The Last Supper* this morning – in the Santa Maria delle Grazie.'

'The Santa Maria delle Grazie!' the old man goes. 'Oh, they sound so happy.'

They do. I get the sudden urge to piss on their parade, though.

'I don't know why everyone bangs on about that painting,' I go. 'I mean, I've seen it in, like, magazines and I always think, who the fock sits down to dinner like that – as in, everyone on one side of the focking table? Would Jesus not have gone, "Goys, could some of you not sit on the other side?" I'm just saying, if thirteen of you went into, say, Wagamama and did that, people would say it was weird.'

The old man turns around in his seat and goes. 'You see, Helen? He's a logical thinker. That's why he's so cut out for business, you see. Oh, if you'd been around, Ross, in Leonardo da Vinci's day . . .'

'I'd have actually said it to him.'

'And it would have been a better painting for it.'

Needless to say, I didn't even know Leonardo da Vinci painted it.

He *is* looking better, in fairness to him, even if the weight *has* been slow in going back on – although with that diet he's on, maybe it never will.

He suddenly goes, 'Now, more than ever, Ross, this country needs people like you.'

'What do you mean, people like me?'

'Well, independent thinkers, of course. Oh, I'm tired of listening to the same old voices saying the same old things about this economic what-not. Fianna Fáil and their developer cronies and their friends in the banks. Allows us all to evade personal responsibility for this thing.'

'Come on, Charlie,' Helen goes, 'you can't get yourself riled up like you used to anymore.'

'I'm just making the point, darling, that it's nearly thirty years since a general election failed to return Fianna Fáil to power. We can't say we don't know them or what they're about. In whose interests did people think they were going to act when it all went bad?'

I look in the mirror again for Helen's reaction but there's, like, none.

'Pull over,' the old man suddenly goes.

I'm there, 'Are you okay?'

This is at the shops opposite the RDS.

'Yes, I just want to get some mints,' he goes. 'Rather odd taste in my mouth.'

I'm suddenly having, like, a panic attack. 'An odd taste? What kind of odd taste are we talking?'

'I'm fine, Ross. It was that salad I had in the hospital restaurant – there were one or two shallots in it. Nothing to worry about.'

I pull in. He gets out and I watch him walk – still with the baby steps – across the road and I realize all of sudden that I'm actually holding my breath.

He disappears into the shop. I turn around to Helen and we both smile at each other – I think the word is, like, *tightly*?

'Now that it's out there,' I go, 'I *did* get a whack of onion off him alright. I was actually going to mention it.'

My phone beeps. It's, like, a text from Regina. 'Can u pop round? I need u rite now!'

I sort of, like, smile to myself. That's when Helen goes, 'He's so proud of you, you know?'

And for a split-second, I wonder did she read it – and Regina's name – over my shoulder.

I'm like, 'Proud? What of? Did he mention specifics?'

'Everything.'

'The business? Because I know for a fact that Hennessy thought he was off his cake trusting me with it.'

'I know. And of course he's proud of the success you've made of that. But he's proud of you, Ross. Of the adult you've become.'

'Okay, was this in, like, reference to something in particular?'

'His illness, I suppose. You've been a rock. Especially in Monaco – I was in no fit state to do anything. You showed real character.'

You can imagine how that makes me feel – lower than whale shit.

'He's my old man – I keep saying.'

I watch him step out of the shop, chewing something. He holds up a packet of Silvermints for us to see. As he's crossing back over the road, he puts his hand over his mouth, obviously testing his breath again.

'Well,' she goes, 'he's proud of the kind of son you are. And the kind of father.'

'I could moorder ye,' Tina goes. 'God fooken help me, Ross, I *could!*'

She's in one of those moods where I'm actually *glad* it's over the phone I'm talking to her.

'Come on,' I go, 'how many times have you said *that* over the years – and, hey, I'm still here.'

I can hear hospital noises in the background. She's obviously at work. 'What do you want?' she goes.

I'm sat in the van on Idrone Terrace, with a Bucky's, taking a time-out before my next collection.

'Ronan hasn't been answering my calls,' I go. '*Or* returning my texts. Do you know has he, like, changed his number?'

'*Changed he's number?*' she goes, like *I'm* the slow one? 'He's not answering because you fooken humidiated him, Ross. In front of tree hundrit people as well.'

'Well,' I go, 'I hordly think I deserve the *entire* blame? What about Blathin? You were totally taken in by *her*, let me remind you. Do you know what I've been racking my brains trying to remember – who was the evil genius in the wheelchair in all the Bond movies? Was it Blofeld, was it?'

'Ross,' she just goes, 'Ine going back to woork.'

I'm like, 'Okay, Tina, wait! Look, do you think you could maybe have a word with him *for* me?'

'And say wha?'

'Just that, I don't know, I had his best interests at hort.'

'Ine hanging up.'

'Tina, please. Look, it's bad enough that Sorcha's stopped me seeing Honor. It's, like, pretty much killing me that now I can't even talk to Ro. I mean, Saturday is the day we usually hit Quirkey's. I stood outside waiting for him, Tina, for nearly two hours.'

She goes, 'Will I tell you where we were last night, Ross? I had to bring him up to de skewill for a meetin of de board of madagement.'

'What are you talking about? It's focking June – school's over.'

'It was an emeerchincy meeting.'

'Emergency meeting – yeah, whatever.'

'We had to sit outside while thee discussed weddor or not to lerrim back next year.'

I actually laugh out loud. That's how disgusted I am. 'What, after the ten A1s he got in his Christmas exams? *And* in his Easter ones! Yeah, like they're so well off for good students that they can afford to expel one who's considered very nearly gifted.'

'He'd be *gone* out of dayer if it wadn't for Mr Moogahy speakin up for him.'

I'm like, 'McGahy? Speaking up for him? Oh, that's very focking nice of him. The kid's a total brainiac, can I just remind you? Blackrock would have your hand off. So would Clongowes and one or two other schools I could mention. *And* they're still rugby schools. I'd have focking said that to the board had I known this so-called meeting was even happening.'

She's there, 'And that would have made tings a whole lot bethor, wouldn't it, Ross?'

I go, 'Sorry, can I just remind you that he didn't actually *do* anything wrong? Er, *they* ripped *his* clothes off, I'd just like to point out? I mean, do we even know yet whether *they* were expelled or suspended? Possibly not.'

That's when I suddenly realize that Tina has hung up and I'm sitting here talking to my focking self.

I know I'm not the man to lecture anyone on the subject of honesty – or lack of – in relationships. But one thing I've always hated is goys who insist on telling their girlfriends, wives, whatever, every little thing – including *your* every little thing.

As if Danuta needs any more reasons to hate me, JP's told her about Honor cheating in the Little Roedean's Sports Day and Ronan getting stripped by a pack of, I don't know, vengeful Mounties. You'd have to wonder what's going on in people's relationships if that's all they can find to talk about. But of course now Danuta thinks I'm a bad father, as well as the man who tried to Frenchie her mother and, well, whatever else happens to be on the rap sheet.

Not only that, roysh, but JP insists on talking to me about it in *front* of her?

He's like, 'This is something you egged him on to do?' a definite note of disapproval in his voice.

Of course *she's* looking at me like I'm focking vaginitis.

'I wouldn't say I *egged him on*,' I try to go. 'The kid had a reputation for being a bastard. He came to me, all upset. I told him how to use it to his advantage. End of. Fock's sake, JP, you'd swear you never even *played* on the S.'

I look at Danuta then. 'Oh, I could tell you some stories about your precious boyfriend there. Except some of us believe in keeping shit to ourselves.'

Still, at least Oisinn is being supportive. He's like, 'Did you remind Ronan that there's other schools?'

I'm there, 'Yeah, I said all that.'

'There's the Loretos . . . Even Muckross.'

'Hey, *I'm* not dissing Muckross. I was always a fan.'

'Did he listen?'

'He won't even answer the phone to me. Yeah, no, he might just need a few more weeks to cool off.'

Danuta looks me up and down. She's a stunner – no question – but *I'd* actually find that anger a turn-off?

'You are fugging eediot,' she goes.

I'm like, 'That's *your* view, Danuta. Maybe your boyfriend shouldn't be telling you funny anecdotes about me if they're going to piss you off to that degree.'

JP decides to break it up then by asking us what we think of the place. It's hord to know what to say, roysh, because there's not exactly a lot to see. It's still a vacant shop unit, even though there's, like, two or three builders in, sawing wood and putting together what I presume will be the counter and pretty much fittings.

I'm just like, 'Foxrock, though. Very brave.'

Of course JP's straight on the defensive. He *would* be – his old man picked the place out. He goes, 'A lot of people in this area are feeling the pinch, Ross. *I* see it day in, day out, doing repossessions. And if anyone has gold lying around the house, it's people in this part of the world.'

I'm there, 'Don't get me wrong. I'm focking delighted. The old dear's book is still number one in the bestseller list – she needs *something* to bring her back down to earth. The focking whelk.'

'I think what Ross is trying to say,' Oisinn goes, 'is to expect *some* kind of local resistance, especially when the sign goes up over the door.'

'Resistance?' Danuta goes – pretty much *laughing* at the word? 'There is nothing they can do to stop it.'

It's *my* turn to laugh then. 'That's what they said about the Luas coming to Foxrock! I'm telling you, when those ladies sit down in The Gables with their cappuccinos and their A4 pads, there's no one in the world who's a match for them. Not *even* the Russian mafia.'

She shoots JP an instant look. And *he* looks like he just chanced squeezing out a fort, then felt it dribble down the back of his leg. I'm thinking, oh, so there are *some* things they don't say to each other, then?

'*Broken, unwanted jewellery,*' Oisinn goes, reading one of the flyers that are stacked on top of what I recognize from TV as a Black and Decker workmate. '*All types of gold, yellow and white, all carats. Damaged, tangled, unmatched and scrap items. Coins, lockets, earrings, pins and bangles . . .*'

'Bangles?' I go. 'Around here? Er, *unlikely?*'

'What does he mean,' Danuta goes, still staring at the J-Dog, 'when he say Russian mafia?'

He's busted, of course. Busted *and* disgusted. Doesn't know what to tell her.

I'm just standing there thinking, yeah, this is the kind of shit you should possibly be talking about instead of discussing what a terrible father *I* supposedly am?

She tries to turn the heat on *me* then. She's like, 'What do you mean, Russian mafia?'

But it's at that exact point that my phone suddenly rings. My caller ID says it's Regina. I could *actually* kiss her.

I'm there, 'I'm just going to take this outside.'

'What do you mean, Russian mafia?' she goes again, except this time she basically *shouts* it?

'Sorry,' I go, 'you goys are going to have to sort your own love life out. And I'm just going to sort out mine.'

I step out onto Brighton Road. It's actually a nice day. First day of the Leaving Cert. – always focking is, of course. I answer the phone, giving it, 'Hey, how the hell are you?'

'Thees fugging man!' I can hear Danuta shout. They're going to love her around here.

'What abicha?' Regina goes. 'Is someone corsing at yee, thor?'

I'm like, 'Yeah, just a Russian bird who hates my basic guts – I wouldn't worry about it. How did that antiqueauction go last weekend?' because I remember that's where she was supposedly headed last Sunday.

That's one in the eye for my critics who say I'm, like, totally obsessed with myself.

'Fane,' she goes.

I'm like, 'Did you pick up that Victorian writing slope in the end?' even though I was never a hundred percent sure what it even was.

She doesn't give me a straight answer, just goes, 'What are yee dee-ing Frayday nait?'

I'm like, '*Friday* night? Er, nothing, as of yet. I'll swing out to Mala-hide, what, ten or eleven?'

'Tan or alavan? What do yee thank ay'm deeing horr – putting in a beety call tee dees in advonce?'

The answer is yes, but somehow I know it's not the answer she wants to hear.

I'm just there, 'Er . . .'

'Yee and may – it's not *jost* abite sax, is it?'

Shit. She sounds mullered. I'm thinking, okay, I definitely don't like where this is going, but I'll maybe just hear her out. 'I suppose not.'

'Ay mean, we *con* actually have a converseeshun, con't we?'

'Yeah, big-time. We've done it loads of times. Proved it.'

'Well, hoy abite danner, then?'

I laugh. I'm like, 'That all depends on what you're cooking,' trying to steer the conversation back to the topic of Ant and Decs.

She's there, 'Ay'm not talking abite cooking onythang. Ay'm talking about us going ite.'

'*Out?* Out where?'

'Where do yee thank? Tee a rastaurant.'

I'm there, 'Have you been drinking?'

'If lafe gavs yee lamons, pour gin on them – thot's what ay see.'

'I take it that's a yes.'

'Ay hod a couple of dranks with lonch – what's thot got to dee with onythang?'

'Nothing, I just . . . I just didn't think we were going to be *doing* public appearances.'

I realize straight away that I've said the wrong thing.

She's like, 'Poblic appearances? Are yee asheemed of may?'

I'm there, 'No.'

'Asheemed to be *seen* with may?'

'*Still* no.'

'Fock yee!' she suddenly screams down the phone. She sounds as pissed off as I've ever heard a girl, certainly since the time Sorcha found out that I stuffed her sister.

'Look, don't take it the wrong way,' I go, 'but going *out* for actual meals together – that's my definition of a relationship getting suddenly heavy. And we said we weren't going to let that happen, didn't we?'

'Och,' she goes, 'a watch worth thorty-*four* thisand – by the way – *isn't* havvy, but going ite for a bate teat is?'

This is a whole new Regina to the one I've been locking crotches with, as the mood suits. Women. They're all as focking mad as each other. Some can just keep the lid on it for longer.

I'm there, 'I can't believe you're bringing up the watch. *You* were the one who said there were no strings. Now it's, like, meals and who knows *what* else you've got planned.'

'So what *am* ay to yee then?'

'Calm down, Regina.'

'Noy, what *am* ay? Some old boot you can pop rind and hov sax with whenever it seets yee?'

'I'd hordly say you're an old boot. I'm on the record as saying Catherine Deneuve.'

'Fock yee!' she practically screams down the phone at me again. Then she just hangs up, leaving me standing in the middle of Foxrock Village, reflecting – I suppose – on the most important lesson that any of us can learn about women. It doesn't matter how perfect they appear at the beginning, there's always – and I mean *always* – a focking catch.

Look who it isn't! Sitting in the window of Cornucopia, that focking veggie place on Wicklow Street, wrapping her big smug face around a slice of – I don't know – baked Portobello mushroom quiche.

It's focking Giovanna.

Now, a lot of so-called sensible people would say, Ross, let it go, take the high road and blahdy blah. Except I can't resist it. You *could* say I'm stupid like that?

So in I go.

I stand over her table for a good ten seconds before she notices I'm even there. Too interested in her magazine orticle, which is about – hilariously – how the floods in Pakistan released 3,000 tonnes of dangerous pollutants into the environment.

'Looks fascinating,' I go. 'Real edge-of-your-seat stuff that,' and that's when she finally looks up. It takes her a second or two to place me, then she goes – not hello, by the way – but, 'Oh, yes,' like someone's just pointed out a knot in the wood panelling that looks vaguely like the face of Jesus.

So I go, 'Do you know what? I used to actually *laugh* at you? Oh, yeah. Back in the day. Ask Sorcha. When you had that focking café of yours in the George's Street Orcade and you were spouting your horseshit about how all the wars in the world were down to basically bad diet, I presumed you were just off your focking cake.'

'Spiritual nutrition,' she tries to go, 'has been accepted as very nearly a science in five American states.'

'Then when Sorcha came home one day and told me you were

taking dogs for yoga, I thought, whoa, maybe this girl's not bonkers at all – maybe she's just clever. And do you know what? That's what I think you *actually* are?'

I've obviously hit a nerve, roysh, because she goes, 'I'm trying to enjoy my lunch here.'

But I'm going nowhere – and I make that pretty much obvious. 'You were the one who told Sorcha to threaten me with a borring order?'

She rolls her eyes at me, actually *rolls* her eyes – I've a good mind to stick her focking face in that bulgur and sprouted bean salad – and goes, 'I counselled Sorcha . . .'

'Ha!'

'I *counselled* Sorcha – and yes, she *was* upset by what happened at the race – that she needed to remove certain negative forces – spiritual tumours, I call them – from her life.'

'You're saying I'm a tumour.'

'In a spiritual sense, yes, that's exactly what I'm saying. When Sorcha first joined my Healing Through Tai Chi class . . .'

'Jesus, how can you even say those words with a straight face?'

'. . . I recognized after barely half a session that there was something almost literally *sucking* the good energy from her.'

'Yeah, it happens to be called the recession. She lost her business.'

'It had nothing to *do* with her shop closing down. It was you.'

'Oh and I know it was you who told her to serve me with the divorce papers in Dax.'

She smiles at me, full of herself. 'In our universe, there are negative forces and positive forces. Or pluses and minuses. Sorcha is a plus. You're a – well, I'm sure you know what you are. Pluses, I told Sorcha, should be with other pluses. Because the only thing that a plus and a minus make is a great big zero.'

'Don't try to bamboozle me with your maths talk. How much do people even pay you for this bullshit?'

She doesn't answer – obviously still has *some* shame. Instead, she tries to have a pop at what *I* do for a living. She looks at the logo on my boilersuit – the words 'Shred Focking Everything' – and pulls a face, as if she finds it, I don't know, *distasteful*?

'I don't think you're in any position to criticize anyone for how they make their living,' she goes. 'I know what *you're* about. Destroying the evidence of how acquisitiveness and materialism brought about the spiritual vacuum that destroyed this country's economy. What a wonderful role model you are for your daughter,' and then she smiles, a real nasty smile. 'And, I gather, your son.'

Sorcha must have heard about Ro. Of course she did. She went to Mount Anville herself. It'll have been all over the past pupil Facebook site inside ten seconds.

'What would *you* know,' I go, 'about trying to bring up children right during the whole current economic blahdy blah?'

'I know it's not a time for – what was it you told Honor? – screwing people over?'

I'm there, 'I still stand by my analysis that it basically is. And you're one to talk about screwing people over. Taking money from poor fockers who've lost their – let's be honest here – *jobs*? Having them spouting nonsense while pulling karate poses in a field in Booterstown. It's a wonder you can keep a straight face long enough to take their credit cord details.'

She shakes her head, roysh, as if *she* feels sorry for *me*? 'You have a very damaged aura,' she goes, 'and I'm not even going to get into your chakra.'

There's no way I'm going to let anyone diss me like that – even though I haven't a bog what she's even talking about. All I know is that she needs to be put in her focking box.

I stick my finger up my nose and rip out – this is going to sound disgusting – but a dirty big nostril goblin, which I then go to dip into her orange, carrot and ginger smoothie.

I've never seen anyone move so quick. And I've played charity sevens with David Wallace, remember. She's up off the stool like it's burning her orse cheeks and she lands – I'm not making this up – in an actual mortial orts pose. Now, correct me if I'm wrong, roysh, but I thought tai chi was supposed to be, like, *defensive*?

Before I get a chance to point out this small fact to Giovanna, though, she reaches out her hand and grabs me by the pretty much windpipe. I'm instantly choking, to the point where I think she might actually strangle me to death, with one hand, here in Cornucopia.

Which is supposedly a health food place, by the way.

She fixes me with this look, roysh – we're talking pure evil – and she goes, 'Eat it.'

I'm like, 'What?' struggling to get the word even out.

I've a good idea where this is going, though.

'That thing on your finger,' she goes. 'That you were about to dip into my smoothie. Eat it.'

I'm there, 'I'll actually just . . . wipe it on my chinos if it's . . . all the same to you.'

I feel her hand tighten around my throat. My actual face must be blue. I look around. Pretty much everyone in the place is staring in our direction. And not one of them steps in to save me, by the way. Yeah, cruelty to animals is wrong, but cruelty to the Rossmeister – well, that's a focking spectator sport.

I'm there, 'I wasn't going to actually . . . dip it in your drink,' which is a lie, of course.

'Eat it,' she again goes.

I can feel my, like, eyes bulging and my face is, like, burning hot. I realize that I'm going to have to do what she says. Otherwise, I'm going to die right here and now.

I look at it, roysh, there on the end of my finger, covering the entire focking tip, all green and slimy, like something you'd see seeping through the walls in a haunted focking house.

'In the name . . . of God,' I try to go, 'don't . . . make me do it.'

She's like, 'If you don't eat it, I can you promise you this, Ross – you've already taken your last breath.'

In other words, I've no actual choice. So I move my finger to my lips. Then I use one or two of my famous visualization techniques from my rugby days to try to convince my brain that it's, like, *guacamole*?

A lot of people in the restaurant go, 'Eeeuuuwww!' and turn away, unable to even watch. And these are, like, vegetarians, remember – imagine the kind of shit that's passed their teeth over the years.

I put it in my mouth, using my bottom teeth to scrape it off my finger, then it sits there on my tongue.

'Swallow it,' Giovanna goes. Everyone in the restaurant has their hands up to their faces. 'I want to watch it go down.'

So I do what I'm told. She releases my windpipe enough to let it slide down – which it does, like a bad focking oyster.

'Now,' she goes, 'tell me it was delicious.'

'Jesus . . . What?'

'Say, "Yum yum."'

'Oh, for fock's . . . Yum yum.'

It's only then that she lets go of my throat. Like I said, the girl's not mad. She's, like, evil.

I see Oisinn walking along Appian Way with a dog. And I'm talking about an *actual* dog. It's unfortunate, but, given the dude's history, it's necessary to add that detail.

I pull over the van, then out the window I go, 'Dude, what the fock?' and even *he* laughs at the, I suppose, madness of it. I'm like, 'What kind of dog even *is* it?'

He goes, 'It's a Chow Chow,' trying to make it sound like the most natural thing in the world. 'It's my old dear's.'

He walks over to the van and the thing storts sniffing the focking tyres.

'I don't get it,' I go.

He's there, 'What don't you get?'

'Well, what's the angle here?'

He laughs. 'There's no angle, Ross. I'm taking my old dear's dog for a walk.'

I'm just like, 'Oh.'

Oisinn looks well, it has to be said. I'm beginning to think that bankruptcy actually suits him.

'So,' he goes, a smile suddenly appearing on his lips, 'how's the, er, Widow Rathfriland?'

I just shake my head. I'm like, 'Do you remember what I used to say about older women?'

He nods. 'They've got tits like balloon animals and they taste of Polident.'

'Okay, I did say that,' I go, 'but that was in specific reference to that focking clunker that *you* were with that night in Leggs. No, what I used to say was that they were no different to younger women. They crack on to be cool at the stort – not interested in a relationship, only looking for a bit of fun and all the usual lines. Then you realize as time goes on that they want the exact same thing as every other woman – in other words, ownership. I just forgot that.'

Oisinn gives the dog's chain a shorp yank. The thing's a bit impatient to be off but Oisinn knows he has to hear this. 'What happened?' he goes.

I'm there, 'She wanted me to go out for a meal with her.'

'A *meal*? Jesus.'

'It's good to hear someone else say that, Dude. Because *she* acted like it was the most natural thing in the world.'

'A *meal*? Did she definitely say go *out* for a meal?'

'Dude, she even mentioned a restaurant.'

'Shit the bed. But you can't afford to be seen out with her.'

'Oh, but she doesn't respect that fact.'

'She's old enough to be your . . .'

'Exactly. I thought it went without saying that it was a no public appearances jobbie. She flipped the tits when I mentioned it, though. She'd a few drinks on her, in fairness. That's when the truth usually comes out, see. Actually quoted to me how much this watch cost her.'

'That's out of order.'

'It's big-time out of order. And she knows it herself. She's left one or two messages apologizing but I'm not going to bother my hole ringing her back. I mean, she was the one who said there were no strings. Which turned out to be horseshit. Like it *always* does with women. They've got more strings than the RTÉ focking Concert Orchestra.'

He smiles. 'What about the sex? You'll miss that.'

'I don't know if I will.'

'You said it was some of the best you've ever had.'

'Dude, I'm still capable of doing better than a widow of, like, sixty.'

'I know – you're still one of Ireland's most eligible married men.'

'Not for much longer once this divorce goes through. And can I remind you that there are still a lot of young, free and single girls out there – and I emphasize the word young – who haven't yet had the pleasure of my company. What are you doing Friday night?'

'Friday?'

'Yeah. Thought I might stort revisiting some of my old fishing grounds – see have they been restocked. I was thinking maybe Dalkey.'

'Can't. I'm Keith Flint.'

'Dude, I'll give you moo.'

'Nah. Like a lot of people out there, Ross, I'm just going to have to learn to live within my new means.'

'Sounds like crazy talk to me. But, hey, I'm a lone wolf anyway. When have I ever needed a hunting portner?'

★ ★ ★

It's obvious that she's never heard of Julianna Margulies, although she takes it as a compliment anyway. I could give a correspondence course in talking women horizontal. And I might yet. Pretty much every goy in The Queens is looking over, in a jealous but at the same time admiring way, obviously thinking, I wish I had his confidence, but all the same, fair focks.

'She's an actress,' I hear her friend tell her out of the side of her mouth. 'I think she's in, like, *Snakes on a Plane*?'

'Oh,' I go, 'you better *believe* she's in *Snakes on a Plane*,' which possibly sounded a lot slicker in my head than when I said it out loud.

There's, like, four of them, by the way, and they're all American, which I knew the second I walked through the door and copped them sitting in their little huddle around a low table. A lot of Septics end up in here because it's in all the tourist guides. Once I saw the pink North Face pac-a-macs and the four glasses of Guinness on the table, untouched, I immediately knew where they were coming from. And where one lucky winner among them is going later.

'The States?' I go, really laying on the chorm. 'I presume you're over here on holiday slash vacation.'

She – as in the bird I've decided I'm going to have a crack at – goes, 'Yeah. We came out on here, like, the DART train? Because we read that the Guinness is, like, *so* amazing?'

I go, 'There's a lot of things in here that are *so* amazing,' just to keep the conversation going. 'The name's Ross by the way.'

'Oh, this is Justice,' she goes, introducing me to her friends, 'Alexia, Leandra. And I'm Egwene.'

She says this just as I'm throwing back a gobful of the old Dutch master and I end up nearly showering them with it. It's true, it really does pay to pack a mac.

'Egwene?' I go, trying to get my shit together. 'Egwene! What a, em . . . What a beautiful name.'

Which it isn't, of course. It belongs on a poster in a GP's waiting room, warning about the dangers of not bagging it up – in between molluscum contagiosum and genital warts.

I don't say that, of course. I just go, 'Can I . . .' and I sort of, like, indicate the seat with my head.

'Of course,' she goes, then Alexia, who's sitting to her right, must know the score, because she throws her legs to one side to let me squeeze in beside – focking hilarious – *Egwene*.

'So,' I go, trying to, I suppose, gauge the size of the job in front of me, 'do you have, like, a boyfriend back home?'

'Yes,' she goes, except she says it a bit *too* quickly? Then I notice this look pass between the rest of them. It's obviously complicated.

It's Leandra who goes, 'Egwene, you have *got* to be kidding,' and then she turns to me and goes, 'She's been with a guy for the past three years who's, like, a total jerk. They're on, like, a *break*?' and she sort of, like, punctuates the word with her, I suppose, *index* fingers?

Egwene's obviously embarrassed. She's like, 'Leandra, he asked for time to decide what he wants and I said I'd give him that time.'

I decide, roysh, that I need to take chorge of the situation here. 'God,' I go, doing my best to look angry, 'why do guys have to *be* like that?' and I can instantly feel all four sets of eyes on me. 'The sad thing is that they end up giving the good ones a bad name.'

One of the things I love about American women is how easily taken in they are. 'Well, *you* seem really decent,' Alexia – as if to prove my point – goes, and I just shrug and try to look all humble.

I'm there, with a totally straight face, 'All I'm saying is that not all goys hurt.'

Justice is the only one who seems to see through me. She's giving me the hord stare and I know she's dubious. In any group of girls, there's always an Ugly Friend with Reservations. They're Mother Nature's way of keeping the human population down. 'I can't believe you're actually buying that,' she goes to Egwene, not giving a shit whether or not I hear her.

Alexia, who's sitting to my right, tries to draw my attention away from the little debate that breaks out between the others. She asks me where I'm from and I tell her that these would be pretty much my streets. Then I ask her the same question and she says they're all students in, like, Gainesville, Florida, and with my other ear I'm listening to the threeway between the others, wondering is Justice succeeding in tamping down Egwene's obvious passion for me.

She's telling her that I'm just another sweet-talker, although I've a definite friend in Leandra, who's saying she thinks I seem like – oh my God – *such* a lovely person.

I swear to fock, I'm suddenly horder than a farmer with a rifle.

'Okay,' Egwene suddenly goes, standing up, 'I need to use the little girls' room,' and she sort of, like, carefully edges herself out of the seat, trying not to knock the drinks over. I point her in the direction of the jacks and off she goes. I'm sat there admiring her fundament when something immediately strikes me as odd. It's, like, the way she *moves*? She sort of, like, shuffles rather than walks. So I look down and I notice – with a fright that actually has me mouthing the word 'Fock!' – that Egwene is pregnant.

I'm not the only one who notices either, judging from one or two sniggers I hear from the other, let's just say, patrons?

Now, shallow as this is going to make me sound, my first instinct is to make like the shepherds in the Bible story and get the flock out of there fast. Because Egwene's way down the road – we're talking seven or eight months from the looks of her, maybe more – and I can't suddenly switch my attentions to one of her mates, just because I've lost interest in her. This isn't Wesley. Although I often think that life would be much simpler if it was.

No, I realize, with the instinct of a man who's found himself in a thousand situations like this before, there's nothing in this for me and I need to bail. Except Justice has noticed that *I've* noticed? She obviously copped me staring and now she's looking at me, roysh, with her eyebrows raised, as if to say, okay, let's see what a decent guy you *really* are.

'Is everything okay?' she even goes to me, obviously loving my sudden discomfort.

I hear, like, more laughter from the other side of the pub.

I'm there, 'I, er, might actually hit the bor,' thinking that if I can just squeeze past Alexia, I *could* make a run for the actual door. My speed over the first twenty yords was one of the things I was famous for back in the day, of course. Yeah, I could be sat at the bor in Finnegan's, enjoying a pint of something responsible, before the first, 'What an asshole!' slips anyone's lips.

'No, *I'll* get the drinks,' Alexia has to go then. 'I've realized I don't actually *like* Guinness? I think I'll get, like, a soda? What do you want?'

I'm there, 'Er – pint of, like, Heineken?'

'Heineken,' she goes, then up she gets.

I'm sat there, thinking, okay, I've *got* to get the fock out of here before Egwene gets back from the Josh Ritter. Leandra tells Justice that they – oh my God – *have* to do one of those *baton mouche* cruises down

223

the Liffey and I take advantage of the diversion to sort of, like, lean low to my right and try to, like, slip out of the seat – I presume *unseen*?

Except Justice is one of those birds with a focking inbuilt motion sensor.

'Where are you going, Ross?' she goes, when I'm, like, three quarters of the way out of the seat. And I just freeze, roysh, staring down at the floor. Of course I don't get a chance to come up with some really, really clever explanation, because she goes, 'He was trying to sneak out.'

Alexia suddenly arrives back from the bor, going, 'Sneak out? What are you talking about?'

'Oh,' she goes, straight out with it, 'he saw that Egwene was pregnant and decided he wasn't interested anymore – exactly like Nathan.'

He must be the father – poor focker.

Of course I end up having to defend myself. 'That's horseshit.'

'I saw him mouth the word "fuck",' Justice goes. 'He's an asshole.'

I'm like, 'I was in shock, that's all. I'd hordly say it makes me an asshole.'

Of course the next thing, roysh, Egwene comes waddling back from the jacks and catches the end of the conversation. She's there, '*Who's* an asshole?'

I should say at this point that the regulars in The Queens are loving this. See, most of them know my M.O. I just roll in there like a focking bowling ball, sending skittles flying everywhere. The entire boozer is glued to what's happening now. It's very much a case of pull up a seat and enjoy the show.

'He tried to sneak out,' Justice goes.

Egwene's like, 'Sneak out? Why?'

'Well, why don't you ask him?'

Egwene turns to me, her big sad eyes looking for an explanation. It's such a pity about the other thing, roysh, because she *is* an actual looker.

You can hear everyone in the pretty much pub thinking, okay, how's the Rossmeister General going to get out of this one? Where's his famous ability to change the direction of the play now and are we going to see any evidence of it here tonight?

Of course, cometh the hour and all the rest of it.

'I wasn't sneaking out,' I hear my voice suddenly go. 'I was, er, looking for my contact lens.'

'Your contact lens?'

'Yeah. On the, er, floor. I actually *thought* I felt it pop out?'

Egwene's hands instantly shoot out, pushing me and Alexia back, while she storts suddenly studying the floor. 'Be careful where you're stepping,' she goes.

I'm like, 'Er, cool.'

Then she suddenly gets down on her knees and – with her big pregnant belly dragging along the ground – storts, like, patting the floor with the palm of her hand.

She's soon joined by Alexia and, seconds later, by Leandra. I can hear, I suppose, *muffled* laughter coming from various ports of the bor and I'm honestly struggling to keep it in myself. I look up and give these two dudes who I know to see – Blackrock, but actually sound – a big wink. They just shake their heads as if to say, will he ever change? And more to the point, would we even want him to? Because we'd miss this.

Of course, Justice cops the dirty big grin on my face. She hasn't budged, by the way. 'Are you not going to help them?' she ends up just going.

I'm there, 'Sorry?'

'Look for your contact lens? You're just going to let *them* do it, are you? Including a woman who's, like, pregnant?'

Obviously, she *knows* there's no contact lens, but what she's trying to do, it's pretty clear, is shame me into getting down on my hands and knees as well. Which, as it happens, is exactly what I end up *having* to do? So I'm suddenly down on all fours too, running my hand over the tiles and now – I can hear it – there's actual out and out laughter everywhere in the bor.

I'm catching various people's eyes and really, like, hamming it up for them.

'I'm practically blind without my lenses,' I go, the big joke being that my vision is, like, twenty-twenty – anyone who ever saw me play rugby realizes that, of course.

'Is that it there?' Egwene goes. She's crawled practically over to the restaurant entrance.

Alexia's like, 'No, it's piece of plastic – I think from, like, a *cigarette* pack?'

My chinos are getting focking filthy, by the way. But in my head, roysh, I'm thinking, okay, Ross, if you crawl *around* the bor, you could actually make a run for the *back* door, then escape through the basically *beer* gorden? With laughter and applause ringing in your ears, obviously.

All of a sudden, roysh, I find myself staring at a pair of black Barkers that seem weirdly familiar. Then a voice above me goes, 'What the hell are you doing down there?'

Oh, for fock's sake!

I look up at him. I'm like, 'I'm, er, looking for my contact lens.'

Luckily, this seems to just wash over him.

'Oh,' he just goes, then he sees Justice sitting there, and the other three birds, I don't know, scrabbling around on the floor. 'I'm Charles,' he just goes. 'Ross's *old dad*, as he famously calls me.'

I sit back on my sort of, like, haunches and go, 'Er, what are you even doing here?'

'Well,' he just goes, looking all proud of himself, 'it's a night for celebration!'

I'm like, 'Celebration? What are you talking about?'

I'll say this for them – the crowd in The Queens are certainly getting their money's worth tonight.

He's there, 'Your sister and Fionn – they're back from Milan. They got engaged, Ross!'

I look across the bor and there the two of them are, laughing away at some private joke. The light catches the chunk of ice on Erika's finger and it ends up nearly blinding me, even from this distance. They both look – I'm going to have to admit it – amazing.

The old man's like, 'It's going to be a wedding, I can tell you, that'll give the lie to all this talk of record budget deficits and rising fears in the bond market as to our ability to repay exchequer borrowings. Full point, new par.'

I notice Helen there as well, with a glass of champagne in her hand, smiling, happy, like the other two – totally full of themselves.

It's Erika who notices me. She practically does a double-take when she sees me down on the floor, with the three birds on their knees around me. Even knowing my rep. She says something to Fionn, which I don't actually catch, then *he* looks over and the two of them just crack their holes laughing – as does Helen, by the way, and she'd usually be the first one defending me.

Erika holds her left hand out in front of her and admires the ring along the length of her orm. Then she turns and she kisses Fionn on the lips. And *he* loves it, of course. He knows how focking lucky he's just got.

The next thing I hear is a splash. At first, roysh, I think that someone's knocked over their drink and it's the sound of, like, Guinness spilling onto the tiled floor. Except all of the girls suddenly freeze. And there's, like, one or two gasps of breath around me as well.

And then I hear another splash – a bigger one this time. And it's pretty much obvious that Egwene's waters have broken.

'Quick,' Justice screams. 'Someone call 911. Or whatever it is for you guys.'

'It's coming!' Egwene goes, as the girls manoeuvre her into, like, a sitting position and tell her to remember the breathing exercises.

I'm just standing there with my mouth open, looking stupid as usual.

'Wait a minute,' the old man suddenly goes. 'Ross, you don't even wear contact lenses!'

So I'm porked outside Donnybrook Fair, the plan being to grab just a quick pastrami on rye for my lunch, between shredding jobs.

I notice I have a missed call from Regina. The third in five days. Came while I was in the back of the van, destroying documents for a company that, let's just say, we all know well.

I hit 171, then listen.

She says long time, no spake, in a sort of, like, jokey way, then says look, she can understand – *wontherstond* – why I'm still mad at her. She was ite of order that tame. Shouldn't have been putting prassure on me lake thot. The drink talking more than onythang. But she really masses me, though – especially us deeing it. I dee it for her lake no mon ever hoz. And good and all as her vaybreetor is, it's nay sobstitute – especially when she has to cheenge the botteries twace a dee!

Anyway, she says, she'd appreciate it if I let her know where she stonds – where *we* stond – one way or the other. She says she's heading to Urlingford tomorrow for the week, presumably to this health and wellness spa of hers, and she'd really appreciate a call before she goes.

It'll tell you what a nice goy I am, roysh, that I actually *do* consider ringing her back. See, I'm a sucker for a compliment and that line she threw in about me being better than her dildo made me think, fock it,

227

maybe I *will* ring her – might even pop out there later for a quick park and ride.

Then I think, on second thoughts, no. Aport from the whole going-out-for-a-meal-together thing, there's something, I don't know, desperate about the way she's chasing around after me. In my mind, she's no longer the sexy, independent cougar she was a week ago.

Lack of self-respect is a quality I love only up to a point.

So I end up deleting her voice message. Then, when I get out of the van, I end up just killing her number as well. I do it just as I'm walking into Donnybrook Fair.

And it's then, roysh, just as I'm answering yes to 'Delete Contact?' that I hear a voice that stops me in my actual tracks.

It's like, 'Oh my God, you are *such* a sap, I'm actually *embarrassed* for you?'

There's no mistaking it. What father couldn't recognize the voice of his own daughter?

From the closeness of it, I can tell that she's on her way out of the shop. Then I hear Sorcha's voice – hassled – go, 'I'm telling you, Honor, tap water is every bit as good as bottled.'

How many parents are going to be telling their kids that in the Ireland of the future?

'You've really upset me today,' Sorcha goes.

Honor's there, 'Yeah, if you're looking for pity, it's between pathetic and *puh-lease* in the dictionary.'

I'm wondering does she pick these sayings up from TV.

'Honor, please stop speaking to me like that.'

'Like what?'

'Like you think I'm stupid.'

'Er, if the shoe fits, buy it in every colour.'

That's when they step through the doors of the shop and they're suddenly stood in front of me on Morehampton Road. They both stand there just staring at me. It takes another good three or four seconds for it to sink in, before Honor comes running straight into my orms, going, 'Daddy!'

It's an amazing moment – possibly one of the best of my life – as I scoop her up and squeeze her nearly to death.

I'm going, 'Hey, Honor!' and she's giving it, 'I missed you!' and I'm going, 'I missed you too, Babes! I missed you too!'

The next thing I hear is Sorcha's voice, all stern, go, 'Honor, get into the cor!'

She must also press the button on the key, roysh, because the headlights on the RAV 4 porked two spaces up suddenly flash. Honor turns around and looks at her, obviously trying to gauge how serious she is.

'Now!' Sorcha goes, so I put Honor down and tell her to maybe just do what her mother says. Which is exactly what she does, roysh, although not without shooting Sorcha a filthy on her way past and asking her under her breath what her actual issue is?

I laugh, trying to keep it light. I'm like, '*Lame*? Pathetic and puh-lease? That's some stock of one-liners she's building up.'

Sorcha narrows her eyes and goes, 'I can handle her, thank you very much.'

'I wasn't saying it as a criticism. She talks like a girl nearly twice her age.'

Sorcha looks incredible. There's no point in me saying otherwise.

I try to keep the conversation pleasant. 'I suppose you heard about Erika and Fionn getting engaged,' I go. 'Although I'm still dubious about it even going ahead. There's still time to stop it, is all I'm saying.'

But she just cuts me off by going, 'What, are you stalking us now?'

I'm like, 'Stalking you?'

She's there, 'Ross, I have my rape alarm – in my bag.'

I go, 'Rape alorm? Sorcha, this isn't us!'

'Anything you have to say to me, Ross, you can say through my solicitor.'

I'm like, 'This is Giovanna's doing. She's, like, brainwashed you against me – because I'm the only one who can see her for the scam ortist that she basically is. Did you hear she made me eat my own snot? This was in, like, Cornucopia, of all places.'

She just roars at me, loud enough for an elderly couple coming out of Hampton Books to stop and ask if she wants them to call the Gords. 'Oh my God,' Sorcha screams, 'just stay away from me!'

I watch her walk back to the cor, then pull out of her space without even checking her rear-view mirror and the driver of a 46A has to practically mill the breaks to avoid hitting her.

I tell the elderly couple to keep their focking noses out of other

229

people's business in future, then I stand there in the middle of Donnybrook with my hort actually breaking.

It takes me a good three or four minutes to get my shit together enough to go into the shop and wander over to the deli counter. It turns out to be the bird who's a ringer for Jennifer Metcalfe who's on sandwich duty today, except for once there's no flirting from me. 'Just tell me you've got pastrami,' is all I go, 'because I don't think I can take any more bad news today.'

Of course, at that point, I don't even know the half of it. See, my advice for people who think they've hit rock bottom is not to worry – believe me, there's always plenty focking further for you to fall.

My phone suddenly rings in my pocket. I answer it because, deep down, I'm hoping it's Sorcha, admitting how bang out of order she just was and asking me if I wanted to bring Honor to Dundrum Shopping Centre or wherever this weekend. But when I hold the phone up to my ear, it's not Sorcha at all. It's the sound of a man crying.

I'm like, 'Hello?' I actually say it two or three times. 'Hello? Who even is this?'

'It's Laddy,' the voice eventually goes. 'Ye fooken pox, Rosser. Ye doorty fooken pox.'

I'm there, 'What?' still hoping against hope that I've got the wrong end of the stick as usual.

'You and me, we were mates, Rosser. We were fooken mates.'

I'm like, 'See, I would have considered us more as neighbours who basically got *along* okay?'

'You fooken gev her the royid. She fooken toalt me you gev her the royid.'

I realize there's no point in me denying it.

I'm just there, 'I'm not sure if this changes anything, Larry, but *she* very much came on to *me?*'

'Changes nothing,' he just goes, between sobs. 'You're a fooken dead man, Rosser. You're a fooken dead man walken.'

7. The getaway package

She moves through the water like a focking eel, in fairness to her. I'm just standing there in the pretty much blackness, watching her do lap after lap of the vitality pool, her little pink swimming hat moving from side to side and her orms – sleek, if that's a word, as well as tanned – coming up out of the water, and just, like, powering her along.

She *has* great orms and I'm only mentioning it as a statement of fact.

She climbs out of the water – wearing the same Ed Hardy tattoo-print bikini that Sorcha has, I notice – whips a towel off one of the heated tiled loungers and storts drying herself off, her face first, then her shoulders and orms. She takes off the swimming hat and shakes her hair loose, then scrapes it all back and ties it up with the bobbin that was on her wrist. Then she dries the rest of herself – stomach, back, legs and, finally, feet.

That's when she cops me, leaning against the door of the amethyst crystal steam-room, caught in the indigo beam of one of the mood uplighters. I catch the flash of her teeth as she smiles and says this is a nice surprise.

A nace suprays.

She's absolutely delighted to see me. All her focking Christmases and blahdy blah.

I wander over to where she's stood and decide to play it, like, uber cool.

'Thought I'd take a day or two out,' I go. 'See what Urlingford had to offer.'

Fock-all is the answer, if the drive through the town was anything to go by. A church, a Centra, two pubs and people with enormous eyebrows being cute with their money.

What a place to stick a hotel. It possibly explains why it's focking empty, despite the fact that it was long-listed for the 2005 Residential Spa of the Year award at the Professional Beauty Awards in London.

'Yee gat may mossige, then,' Regina goes, handing me a bottle of

231

moisturizer while *she* lies face-down on the lounger. I take it as an invitation to rub this shit into her back. 'Ay dudn't thank yee were going tee come.'

What I don't mention, of course, is that I had to get out of Dodge for a few days, because one of Ireland's most ruthless gangland killers is threatening to murder me for giving his girlfriend the beans. News like that might really spoil the atmosphere of – what is it the ad on the radio called it? – relaxed timelessness and contemporary grace?

'Look, I'm sorry I haven't been returning your calls,' I go. 'It just weirded me out – all that talk of meals and, I don't know, whatever else was going to follow on from that.'

I squeeze the tube and the stuff squirts into my palm. It smells of, like, ginseng and, you'd have to say, juniper. I rub my hands together and warm it up.

'Look, *ay'm* sawry,' she goes. 'Ay shouldn't have been putting prassure on yee like thot. Toddy always said thot abite may – always want tee moch, tee seen.'

I'm there, 'Hey, don't get me wrong, the sex is fantastic. But as for the whole wandering-around-town-like-we're-an-actual-couple thing, I'm just not there yet. There's a hell of an age difference. I hate to keep reminding you of that fact.'

I stort massaging the cream into her back and neck. She doesn't say shit for about a minute or so, then she goes, '*Ay've* got tee learn tee enjoy thangs for what they are. See, *ay'm* a plonner – always thanking one step ahead. That's why *ay* was always the breens behaind the basniss. Always thanking of the naxt steege. It's hoy may breen works, see.'

I just nod. 'If I was asked to come up with a really short sentence to sum up *my* whole – I'm going to call it – philosophy on life, it'd have to be just enjoy the moment.'

She laughs – I think in a good way. 'Ay'm not going to denay it – you've hod an amazing affect on may.'

'Hey, *don't* deny it, then.'

'Do you know what may frands keep seeing?'

I focking knew that her friends were involved. This all storted after she had lunch that day with Levinus – or whatever the fock he was called – and his wife. I can tell you from long and sorry experience that

232

it's always *friends* who put the pressure on to define relationships beyond the actual physical.

'They keep seeing, "When are we gonna meet this nee mustery mon of yeers?" They thank *ay've* cheenged, see.'

'In a good way?'

'Ay don't know. They jost see ay've cheenged.'

There's, like, silence for a couple of minutes, then she suddenly goes, 'Jesus, will yee put some meat intee ut. Supposed tee be a massorge – you're nat slapping cheap emulsion ontee a wall, yee know.'

I'm like, 'Sorry, I'm just a bit cream crackered from the drive. By the way, what even county are we in?'

'Forget you're in any cointay,' she goes. 'You're in a unique hadeaway of devane alagince that will help yee reconnact with your sanses.'

I laugh. 'Yeah, no, I actually heard the ad on the way down here.'

She turns her head around to look at me. The next thing, she's suddenly propped up on one elbow, sizing me up.

'Hey,' she goes, a definite smile in her eye, 'do yee know what *ay* thank would relox yee?' and she makes an instant grab for the belt of my chinos, her mouth already working like she's bobbing for apples.

'No!' I go, pushing her away.

There's no hiding the disappointment on her face. She's like, 'Yee've naver said no before.'

The truth is, roysh, that since she revealed her whole desperate, post-menopausal side to me, I wouldn't be a hundred percent sure I could achieve and sustain. She's no longer Catherine Deneuve in my mind. I suppose a nice way of putting it is that it'd be like trying to thread a wet noodle into a Chubb lock.

'Not *here*,' I just go, which sounds weak, I realize.

'Jesus, yee've naver been packy abite where we dee ut before.'

'Er, this is the swimming pool?'

'Vatoloty pool.'

'Vitality, then. My point still stands. What if someone walks in?'

She makes another grab for my general crotch area but I managed to, like, fend it off.

She's like, 'Hoy's gonnee walk un?'

I'm there, 'Er, another *guest*, for example?'

'There *aren't* any other gasts. *Ay* own the place, remambor?' and she makes a third grab for me. This time she manages to rip open my chino buttons and worm her actual hand inside.

From her reaction, it's pretty obvious she's surprised to find it so quiet in the old Beacon South Quarter.

'I possibly need to just chillax first,' I go and she just nods, roysh, cracking on not to be disappointed – we *all* know that look – then says, well, I'm definitely in the right place for that.

She stands up, picks her robe off its peg and puts it on, tying the belt in a way that I'd have to describe as *frustrated*? 'Come on,' she goes, walking off, 'let's get yee *ite* of those clothes for storters.'

I follow her through a door into what turns out to be the meditation room. There's, like, nine or ten low beds facing an entire wall of, like, floor-to-ceiling windows, through which you can stare out at the Zen gorden while breathing in spearmint and eucalyptus oils and listening to the music of The Eagles played on the Andean panpipes.

It *would* actually chill you out – if you didn't know that on the other side of that little gathering of tall bamboos out there is the focking cor pork for Horvey Norman.

Regina is rooting around for a robe for me.

I notice a little table laid out with herbal teas and fresh fruit and jugs of iced water and little bowls filled with, I don't know, Brazil nuts and dried apricots and sunflower seeds. It makes me think of Sorcha and how much she loved places like this, and how she always bought a candle for thirty or forty snots in the spa, and said that she was going to remember to, like, breathe more when she got home and to – oh my God – *actually* relax, and how she always got me to stop at a petrol station on the way home to buy dried banana chips, which ended up never being opened and are probably still in the focking cupboard in Newtownpork Avenue.

That was the Celtic Tiger, though – we all did that kind of thing.

'Yee're nat gonna put thos on over yeer clothes, are yee?'

Regina's found me a robe.

'Sorry,' I go, suddenly remembering to undress, 'I was just feeling a bit – I don't even care if it's a word or not – but *notalgish*?'

She laughs. 'Tell me abite ut. See thos room? Ay remambor dees when there'd be thortay, maybe fortay people, sitting iteside thot door, waiting for a bad to lay dine on.'

234

I take off the old Apple Crumble and just shake my head. I'm like, 'Queuing to get into a relaxation room. Would that be considered ironic? Because it certainly sounds like the kind of thing that should be.'

She goes, 'Modness, is what it was,' and I end up having to agree with her.

I'm there, 'It *was* an amazing thing in our lives. In all of our lives.'

I step out of the old boxer shorts and her eyes – I can't *help* but notice? – linger on the old people-pleaser. She's seriously gumming for me and she looks – I'm going to have to admit this – still disappointed that I'm not trying to actually hop her.

I decide I should offer her maybe one or two words of comfort. 'Give me, like, a day here,' I go, pulling on the robe, 'and I guarantee you, we'll be at it like knackers' dogs.'

'Just go and lay dine,' she goes, 'and give your mithe a rast,' which is exactly what I end up doing. I close my eyes and do the whole chilling-out thing for ten, maybe fifteen minutes, with Regina lying down on the bed next to mine.

'Sorcha's a massive fan of the old panpipes,' I, at some point, go. 'Remember the wife I told you about? I don't know if she has this particular album, but she's definitely got, like, Simon and Garfunkel, Disney, Andrew Lloyd Webber – all that shit, like I said, played on the actual panpipes.'

'They're vory relaxing.'

'I don't know if that's true in Sorcha's case. Most of them she hasn't even taken out of the plastic . . .'

Regina laughs, in fairness to her.

'Honestly, she has a big stack of them next to the panini press. Every time she goes to make herself a sandwich, she gets stressed about not having made a dent in those CDs she bought to – oh my God – *supposedly* relax . . .'

She *really* laughs at that. I think she finds me genuinely hilarious – possibly another reason why she's obviously fallen so hord for me.

I'm there, 'I mean, it's all pressure, isn't it? It's like all those books you see. 1001 *Albums You Have To Hear Before You Die*. 1001 *Books*. 1001 *Films*. Jesus! Before you *die*? Someone's always reminding you that you're on a focking clock . . . Sorry, Regina, I can be quite deep. I don't even know where it comes from half the time.'

235

There's, like, silence between us then for a couple of minutes. 'Ay *hod* to get away,' she eventually goes, totally out of the blue, 'from that wee batch.'

She means her daughter – I know that without even asking. Hedda. Focking *Header* is possibly more the case.

'Jesus Craist, the otmosphere in the hise is unborrable.'

I end up losing it, despite the whole supposedly relaxed vibe. '*What is her issue?*' I go. 'You'd think she'd be focking delighted for you, pulling a goy – not being big-headed – but thirty years younger than you.'

'She's jallous.'

'Jealous? I don't know about that. I'm usually good at picking up vibes when a bird is into me. I have to admit, I got very few from her.'

'Ay don't mean she's jallous of yee. She's jallous that *ay'm* gatting some and she's nat.'

I'm thinking, we don't know for definite that you're getting some. I maybe shouldn't have promised her that I'd be back on the case tomorrow. It's like a focking drum-roll in my ears.

'How do you know she's not getting any?' I go. 'I mean, she's, what, eighteen, nineteen?'

She goes, 'Because she's celibate,' and she says it in a sort of, like, a sneery way?

Well, I'm one to talk, because I end up sneering as well. I'm like, 'Celibate? Jesus, what's the focking point of that?'

'A lot of these – emos, they call thomsalves – they cheese tee obstain from sax.'

I just laugh. 'It's no wonder they look so focking miserable, then. Outside the Central Bank on a Saturday afternoon. God, I've been at Protestant funerals with more focking smiles.'

That's when I suddenly remember Toddy.

'Sorry,' I go, 'I didn't mean any . . .'

She cuts me off – either didn't cop it or it didn't bother her. 'Ay thank you're rait, though. Bloody good seeing-tee is what the gorl needs.'

I laugh. Then a sudden thought enters my head. Ah, you can probably guess what it is because you know how much I love a challenge. Except then I picture her – she looks like she's been rescued by the Order of Malta from the mosh pit of a Sleater Kinney gig – and I quickly banish the idea.

I'm like, 'I don't know any goy who'd be brave enough to go there. No offence, Regina, I know she's your daughter and everything, but she's actually behaving like a – well, you used the word yourself – basically bitch. She's practically driven you out of your own home.'

'She's still bleeming may for Toddy's dath.'

'That's horsh.'

'It's tree, though. She thanks if *ay* hodn't asked him for divorce – if ay'd forgaven him, you know, for your soster – then he'd still be alave todee. And meebay she's rait.'

'You shouldn't think like that.'

'Well,' she goes, 'ay jost needed a breek from her, is all. A dee or toy here and ay'll be fine.'

I continue just staring out into the old Zen gorden, breathing in the eucalyptus and listening to a tune I recognize as 'Hotel California'. Through a gap in the tall bamboo, I can see a dude pushing the back seat of his Saab 9-3 forward to fit a Samsung 42-inch plasma into it. 'I've the exact same TV as that,' I hear myself go, 'except mine's not HD ready.'

Then I must fall asleep, during the silence that greets this news. Because the next I know, Regina is standing over me and she's sort of, like, shaking me awake, going, 'Ross! Ross! Ross!'

I open my eyes. Must have been more wrecked than I actually thought.

'Hoy's Lorry?' she goes.

It would not be an exaggeration to say that my bowels pretty much nearly give way. I'm like, 'What?'

'Lorry,' she goes.

I'm there, 'Is he here? He's no one. How the fock did he find me?'

'He dudn't,' she goes. 'You were just saying his neem in your sleep. *Lorry, I'm sawry. I'm sawry! You've gat to forgav may.*'

Kathleen has miracle hands. There's no other way to describe what she's actually doing to me. I'm laid out flat on the massage table and she's, like, working all of the tension out of my neck and shoulders.

She goes, 'You're *full* of knots,' except she says it in a sort of, like, funny accent, which I'm not even going to attempt to do. 'Have you had a recent shock or trauma?'

I'm like, 'Just keep doing what you're doing. Don't change an actual thing.'

Kathleen, by the way, is an absolute ringer for Rosie Huntington-Whiteley, except an Irish countryside version of her, if you can picture that.

With a masseuse like her on the payroll, though, it's a wonder this place isn't still packing them in.

I'm like, 'No offence, but did you train in, like, Thailand or one of those?'

She laughs. 'No, I'm not even qualified at this. I'm studying it part time, two evenings a week.'

I'm like, 'What do you do full time, then?' because I've got a skewer under this towel that would kebab a focking pig.

'I work on reception,' she goes. 'Sure, didn't I check you in yester-day?'

I thought she looked familiar alright.

'Kofryna,' she goes, '*was* the senior therapist here but she went back to Lithuania – there just wasn't enough work.'

'It's the same story everywhere,' I go, at the same time pulling what I hope is a sympathetic face, although she can't see it, of course, because I've got my boat stuck in that foam loop thing. 'Must be weird,' I go, 'working in a hotel where there's, like, literally no guests.'

'Well,' she goes, 'we've two couples arriving at the weekend.'

I'm like, 'Two couples, though. Jesus, this place has got, like, two hundred and fifty rooms.'

'I know. Did Mrs Rathfriland tell you what it used to be like?'

'Out the fockng door, by all accounts. I mean, you'd have to wonder is the whole Celtic Tiger thing *ever* going to come back, wouldn't you?'

'It doesn't look like it. Things are very bad out there.'

'That's certainly what everyone seems to be saying.'

'My younger brother now – Fachtna – he just finished his Leaving Cert. there a while back and he's probably going to have to emigrate.'

'Emigrate? Jesus! Where did it all go wrong? That's what I'd love some of these so-called economists to explain to me in words I can understand . . . Actually, here's another question for you, which I'd say came up a fair bit during the whole boom thing – what county are we even in?'

'Our motto is, forget you're in any county.'

'Yeah, no, I get *why* you'd say that, but which one actually is it, of the thirty-six?'

'Kilkenny.'

I'm like, 'Kilkenny?' and then I actually laugh. 'Well, that's another one ticked off the list, then. Must be in double figures by now.'

The next thing I know, I'm looking through the – like I said – loop, at a pair of slippers with 'Bel Eire ®' embroidered on them and I hear Kathleen go, 'Good morning, Mrs Rathfriland. Did you have a nice run?'

That's where Regina's been, by the way. I woke up to a note telling me that she was spending the morning in the gym and that she'd booked me in for an 11 a.m. deep-tissue head, neck and shoulders.

She doesn't answer Kathleen's question. I get the impression that she's a bit of a wagon as a boss.

'What abicha?' she just goes to me. I look up, roysh, and there she is, suddenly stood in front of me, freshly showered, with her face all red and shiny from a morning's exercise. 'What are yee gonna hov for brackfist?'

'I have to admit,' I go, 'I had a look at the room service menu and I very much like the sound of the baked eggs Florentine on, like, a toasted bagel.'

She goes, 'Did yee hear thot, Kathleen?'

Kathleen's like, 'Yes, I'm just finishing up here, Mrs Rathfriland.'

Jesus, she has the girl cooking as well. This place must be royally focked.

'And *ay'll* hov the seared tuna Niçoise and a glass of paneopple juice. Sand it op when it's roddy. Ross, ay'll be opstors in the room.'

Then off she focking toddles.

'Jesus,' I go, 'how do you put up with that?'

Kathleen's like, 'Oh, she's okay – at least you know where you stand with her.'

I'd have said the same about her until a week ago.

She finishes whatever magic she's been working on my neck, then goes, 'Okay, I'm going to leave you now, just while you put your robe back on and . . .'

'Whoa, wait a second,' I go, suddenly turning over on the bed. I'm hoping she doesn't notice that I've got the old handbrake on, though I suspect that she does – it's kind of hord to miss, even under the towel.

'Look, I hope this doesn't come across as sleazy but I'm going to *have* to ask you for your phone number.'

She's like, 'What?' like I'm a focking monkey speaking Spanish to her.

'Hey, I'm not going to mince words here. I think you're a sort of, like, Irish verision of Rosie Huntington-Whiteley.'

'Who?'

'Google her later if you want. There's an attraction, is what I'm saying.'

The look of shock on her face. You'd swear no one had ever hit on her before. Get used to it, I'm thinking, if you're going to touch people like that.

'I'm married,' she goes.

I actually laugh at that. I'm there, 'Well, *I'm* not prejudiced.'

That'd be a classic line of mine.

She looks over her shoulder at the door, presumably worried that Regina is about to walk back in. Or maybe it's a reminder to *me*, that I'm her boss's current plaything.

'Hey, don't worry about *her*,' I go. 'That's very much a use and abuse situation. Look, I'm laying my cords on the table. I'm actually turned on here,' and I nod at the bulge in the towel.

Most birds I know would take that as a compliment.

'I'm married!' she again goes, except this time she actually *shouts* it at me? Then storms off out of the treatment room.

I'm thinking, hey – speculate to accumulate. That's how much the massage has actually chilled me out. I'm even having a chuckle to myself, wondering will I ever change? I mean, you'd *imagine* I'd lay off the ladies for a while, given the amount of shit that I'm currently in.

That's when I hear my phone suddenly ring in the pocket of my robe. Every muscle in my body instantly freezes up again, because the first thought that enters my head is obviously that it's Larry.

I reach into my robe and take it out slowly, my hand actually trembling. I don't know why – he can't actually do anything to me here. But then I notice from the screen that it's not him at all. It's my old man and I end up just answering it, as I always do when he rings these days, just in case there's something wrong.

'Ross!' he just goes. He actually sounds relieved. 'Where are you?'

'Well, the story *I'm* being told,' I go, 'is Kilkenny.'

'Kilkenny? Good heavens!'

'What's the Jackanory?'

'Well, Helen and I just called up to see you. See did you fancy having a spot of brunch with us. We're meeting Erika and her bethrothed . . . The thing is, it's your apartment, Ross, it's been – what's the phrase? – *trashed*?'

I'm like, 'Trashed?'

'True as I'm standing here,' he goes, 'in what would appear to be the scene of some class of earthquake – or other such natural disaster. It's a scene of devastation, Kicker. Naturally, I was worried. I said to Helen, I just hope he wasn't here when this happened. Everything you own, Ross – clothes, furniture and whatever else – has been torn to shreds or smashed to bloody smithereens. And your BMW Z9, Ross . . .'

That, as you can imagine, stops me dead in my tracks. I'm like, 'My BMW Z9? Whoa, what are talking about?'

'The same thing,' he goes. 'Down in the carpark. Destroyed. The tyres slashed, the windows broken, the bodywork – oh, someone looks like they went at it with a bloody sledgehammer . . .'

I feel a genuine tear suddenly slip my eye. I loved that focking cor. They've crossed the actual line there. And in a major way.

I'm there, 'Could, like, a panel-beater do anything with it?'

He goes, 'Good Lord, no. It's a write-off, Ross. A bloody write-off.'

'Walk?' I go. 'Walk where?'

Regina reacts like it's the most ridiculous question she's ever heard.

'Does it motter where? I'm talking abite just gatting some frash orr.'

'But it's, like, pissing down,' I go, opening a crack in the curtains. 'Or it *has* been pissing. Another poxy summer, huh?'

I open the door of the mini-bor but she stretches out her leg and kicks it shut with one of her MBTs. 'Is someone cheesing yee?' she suddenly goes.

I'm like, 'Excuse me?'

'Yee hord may. Cheesing after yee. Ay mean, you arrave here onaxpactedly . . .'

'I wanted to surprise you.'

'Yee jomp abite ten feet in the orr every tame the phone rangs . . .'

'Like I said, I came here to try to chillax.'

'You won't lat me open the cortains, even during the dee. Then the neetmares – another one last nait, bay the wee. Lorry – again. *Don't sheet may?* There *is* someone after yee, isn't thor?'

'There's not.'

'So way won't yee go ite for a walk with may thon? You don't want to be seen ite with may – even in Urlingford.'

'Look, I agree, a walk isn't as big a deal as a meal in a restaurant – but it's in the same postcode.'

She shakes her head and laughs – the word is . . . I'm going to say it – *bitterly*?

'Well,' she goes, 'ay don't really know *what* ay'm getting ite of this then,' which is a definite reference to me not being able to perform again this morning.

I end up just rolling my eyes and going, 'Fine! I'll *go* for a walk with you if it's that important to you.'

'Och, don't bather!' she goes.

See, she still wants me to come with her, but at the same time she wants to, like, play the mortyr? That's focking women for you. Age, race, colour or creed – they all do passive aggressive the exact same way.

Off she focking storms.

I just shake my head, then I follow her, from a safe distance, down-stairs, through the lobby, then out onto the N8.

What even *is* creed, by the way? Probably doesn't matter.

I stay maybe twenty or thirty metres behind her, but I make sure she knows I'm there. 'Look, Regina,' I shout ahead to her, 'we're out in public together for the first time,' trying to make a joke of the whole thing.

She's in, like, no mood for my bullshit, though. She doesn't even turn around – I just hear her go, 'Awee to focken Doblin with yee.'

Of course that's not an actual option for me, what with a death threat hanging over my head, which I can tell you is the only reason I continue following her along the hord shoulder, trying to make it up with her

'Regina!' I go.

She's like, 'Awee to fock!'

She suddenly has a quick look over her shoulder, to make sure there's a break in the traffic, then dorts across to the other side – this is the main Dublin to Cork road, bear in mind. I wait for another break, then I do the same.

I'm thinking she can't be *this* upset over me not wanting to go for a walk. Then I'm thinking, is it the other thing – the obvious thing. I know birds don't get actual periods at her age, but do they still get all the shit that goes with them? It's one focking tough break if they do.

She takes a hord right and I follow her up another road for maybe a full K, staying maybe twenty metres behind her, even when she quickens the pace. It'd take some burst of speed to burn me off. Denis Hickie's possibly the only person who's ever done it.

'Come on, Regina, this is stupid,' I go. 'And it *is* raining, by the way, just to prove my original point.'

She says something I don't quite catch. Possibly some shit about being tired of babysitting – *beeby-satin* – me.

She *has* a cracking little tail on her, I might have already mentioned. Although with those thermo leggings they wear you can never really be sure. A girl could have a hoop like two bulls running for the same gate and you wouldn't know until you got her home.

Adidas. New Balance. Ronhill. I'd focking prosecute the lot of them.

We cross a river and that's when the rain really storts chucking it. She puts her head down and finds another gear. I shout the thing about Denis Hickie and, if she answers, I don't actually hear it.

We go on another few Ks, taking various twists and turns. There's fock-all to see – which is one of the reasons I'd be anti the whole walking thing in general – except fields and this sort of, like, forest?

It's probably out of boredom that I actually whip my phone out of my pocket and I notice I've had two or three missed calls from – fock! – Larry. I listen to the messages. I don't know why. Maybe half of my mind is thinking, okay, I need to know exactly what I'm facing here, because they always say – don't they? – that forewarned is foreormed? Then the other half of me is possibly hoping that the shit-storm has somehow passed, that he's going to be on my voicemail going, 'She was a bleaten skank, Rosser – in utter words, not wort you and me falling out over. Ye actually did me a favour when ye tink abourrit. Fact, I owe ye one, Buddy.'

It's, like, wishful thinking, of course.

In terms of, like, content, I'd say his messages swing in step with what I'd imagine to be his mood. In other words, all over the gaff. I mean, we all know what it's like to break up with someone – you end up experiencing all sorts of emotions.

'Ine coming arthur ye,' one message, from yesterday afternoon, goes. 'Wherever you're fooken hiding, Rosser, you'd bethor make it good, because Ine gonna hunt ye dowin and Ine gonna fooken kill ye.'

In the background, I can hear the sound of, like, glass breaking, so I'm presuming this was while he was in making shit of my gaff.

The next one – five hours and eight or nine cans of Galahad later – is more, I suppose, *tearful*? He's all, 'I fooken loved ye, Rosser. Me *and* Tetty did. Like a fooken brudder, man. But ye broke the code of honour. I don't want to hoort ye, Rosser, but you're arthur giving me no utter choice.'

Then this morning – around the time, presumably, when his hangover was introducing itself – he left another one, more manic this time. 'If you've addy fooken balls, you'll come and you'll fooken face me. And we'll sort it, reet – like two adults. Any weapon you choose!'

Hearing his plans for me helps me focus on my – I suppose you could say – *plight*? I need a bed for a few nights. Which is why I break into a sudden trot and catch Regina up.

I'm pretty shocked, I have to admit, to find that she's in, like, tears. I grab her by the orm and sort of, like, spin her around. I'm like, 'Regina, what's the story? I *came* for the walk, didn't I?'

As I suspected, though, the walk had fock all to basically do with it. 'Ay jost don't know where ay om with yee,' she goes, that whole conversation we had yesterday by the vitality pool – about wanting too much too soon – totally forgotten.

I'm like, 'What?' because I really didn't expect to be having this conversation again.

'Look,' she goes, 'ay don't corr what *ay* said yasterdee. Ay con't contanyee lake thos. Nat knowing when ay'm gonna have yee. Rapping each other's clothes off one manute, the naxt, nathing.'

'If it's the sex thing,' I go, 'normal service *will* resume, I can assure you of that.'

'It's nathing to dee with sax. Look, *ay'm* used to being in control of sat yations. Hadda says ay'm a control frake and she's passibly rait. She *is* rait. Work and whatever alse – thot's the wee *ay've* always been. But yee and may is the only part of may lafe where ay *don't* feel in control. And *ay* thought ay could hondle thot. Trayed to persuade mayself that ay could – what's thot word yee use? – chillax. But *ay* con't.'

I'm like, 'Sorry, what's your basic point here?'

'Like ay told yee yasterdee, *ay've* cheenged since ay met yee. Ay'm talking abite *me* – finally being mayself. Ay've come ite of may shall. And you've been a huge port of thot, because, for once since Toddy dayed, I've find something that's nathing to dee with hum and what hoppened tee hum. Do yee ontherstond what ay'm seeing?'

'I think so.'

'Do *ay* hov tee prostrate mayself on the wet grind thor and see it – ay'm in love with yee, Ross.'

Jesus. I knew it. See, people think I'm being big-headed when I say it, roysh, but I *make* women fall in love with me. I don't know exactly how. There's possibly nothing I can even do about it. But *it* happens.

'That's way,' she goes, 'ay've decided to fanish ut. Whatever *ut* ever was. Ay want yee to go home, Ross, and ay don't aver want tee see yee again.'

I'm like, 'What?' although what I actually mean is, 'Shit!'

'It's for the bast,' she goes. 'Och, it'll seeve me a lat of hort eek in the lawng ron.'

That's when it hits me. Like a bolt of lightning. One of my world-famous ideas. It's a fact that I need somewhere to live. Somewhere that Larry and, I'm presuming Terry, won't find me. Preferably somewhere with a big wall around it and big wrought-iron gates, with the various comings and goings monitored by twenty-four-hour CCTV.

I'm thinking, okay, Rossmeister – you need to get your focking game face on here.

I unzip the old Henri Lloyd jacket and invite her to shelter inside. It's actually a pretty romantic moment, with the rain splashing up off the road. She thinks about it for a second, then sort of, like, nestles into me. The wet from her hair soaks straight through my T-shirt to my chest.

'Ay thank we could have really hod something,' she goes. 'But it's batter that thus happens noy than dine the road. Because ay'd want thos tee last foraver. And one obstacle we could naver get arind is the fact that *may* foraver mait nat be as lawng as *yeer* foraver . . .'

Jesus, the woman's bananas.

I put my finger over her lips. I don't *know* why? Possibly because I know it's what'd happen if this was a movie.

'Why don't we, like, move in together?' I suddenly go.

Her face just drops. It's a hell of a lot more than she expected – although don't get me wrong, she's focking delighted with herself. 'Intee may hise?' she goes, still in basic shock.

I'm like, 'Why not? Like you said, you don't know how much time you've got left on this Earth.'

'Well, that's nat exactly what ay said.'

'Well, what you meant – I *think* – is what's the point in wasting time? You're at an age now – sixty – when you see something you want and you know you've no option but to just go for it. But I'm going to say something now that's going to possibly shock you – whatever you're feeling, I'm pretty sure I'm feeling it too.'

See, this is me doing what'd be known as my thing. This is, like, old school Ross.

'I'm not one to just bandy around the old L word,' I go. 'But that's very much the direction I feel I'm headed in. And I'm not fighting it anymore, Regina. I'm done. I'm tired. You could say you've blown away my defences.'

She's lapping this shit up, her mouth and eyes wide open.

'Look,' I go, 'I can't claim to know women. Who can? But this I *do* know – I'm ready to take whatever we have to the next level. Blah blah blah.'

She smiles at me. She's putty in the hand. She's like, 'Meeve *an* togather?'

'The sooner the better. The second we go back in fact.'

'Ay con't believe ay'm abite to see yass.'

I'm thinking, yeah, what the fock else are you going to say? I'm holding out for George Clooney?

I'm like, 'Say it, then.'

She goes, 'Yass!' and then she gets all excited and, like, throws the lips on me. We kiss for a bit, then she suddenly turns almost fully around and goes, 'Thot's what ay wanted to show yee, bay the wee?' and I follow her line of vision to this, basically, castle in the distance.

I don't get it.

'*Ay* jost love ut,' she goes. 'It was built bay a Caltic chieftain in the fofteenth cantury.'

I just nod, cracking on to be interested. 'It's one of the better ones, in fairness to it.'

'Do yee want to teek a closer look?' she goes. 'There's a romontic storay behaind ut.'

'Or,' I go, giving her the old mince pies, 'we *could* just go back to bed.'

She doesn't say anything. She doesn't need to. Her face lights up like Christmas come early. I go to grab her hand but she pulls it away and sticks it in her skyrocket, then we follow the road – still in the pissings of rain – back to the N8.

I get, like, a text while Regina's in the old Jack Bauer. I can see straight away that it's from Honor. It's her opening line that has me suddenly sitting bolt upright in the bed.

It's like, 'Daddy theres somethin rong wit mommy : ('

So I fire straight back with, 'Hon wot actually is it?'

She goes, 'Omg she's turnin off all d radiators in d rooms we dont use.'

I'm like, 'Er why exactly?'

'She says we hav 2 sav energy, espesh wit d current price of oil. And also 2 preserve d earths precious resources.'

I'm there, 'I don't tink ur mothers well. Shes havin possibly sum kind of breakdown.'

Where are social services? That's what *I'm* wondering.

Honor – the poor frightened kid – goes, 'Shes like, er, it's july, as in d middl of d summer, theres no sense in heating all thes rooms – and who 4?'

I'm there, 'Honor, lock urself into a room, preferably 1 of d 1s that has d actual heating on, and stay ther until she snaps out of it. Itll pass, I promise.'

She asks me what I think of the miniature chocolate éclairs and I tell her I love them. Because I went straight *for* them, totally ignoring the free-range, corn-fed egg and cucumber finger sandwiches, the freshly baked scones with strawberry preserve and the Palm Court Tearoom's famous smoked Atlantic salmon with capers on farmhouse brown bread. Focking horsed them all as well. She smiles and says the secret is brandy in the cream.

'Toddy worked for a year in The Rutz,' she goes, 'when he was in his twanties. *Ay* thank that was one of the reasons ay fell for him at the stort. Ay most have been in awe.'

I stare out the window at one of those giant gorden chess sets – getting totally pissed on. I don't actually play the game but even I can tell you that there's, like, one or two pieces missing. 'Hey,' I go, 'which are the two – I suppose – characters that usually go in the middle of the back row?'

She turns her head and looks to where I'm looking. 'The kang and queen,' she goes. 'Aye, someone stole them. Abite a year ago, we storted advertasing for stag portays. That's hoy dasperate we were for basniss. Noy, *ay'd* rother the place was amptay.'

I nod. 'Did anyone ever play actual chess on it?'

She laughs. 'Not that *ay* saw.'

'So it was just, like, a feature?'

A feature – that was a word you always heard when there was stupid money washing about the place?

She looks around the empty lounge room. Some ladies' shoe designer is supposed to have come up with the concept, modelled on the drawing room in the doll's house that was owned by, I don't know, Queen Mary, I think it said in the brochure.

'Ay know ay con soind morbad at tames,' she goes, 'forever talking abite the past, but ay remember when this room was *always* full – even on Mondee and Tuesdee afterneens. We used to chorge a hondred euros per head for thot – a pat of tea and a plate of wee cakes and sondwiches – and we'd a four-week weeting list for a teeble.'

'That was the beauty of those days. You could rip the focking piss out of people and they'd actually say thank you for it.'

'Och, they came from averywhere. Clarmallagh. Garrycastle. Even Portnahinch. And see Christmas? We hod to teek on axtra staff jost tee sell gaft voychers . . .'

Her eyes fix on the grand piano, which I doubt anyone's played since the country went to basic shit.

'Ay'm sorray ageen abite yasterdee,' she goes, meaning presumably the focking piss-fit she threw on the N8 – well, actually, just off it. If you want to be exact about it, it was the R-5-something or other. 'Ay jost – well, lake ay told yee . . .'

'Foget about it,' I go. 'Look, the important thing is that you said how you felt about me. And luckily I happened to be feeling the exact same things. And now it's out there. How can that be a bad thing?'

Like I said, I don't *play* chess? But when it comes to this game, I'm a focking grandmaster.

'Yee certainly hov your mojo back,' she goes, with a smile, 'if last nait's performance is onything to go bay. Ay'm trying to remambor what it was ay dud to turn yee back awn lake thot.'

She's flattering herself there. I was actually thinking about Kathleen the whole time we were doing it.

I go, 'I'm sorry I didn't last longer. There'll be plenty more where that came from, though. Especially when I move into your gaff,' and I mention it only as a subtle reminder to her.

She's *in* two minds about it, though. I can see the doubt in her face as she sips her Darjeeling. But she still wants me – the famous L word slipped her lips again while I was setting the hounds on her last night – and I know she'll do literally anything to please me. 'Hedda's nat gonna be hoppay,' she goes.

I'm like, 'She's an emo. They never focking are.'

'*Ay* mean, she's going to goy absolitely mantle.'

'Let her.'

'What, savan months after her fawther days, her mother meevs in her wee toyboy . . .'

'I'd hordly call me a toyboy.'

'*Ay'm* jost seeing, that's hoy *she's* gonna see ut.'

Shit. I'm losing her. I realize that I'm going to need to do something here.

'Look,' I go, giving her the old Sacred Hort of Jesus eyes, 'these feelings I have for you are so – oh my God – basically huge, that I've decided there's no point in me even *trying* to resist them? I'm just not strong enough – not in that way. I don't care about the age difference. I don't care that we've only known each other, what, a few months? I'm going for this thing and I'm going for it in a major way. And God help anyone who tries to tell me it's wrong.'

See, I'm like a focking wordsmith when I need to be.

She smiles at me, suddenly remembering how actual lucky she is. 'Gat your stoff,' she goes, 'and meev it un – the sacond we gat back to Doblin.'

My stuff. From what the old man said, I don't actually have any

251

anymore. And I'm not brave enough to go back and sift through the rubble of my gaff to find anything that might be salvaged.

'She'll be away at thot Axegen Fastival. Nat that I even curr what she thanks.'

'All that *actually* matters,' I go, 'is the way we feel about each other. And it's out there now.'

She moves in then and kisses me. Actually, we *both* kiss, for a minute or two and I get the taste of capers from her tongue. When she comes up for air, I make a point of going, 'What's the story with that bird Kathleen, by the way?'

There's badness in me. I'm convinced of that.

Regina suddenly straightens up in her focking embroidered antique chair, roysh, her face all serious. She's like, 'What abite her?'

I'm there, 'Look, I don't want to cause trouble – because it looks to me like she's very much running the show around here.'

'There's thisands ite thorr would be glod of her job – what hoppened?'

I sigh, like I'm sorry I even brought it up. Then I sort of, like, steel myself to break the bad news. 'When she was giving me my massage yesterday, I just felt that . . . okay, let's just say that she seemed to get a lot more out of it than I did.'

Her mouth just drops. 'What are yee talking abite?'

'She really got into it, if you know what I'm saying. I mean, the poor girl, she obviously couldn't help herself. But she was even groaning.'

'Groanen?'

'Yeah, no, like I said, she was getting her definite jollies from it.'

'But she's morried!'

'I did point out that fact to her. I also pointed out that I had an obvious thing going with you, her boss – the woman who could sack her on the focking spot if she found out . . .'

'The wee hossay.'

'Didn't seem to dampen down her ardour, I can tell you that for nothing. I mean, let's call a spade a spade here – she's been pretty much salivating over me from the minute I arrived.'

She stands up. She's there, 'The doortay wee . . .'

'Like I said,' I go, 'the last thing I want to do is cause trouble for the girl,' except Regina doesn't hear me, roysh, because she's already on her way out to reception and I think about maybe hitting the old Himalayan Spring Hydrotherapy suite until the smoke clears.

That's when my phone all of a sudden vibrates on the table. I have it switched onto, like, silent. Not only because of Larry. There's been a lot of customers ringing the last couple of days, wondering where the fock I am. Except it's not them at all, because it's a photo of – believe it or not – Ronan that's lit up on the little screen, the one of him taking a sneaky sip of my pint the year I went with him and Tina to Santa Ponsa.

I can't believe it. He's back talking to me.

I answer by going, 'I presume you got my text about Paul Williams moving to the *News of the Wurdled*?' because I never gave up making the effort. Never. 'I think *someone's* going to be switching Sunday newspapers.'

He's like, 'Rosser, where are ye?'

'I'm actually getting that question a lot,' I go. 'Kilkenny seems to be the general talk – but from the scenery it could be literally anywhere outside Dublin.'

'When are you coming home?'

That's when it's suddenly obvious to me – the upset in his voice. I straight away stand up. I'm like, 'Ro, what's wrong? You haven't run into Terry and Larry, have you?'

He goes, 'No.' Then he ends up just blurting the reason out. 'Me ma's going out with McGahy.'

Of course, I end up nearly tripping over an antique pouffe – that's how much in actual shock I am. 'Going out? What the fock are you talking about?'

'They're going out wit each udder, Ross.'

'As in, like, boyfriend, girlfriend?'

'Yeah.'

'Are you sure, Ro? I know she had to talk to him once or twice to talk him out of expelling you for the other thing.'

'Thee went to the fooken theatre last night.'

'What? I mean, what did they go to see? Actually, don't even answer that – it wouldn't mean a thing to me either way. I'm pretty much babbling here while I try to get my head around it.'

'I found the tickets in me ma's drawer this morning.'

I shake my head – I think the word is, like, *ruefully*? 'Yeah, no, certain things *are* storting to add up here, Ro. I thought they looked a bit too

253

cosy the night of the musical. It was her stopping his mother from dying that time. That's what kicked it off, whatever signals that sent out to him.'

'I only found out last neet, Rosser. Just happened to look out the window when he dropped her home . . .'

'In his Nissan focking Storlet – don't even finish that sentence, Ro. Jesus Christ, Tina and McGahy!'

'Then I found the tickets. I don't want me ma going out with him.'

'I don't focking blame you. No offence, but what could *she* possibly see in *him*? Er, McGahy? God, I'm just trying to think of some of the nicknames we used to have for him.'

'If this gets out . . .' he goes, then he doesn't need to say another word after that.

The embarrassment of being stripped naked on stage by a, I don't know, *coven* of vengeful Mounties is nothing compared to the humili-ation of everyone in Castlerock knowing that the headmaster is banging his old dear.

'It won't,' I go. 'Leave it to me.'

The door slams and I watch Regina's face tighten. Even though she *says* she doesn't care what her daughter thinks, I know that, deep down, she actually *does*? Which is why I'm going to have to be strong for her. Strong for both of us.

Hedda lets her bag just fall, then I hear her coming down the hall, dragging her feet along the parquet floor.

She walks into the kitchen – she's got that washed-out, post-festival look – and the first sight that greets her is the old Rossmeister General standing at the entrance to the conservatory in his boxer shorts and the new Leinster pro training jersey.

Well, you can imagine the disgust on her face. It's like someone stuffed her focking mouth with wasabi, then wired it shut.

She totally blanks me, and totally blanks her mother, who's stand-ing in her dressing gown, with her back against the two-door American-style fridge freezer. She pulls the cupcake-shaped cookie jor from the cupboard next to the dishwasher and helps herself to a Tracker bor.

You could literally cut the air with a knife.

'How was Oxegen?' I go – you *know* me, I like to make the effort. 'Who was even headlining this year? Was it Jay-Z or Kasabian?'

She just looks at her old dear then and laughs, except in, like, a *sarcastic* way?

I know my music, though – that she can't deny.

She's like, '*Really*, Mum? He's *still* here?'

Regina just folds her orms, which I recognize as, like, a defensive gesture. So I jump straight in there.

'Oh, *I'm* still here,' I go. 'Matter of fact, I *live* here now.'

You can nearly see the cracks appear in her white foundation, she's that angry.

'That's right,' I go, with a dirty big smile on my face, 'I've moved in.'

'Lat *may* hondle thos,' Regina goes and, to be honest, roysh, I'm more than a little bit put out. She wasn't doing a great job of handling it before I came to her sudden rescue.

'It's troy,' she goes. 'Ross has meeved un. *Ay'm* nat awsken yee to lake it. *Ay'm* jost talling yee as a motter of sample courtesay.'

'*Courtesy?*' Hedda goes. 'That's *got* to be a focking joke.'

'We love each other!' Regina practically screams at her.

That stops Hedda dead in her tracks. She just stares at her old dear for maybe ten seconds, then this sort of, like, smile basically erupts all over her face.

'You've lost it,' she tells her. 'You've lost the *actual* plot,' and then she turns and says that if I've moved in, then she's moving out. Then she stomps out of the kitchen.

'Meeve ite, than!' Regina shouts after her. 'Go noy! Jost get ite! Get ite and don't come bock!'

She may or may not mean it. All I know is that she's upset, so I do the gentlemanly thing. I take her in my orms and I hold her and run my fingers through her hair and tell her that everything's going to be okay, because we love each other and blahdy blahdy blah-blah.

After a couple of minutes, she pulls away and says she's going to try to get herself centred, which presumably means an hour or two of yoga, so I tell her that I'm going out.

See, I've got one or two family matters to sort out myself this afternoon.

I tip out to the garage, where the van is stashed. There's, like, a stack of paperwork on the front passenger seat, which reminds me that I'm going to have to get back to the whole *work* thing at some stage? I've no idea how many clients I've lost in the few days I've been missing.

I'm actually backing Old Amnesia – as the old man calls it – out of the driveway when Hedda's face suddenly appears at the window on the passenger side. She's got her rucksack on her back – she's obviously just taking whatever she brought with her in Oxegen.

I can't resist it, of course. I lower the window and go, 'Can I give you a lift somewhere? The focking laundrette maybe?'

She calls me a few names, though nothing worse than the names Kathleen called me through the door of the Himalayan Spring Hydrotherapy suite after she'd been handed her cords.

I end up just laughing in her face.

'Oh,' she goes, 'you must be very proud of yourself, forcing a young girl out of her own home.'

'Possibly for the best,' I go. 'You'd have been driven mental with the sound of the headboard banging off the wall all night!'

I'm expecting more abuse out of her mouth but instead she looks at me calmly and goes, 'You know she's grieving?'

That, for some reason, hits home harder than any bad words she can throw at me. Because it speaks to that tiny little part of my brain that knows, deep, deep down, that I'm not a complete and utter write-off as a human being.

I go to quickly close the window but she stops it with her hands.

'She's having some kind of breakdown,' she goes, 'and you're taking advantage of that. Do you know what that makes you?'

I tell her she hasn't a clue.

'It makes you a vulture!'

She takes a step backwards and I'm out of there in, like, a spray of gravel.

'You're a fucking vulture!' she shouts after me.

A few minutes later, I'm driving through Malahide Village, just storting to calm down again, when Larry makes one of his, by now, three-times daily calls to me. This time, I actually answer it. Don't ask me why. I just decide that, look, it's getting on for nearly a week now – it's about time he storted getting his head around it. I mean, I've scored loads of my friends' girlfriends – ask Oisinn, ask Christian, ask JP – and it'd usually be forgiven and forgotten by now.

'Larry,' I go, 'tell me you're calm.'

He's not. He's, like, roaring down the phone at me. 'Where are ye? Where the fook are ye?'

I'm there, 'I'm hordly likely to tell you that, am I?'

'I'll find ye, Rosser – and it'll be ten toyums woorse for ye when I do.'

'Believe me, Dude, I'm in the last place you'd even think of looking.'

It's true. I mean, who'd believe I'd be hiding out on this side of the world.

'Oh, me and Tetty have ways of gettin to ye – don't you woody about tat.'

I end up nearly breaking the red light outside the Malahide Marina Village. 'Are you threatening my family?' I go.

He's pretty hurt by the suggestion. 'Ine not gonna lay a finger on anyone except you,' he goes. 'What do ye tink I am, Rosser, a fooken scumbag?'

When I don't answer, he goes, '*You're* the bleaten scumbag, remember . . . I fooken luffed that geerl.'

The light goes green and I ease my foot onto the accelerator. 'Look, what happened between Saoirse and me, it was nothing. It actually happened in the blink of an eye.'

'Dat's not what she said. She said ye made her feel tings.'

'I wouldn't be so sure about that.'

'Tings no fedda had ever made her feel.'

'Dude, I think a lot of that might have been down to the buildings collapsing around us. The vibrations and blah blah blah.'

'Ye still gev the royid, Rosser. You still gev her the royid. And you *knew* I luffed her.'

I try to change the angle of the play. 'Do you definitely know there's not still a chance for you two, though? As in, do you think you might even get back together again?'

He roars at me. 'Do ye tink I'd want her now? The doorty fooken slut.'

'Well,' I go, 'that's kind of what *I'm* driving at? She wasn't *for* you, Larry. I'll tell you what, why don't you let me fix you up with one or two birds I know,' because I could think of a dozen regulars of mine straight off who'd – pordon the pun – take a bullet for me. Chloe and Sophie are just two examples.

'Ye tink I want your filty cast-offs?' he goes. Then he really loses it with me, to the point where I think he must be *on* something. Coke would be my bet. 'Is dat what ye tink of me? Ye royid a bird who I fooken luffed and den ye offer me yisser fooken trowbacks . . .'

'These are really good-looking birds, Larry. I can text you one or two pictures . . .'

'Rosser,' he goes, 'Ine gonna break your back, then Ine gonna cut your balls off and feed them to ye while you're still aloyuff,' and that's the point at which I decide to hang up.

I drive on and get back to thinking about what you might call the job in hand.

Malahide and Finglas are actually a lot closer to each other than you'd think. It's a wonder that fact has never got out.

I pull up outside the gaff, then I wander up the driveway and I try ringing the doorbell. Of course, it doesn't work. Tina took the batteries out of it – *and* the smoke alorm, by the way – to put in the *Pirate Pete, The Repeat Parrot* that Ronan got her on Henry Street for Christmas. Which is, what, seven months ago now?

Jesus.

I end up having to knock two or three times on the wire glass window beside the door. I look back out at the road. I still can't believe I'm allowing my son to be raised in this focking Legoland Ghetto. Ten seconds later, the door opens and it's Tina – I know I'm one to talk – but still in her focking pyjamas.

'Ronan's not hee-er,' she goes. 'He's playing poker wit Buckets of Blood. You'll gerrim on he's mobile.'

I end up having to put my foot in the door to stop her closing it on me.

'Don't play the innocent with me,' I go. 'You know why I'm here.'

She rubs her face with her hand. Doesn't invite me in, by the way. She's like, 'Ross, Ine worken nights dis week. Just tell me what de fook it is you want.'

'Okay, I'm going to come straight out with it, then. I'm not happy with your latest boyfriend.'

This isn't jealousy, I should add. If me and Tina were the last two people on Earth, I'd breed outside my focking species.

'Boyfriend?' she goes. 'You mean Tom?'

I laugh. 'Not even an *attempt* to deny it.'

Her expression goes all hord then – you might have met women from this port of the world yourselves – like she'd glass me if she had the necessary weapon to hand. 'What does it even have to do with you?'

'I think it's got plenty to do with me. The headmaster of my son's school is giving his mother a serious sticking. Do you know what it'll do to him if that gets around Castlerock?'

'No woorse, I'm shewer, than having he's clothes ripped off him in front of three-hundrit-n-odd people.'

'I wouldn't be so sure.'

She goes, 'Look, just mind your own fooken business,' and again I have to stick my foot in the door to stop it being slammed on me.

'He's upset,' I go. 'He rang me.'

'I'll talk to um.'

'Personally, I think you should finish it.'

'I don't give a fook what you *peersonally* tink. Who I see and when I see dem is *my* business and nutten to do with you. Now fook off, Ross, and let me get some sleep.'

Then she really does slam the door on me. I'm wondering does she swear like that in front of *him*. Maybe when they're coming out of the theatre. 'Dat fooken Shakespeare, der's no doubt de fooker could write playiz, Tom.'

I push open the letter box with my thumbs and I shout through it as she disappears back up the stairs. 'You're my witness, Tina, that I tried to be reasonable.'

She said it was none of my business. Even Oisinn is struggling with that one. 'But he's your son!' he goes.

I'm like, 'Appreciate the back-up, Dude. The language out of her mouth as well. Swore at me like a focking builder's labourer.'

This is us back in, like, Slattery's by the way? Which is my new local for the duration. Larry would know to look for me in Kielys, see.

I'm there, 'Dude, do you have any idea what it's going to do to Ro if he goes back to school in September and this is still going on?'

'I know.'

'I mean, how would you feel if he was banging *your* old dear?'

That's possibly not a fair comparison. Oisinn's mother isn't great.

'So what are you going to do?' he goes

I'm there, 'What do you think? I didn't get any satisfaction out of her, so I'm going to turn my sights on him – see will *he* listen to reason.'

Oisinn just laughs. 'You and McGahy are, like, fated to be enemies forever.'

He's possibly right. See, just to fill you in on the old back story, it all goes back to the time he pretty much humiliated me in front of the class for not knowing some fact about, I don't know, algebra or Yeats – I can't even remember what it was he even taught, which will tell you how little interest I had in his class. Anyway, Father Fehily got wind of it and threatened to sack him unless he apologized to me in front of an entire assembly. I'll never forget the look on McGahy's face when Fehily stood up and went, 'Now – one of *the staff* has something he wishes to say to Ross O'Carroll-Kelly, the captain of our all-conquering senior rugby team . . .'

I made his life a pretty much misery after that, knowing that he couldn't basically do anything to me. But then, of course, he got his own back when he became principal himself, agreeing to have the result of the 1999 Leinster Schools Senior Cup final reversed, all because I *happened* to be taking metamphetamine at the time we won it. I'm wondering is the Tina thing a case of him upping the ante.

'I think it might be a spite ride situation,' I go.

Oisinn looks Scoobious. 'Doesn't sound like McGahy's style.'

'Well, what could he possibly see in her?'

'Can I just remind you that *you* saw something in her once? Otherwise there'd *be* no Ronan.'

'Well, what does *she* see in *him*, then? This is a man who still lives with his old dear, can I just point out? Sorry, no offence, Ois.'

'None taken.'

'Then there's the age difference. She's what – thirty-three, thirty-four? *He's* in his actual fifties.'

Oisinn laughs. 'Yeah, you're one to talk about age-inappropriate relationships,' except he's obviously only saying it to get a rise out of me. 'What about that woman you were banging up until a few weeks ago?'

I let it go. Then one or two pints later, I go, 'Yeah, no, it's funny you should mention the whole Regina Rathfriland thing, because we've actually, er, moved in together . . .'

I can tell from his reaction that he thinks he's, like, *misheard* me?

I'm there, 'I shit you not.'

He's having serious trouble getting his head around it. He's like, 'Dude, what the fock? I thought she was a burner? Use and drop, you said.'

I laugh. 'Nah, it's nothing to worry about. It's just that somebody's trying to kill me at the moment.'

'Kill you?'

'Well, not just kill actually. Slash my throat and pull my tongue out through the slit. Force-feed me my balls. That general thing.'

His eyes go wide like actual saucers. I suppose one of the things you'd have to say in my defence is that there's never a dull moment with me around.

'Yeah,' I go, 'do you remember Terry and Larry who live next door to me in Rosa Porks? *Prime Time* did that special investigation on them.'

'Murder Incorporated?'

'Yeah. I mean, it's *all* about nicknames, that world, isn't it? Anyway, did I ever mention to you that Larry had this, basically, girlfriend?'

He actually just stares at me. 'Jesus focking Christ . . .'

'Called Saoirse.'

'Ross, tell me you didn't.'

'Well, that'd mean lying to you, my friend.'

He just shakes his head, like he thinks I'll never learn. He's possibly right. 'Shit the bed!' he goes. 'Ross, you'd stick it anywhere there's moisture.'

I laugh – just playing Jack the Lad, if I'm being honest. 'Well, you know Little Elvis here – he'll play any venue.'

In normal circs, Oisinn would crack his hole laughing at a line like that. Instead he goes, 'Ross, this isn't Rob Kearney threatening to slap you for making a move on Susie Amy in BTs two Christmas Eves ago. These guys are supposed to have, like, ten murders to their name.'

'*Hello?* Do you not think I *know* that?'

'Well, it certainly explains why you've been looking over your shoulder all night. And why you asked the barman to point out the emergency exits when we came in.'

'Yeah,' I go, 'does that not prove to you, Oisinn, that I'm taking every focking precaution? Look, it was a mistake. She was vulnerable and I got in there. Ninety-nine percent of goys would have done the exact same thing. But now I'm trying to focus on the long game. The girl was an obvious scuzzbucket. I'm hoping that down the line, Larry's going to decide that I did him an actual favour.'

'You better just pray he doesn't catch up with you in the meantime.'

'See, I've reasoned it all out – how likely even *is* that? I mean, we don't exactly move in the same circles, do we? Although I heard one of those so-called economists on the radio today saying we're all going to know at least five working-class people by the time this recession is over.'

'He'll find you, Ross.'

'Not shacked up in Malahide he won't. Think about it – the northside! Who'd ever look for me over that side of things? I've got the old Reet Petites firmly under the table there, by the way. Regina's fallen in love with me.'

'I focking knew she would.'

'Well, don't worry, I'm telling her that I love her as well. And her place is a focking fortress, by the way. We're talking gates. Security cameras. Blah blah blah.'

He's there, 'Look, no offence, Ross, but what a focking way to live.'

I laugh. 'Dude, it's not exactly the Iveagh Hostel. I get all my meals cooked for me as well. This will have all blown over by the end of the summer – you mork my words. All I've got to do in the meantime is keep a lust-maddened sixty-year-old woman purring. Hordly a big ask.'

I text Honor, still worried sick about her, of course, wondering has her mother storted feeding her pasta shells and focking Ragú. Because that's the direction that things seemed to be headed a week or two ago.

I'm like, 'Hey Hon, howr things? Is d heatin back on?'

She's there, 'Omg yeah like a week ago.'

I go, 'Cool. Ev back 2 normal so?'

'Er no,' she goes, 'she keeps burstin in2 tears.'

'In2 tears? Why?'

'Cos shes a sad bitch.'

'That mite b a bit horsh Hon.'

'A sappy cow then.'

'Well thats a bit beter i suppose. But u dont kno why shes cryin no?'

'Er who cares? Shes bringin me 2 Paris btw! :)'

I'm like, 'Paris?'

She goes, 'Er yeah are u thick? For winnin d race.'

I've honestly never seen the seafront in Sandycove so rammers, especially on a weekday afternoon. *These* must be the new unemployed that everyone's banging on about, just saying fock it. The misery. The mortgage. The national debt that everyone seems suddenly obsessed with. Fock it all. Let's just hit the beach.

I'm sitting on a bench with the old man, staring out at the sea. It's a bit of a focking Hallmark moment, I'm prepared to admit, but *he* wanted to grab some fish in Cavistons, and *I'd* no jobs this afternoon, so I said I'd bring him in the van.

Anyway, it ended up turning into a walk along the seafront – I'm not making excuses, I'm just telling you how it happened.

We sit and watch the Stena go out until it's just a speck on the horizon.

'Gone,' he goes and I get this instant, I don't know, flash of memory from my childhood. Did we *used* to sit here?

'No,' I go, 'I can still see it.'

He's there, 'Can you really?' and he seems seriously impressed.

I'm like, 'I can,' and I don't know why, roysh, because I actually *can't*?

'One of the things that made you the rugby player you were, Ross – your vision.'

'Even now I can see it . . . Still . . . Still . . .'

'Extraordinary.'

'Now! *Now*, it's finally gone!'

'Absolutely extraordinary.'

There's, like, silence between us then.

There's a bunch of people behind us playing beach volleyball on the grass. Nearly all men, though – I've already *had* a look? I've never seen the point of *men's* beach volleyball.

He goes, 'You heard the news this morning, I take it.'

Weirdly, I did. I automatically take it that he's talking about Sean FitzPatrick.

'Bankrupt,' he goes. 'This morning.'

I'm there, 'Sorry. I know you two were friends. I mean, you even played rugby together, didn't you?'

He's like, 'That we did,' and then he gets this sudden distant look in his eyes. 'Rest easy, silver fox – they can't hurt you anymore.'

He takes a breath. 'Of course, the newspapers will be full of it tomorrow,' he goes. 'Reporting the man's troubles with ill-concealed joy.'

I stare at the yachts in the . . . Isn't it mad to think that I've lived in this area all my life and I still don't know what that sea's actually called?

He goes, 'Why do people have to know that Seanie is suffering? I'm not an iceberg, Ross. I know there's a lot of people out there in trouble – jobs, mortgages and so forth. But forget Moody's cutting our credit rating to Aa2. Forget the rising cost of exchequer spending. When you find yourself experiencing joy watching another man – whatever he's done – lose everything, that's the time to ask, my God, what has happened to this country? What have we become?'

I'm there, 'Have you rung him?'

He shakes his head. 'He'll be busy with his legal chaps, I expect. Although he's not far from my thoughts. No, Charles O'Carroll-Kelly and that famous solicitor sidekick of his, Mr Hennessy Coghlan-O'Hara, brackets BCL, are already on the case. We're going to see to it that this country pays proper homage to the man who put me and thousands of entrepreneurs like me on the road to success.'

'What are you going to do?'

'We're collecting signatures, Ross, for a petition, which we intend to present to Iarnród Éireann, calling for Greystones DART station to be renamed . . . Sean FitzPatrick Station.'

I laugh. I can't help it. 'Greystones is a good idea,' I go, 'seeing as it's the end of the focking line for both of them.'

He laughs at that, in fairness to him. Then he asks me how things are with Ronan. He knows the story – just as he knows the Jack with Honor – although it's the closest he's come to actually acknowledging what happened at the musical that night.

Helen ushered him out of the concert hall for fear he'd have a focking recurrence with his hort.

I'm there, 'He's back talking to me again at least.'

'There you are,' he goes, 'that's wonderful. And little Honor?'

'Sorcha still won't let me see her. Ah, I focked things up there in a major way. It's just I wanted my kids to be . . . Fock it, I don't even know anymore.'

He looks at me sideways, smiling. 'You wanted to live your life through them – what's this they say, *vicariously?*'

I don't even get a chance to react to that, because he sees my face and instantly goes, 'I'm not judging you, Ross. I did the same thing with you, remember. Bringing you to the park in all sorts of weathers and throwing that bloody ball at you. Do know how many concussions you had by the time you were Honor's age?'

'How many?'

'Well, maybe it's best all round that I don't tell you.'

'Jesus,' I go, just shaking my head. 'it'd certainly explain a thing or two about how I turned out, wouldn't it?'

The two of us just crack our holes laughing. I honestly can't remember the last time we laughed like this. Maybe we *never* did?

'We want our children to be happy,' he goes, 'so our instinct is to give them the kind of things that *we* associate with happiness. That's all *you* did. With Ronan, it was girls. With Honor, it was success in the old realm of sport.'

I just nod. 'I think the word I'd have to use about you is, like, *insightful?* I'm just pointing out that things might have been different if I'd actually listened to you more. End of.'

He laughs. 'Why would you listen to *me?*' he goes, shaking his head. 'Why would you listen to anyone? There's no perfect way to raise children, Ross, despite what these, quote-unquote, experts tell you. It's rather like golf, you see. There's never a time when you think, "That's it! I've got this bloody thing cracked!" And there shouldn't be. Because Ronan and Honor are your *life's* work, Ross! Your bloody *life's* work! Just like you and Erika are mine.'

Oh, shit. I'm on the point of telling him about Regina. It's my focking conscience. It happens from time to time. I can feel myself actually about to say the words. I end up having to bite my lip.

'Being a parent,' he goes, 'means having to forgive yourself all sorts of bloody things.'

I'm there, 'Rugby was possibly the only thing in life that I've ever been really, really, really amazing at.'

He stares out to sea and smiles, as if reminded of something. 'I'm just thinking about something that poor old Denis Fehily used to say to us – I'm sure he said it to you chaps as well. "You're getting it wrong. You're getting it *all* wrong. But by God, you're making all the right mistakes."'

Shit. Here it comes again.

'I have a confession to make,' I suddenly hear myself go.

I'm going to focking do it. I just can't keep it to myself anymore.

He's like, 'A confession? What are you talking about, Kicker?'

'Do you remember . . .'

'Do I remember what?'

What if he keels over, here on Sandycove Green.

'Do you remember . . . that signed Tiger Woods picture I gave you for Christmas a couple of years back?'

'Of course – is it not pride of place in my study?'

'Well, it's a fake. I actually signed it myself. Woke up Christmas morning, seriously hungover, realized I'd fock-all to give you, cut the picture out of one of your golf magazines and scribbled the focker's name on it using your Mont Blanc.'

He looks totally and utterly bewildered. 'Yes?'

'Are you even listening to me? I'm saying it's not Tiger Woods's actual autograph.'

He laughs. 'Well, of course it isn't! I know what Tiger Woods's signature looks like. Didn't I get it myself at the JP McManus Pro-Am in 2000?'

Of course, that totally throws me. 'Well, why have you got my one framed on the wall of your study if you know it's a fake?'

And he just goes, 'Because *you* gave it to me, of course.'

I'm like, 'Oh,' and I have to turn my head and pretend to take a sudden interest in the Joyce Tower so he doesn't see my eyes suddenly filling up with actual tears.

And in that moment, my mind is made up.

I step out into the gorden and the sight that greets me is Regina's rump in the air – I think the phrase they use for animals is, like, *presenting*?

Although Regina's not presenting. At least I don't think so. No, she's actually *weeding*?

I've decided to end this thing. If it ever really was a thing. I just can't risk the old man finding out, which is why I've got my bags already packed upstairs. I was going to leave, like, a note. Then I was going to maybe just drive away and possibly text her later on.

But for once in my life, this is me about to do the decent thing.

'Hey,' I go.

She has a fantastic orse, in fairness to her.

She turns around, roysh, and looks at me and I'm going to have to admit, roysh, that I get a bit of a fright. Because she's had her hair cut short. Not just *normal* short? We're talking Sharon Stone short. I think Sorcha said it was called a boy cut.

She must cop my face, because she goes, 'Do yee lake ut?'

The thing is, roysh, I kind of *do*?

I'm like, 'Yeah, it's nice.'

But she still goes, 'Do you nat thank ut teeks yorrs off may?'

'I do, definitely. What, er, prompted it?'

She gives out a little groan as she climbs up off her knees – it's, like, another reminder that I'm doing the right thing here. She might be only a few years away from assisted living.

'What do yee mean, what prampted ut? *Ay* jost foncied a cheenge, is all.'

'Hey,' I go, 'I only asked. I said I actually like it.'

I look at her. She's got two big sweat patches under the orms of her turquoise aertex and her MBTs – I'm going to be honest with you – are doing literally nothing for me now.

'There's, er, something I need to say to you,' I go.

She's standing there with, like, weeds spilling out between the fingers of her gorden gloves. And she knows what I'm about to say. Girls, like front-row forwards, can just sense when they're about to be corded.

Except she gets in there before me. That's the experience showing, see – old head on, well, old shoulders. Or maybe old head with a young haircut on old shoulders. She goes, 'Thor's something *ay* need tee talk to yee abite, tee.'

Naturally, that throws me. I'm like, 'Er, okay – you first, then,' because obviously mine's a total conversation-stopper. I don't want to go, 'This was actually a mistake. I'm out of here,' if her thing ends up being that she picked up a beautiful, I don't know, Empire three-branch candelabrum today.

She twists the weeds into her hands, then drops them into a little pile at her feet. 'Hedda called arind todee.'

I actually laugh. 'I thought she moved out.'

'She said she'd been talking tee Kathleen.'

'Kathleen? As in, Kathleen who came onto me in the hotel?'

'They're frands, see – jost from Hedda going dine thor all the tame, when her doddy was alave.'

'Okay.'

'And she's seeing ut was the other wee rind – thot yee came on tee hurr.'

'That's what she said when you sacked her, can I just remind you.'

'Aye. And she's stacking tee her storay. She said yee beesically prapositioned her and when she told yee she was married, yee made up a storay.'

'Well,' I go, 'if you knew me half as well as you thought you did, you'd know that's total horseshit.'

'Thot's what ay told her. Ross, it's *yee* ay believe.'

'Okay, well, that's cool. Probably my turn to speak now . . .'

'We hod a heege roy. Lot of bawd thangs said.'

'Like what?'

'Doesn't motter.'

'Just as an example, though.'

'She called may a dasperate old coy who was traying to hold bock the yorrs and meeking a obsolete fool of maysalf in the process . . .'

Ah, that'd explain the trip to the focking hairdresser's.

'She said *ay* should be grieving for Toddy instead of running arind with some gay who's luterally half may eege.'

'Okay,' I go, 'on that exact point . . .'

'So *ay've* come tee a decasion . . .'

Happy focking days, I think. She's going to do the deed, saving me the trouble of making a big speech and allowing me to take – for once in my life – the moral high-ground.

'A decision?' I go.

She looks away from me. 'It's, well, the toughest dacision ay've ever hod to meek in may lafe.'

'Well, it would be. Continue.'

She fixes me with a look and goes, 'Ay'm wrating Hedda ite of may wull.'

You can imagine my reaction. I mean, it's not exactly what I was expecting. I'm like, 'Er, can you do that?'

'*Ay* can dee onythang ay want. It's *may* mornay – may basniss.'

'What are you going to do?' I go, proving that my legendary slowness is still intact. 'Leave it all to the dogs and cats home?'

Then I catch her smiling at me in, like, a certain way and I know what she's going to say before she even opens her mouth.

'Ay'm gonna leave it all tee yee.'

I can actually feel my hort suddenly quicken.

I'm like, 'Er, *say* that again?'

'Well, way nawt? Yeer the one person in the world at the moment who meeks me hoppay. Way *wouldn't* ay leave it all tee yee?'

I try to say something, roysh, except my mouth won't form actual words.

She steps up to me and, like, kisses me on the lips. She smells of Gucci *Envy Me* and B.O. The next I know, roysh, she's kissing my neck, then undoing my belt and my chino buttons and – with her gorden gloves still on, remember? – having a root around below-deck.

'Noy,' she whispers in my ear, 'what dud *yee* want to see to *may*?'

I can feel myself firming up. 'Nothing,' I go. 'It can possibly wait.'

Years.

8. Where there's a will . . .

I've already seen the ring, remember – although I still make a major fuss of it, like you're supposed to when two people who you know make it official. I tell them the truth. It's a focking beautiful ring. Way nicer than I expected a schoolteacher – albeit one in the Institute – to be able to afford.

Fionn's like, 'Thanks, Ross,' except he sounds like he doesn't actually *mean* it?

'Dude,' I go, 'that's an actual compliment.'

JP asks if they've set a date yet – or if they even have one in mind. Erika says some time next summer, although they haven't even considered venues yet.

'How deed eet happen?' Danuta goes, wanting to hear the story, which I've already heard at least five times from the old man. 'How does he propos to you?'

Erika just smiles at Fionn. She looks amazing, by the way – and I'm saying it in a brother-sister way. That dress she's wearing really shows off her high-beams. 'Well, we were sitting out on the balcony . . .'

I'm there, 'Of Fionn's gaff in Pilot View.'

I can feel Danuta giving me daggers. *Why* the fock? All I'm doing is, like, filling in the background.

'It was early evening and I was just sitting, watching the rain fall on the sea – oh, and I was a reading a book that Fionn recommended . . .'

'It's about Gideon Mantell and Richard Owen,' *he* goes, hoisting his glasses up on his nose with his finger, 'two nineteenth-century geologists whose obsession with unlocking the secrets of the dinosaurs set them on a course of bitter rivalry.'

How can anyone say she *hasn't* just settled?

'Then he stepped out on the balcony,' Erika goes, still smiling at him, 'and he said, "I've got a question for you." When I turned my head, he was down on one knee.'

One knee? The cocky focker. By rights it should have been two.

She's like, 'I'm so lucky.'

Then *he* goes, 'I think everyone here would agree that *I'm* the lucky one.'

'Agreed,' I go, then I try to move the conversation on. 'So, this, er, so-called business idea of yours, Fionn – has it gone anywhere or has it turned out to be a total and utter flop?'

JP *and* Oisinn both roll their eyes.

I go, 'Hey, I'm only asking out of concern for my sister. What *he* earns in a month as a focking teacher, she'd spend in an hour in BTs.'

'*Our* business idea,' Erika goes, subtly correcting me, but still all smiles, 'is progressing very nicely, thank you for asking. We've just signed the lease on that field in Mullinavat, public liability insurance hasn't been nearly as costly as we expected it to be and we've expressions of interest from thirty-six schools.'

'And there's bound to be more,' *he* goes, 'when the summer holidays end. Erika's taken charge of the administrative side of things, while I've been more concerned with matters of historical accuracy, ensuring that the re-enactments remain faithful to the facts as they happened. But at the same time, trying to figure out – in the case of say, the Somme – how do we re-create the sense of horror and the mind-numbing stasis involved without shaving students' heads, amputating their legs, infecting them with Spanish flu and asking them to sit in two trenches filled with rats and rainwater for a month!'

Everyone laughs. It's not immediately clear why.

Fallon & Byrne is packed, in all fairness, even though it's only, like, *wine* they're serving? I let my eyes do a sweep of the place. There's a lot of familiar faces. A fair few ghosts of – let's just say – situations past. I spot Larissa Brinckman with two or three more of Erika's equestrian friends, all of whom I've covered over the years. And Fionn's surprisingly foxy sister – was it Elinor? – who I'm tempted to have a crack at tonight, on a point of pure principle.

That's when I cop Sorcha, coming up the stairs, looking incredible in just her skinny Sevens, her Kate and Kass giraffe print halter and her Stella sunnies holding back her hair – she's obviously just had her roots done as well.

My first instinct is to walk away – maybe go and talk to my old man, who's wandering around asking random people to sign his petition for Sean FitzPatrick Station.

Then I just think, fock it. It's Erika and Fionn's engagement porty – we can at least be civil to each other.

'Hey,' I go, 'I suppose you're going to be a bridesmaid if the whole thing ends up going ahead?'

Her reaction actually surprises me, although shocks is possibly *more* the word? She gives me – I'm not making this up – an actual hug and then, like, air-kisses me.

I'm wondering is she pissed.

'Erika told me about the break-in,' she goes, obviously feeling the need to explain herself. 'She said your place was destroyed. I admit it, I was worried about you.'

See, Sorcha actually cares about me. It's the reason I've always been able to worm my way back in there.

'Well,' I go, 'to be honest, most of my shit – for instance, all of the stuff *you* bought me over the years? – was still in the old dear's gaff in Foxrock.'

She doesn't react to this, even though I can tell she's secretly pleased. She's like 'Do you have somewhere to stay?'

I'm there, 'Yeah, I'm staying with, er . . . well, you *could* say a friend.'

She doesn't bother asking who – she wouldn't give me the pleasure of telling her that it's a bird. Instead, she tries to go, 'The whole *crime* thing is supposedly storting up again – that's how desperate people are becoming out there. Do the Guards have any leads?'

Fock, I didn't bother my hole even ringing them. I did what I should have done the day those two lunatics moved in next door – just walked away and left the place to the elements. I'm like, 'Er, yeah, they just think it was basically burglary.'

I'm suddenly thinking, hang on. This is, like, *too* weird? How did we get from her threatening me with the Feds outside Donnybrook Fair that day to us shooting the shit like this as if nothing ever happened? It couldn't be down to just the break-in.

'Burglary?' she goes. 'Oh my God, it's all these cash for gold places that have suddenly sprung up.'

I laugh. 'Well,' I go, 'Foxrock's getting one in a few weeks' time. I don't know if you've heard.'

She obviously has, roysh, because she has a look over my shoulder to make sure that Danuta's out of earshot. 'Has anyone told your mum yet?'

'Nah, she's too busy promoting that horseshit book of hers. Did you see her on Miriam O'Callaghan, by the way, saying that people who are spending money like it's still the Celtic Tiger are actual patriots?'

Sorcha, who's always sucked up to my old dear, goes, 'The reviews have been – oh my God – amazing. The one in the *Times* said that the story of little Zara Mesbur's struggle to come to terms with the country's altered economic topography is a modern-day allegory that recalls the works of George Orwell.'

I'm like, 'Look, take it from someone who's read the back cover and one or two inside pages – it's shit. It's going to be hilarious when she finds out about the cash for gold shop, though. Hi-focking-larious. This is really nice, by the way – as in, us back to normal?'

'Don't stort getting ahead of yourself, Ross.'

'I'm not,' I go. 'I'm just making the point.'

A passing waitress stops to top up my glass and – I can't help but notice – check me out in a major way. Sorcha definitely notices. I'm there, 'How's Honor, by the way?' playing the total innocent.

She goes, 'Same as usual. Cheeky. Disrespectful. We're going to Paris in the morning.'

I'm like, 'So, you decided to actually bring her in the end?' cracking on that I didn't already know.

She looks amazing, by the way. Astonishing, in fact.

'Well,' I go, 'I'll pay for it. I mean, I was the one who promised her that if she won that race and blahdy blah . . . Blah blah blah.'

She's there, 'It's fine,' and then, roysh, a few seconds of silence pass – maybe even ten – before she goes, 'She really misses you.'

I'm, like, totally bowled over by that – but not so bowled over that I can't suddenly see an *in*?

'Hey,' I go, giving her one of my famous big softie looks, 'when you goys get back, maybe I could swing out to the gaff to see her, even for an hour. I'm talking about supervised – you can have witnesses there to prove that I'm not training her in any way.'

'That'd be nice,' she goes. 'That'd be really, really nice.'

Then she just, like, waves at Erika over my shoulder, then tells me to ring her next week, before she tips over to her friend.

I'm left standing there thinking that was easy. That was actually *too* easy? There's something up. There's something definitely up. Except I don't get a chance to figure out what it is, roysh, because the next voice I hear is Ronan's.

'Alreet,' he just goes.

I spin around and there he is, stood in front of me, dressed like a focking joyrider, sucking on one of those little plastic cigarette placebos – the son I haven't seen in pretty much six weeks.

'Well thank fock you're not back on the smokes,' I go. 'Which is no thanks to me, I realize that.'

He shakes his head. 'It's forgotten, Rosser, I told ye.'

'Of course, I definitely look less of a villain now compared to your old dear. Oh, she's let her standards seriously slip. No offence, Ro, but I'm actually insulted I ever went there myself.'

He looks sad. 'She brought him into the gaff last neet.'

I'm like, 'What?'

'Was the foorst time. Thee must be getting seerdious, Rosser.'

'I'm not asking this in, like, a jealous way, but did he stay over?'

'No. He bought her a rose, but. It was on the kitchen table when I got up this morning.'

I laugh. 'He buys her a rose, gets invited in and *still* fails to seal the deal. What a focking sap.'

He looks at me, roysh – okay, it's a word I've invented – but *pleadingly*? He's like, 'Rosser, we have to think of a way to break them up.'

Larissa Brinckman gives me a wave. She told me at her twenty-first birthday porty that she was, like, deeply in love with me, then tried to claim afterwards that someone spiked her drink. Yeah, the focking borman did – with the double shots of vodka you asked him for. I give her a wink. Supposedly married with two or three kids now, but I'll always have that to hold over her.

'Rosser, are ye even listening?'

'Sorry, Ro. Look, I didn't have much luck last week in trying to talk your old dear round. But I still firmly believe it's just a summer fling – either that or a use and abuse situation.'

'It's not, Rosser. Arthur you called out that day, she steerts aston me all these questions.'

'What kind of questions?'

'Do I like Tom? Do I not tink it'd be nice to have a stable, responsible authodidy figure in me life?'

'Okay, I'm taking *that* as a personal dig at me.'

It's what Ronan says next that brings me to my sudden senses and makes me realize, roysh, the seriousness of the situation. 'What if he ends up being me stepfadder, Rosser?'

'That's not going to happen,' I instantly go. 'I'm telling you *now* that's not going to happen.'

'Then fooken *do* something,' he goes. 'I'm going over to say congratulashiddens to Fionn and Edika.'

Before he does, he fixes me with a look, again *pleadingly* – copyright, Ross O'Carroll-Kelly 2010 – and goes, 'Ine trusting ye, Rosser,' which gives me, all of a sudden, an amazing sense of, not only responsibility, but you might also say pride.

It's amazing the difference that a few days can make.

As in, I've got a safe place to stay – rent-free – with a rich, sex-mad woman who's promised to put me in her will. My wife is back talking to me again, even though I'm still not a hundred percent sure why. There's a very good chance I'm going to be allowed to see my daughter, albeit supervised. And now I have a shot at winning back the trust and respect of my son.

In fact, if I didn't have one of Ireland's most ruthless gangsters threatening to – in his latest voice message – cut me into little pieces, put me in a suitcase and throw me in the focking sea, I'd say that it's turning out to be a pretty alright summer.

I see her through the stained-glass window in the front door, shuffling up the hallway, telling me she'll be right there – not as fast on her feet as she used to be. I suppose she's got to be the best port of, what, eighty?

She opens the door. Cordigan. Glasses. Grey woolly afro. She's actually not *that* unlike Sorcha's granny. Even has one of those unexplained bandages that old people have on their shins.

She screws her face up, like she's having trouble focusing on me, even from, like, three feet away.

'Is this the McGahy residence?' I go, even though I already know it's the right place.

We're talking Albany Avenue off the Monkstown Road.

She's like, 'Yes!' except she sort of, like, shouts it. 'What is it you're selling? Whatever it is, we've enough.'

'I'm not actually selling anything,' I go. 'This is basically a *social* call? I'm a past pupil of Castlerock College.'

'Oh, you've come to visit Thomas!' she goes. Her face is suddenly all lit up. Her son's an obvious Billy No Mates – she possibly sees me as a potential friend.

'That's right,' I go. 'He actually taught me. What a teacher as well! Jesus!'

Her face suddenly drops. At first I wonder is it because I swore. But then she goes, 'Oh, you've just missed him . . .'

Which I already know, because I watched him leave in his cor, with a sticker on the back that says, 'No one ever repossessed on a Starlet!'

You're not focking wrong there.

'Oh,' I go, 'what a nuisance! What a thundering nuisance!'

She's there, 'He'll only *be* an hour.'

Which I *also* know, because he has a coffee and reads the papers in Insomnia in Dun Laoghaire every Sunday morning. It's not the first time I've had to keep tabs on him is all I'll say.

I'm like, 'Oh, really?'

And picture me, by the way. I've dressed up as a right focking dork – grey slacks, white shirt, purple cable-knit sweater tied around my shoulders and my hair side-ported, to the point where she just turns around and goes, 'Why don't you come in and wait?' because that's how believable I am as an actual dweeb.

'I'm really sorry for the intrusion,' I go, stepping into the hall. 'I'm sure you get this all the time. Past pupils of his wanting to come back and pay, I suppose, homage.'

'No,' she goes, 'none of his students *ever* call.'

I nearly laugh in her face. That's because he's a cock, I think.

I follow her down to the kitchen, which, by the way, takes practically forever. She's that kind of slow on her feet where, if you were behind her getting off the bus, you'd feel like nearly giving her a shove in the back, even though deep down you'd know that it was possibly wrong.

She's like, 'Will you have tea?'

And I go, 'Tea . . . would be . . . delightful,' with my two hands joined, as if in prayer. It's a performance-and-a-half, even *I* have to admit it.

She lashes on the kettle, then, like, indicates for me to sit in the comfy chair next to the fire, which I do. I'm there, 'I have to tell you, Mrs McGahy . . .'

'Call me Mellicent,' she goes, counting three teabags into the pot.

'Mellicent, then. Your son is some teacher. I can still remember loads of the . . .'

What the fock *did* he teach again? I take a punt.

'. . . poetry we learned.'

She's like, 'Poetry?' her face all scrunched up again. I'm beginning to think it has fock all to do with her eyesight – it's just something she does when she's confused. 'But he's always taught geography.'

Geography – that was it.

'My point was,' I go, quick as a flash, 'he made it *sound* like poetry? All the names of the different countries. Holland and blah blah blah. Things that'll stay with me forever – and that's being honest.'

She seems happy enough with that, because she nods as she pours the boiling water in the pot, then while it's drawing she whips out the biscuits. Old people in this port of the world always have good biscuits in – in case a priest or a county councillor should call.

'Do you know what,' she goes, 'you remind me a lot of Thomas when he was younger.'

I crack on to find that hilarious. 'Really?' I go. 'I'd consider that a basic compliment.'

She's actually sound. She can't help who her son is, I suppose. 'Oh,' she goes, 'he had lovely manners, just like you.'

I'm there, 'Well, it's nice to be nice would be a catchphrase I constantly use.'

Then she stops, roysh, as if remembering something. 'I must show you some photographs of him – I'm sure he won't mind.'

Off she shuffles, presumably into the living-room, and I end up just punching the air. I pour the tea, to save her the trouble, then grab the biscuits and sit back down. I'm horsing into my third Bourbon cream when she arrives back into the kitchen with this humungous, black, leather-bound album, which she then drops in my lap.

The focking motherlode.

I honestly can't get it open quick enough. You can imagine my excitement, I'm sure. I'm suddenly sat there, in McGahy's kitchen, leafing through the focker's life, while his old dear is stood behind me, providing a running commentary.

I'm suddenly staring at a photograph of him – he's maybe Honor's age – bawling his eyes out, sitting on the shitter. 'He would *not* be toilet trained,' she goes.

I'm like, 'No way!' trying but failing miserably to hide my delight.

'Oh, he'd have tried the patience of the entire communion of saints. The angels as well. Sure, he wore a nappy until he was seven years old . . .'

Jesus Christ. I'd have paid ten grand for that kind of info when I was at school.

'In fact, his sister, who was three years younger than him, she used to call him Shippy Pants. Because she couldn't pronounce the real word.'

I'm there, 'I'm presuming *shitty*.'

And there it is! A photograph of him as an actual boy – he was even *tall* for seven – wearing a proper, full-on nappy!

'Hey,' I suddenly go, 'you wouldn't have any more of those Bourbon creams, would you, Mellicent?' and she straight away goes, 'Of course,' and then, as soon as she turns her back to go to get them, I rip the photo out of the album and stick it in the sky rocket of my – hilariously – slacks.

'I don't see any photographs of him playing sport?' I go. 'Was he rubbish at it or something?'

'Sport?' she goes, like even the *idea* of him playing anything is too ridiculous for even words. 'He was too interested in his schoolwork. Of course, his father – Lord have mercy on him – he wasn't happy with that.'

I shake my head. 'I'd say he wasn't, Mellicent. Please, continue.'

'I remember he used to say to me, "It's not normal – him stuck in his room with his nose in a book."'

I laugh – well, chuckle is more the word. 'He might have had a point there, in fairness to him.'

She hobbles back over with Bourbons – she brings the whole packet this time, to save herself another trip. I'm thinking, Jesus, you'd think McGahy would buy her a focking zimmer. Or even a cane.

'One thing I definitely do remember about him,' I go, 'is that he always hated rugby. He was very much *anti* the sport?'

She rolls her eyes in a sort of, like, knowing way. 'Well, that was the game his father *wanted* him to play.'

'Ahhh, certain things are storting to add up now.'

'Because my Eamon played prop, you see, for Roscrea. Back in the fifties. But he always thought Thomas was a physical coward. He said that about him from a very early age.'

I laugh. 'Jesus – no wonder he hates rugby, then.'

'Well,' she goes, 'later on, of course, we had all that trouble with the boys from the school team. That'd be another reason.'

'Trouble?'

'Oh, they used to throw all sorts of things at the house. Eggs. Dogs' dirt. One night, they wrapped his entire car in clingfilm.'

I just shake my head. 'That's bang out of order. And I *mean* bang. Do you mind me commenting, by the way – I don't see any girlfriends in here. Were there ever any women on the scene?'

She reaches for the book and turns ten, maybe twenty pages, for me. *He's* obviously her pride and joy – a whole album dedicated to the focker.

'There,' she goes, 'that's Peggy – that was the girl he took to his debs dance,' and I have to put my hand over my actual mouth to stop myself from laughing. I swear to fock, she looks like Martin Johnson with an overbite. 'Peggy went to live in South Africa. She's married to a chiropractor now. Oh, he was broken-hearted.'

And that's it? No one since. Jesus. I point at the window. 'God, that rain is really coming down now, isn't it, Mellicent?' and, when she turns to look, I tear that photograph out as well and stick it in the old *phóca*.

'What about now?' I go, wondering has he told her. 'Is he with anyone? As in, *with* with?'

'Oh, yes!' she goes. 'He's met a beautiful, beautiful girl. She's a nurse. I have diabetes, you see, and she was the one who managed to get my blood pressure down . . .'

The next thing I hear, roysh, is the front door slamming, then footsteps in the hall, then McGahy's voice going, 'I'm home, Mother!'

Hilarious.

'Thomas,' she goes, 'come in here a minute. Look who's come to visit,' and then she turns to me and goes, 'I didn't even ask you your name.'

'What the hell are *you* doing here?' are the very next words I hear. He's suddenly stood at the kitchen door, the Sunday papers under his orm, madder than the Old Testament.

'Thomas!' *she* goes, giving out to him, which is hilarious.

He's like, 'Mother, go into the living-room,' and then when she doesn't immediately, he shouts it, 'Mother, go into the living-room!' in the exact same way he used to shout in class.

She waddles off out of the room. I'm like, 'Cracking cup of tea, Mellicent,' really rubbing it in.

He morches straight over to where I'm sitting. 'What the hell are you doing in this house?' he goes, playing straight into my hands.

I stand up. I'm at least three inches taller than him, see, which has always pissed him off. I'm there, 'Not nice, is it? When someone intrudes on your, I suppose you could say, family life.'

He knows straight away what I'm talking about. 'Tina,' he goes, 'is not part of your family life.'

I'm there, 'Yeah, but Ronan is – which is why I'm telling you to stay away from her. From both of them.'

'How dare you!'

'No, how dare *you*! Handing back our Leinster Schools Senior Cup winners medals, that was one thing. But this? This is stepping way over the line.'

'What the hell are you talking about?'

'Don't act the innocent. This is a spite ride situation – that much is obvious.'

'I don't have to justify my relationships to you or anyone else.'

He's really shouting now.

I'm there, 'Finish it with her – or you'll be sorry.'

'Get out of my house this instant. I'm calling the Guards.'

I laugh in his actual face. 'Oh, don't worry, Shippy Pants. I'm going. But remember, I *did* warn you.'

Half eight on Monday morning, Fionn rings, sounding majorly pissy with me. He goes, 'When you called out to the apartment yesterday . . .'

I'm like, 'Whoa, what are you talking about?' because I can sense an accusation in the post.

'You called to my door at ten past nine on a Sunday morning, Ross. That's a memorable enough event in itself.'

'Bringing muffins from focking BB's. Which neither you nor Erika thanked me for, by the way.'

'Did you steal my purple cable-knit sweater?'

'Jesus Chirst,' I go, 'you're worse than my old dear with her fur coat.'

'Did you steal my purple cable-knit sweater?'

'Yes.'

He tuts. I'm telling you, he's lucky this conversation is taking place over the phone. 'Erika said she saw you disappear into the bedroom alright. And my trousers as well, I presume?'

I laugh. 'I wouldn't give them the pleasure of calling them that – they're focking slacks if they're anything.'

'Well, do you mind me asking – why are you stealing my clothes?'

'It's nothing focking kinky, if that's what you're implying. Look, it's not a major deal. I had to pass myself off as a total nerd for a couple of hours. I don't have time to go into the whys and the whatnots. What the fock are you doing out of bed, by the way? School doesn't stort again for another, what, three weeks?'

'I'm on the way to Mullinavat,' he goes. 'I need to measure that field. We've decided to start with the Battle of the Boyne.'

'Interesting. *Very* interesting.'

He's there, 'Do you really think so?' the sweater business totally forgotten.

I laugh. I'm like, 'Don't get carried away with yourself, Dude, I'm not talking about that,' because I'm porked – I should have mentioned – in the little, like, bus bay opposite Blackrock College. 'I'm sitting here looking at the circus field. There's no sign of Sorcha . . .'

'Isn't she in Paris with Honor?'

'Well, there's no sign of Giovanna either. There's no sign of *any* of the Healing Through Tai Chi crew. It's back to being just a field again.'

'Maybe they've broken for – yeah – summer holidays.'

'It's not that. There's something seriously iffy about this.'

He sighs, roysh, and tells me to bring his clothes back tonight, then just hangs up on me.

I pull back out onto the road, my mind suddenly racing. There's something going on. You could almost say I have a fifth sense for these things. Somehow I know that Sorcha being so suddenly nice to me in Fallon & Byrne that night is connected to that field being empty this morning.

But how? That's what I'm going to have to find out, I think, as I pull up at the red light where Mount Merrion Avenue meets the Rock Road. I'm sat there in a daze, roysh, this thing taking up pretty much all of my brain power, when all of a sudden it happens – *the* most terrifying thing that's ever focking happened to me.

Now, I don't say that lightly. I've been around a few corners in my time. I've had husbands who've walked into the room and caught me conkers-deep in their wives – some of them you'd even know from the old celebrity pages. That's a fear you never learn to master, no matter how many times it happens to you.

But this is something different. I can honestly say I've never experienced anything like the hort-pounding, toe-curling, orse-emptying terror I feel – as Terry and Larry cross the road right in front of me.

Okay, don't ask me what they're even *doing* in Blackrock at half eight on a Monday morning. I think we can take it for granted that it's criminal. I actually don't *give* a fock? All I can think about is that scene in *Pulp Fiction*, where pretty much the same thing happened to Bruce Willis. And like him, roysh, I'm sitting there thinking, okay, don't notice me, please don't focking notice me.

And for a second, roysh, I think my prayers might be actually answered. See, it often happens that you can't find something you've maybe lost because it's, like, right under your nose. It's almost like it's *too* obvious? *And* they're, like, deep in conversation. Terry has a stop-watch and Larry is quoting times in military hours, so they must have been casing a possible job.

Against all that, I'm sitting in a yellow Transit van with Shred Focking Everything painted in blood-red letters on the side. And, yeah, halfway across the road, the two of them stop – it's like they've sensed me, rather than seen me – and they both turn their heads slowly and I'm suddenly looking at them through the front wind-screen, Terry mouthing the words, 'Doorty fooken . . .' and Larry just staring at me with a big blue vein, I don't know, *pulsing* in his focking forehead.

Except they don't move. Not straight away. It's like they're trying to work out are they actually hallucinating – could anyone get this basic-ally lucky?

Then they move. Quick as well. But not as quick as I do. They each run for a door – Larry the driver's side, Terry the passenger's. I reach for my key and hit the button for the central locking, not a second too soon. Larry thumps the window and the entire van shakes. I reckon if he hit it a second time, he could put his fist clean through it. But he doesn't get the chance. I hear a beep behind me and I notice that the lights have turned green again, so I put my foot down and, with a screech of rubber, I'm out of there, looking at the two boys pointing and shouting threats in my rear-view mirror.

I breathe a sigh of relief as I watch them shrink into the distance. What I'm forgetting, of course, is that this is Blackrock, where you can't drive more than twenty focking yords without hitting a set of lights.

The next red I get is at that little focking pedestrian crossing between Blackrock Shopping Centre and the Frascati.

Shit!

I look in the mirror. In the distance, I can almost hear Terry turn to Larry and go, 'Hee-er, dis is Blackrock, remember!' and suddenly, roysh, the two of them are, like, tearing towards me again, as fast as their Nike Air Max runners will carry them.

They catch up with me, roysh, just as the light turns green again. Larry appears on the passenger side this time and goes, 'You're a fooken dead man – ye filty fook,' but I just slam my foot on the accelerator again, nearly flattening this woman who thought she had time to, like, tiptoe across, all apologies.

'Keep arthur him,' I hear Terry shout, because they can see there's another red light just before Eagle Stor. I'm looking at them, roysh, closing on me fast and I think, okay, if this light doesn't turn green in the next five seconds, I'm going to be fish food by lunchtime. And that's if I'm lucky.

Five, four, three, two . . . Green.

Go!

Someone kicks the back of the van, presumably Larry, because I also hear him go, 'I luffed her. I fooken luffed her.'

I give the accelerator some serious welly, but then I'm stopped again just after the Permanent TSB. I punch the actual steering wheel, going, 'It's supposed to be a focking *bypass*!'

The next thing I hear is the sound of breaking glass. It's actually a humungous explosion and my first instinct, of course, is to duck. And it's as I do that I realize that the back window has gone. I don't know whether they shot it out or if they just threw something at it. I don't wait around to find out either. I lead-foot it, even though the light is still red, and a silver Ka coming from Carysfort Avenue ends up having to swerve to avoid being creamed.

The two boys keep coming. I take the bend in the road at, like, a hundred and fifty Ks, but then I end up *having* to stop at the lights just before Maxwell Motors, because there's, like, traffic coming the other way.

I notice that I'm, like, shaking – it's the adrenalin, see.

The next thing, roysh, I'll never know how they made up the distance so quickly, but they're on me – they're literally on me. The van suddenly shakes and I realize they've jumped up on the rear bumper and I know there's no escaping them now. Then I hear feet clambering around on the roof. So I put my foot down – thinking, fock it – and I stort swerving from lane to lane to try to, like, knock them off.

They somehow manage to hang on all the way up the hill and I can hear Larry going, 'You're dead, ye doorty fooken pox! You're fooken dead!'

I drive straight through the lights at Temple Hill, then realize – fock it – I should have veered left onto the Monkstown Road, because there's always a back-up of cors at the bottom of Newtownpork Avenue.

But my ability to process information quickly and make the right decision in a split-second was one of the things that made me – and these are George Hook's words now – *the* greatest unfulfilled talent in the history of Irish rugby. And I'm happy to tell you that I still have it. I fly up the hill – with Larry on the roof, I discover, and Terry standing on the rear bumper, I *presume* gripping onto the frame of the broken window? Then, roysh, at the very last second, just before the Butler's Pantry, I pull the wheel shorply to the left, turning into Montpelier Place – a little *cul de sac* I remember from my time as an estate agent – at the same time sending Terry and Larry flying through the air.

I don't even stick around to see where they land. I throw open the door and the next thing I know I'm clambering over someone's front railings, then making my escape through a back gorden. And in the distance, I can hear Larry – obviously regathering his wits – go, 'Remember, Rosser, we only have to be looky once. You have to be looky all the toyum.'

★   ★   ★

Shit, is there no satisfying this woman? Twice yesterday evening, either side of Gok Wan, then once when she woke up in the middle of the night. Now it's nine o'clock the following morning and I'm trying to get dressed, but she's staring at me with those hungry eyes and her tongue sticking out of the side of her mouth, like Sorcha's granny when the focking Angelus is on.

Maybe Regina is my punishment for the life I've so far lived. A woman who's giving me so much Posh and Becks that it's actually beginning to feel like work.

She's like, 'Do yee hov tee go?' throwing back the sheets, then rubbing her hand up and down her bare leg, like she did that very first morning, downstairs in the kitchen.

I try to blank it out. I go, 'Bit of important business, to be fair,' and then I sit down on the side of the bed and stort putting on my Dubes.

She, like, drapes her orms around my shoulders from behind and goes, 'What if ay told yee thot *ay* want sotisfaying?'

I know entire rugby clubs who couldn't satisfy her.

I'm like, 'Regina, honestly, this shit I've got to do is, like, really, really important,' and I sort of, like, struggle free of her.

'Och,' she goes, 'you're nee fon,' and I can't work out whether she's ripping the piss or genuinely pissed off.

Two minutes later, roysh, I'm on my way out the front door, when she shouts down after me, 'Ay love yee,' and of course *I* end up having to say it back to her.

'I, er, love you as well.'

The next thing I know, roysh, she's stood at the top of the stairs. And that's when – they're so focking clever, see – she hits me with the line 'Lat's go ite for thot meal we talked abite so.'

And of course I can't say anything, because if I love her – and if she's leaving me all her moo when she falls off the perch – then what's the problem with us doing public appearances?

They're tactical focking masters.

'Er, cool,' is all I can go.

She's like, 'Fraydee?'

And I'm there, 'Er, yeah, whatever.'

'And horry home,' she goes. 'Ay'll be weeting for yee.'

Oisinn's also waiting for me – outside the gate, as arranged, in his old dear's Peugeot 206. He seems genuinely shocked when he sees the

state of me. He's like, 'Shit the bed – those two goys must have really put the shits up you.'

My face is, like, totally washed out and I'm a bit unsteady on the old Amanda Peets.

'Dude,' I go, 'this is fock-all to do with Terry and Larry. This is her, in there. Jesus, she's insatiable.'

He just laughs. 'I can't believe you're still hanging in there. Dude, there must a thousand beds in this town where you could find refuge.'

'That's a nice thing to hear. Yeah, no, but things have moved on since we last spoke. She's sticking me in her will.'

He's pretty shocked, it has to be said. 'She's what?'

'She changing her will. She says she's going to leave me everything. Dude, she's worth millions.'

He laughs. 'Am I hearing this right? Does she not have a daughter?'

'Yeah, but she's an actual bitch. They fell out in a big-time way.'

'Ross, is this woman all there?'

'Being honest, I don't think so. She's supposedly grieving. But – again – she's worth millions.'

'But even if she changes her will and it's allowed to stand, she could live for another thirty years.'

'The way she rides, she won't.'

'Ross, I'm serious. What the fock are you playing at? You could end up as her full-time carer.'

I laugh. 'I'll be long gone before that ever happens. Look, I've thought about this. I know what I'm doing. I've decided I might as well become an actual gigolo . . .'

'Jesus Christ.'

'Even if she doesn't die in the next two or three years, this is a woman who likes spending money on me. I just decided, fock it, you've done the whole love thing, Ross – where did it get you? You're thirty and you're still on your focking Tobler. Okay, I never thought I'd hear myself say these words but why not have sex for money?'

'Dude, I don't know what to say to that.'

'You don't have to say anything. Thanks for doing this, by the way.'

He shakes his head and says it ain't no thing but a chicken wing. And by that he means that I was the one who came and got him when he was, like, scared and on the run in the south of France. He owes me.

Except there *are* no debts between friends, especially ones who played rugby together.

We drive on in silence. Oisinn was never a morning person.

'I've got something that's going to put a smile on your face,' I eventually go, then I reach into my chinos for the photographs.

This is as we're passing the Yacht in Clontorf. When I show him the one of McGahy in a nappy, he ends up nearly driving us into the focking sea. He's there, 'Is that . . .'

And *I* laugh. I'm like, 'You better believe it's him!'

'Fock,' he goes, 'how old is he there?'

'Seven.'

'Seven? Wait a minute – no, that's got to be him dressed up for Halloween.'

'Dude, he wore a nappy until he was seven – that fact came straight from his old dear's mouth.'

He looks all of a sudden confused. 'How did you meet his old dear?'

I'm there, 'Long story. Now, have a look at this one,' and I hand him the second photo.

'Dude,' he goes, 'this is a picture of Martin Johnson.'

I'm like, 'Is it, though? Look again,' which he does.

'Shit! The Bed!' he goes.

I laugh. '*That's* what he brought to his debs.'

'Fock, I can see the dress now. Jesus, she's horrific.'

I shake my head. 'And you're saying that, bear in mind, as a man who's been with some of the ugliest things to ever come down the pipe. No offence to you.'

'So what are you going to do with these?'

'Oh, I've one or two ideas floating around up there in my, I suppose, *mind*?'

A few minutes later, we're crossing the East Link Bridge. As Oisinn winds down the window to pay the toll, he goes, 'Did I tell you about my new job?'

I'm like, 'Job?' obviously concerned about the goy.

He laughs. 'You know I've been walking my old dear's dog?'

'Yeah, I've seen you – what about it?'

'Well, one or two of the neighbours asked me if I'd take theirs as well – for a few yoyos. So then I started thinking, it's as easy to walk ten as it is to walk three. So I stuck an ad on the noticeboard in that supermarket of Gayle Killilea's.'

'*That's* your new job? And what are you earning – pocket money?'

'Well, I'm not pulling in anything like, say, a male prostitute . . .'

'Gigolo.'

'But I'm earning exactly what I'm allowed to earn under the terms of the bankruptcy.'

I don't know what to say. I'm actually hurting for the goy. I'm like, 'Walking dogs? Dude, that's, like, babysitting – Jesus, it's a job for a teenage girl.'

'Ross, don't,' he goes. 'I'm earning again – you've no idea how good that is for my sense of worth. Plus it gets me out into the air. Gives me time to think.'

I'm there, 'As long as you're happy.'

When we hit the Rock Road, he asks me if I'm okay, as in nerves-wise? I tell him I'm coola boola. I doubt if they're going to be still hanging around. This is Montpellier Place we're talking – the Feds would have been on the scene in, like, five minutes.

We pass the circus field again. Still no sign of Giovanna and her cult members. Which reminds me that Sorcha and Honor are due home tomorrow.

We take the bypass and – wouldn't you know it – every focking light on it is green. As we reach the top of the hill, Oisinn asks me again if I'm okay.

I'm like, 'Dude, if you can be brave, then I can be brave too.'

I'm ready for it. Whatever *it* actually is.

He takes the left turn at Butler's Pantry and, despite my fine words, it turns out that I'm not actually ready for it.

'Fock, no!' I hear myself just go. 'Fock, no!'

Old Amnesia is just, like, a blackened lump of twisted metal.

'You must have known they'd burn it out,' Oisinn goes.

I don't know if I even answer him. I open the door of the cor and the smell of, like, wet ash fills my nostrils straight away.

I get out and make my way over to what's left of the old man's van. Which isn't much, as it happens. The springs from the front seats and the outer metal frame of the actual shredding machine are the only things that are still even recognizable. The rest is just a chorred and mangled mess of metal on four pretty much melted wheels.

I laugh. It's possibly, like, *nerves*? I turn to Oisinn and I go, 'Any dog-walking jobs going?'

He can't believe it either. He's like, 'How much did all this cost?'

I just shrug. 'Seventy for the van? Maybe the same again for the equipment? Your guess is as good as mine.'

'Well,' he goes, 'it's lucky you're insured.'

Oh, shit. What with everything that's been going on – Ronan, McGahy, Terry and Larry trying to murder me – I forgot to actually renew it. I was actually going to do it that focking day.

Oisinn can read me like a book – a pretty basic book as well. 'You were driving around uninsured,' he goes.

I'm there, 'I had the form filled in and everything. Kept meaning to send it off. It was in the actual glovebox.'

'A hundred and forty Ks,' he goes. 'Do you have it?'

I'm like, 'What do you think? There's only, like, five in the company account. And obviously I can't tell the old man that the company he gave me has gone up in literally smoke – all because I couldn't keep my sword in its scabbard.'

Oisinn looks at me then like he's just realized something even *more* serious?

He's there, 'Dude, you've got to get out of this country.'

I'm like, 'Er, where am I going to go?'

'Go and stay with Christian in the States.'

'Yeah, I left there in handcuffs the last time, remember? There was that whole deportation order and blahdy blahdy blah.'

'What if they come after your family – have you thought about that?'

'They won't. Larry's got this thing about honour. That's pretty much why he wants me dead.'

'Why don't you go to the Feds?'

'That'd only make it worse. Do you think they couldn't – I don't know – *put a hit on me* just because they were locked up?'

'Well, what about Liechtenstein?' he goes, sounding desperate now. 'Didn't they want you to coach their women's national team?'

I'm like, 'Dude, my kids are here. I'm not letting two – admittedly sound – scumbags drive me out of my own town. No, it's like Larry said. I only have to be lucky all the time.'

★　★　★

How Tina got to work in a hospital with a mouth on her like that I'll never know. She honestly belongs down the focking docks, loading crates onto ships. She calls me a bastoord, then a doorty fooken bastoord, then a pox. I just hold the phone away from my ear until she pretty much blows herself out.

Then I'm like, 'Finished?'

'You put dem pitchers of Tom on de internet,' she goes, no proof or anything.

I'm like, 'Okay, just say for orguments sake that you're right – do you not think I was fully justified?'

'Dat was a medical condition he had.'

I laugh. 'Oh, I forgot I was talking to an actual nurse. And what about the other one? That was the last girlfriend he had and she was a total munter.' I'm sitting in the study in Regina's gaff, with the Facebook page open. 'That's his standard, Tina – and that was, like, thirty *years* ago?'

She's there, 'If ye tink ye can break me and Tom up dat easily, you've anudder tink comin.'

I'm there, 'Have you seen how many have already liked it? We're talking thirteen. Can you imagine what that figure's going to be by the end of the month, when the schools go back?'

'Ye doorty fooker . . .'

'And when I stick it on Twitter – it'll possibly end up trending.'

'Bastoord!'

'Tina, I can make this stop right now. All you've got to do is break it off with him.'

'Why? Because you caddent beer to see me happy?'

I'm like, 'Whoa, don't flatter yourself. *So* don't. What I can't stand is to see Ronan upset.'

'Ine tellin you what Ine arthur already tellin him. Ine entitled to a birra happiness. God knows, arthur all the wankoors I've been wir over de yee-ers.'

I know she's including me in that.

I'm like, 'So Ro's feelings don't matter, is that what you're basically saying?'

'What Ine sayin is dat he's going to have to come to teerms wirrit – just like you are.'

I laugh. 'Of all the men in the world, Tina . . .'

'We enjoy each udder's company.'

'Oh, do you?'

'Yeah.'

'Even though there's real badness in him?'

'There's no fooken badness in him. He's a lovely fedda.'

'Oh, there's badness in him alright. I could tell you some stories. I've always considered him a kind of evil Dumbledore – who hates actual rugby.'

'Look, I don't have to explain meself to you in anyhow.'

I try to, like, reason with her then. 'Tina,' I go, 'forget that it's me who's saying this and just try to see it from Ronan's POV. Do you know what *we'd* have done at school if we found out that one of the other kids' mothers was banging the principal?'

'What?'

'Well, we'd have made his life miserable, I can tell you that for nothing. And I'd have been the first in line when the wedgies were being dealt. All I'm trying to do, Tina, is protect him.'

'Protect him from people like you, then?'

She sort of, like, wrong-foots me with that line of orgument. I'm like, 'Yeah, I suppose.'

She's just there, 'Well, just to let ye know, your little stunt didn't woork. If anyting, it's arthur bringin me and Tom closer togedder.'

Another one.

'Hello, is that Shred Focking Everything?'

It's, like, the fifth call today. I'm going to have to arrange some kind of voice message to tell people the news.

'We're, er, not taking on any new client work at the moment,' I go.

The dude on the phone ends up being a bit snippy with me as well. He's like, 'What does *not taking on any new client work* mean?'

And I thought *I* was slow. 'Means you're going to have to ring someone else.'

He sort of, like, tuts to himself, then tries to give me a lecture. 'I would have thought, given the current state of the economy, that you'd have been desperate for any work you could get.'

People love to focking think that, don't they?

'Not so desperate,' I go, 'that I need to listen to shit from tossers like you,' and then I hang up on him.

Yeah, I think some kind of voice message might definitely be the way to go.

No sooner am I resettled in front of the TV than the house phone suddenly rings. Between it and the intercom doorbell, I'm getting no focking peace at all today. All I'm looking for is a quiet focking morning. Regina's out – shopping – so I let it ring out once or twice.

Except whoever it is, roysh, they seem pretty, I don't know, persistent, insistent, whichever of the two means being a total and utter pain in the hole.

I eventually answer by going, 'This better be focking good,' and the voice on the other end – Irish countryside, from the sound of it – goes, 'This is Malahide Garda Station. There's two of our fellas outside the gate there. They're pressing the intercom button but no one's answering.'

I'm like, 'Excuse me?' bringing the cordless out to the kitchen, where the CCTV screen is.

'They're looking to get in,' he goes. 'Can you buzz them in?'

There's two Gords outside alright, one sitting in the front of a squad cor, the other pacing up and down in front of it.

'Okay,' I go, 'can you tell me what it's in connection with?' thinking, what if it's Terry and Larry and this is, like, a trap.

'Open the gates,' the dude goes, 'or I'll tell the fellas to drive right fucking through them.'

So I press the remote button and the gates open and then I suddenly stort to shit myself. I'm thinking, why didn't I at least ask them to flash their badges. I mean, it *could* be a trap. Maybe they've found out where I'm staying and these two dudes are, like, contract killers who they've sent to do the job.

It's an awful lot of trouble to go to, but then they *are* seriously pissed off with me.

My hort, I don't need to tell you, is beating like a focking drum as I hear the sound of tyres crunching on the gravel. A few seconds later, the doorbell rings – bing-bong – and I think about maybe hiding, in the wine cellar, under the bed, anywhere.

But then I think, come on, Ross, you've been watching too many Bourne movies and you're letting your imagination run away with you.

So I end up just opening the door. And you can imagine what goes through my head when I look at the two Gords, both of them smiling, and I notice that the one on the left is holding a gun.

I don't actually remember deciding on a course of action. All I know is that I throw my hands in the air and I drop to my knees and I stort pleading for my actual life. I'm going, 'Please!' in verbal diarrhoea mode. 'It was a five-minute job on the stairs. It honestly meant nothing. I've got kids. Please. I don't want to die.'

The two goys look at each other, then crack their holes laughing.

'We're returning Mr Rathfriland's shotgun,' one of them goes. He's the one who actually hands it to me. 'It's not needed anymore as evidence.'

I'm like, 'Oh.'

'And who are you?' he goes.

I'm there, 'Ross,' the voice still a bit trembly. 'Ross O'Carroll-Kelly.' I'm still down on my focking knees, by the way.

He goes, 'And who are you in relation to Regina Rathfriland?'

'I'm her, er . . . her friend.'

The two of them look at each other and a definite smile passes between them.

'Her friend,' the second goy repeats. 'Well, friend, tell her to make sure and put that thing away somewhere safe. I'm sure she's not going to want to be looking at it anyway. But we have to return items to their legal owners once they're no longer part of an official investigation.'

'Her friend?' the original dude goes, chuckling to himself, as they're getting back into the cor. 'I'd say he's her toyboy if he's anything.'

'Oh, I'd say so,' the other one goes. 'I'd say he's giving her the right root.'

'Oh my God, Amanda Holden is a waste of focking make-up.'

I can't tell you how good it is to hear my daughter's voice again.

Sorcha is holding the front door open for me and I step into the hall. I'm there, 'Does she know I'm even coming?'

She smiles and goes, 'I thought I'd let you surprise her,' and then she leans towards me and air-kisses me, once rather than the traditional twice. And in pretty much the same movement, she looks over my shoulder, out onto Newtownpork Avenue. 'Ross,' she goes, 'where's your van?'

Of course, what do you say to that? 'It's, er, pretty much out of commission for the moment,' I go. 'I actually came here on the bus.'

She's suddenly full of concern for me. 'The bus? Ross, is everything okay?'

I laugh. 'Ah, the old so-say's not so bad. You actually get used to the smell.'

That seems to put her mind at ease. She's like, 'Go in and see her.'

I pop my head around the door of the living-room. She's sitting on the floor, about six inches from the TV, totally glued to E! News. Like mother, like daughter, I just think.

Actually, like father, like daughter as well.

'Oh my God, Madeline Zima is *such* a wound,' she's going. 'If I was throwing that dress out, I'd leave it with next *door's* trash? That's *so* lollers!'

I'm just there, 'Now what way is that to be talking about other people?'

She turns her head and practically screams, 'Daddy!' She jumps up and by the time the third 'Oh my God!' slips her lips, she's crossed the living-room floor and pretty much jumped into my orms.

It's a genuinely amazing moment – a real tear-jerker, if you were there to see it.

We sit down, Honor on my knee. 'How was Paris?' I go. 'I want to hear all about it.'

'Oh my God,' she goes, 'Lake Bell was staying in our hotel and we saw Zoey Deschanel coming out of the George V in a red dress that – not being a bitch – did nothing for her. And Mom *thought* she saw Joy Bryant going up the escalator in Anna Lowe but when we chased after her – oh my God, *toats* embarrassing – it wasn't her at all, just this, like, woman who *looked* like her? And the fashion was, like, *so* amazing. You can see all the new styles – oh my God – months before they come out here, especially the new trend in colours. The French just know how to do things. Mom bought me my first little black dress and she says that, no matter how bad things get with the economy, it's the one thing that a girl can't afford to be without. And we had dinner in a restaurant where they called me Mademoiselle, but Mom – oh my God, she can be *so* retorded – wouldn't let me have the foie gras because they couldn't provide a certificate to say that it was ethical . . .'

I just shake my head in, I suppose you could say, *wonder*? 'Sounds like you two had an amazing time,' I go. 'And how was that street you were banging on about before? The *Champs* . . .'

She screws her little face up at me. 'The *Champs Elysées*?' and it's hilarious, roysh, because she says French words now with an actual accent, the exact same as Sorcha does. 'You're *such* a tord, Dad. The *Champs Elysées* is – oh my God – *so* lame. As in, like, Toats McGoats.'

I'm like, 'Is it? I thought it was, like *the* place for fashion?'

'Er, yeah!' she goes. 'If your idea of fashion is, like, Zara, Gap and Benetton – oh my God, it's, like, *so* high street. For, like, *haute couture*, you have to go to, like, Avenue Montaigne or Rue du Faubourg Saint-Honoré . That's where they *all* are – Christian Dior, Yves Saint Laurent, Chanel, Hermès . . .'

I'm there, 'Oh, my mistake.'

She's like, 'Prada, Gucci, Versace. And look,' and she suddenly rolls up her little sleeve and sticks the back of her wrist practically in my face. 'Smell, Daddy!'

I'm like, 'Jesus!' and then I take a breath. It's nice actually. 'What's that, Honor?'

'It's Shalimar. Mom said it was, like, *her* first ever perfume as well? You get it in the House of Guerlain. Actually, that's, like, the only good thing on the *Champs Elysées*. The rest is, like, *so* lame. Oh my God – *and* the Louis Vuitton store.'

'Oh, *they're* there as well, are they?'

'Hello? It's, like, their flagship store?'

'Is it?'

'Oh my God, everyone in the world knows that, Dad. And Mom bought me a Vuitton make-up pouch which she says I can use for a pencil case when I stort in Mount Anville. And she said I can have an actual bag when I'm, like, thirteen. When will that be, Dad?'

'Jesus, you're asking the wrong man, Honor. How old are you now?'

'I'm nearly five.'

'Well, then you're talking six, seven years. Something in that ball-pork.'

'And the House of Guerlain has an in-house spa. And I had my first ever mani-pedi. And when I said I wanted an extreme facial, the lady said I didn't need one because I had the nicest skin she'd ever seen. And then Mom storted crying. Oh my God, *so* embarrassed for her.'

I look over my shoulder. I don't *know* why? 'Your mother was crying?'

'Er, are you deaf? That's what I said, wasn't it? The woman said I didn't need to cleanse *or* exfoliate and Mom just, like, burst into tears. Er, *overshare?*'

I lift her off my knee and plonk her down on the sofa beside me.

I go, 'You sit and listen to Ryan Seacrest for a minute, will you? I need to go talk to Mommy.'

She seems happy enough with that. On the way out of the room, I hear her go, 'Gabby Sidibe – oh my God, they can do *nothing* with her.'

I wander out to the kitchen. Sorcha's cooking lunch. It smells very much to me like her famous avocado and goat's cheese torte. I lean against the door frame and I go, 'I can't believe how like you she's become. It's lovely to see.'

She accepts the compliment, then says she has her moments, even though she can be so rude sometimes.

I laugh. I'm there, 'So she's inherited at least *some* of my genes, then?'

She's standing with her back to me, chopping basil. I walk up behind her and – I know I shouldn't, roysh – but I go, 'So, how's the old healing going – through tai chi or otherwise?'

'Fine,' she goes, a little too eagerly.

I'm there, 'And Giovanna – she's well, is she?'

She doesn't answer. After, like, a moment of silence, all I can see is her two shoulders going up and down and it's obvious she's crying. The next thing, roysh, she lets out this – I'm going to call it an anguished howl, then she turns around to face me and I make an automatic grab for the hand that's holding the Stellar Sabatier herb knife.

It's not that I think she'd *intentionally* stab me? But it's a fact that I inspire strong passions in women. It's my instinct for self-preservation as much as anything.

I sort of, like, pull her into a clinch and she storts literally crying on my shoulder, going, 'She ran off with our money, Ross. She ran off with all our money.'

I'm just holding her, going, 'Hey, it's okay. It's okay, Babes.'

'It's not okay,' she goes. 'She *was* a con woman. You were right, Ross. You were right all along.'

I'm like, 'Believe me, that gives me no pleasure whatsoever.'

Well, it actually gives me a lot of pleasure – though you're not supposed to show it.

She pulls away from me, her face an absolute mess, and looks me in the eye. 'I confided things in her, Ross. I mean, things about us – about our break-up, about my feelings for you. And I let her say the most awful things about you. She said you sucked the life force out of Honor and me . . .'

'Because I was the only one who pulled her up on her horseshit.'

'And all the time she was scamming me. Scamming all of us.'

I'm like, 'How much? How bad are we talking here?'

She closes her eyes, sending more tears spilling down her face. 'Five grand,' she goes.

I'm like, 'Five *grand*? From each of you?'

'She said it was for the next phase of our healing.'

'I wouldn't focking blame her. So where is she now – have the Feds any idea?'

'They think she's probably left the country.'

'I'd say they're probably right. Five grand from, what, two hundred and fifty people . . .'

'It's one point two five million.'

'Thanks. I'd have got there in the end. One point two five. Fock!'

She goes, 'They're saying her name might not even have *been* Giovanna, Ross,' and that kicks off another round of tears. 'They think it might have been an alias.'

'I'll give it to you,' I automatically go.

She's like, 'What?' wiping her face with her open palm.

'The five grand.'

'No,' she goes, shaking her head. 'You won't.'

'There's five Ks in the company account. I can write you a cheque – this actual minute.'

'No, Ross. I can't have you constantly picking up the pieces for me. Otherwise, what's the point in us getting divorced? Thank you, Ross, it's very much appreciated, but I'm going to have to learn to stand on my own two feet.'

I just shrug my shoulders. 'You don't have to.'

'Look, I'm just sorry I let that woman keep you from your daughter. She got inside my head . . .'

'Doesn't matter.'

'Why do I put my trust in these people? Why am I always looking for gurus?'

I wipe a smudge of mascara from her cheek with my thumb. 'You want to believe in something,' I go. 'That's not a bad thing. Especially with the way the world is going out there. To shit, in other words.'

'Well, that's another thing you were right about. We do all have to become tougher if we're going to get through this thing that's happening.'

I shake my head. 'I wouldn't listen to what I say, Sorcha. If you knew some of the things that have happened to me recently – I mean, I don't know shit.'

She forces out a smile. 'Where are you living?' she goes. 'Oh my God, you're being so mysterious about it.'

'I told you, just with a friend.'

She's like, 'A *female* friend?'

I just nod.

Then *she* nods, *processing* this information, if that's the word.

I'm like, 'She's not someone you need to be jealous of, in case you're wondering.'

Her face becomes suddenly serious, like she's concentrating on something. 'I don't think I am,' she goes and I can't work out whether she's telling the truth or not.

A few seconds pass. She smiles at me then. 'You are *so* a good person,' she goes. 'It makes me – oh my God – *so* sad when people can't see that.'

'Yeah,' I go, 'I suppose if I had to define myself, I'd say, Ross O'Carroll-Kelly, yeah, his hort's in the right place, but his brain – who knows where the fock they put that. Although that might well be it, swinging between his legs.'

She laughs – she thinks it's genuinely hilarious – but then she gets suddenly serious again. 'All these fads. All these so-called lifestyle experts. But at the end of the day, Ross, you're the one who's always here.'

I'm like, 'Hey – and I always will be.'

And then Honor suddenly walks into the kitchen and goes, 'Oh my God, Sandra Bullock *so* has an issue with cellulite – it's, like, eeeuuuwwww!'

And what can we as proud parents do except just smile.

It's funny, roysh, because Sorcha was always talking about coming here – as in, like, The Truite Meunière? But now she's *never* going to get a chance to eat here because, according to what Regina's saying, it's closing tonight for good – and *she* should know, because she owns the focking place.

Yeah, no, she's decided – with the whole current economic thing – to close it down. Although she's keeping the others open, she says, including The Papaya Tree on Dawson Street and Lush in Rathgor, which are still making decent moo, which is down to the fact that they both introduced a special set menu – three courses, plus half a bottle of wine, for, like, thirty-five yoyos.

She wanted to do something similar here, she says, except Arnaud, the head chef – who's been here for, like, thirty years – begged her to close the place down rather than sell his creations at those kind of prices.

'What could ay dee?' Regina goes, pronging a scallop with her fork, then dipping it in garlic vermouth sauce and offering it to me across the table. I eat it. It's incredible. 'We've been frands forever. Arnaud and Toddy were in callege togather. When *ay* mentioned the words orlay bord, he crayed for an orr. He's vary emotional – Franch, see. Och, he bagged me, said please don't sell may food so cheaply. Said he'd rother give it ite for fray to the homelass.'

I have to say, roysh, he certainly *seems* to know what he's doing, because this is *the* nicest rib-eye steak with bordelaise sauce that I've possibly *ever* had?

'Still,' I go, 'it must be pretty hord, seeing the place close.'

She smiles. I think she really appreciates me saying it.

'The Truite Meunière,' she goes, 'was always *may* favourite. Because of Arnaud meenly – the gay's a genius . . .'

See, I was actually dreading tonight, the whole date aspect that she's suddenly introduced to our – for want of a better word – relationship. But it's not as bad as I expected. There's very few witnesses in the restaurant and it's not going too badly conversation-wise.

'I'm sorry again,' I go, 'about leaving Toddy's gun on the kitchen table like that.'

She shakes her head. 'It's fane. What were the Gords even thanking branging that rind to may hise lake thot? What do *ay* want it for – a seevenir?'

'Well, again, sorry – I can fully understand you flipping the tits like you did when you saw it.'

She smiles. She has a piece of spinach linguini stuck to her top teeth, although, being a gentleman, I don't mention it. '*Ay* thank ay could forgav yee for onythang,' she goes, then I feel something – her stockinged foot, presumably – move slowly up the inside of my leg. 'Yee more thon meed up for ut leeter awn. Ay'm walking wonkay all dee, so ay om.'

She seems well on. I'm pretty sure she skulled a few before we came out.

I try to distract myself by going for the gratin potatoes – Arnuad does them with, like, Gruyère. I'm trying to remember the last time I had gratin potatoes of *any* kind. I suppose that's another way in which the recession has affected me.

'So, er, any word from Hedda?' I go. And I'm only asking as someone who has a daughter himself. 'Do you know where she's even staying?'

'Don't knoy, don't curr,' she goes. 'She can dee what she lakes. Ay'm fanished with her. And I meant what ay said, bay the wee.'

'About?'

'Abite may wull. Ay've made an appointment to see may solicator.'

I top up her wine glass – a good, decent whack as well.

I'm like, 'You don't have to do that, you know.'

She goes, 'Ay want tee. Ay'm *deeing* ut.'

'Okay,' I go, 'I'm not going to argue with you. Just as long as you know, I'm not in this for old do-ray.'

She smiles. 'Yee *dee* love me,' she goes, 'don't yee?'

Shit. That bit of linguini on her teeth is really beginning to piss me off now.

I'm like, 'Of course I do. Big-time. Feelings. Blah, blah, blah,' and I reach across the table for her hand.

Again, she pulls it away, roysh, like she thinks it might burn her.

'Ay'm sorray,' she goes. 'Ay jost hov a thang abite may honds. It's sully, ay know.'

I suddenly remember reading something, maybe in one of Sorcha's magazines, about how the hands are the one place that women can't hold back the signs of ageing. That's why all these older celebrities who've had, like, work done are constantly trying to hide the old Christian Andersens. Madonna, for instance, hasn't got a line on her face, but she's supposed to have hands like a focking silverback gorilla.

I'm just there, 'Hey, it's not a thing.'

Regina decides to change the subject. 'Bay the wee,' she goes, 'where's your von?'

I'm like, 'My what?'

'Your von? It's nat in the goroge – or it wasn't when ay put Toddy's gun ite thor.'

I decide to just come clean. 'Yeah,' I go, 'it was actually stolen.'

'Stoolen?'

'Yeah, no, it was found, like, burned out?'

She stares hord at me for a few seconds. 'Ross, are yee talling may the treeth when you see thot no one's after yee?'

'Yeah, of course.'

'Because forst it was thot aportmant of yurrs. Then it was yeer cor. Noy, your von . . .'

'Well,' I go, 'it's like the Holy Inquisition was saying to me recently, the whole crime thing has suddenly kicked off again – yes, *even* on the southside. People are becoming basically desperate over there. You know that yourself, with the whole early bird thing you were talking about. In Rathgor? I mean, who ever thought that'd happen?'

This seems to satisfy her.

'So,' she goes, 'what are yee living awn?'

'What am I living on?'

'Aye, ay presume yee've no ancome if yee've no von.'

'That's, er, true.'

'Rait,' she goes, 'ay want yeer bonk details.'

'My bank details? Er, *why* can I just ask?'

'Ay'm gonnay tronsforr some mornay to yee – avery week. Will we see tee grond?'

'Two grand?'

'Three, thon?'

'Er, that'd be great.'

'Okee, four grond. Ay'll sat up a stonding awder. And yee can teek thot gulty look off yeer feece. It's all gonnay be yours one dee onywee.'

Arthur, Joxer, Marianne, Buster, Orville, Zaccy, Tarja and King.

Oisinn breezes through the introductions and I have to say I'm impressed. I've never been much into dogs myself, but he must be seriously into this new job of his if his ability to remember names is anything to go by.

Even JP comments on it. 'You seem really, I don't know, at peace,' he tells him.

Oisinn just laughs. It's nice to see even that.

This is us in, like, Stephen's Green, by the way. While Oisinn's exercising his mutts, me and JP have just been, like, throwing the old

Gilbert back and forth. The magic's still there in my wrists. JP even vouches for that, roysh, because he at one point goes, 'God, if Johnny Sexton passed like you, I think we'd have a very good chance of beating New Zealand in the Autumn series.'

That kind of shit helps with my confidence, even though it also makes me think how history could have been so much different if I hadn't been so into the birds and the pop.

'Any news on your gaff?' he goes.

I'm like, 'What?' and I end up throwing him a total hospital pass.

'Your gaff,' he goes, after running, like, twenty yords to retrieve it. 'When it's gonna be habitable again?'

'Er, no news yet, no.'

He's like, 'Where are you staying, by the way? You know, in the meantime?'

I hate not being able to tell him. He's, like, one of my best friends. But it's like Ronan always says – keep the circle of knowledge tight.

Plus, I don't want it getting around town that I'm romping a sixty-year-old woman. It could do untold damage to my rep.

'You know me,' I go, 'one thing I'll never be short of in this town is a bed.'

He laughs, in fairness to him.

'So what's the Jack with you?' I go. 'What have you been up to?'

He's there, 'I'm actually just back from the airport. Danni's old pair are gone back to Russia.'

This time I laugh? 'Fock. I never even got a chance to kiss her old dear goodbye.'

'Ross, don't even joke about that.'

'Hey, she loved it. I know when a woman's aroused. She had focking stors in her eyes.'

'Just please don't say things like that in front of Danni. Ross, they were still talking about you as they were walking through the departure gates.'

'Sounds like I made quite an impression.'

'Danni's old man kept telling her to watch you.'

'Jesus, as if she didn't already hate me enough. What's the deal with the shop, by the way?'

'Well,' he goes, 'the sign is going up over the door this afternoon.'

I'm like, 'Fock!'

I'm not the only one who feels this way either because Oisinn says the exact same thing.

JP's still trying to put a positive slant on it, though. 'I don't know,' he goes, sending the ball spinning through the air towards me. I catch it brilliantly, it has to be said. 'I think Foxrock has changed quite a bit from the days when the locals objected to every little thing they thought might affect the value of their houses. I mean, the people there are going through the same financial agonies as everyone else. Worse, from a lot of what *I've* seen. I think a lot of locals are going to consider what Danni's doing a vital social service.'

'Dude,' I go, launching it straight back at him, 'if my old dear looks out of the window of The Gables tomorrow morning and sees a sign across the road saying "End of the Rainbow – Cash for Gold", she'll shit an egg so big, it'll keep Foxrock in frittatas for a month.'

Oisinn laughs. I *can* be very funny. So funny, in fact, that the dude must accidentally let go of one of the eight leashes he's holding and Orville – a Jack Russell that belongs to a woman on Morehampton Road – makes a bolt for it.

JP, who *used* to be one of the best full-backs for his age in the country, lets him slip right through his legs, then he turns and chases off after him.

Oisinn doesn't seem too worried. Like I said, he's unbelievably chilled these days. 'Do you remember JP did the exact same thing against Monkstown in the Junior Cup?' he even goes and of course *I'm* the one who ends up laughing then.

I wander over and sit down on the bench beside him.

Buster tries to stick his nose in my crotch and I end up having to slap him twice on the nose, hord, before he accepts that there's nothing down for him.

Oisinn goes, 'Sorry, Buster. He's got someone who looks after him in that department these days. How is she, by the way?'

I'm there, 'Regina? She's fine.'

'Sex still good?'

'There's plenty of it, is all I'll say. And as well as that . . .'

'What?'

'She's giving me four grand a week.'

He laughs, roysh, like he can't believe his ears. 'Dude, say that again.'

'She set up a standing order for me. Four grand – it's no biggie.'

'In other words, she's put you on salary.'

'She's *hordly* put me on salary.'

'You're on the payroll, Dude, as her paid lover.'

Then he cracks his hole laughing. And that's when my phone all of a sudden rings.

I answer it, roysh, and the next thing I know I'm listening – well, *half* listening – to the old man banging on about some dude called Frank Hoppel, whose name certainly rings a bell.

I'm like, 'Does he drink in, like, the Royal St George or something?' still not sure why I should give a fock about him one way or the other.

'Well, yes,' the old man goes. 'But listen to what I'm telling you, Ross. He's been arrested.'

I'm like, 'Arrested?'

'Taken in for questioning . . . Crumlin, if you can believe it! Hennessy's on his way out there now.'

I step out of earshot of Oisinn.

'Sorry,' I suddenly go, 'what's this even about?'

'Well,' he goes, 'I shouldn't say too much over the phone. Let's just say that a connection has been established between him and a certain financial institution. And, well, the exact nature of the relationship, he'd rather not have shared with the authorities.'

Of course I'm *struggling* to keep my rag here. 'Er, when I said what's this even about, I meant how is it any of my beeswax?'

'Well,' he just goes, and I have to admit that his answer leaves me pretty much speechless, 'you were supposed to collect seventeen bags of documents from him the other day.'

I'm like, 'What?'

'Yes, last week,' he goes. 'Don't you remember?'

Shit, he must have been the dude I told to go fock himself.

'He rang your number when you didn't show. Said whoever answered was terribly rude to him.'

I'm there, 'Doesn't sound like me. He must have rung the wrong number.'

'That's what I thought. Anyway, the postscript to the story is that the Criminal Assets chaps showed up an hour after you were due. Oh, it was easy for them. Well, all the evidence was bagged up and waiting in the hallway.'

I know the question is coming – that's as sure as I'm about to make my voice sound all breaky-uppy and crack on that I've lost my signal.

He goes, 'Hennessy wouldn't be half the solicitor he is, Ross, if he didn't, well, ask what happened to you? That's how a legal mind works, you see. Clinical. Etcetera.'

Of course I can't bring myself to tell him the actual truth, that the business he basically entrusted to me – the company that he predicted could be worth between fifteen and twenty mills inside three years – is already focked, just like Hennessy said it would be if the old man handed it over to me. And why? The usual. I couldn't keep the old heat-seeker to myself. I don't know how I'd even begin breaking the news to him. If that makes me a sentimentalist, then, hey, I'm guilty.

'Of course,' the old man suddenly goes, 'I know the truth, Ross.'

My blood goes instantly cold. I'm like, 'What?'

'Come on, Ross, you can't get anything past your *old dad*. I know what really happened.'

I'm looking at JP walking back towards us, with Orville struggling in his orms.

I'm like, 'Yeah, you're actually just breaking up there. I think the signal's about to . . .'

He goes, 'You *knew* that a raid was about to happen, didn't you?'

I'm there, 'Errr . . .'

'Oh, I said as much to Hennessy. I said the chap will have *sensed* that something was about to happen. Wouldn't want to be caught with the evidence on him. No, no, I said. Young Ross, he's as astute as they come. He senses things. You only have to remember the way he used to create space for himself on the rugby field.'

I don't give him an answer either way. I'm actually still there going, 'Errr . . .'

And he's like, 'Oh, your godfather *will* be relieved,' then *he* ends up hanging up on *me*.

There's a turf war raging on the streets of Dublin 15 – that's according to Paul Reynolds, who, I think it's generally accepted, knows his shit. I higher up the sound.

On the screen, they're showing the outside of a pub in a place called Corduff – yeah, it's a new one on me as well – with two Feds standing gord on the door and the whole place roped off with, like, scene-of-crime tape? Then they show the inside.

He gets the access, Reynolds – that's why Ro's always been a fan.

There's, like, pools of blood all over the floor, roysh, and broken glass everywhere. Then the camera sort of, like, zooms in on a bullet hole in a painting of four or five dogs playing snooker.

I listen, roysh, because somehow I know – you could call it, like, *instinct?* – whose handiwork this actually is.

'Today's attempted killing,' Paul Reynolds goes, 'marks the escalation of what Gardaí say is a power struggle within the self-styled New Westies. Members of the notorious criminal gang are fighting for control of Dublin's ever-dwindling cocaine market. Garda sources believe the attack, which happened in broad daylight in front of dozens of lunchtime customers, was ordered by the two brothers who head the gang. The victim, who is recovering in hospital, is known to have served under them as a lieutenant and, according to sources, was expected to assume control of the criminal organization in May, when the brothers planned to move to Alicante. However, they changed their minds about retirement, creating ill-feeling within the gang and resulting in what happened today – the first shots fired in what Gardaí fear will be a long and bloody battle for control of West Dublin's streets. Paul Reynolds, RTÉ News, Corduff . . .'

It's at that exact moment that the room goes suddenly dork. I end up pretty much shitting myself . . .

Someone has their hands over my eyes.

I let a scream out of me. Not a shout, either. A scream, like an actual girl.

I grab the two sets of fingers and pull them back, then – in pretty much the same movement – I scramble to my feet and spin around.

Shit. It's only Regina.

'What's the motter with yee?' she has the actual cheek to go.

I'm there, 'Jesus, I'm shitting like a flock of bats here.'

She looks at the TV screen. 'Maybe yee shouldn't watch the sax o'clock nees if it meeks yee thot jompay.'

I'm like, 'Sorry,' my hort beat returning to something close to normal. 'You, er, frightened me, is all.'

'Well, *ay've* got a surprays for yee,' she goes. 'Come on – itesade.'

308

I'm still a bit shaky on my feet actually. My nerves have been shot to bits, I realize, since that day in Blackrock.

She covers my eyes again, then sort of, like, slow-walks me out to the front door.

I'm like, 'Do we have to go through this entire routine?'

'Nee peeking,' she goes.

I step blindly out onto the front step, then out onto the gravel drive-way. That's when she removes her hands from my eyes and I'm just stood there, staring, in total and utter awe.

It's, like, an Audi A8. Brand focking new. And presumably a present for me.

I run my hand along the smooth gold bodywork, which I can see my actual face in, by the way, then I look through the driver's window at the cool grey upholstery and the brushed aluminium and walnut detailing.

'I don't know what to say,' I go.

'Well,' she goes, 'thonk yee would be a good pleece tee stort.'

I'm like, 'Well, definitely thank you,' and I go to kiss her on the cheek. She catches me by the back of the neck and tries to force her tongue into my mouth but I pull away, roysh, cracking on to be too excited about checking out the cor's features to even think about sex.

She laughs. 'It's tree what thee see – the love rayvel you really have tee worry abite is a cor! Go on, gat in thor!'

It's an un-focking-believable piece of work. We're talking direct-injected, four-point-two litre, V8 engine. We're talking all-wheel drive, automatic torque-vectoring rear differential, collision-mitigation system and then – the crème de la mer – a 1,400-watt Bang & Olufsen sound system.

I'm just sitting there, shaking my head, going, 'This is unbelievable.'

'Well,' she goes, 'ay hope yee've no objactions to me baying it for yee.'

I laugh.

'Er, no,' I go.

'It's jost ay felt sorray for yee. All the bod lock yee've hod. Yeer aportmant, yeer cor, yeer von, yeer basniss. I was draving pawst a showroom yasterdee – it was just a spor of the moment thang.'

I run my hand along the dash. 'No,' I go, 'I, er, love it. You're defin-itely not taking it back.'

She hands me the key then. 'Ay suppose ay'm ite of the pacture tonate so. Ay'll be in the sunroom – see can ay gat may *prana* roteeting in corcles of positive *chi*. Ay'll open the front geet for yee.'

I turn the key and the beast comes to life. It doesn't roar. It's one of those strong but silent animals.

I wait for the gates to open, then I put the accelerator to the floor and I tear out onto the road, spewing gravel everywhere.

I've never driven anything like it before – the thing corners like a focking rollercoaster ride – and I'm suddenly out on the Malahide Road, opening it up, seeing what it's got, with the radio on full blast – classic Kings of Leon – just to keep the old guilt feelings at bay.

That's when I feel my phone suddenly vibrate against my leg. I reach into my pocket and grab it. It's Ro. He sounds, if I'm being honest, a bit down. I try to cheer him up, of course.

'Ro,' I go, 'you wouldn't believe the cor I'm breaking at least two laws in at this exact moment in time.'

He's not interested. 'Ine back to school tomoddow,' he goes. 'You never did athin, Rosser. Me ma's still going out with McGahy – they're at the fooken pitchers toneet – and *you* did fook-all abourit.'

I'm like, 'Are you smoking there, Ro?' because I can tell from the way he's breathing.

'I am, yeah.'

'I thought you quit.'

'Well Ine back fooken on them.'

'Look,' I try to go, 'I did my best.'

He's like, 'What did you do?'

I'm there, 'Hello? I stuck those photos on Facers. The one of him in the nappy. Then the one of that focking jackpine savage he used to go out with. I did send you the link, didn't I?'

'What good did it do?'

'Well, obviously none,' I'm forced to go, 'if they're at the flicks tonight. To be honest, I didn't come up with a Plan B because I didn't figure on Plan A actually *failing*? Whatever about him in the nappy, I honestly thought when your mother saw the focking cronk he brought to his debs, she'd get sense and dump his ass.'

'She didn't but. It's the fooken opposite if athin. She's just arthur showing me a brochure.'

I'm like, 'A brochure? Is she threatening you with that juvenile care home again? Oh, that'd really suit her, wouldn't it? Get you out of the way.'

'No, it was a travel brochure, Rosser. Authumn breaks.'

I relax a bit then. 'Look,' I go, 'a lot of birds do that in relationships, Ro. They book holidays months and months in advance – just to keep the goy hanging on in there. Doesn't mean shit.'

'She's talking about the October bank hoddidee weekend.'

I laugh. 'Look, Ro, I have to be honest with you, I still don't know what *she's* playing at – she's possibly flattered. Older man. He's also the first goy she's been involved with since me who hasn't done jail time. There's possibly a novelty element involved. My hope is that she'll have seen sense *long* before the two of them go off on this, I'm pre-suming, city break.'

'Not *two*, Rosser. She wants the tree of us to go away togedder.'

I'm like, 'What?'

'She's talking about Copenhagen.'

'Whoa, whoa, whoa – as in, you, her and *him*?'

'Yeah – she said we'd be like a little family.'

'Family? Did she use that actual word?'

'I think so.'

'Rack your brains, Ro, I'm going to need a firm answer on that one.'

'Family. She said it, yeah.'

I end up having an absolute shitfit. 'No focking way,' I go – this is while I'm still at the wheel, remember. 'That's not going to happen. What, the three of you, playing happy families over in – what even country is it in? Or is it a country in itself? Is there even a website where we can find that out?'

'It's in Denmeerk, Rosser.'

'Denmork, then. Wherever. It's not happening. Look, I'll sort this, Ro. I'll come up with another plan.'

'Yeah,' he just goes, 'you said that befower. You're all fooken talk, Rosser.'

And even sitting in a machine with a horse power of three hundred and seventy-two, I can't tell you how bad that makes me suddenly feel.

9. The Battle of the Boyne II

Sorcha says that the cost of Government borrowing has, oh my God, soared – to, like, nearly three *times* the German rate? Which will tell you, she says, how little faith the international morkets have in our ability to pay the money back. She's bending down to grab a probiotic yoghurt from the fridge and, out of the corner of my eye, I get that flash of knicker that no man can resist – no matter who the woman happens to be – riding up above the waistband of her Genetic Denim skinny jeans.

'Dad thinks there's, like, *no* way the IMF are going to stand by for much longer,' she goes, 'especially with the ongoing uncertainty over what the bank bail-out is going to even *cost* the country?'

I'm trying to work out is that a G-er she's wearing or the regular Diana Vickers.

She stands up again, slips the yoghurt into Honor's little schoolbag, then stares hord at me. 'Dad says that what we're looking at now is an actual sovereign debt crisis.'

I end up just rolling my eyes, which is the reaction I think she expects from me. The fact is I'm not here this morning to get into a big intellectual debate. I'm here because today is my daughter's first day in Mount Anville – as in, like, the *junior* school? – and I want to be there to see her off.

It's like Sorcha says, aport from getting married, it's possibly *the* biggest day of her actual life. I know when Sorcha storted there, she didn't sleep a wink the night before – her old dear told me that she was dressed in her uniform and sitting on the edge of her bed waiting to go from about half five in the morning.

No such luck with Honor, though.

'She must be excited,' I happen to go, which automatically reminds Sorcha that the girl isn't even out of bed yet. She walks out to the foot of the stairs and shouts up to her, 'Honor Angelou Suu Kyi Lalor-O'Carroll-Kelly! Switch off that television this instant and come down for your breakfast!' and then she turns around to me and goes, 'She's – oh! my God! – addicted to that entertainment channel.'

I'm tempted to remind her whose idea it was to bring her to LA to live for the first two years of her life. Except I don't.

The next thing I hear is her tramping down the stairs, going, 'Ryan Phillippe is, like, *toats* hot!' and then she steps into the kitchen, cops me standing there and pretty much jumps into my orms, going, 'Dad!'

Like I said, I'm a total sucker for her, and you'd have to say, the feeling's obviously mutual.

'Daddy's coming to school with us this morning,' Sorcha goes. 'Now, are you going to eat up your muesli like a good girl?'

Honor's like, 'Muesli? *Eeeuuuwww!* Who's driving?'

Sorcha looks at me. 'Do you want to?'

I'm there, 'I'm easy like a Sunday morning, Babes.'

Honor looks suddenly worried. 'Not in the van, right?'

I laugh. You'd have to. 'No, the van's, er, still off the road. Yeah, no, I'm driving a brand new A8 these days.'

Honor claps her hands together and goes, 'Oh! My God!'

She knows a good cor from a bad one – just like her mother. She even sits straight down and gets bet into the muesli, even though it looks like a focking kitty-litter tray.

Deep down, I think Sorcha really loves the effect I have on her.

Fifteen minutes later, after Honor has, like, made her bed, then stacked her breakfast things in the dishwasher, we're on the road to Mount Anville.

Sorcha, it has to be said, is seriously impressed with the new wheels. She manages to hold her piss all the way up Newtownpork Avenue, but then, when she sees me corner the turn onto the Stillorgan dualler, she can't help herself. 'It *is* an amazing cor,' she goes. 'The business is obviously doing well.'

I decide to tell her the truth. I don't want her getting her hopes up for a big divorce settlement. I'm there, 'I wouldn't say that. It was actually a present.'

'A present?' she goes. 'Oh my God, from who?'

'From this girl – well, woman – that I'm sort of, like, living with. I mentioned her before.'

'So who is she, Ross? I don't understand why you won't tell me. Do I know her? Oh my God, she wasn't in, like, H.C.K., was she?'

'I don't really want to say at the moment. See, we haven't really defined what it actually *is* yet?'

'Hello? You're *living* together?'

'Yeah, no, that's only because my gaff got wrecked.'

'*And* she bought you an Audi. It sounds like it's pretty defined in someone's mind. I mean, I didn't want to say anything but this is the exact same car my dad was thinking about getting this year but then changed his mind because we're supposed to be in a recession.'

I feel a big, shit-eating grin break out across my face. I know how much that's going to piss him off.

She goes, 'I don't know why you won't tell me what even *school* she went to?'

Because she's that old, I think, it was probably a focking hedge school.

That's when Honor, sitting in the back, roysh, totally out of the blue, pipes up, 'Mom, do you think Jennifer Aniston and Brad Pitt will ever get back together again?' and you wouldn't need to be a child psychologist to know what she's *actually* asking?

Sorcha looks at me sideways – this is, like, halfway up Fosters Avenue we're talking – and goes, 'No, sweetie. He's with Angelina now. I think they might eventually end up being really amazing friends, though.'

'But Jennifer's still, like, toats obsessed with him. That's what it said on *E!*'

Sorcha goes, 'She's not obsessed, Honor,' not taking her eyes off me. 'She's just interested in what happens to him. They have a shared past, you see.'

'Well,' Honor goes, 'I think Jennifer Aniston's a sappy bitch.'

'Honor, your language! And I've told you – haven't I? – that we don't talk about people in those terms.'

'All I'm saying is that she actually just *let* Angelina take Brad away from her? That's why she's a sap.'

'None of us knows what actually went on. That's why we shouldn't be so quick to judge celebrities.'

'Yeah, whatevs! Angelina's, like, way hotter anyway? That haircut did Jennifer Aniston – oh my God – *so* many favours.'

I just smile at Sorcha. I know Honor's going to love Mount Anville. Then Sorcha can't help but smile, obviously thinking the exact same thing.

We pull into the corpork. Sorcha lets Honor out of the back while I don't stir. She asks me am I not going to walk Honor to her classroom and I tell her that I might not be welcome after the whole *Seven Brides* fiasco.

She just nods and goes, 'You're probably right.'

I give Honor a bit of a spiel about what an amazing journey she's about to embork on – jazz piano, three-day-eventing, the Ougadougou Cultural Immersion Programme – and that she should enjoy every minute of it. I give her a hug and off she trots and I'm left just sat there, thinking about that old line about how quickly they grow up.

I don't know which of them looks prouder – my daughter or my, still, technically, wife – as I watch them cross the campus to the junior school building, Sorcha pointing out various things and obviously filling her in on a bit of the history of the place – Mary Robinson, Alison Doody, blah blah blah – along the way.

I whip out my iPhone. It's on, like, silent, although I felt it vibrate in my sky rocket just before the Radisson. A missed call from, like, Larry. He's left another message, although I decide not to bother listening to it. I actually ring him back, roysh, to try to make one last appeal to the crazy focker's better nature.

'Where are ye?' is his opening line.

I'm like, 'Dude, you ask me that every single time we talk. Do you think I'm that stupid that I'm just going to, like, blurt out the answer one day?'

I probably focking will, knowing me. Deep down, he possibly knows that too.

'You're a dead man, Rosser – a fooken dead man walken . . .'

I'm just like, 'Whoa, whoa, whoa – you've been saying that for months, Larry. You still haven't found me.'

'It's oadley a mather of toyum.'

'Yeah, whatever.'

'Ine gonna hunt ye dowin, Rosser – oh, you'd bethor believe it. There's feddas taught thee could hoyud from us befower. We found feddas in Amsthordam, Spayun, all over the wurdled. We'll foyunt you – believe me.'

'From what I've seen on the news, you've got bigger shit to worry about than finding me. I think I'm actually distracting you from whoever the real enemy is.'

315

'*You're* the real fooken enemy. Wadn't for you, I'd be in Ali-fooken-cante be now with Saoirse, retoired ourra the gayum. If it wadn't for you and your fooken dick. And now Ine gonna hack that dick off with a bleaten . . .'

I hang up, roysh, because I spot Sorcha walking back towards the cor, dabbing at her eyes with a piece of, like, tissue. I hadn't realized how seriously emotional it was going to be for her.

She gets in and I ask her if she's okay. She goes, 'The next thing we know, she'll be a young woman.'

I rub her forearm, a thing I used to always do when she was upset, and she takes, like, a deep breath, then immediately changes the subject, a thing *she* always did.

'You only have to look around the carpark,' she goes, 'to see that we're living in an all-of-a-sudden different country. Even a year ago, it would have been all Mercedes CL500s and Volkswagen Touaregs. I saw a Qashqai over there.'

I just nod. 'It *is* sad, I suppose.'

'I mean, an *actual* Qashqai, Ross!'

'I'm agreeing with you, Sorcha. I think – I don't know – there should be a tribunal set up to invetigate the whole thing.'

I go to turn the key in the engine, except before I get the chance to, she goes, 'Look, I probably should tell you, Ross – I've come a decision.'

She pulls these lines out of focking nowhere.

I'm there, 'What kind of decision are we talking?'

'A life one. And I'm only telling you because I don't want you to hear it from someone else.'

'Go on.'

'Well, I've decided to, like, sign on.'

I'm there, 'Sign on?' in my innocence. 'Sign on what?'

She laughs. 'The dole, silly.'

I don't know what to say. That's how much in actual shock I am. 'The dole?' I manage to blurt out. 'But . . . But you've got an Orts degree.'

She shakes her head. 'There's no shame in being out of work, Ross. Especially in the current economic climate. Even Mum was saying this morning that unemployment is no longer the fault of the *actual* unemployed? Half my class from UCD supposedly don't have jobs.'

I could literally cry for the girl, although I try to be as supportive as I *can* be?

'Where does this – okay, I'm going to say it – *signing on* even happen?'

'Cumberland Street,' she goes, straight out with it, 'in Dun Laoghaire.'

I'm like, 'Jesus,' and I ask the obvious question then. 'I mean, is it safe? For a girl like you, I'm talking.'

She just shrugs. 'I don't know. What I do know is that I can't live on no income.'

'I'll give you a bit extra, then. Look, just between the two of us, the business hasn't been going great recently. But I've got money.'

She's like, 'Thank you, Ross, but this is all about me finally facing up to reality. I don't want to be a coward for our daughter.'

I just nod. Then I think, okay, if she can be brave, then so can I. I'm there, 'Do you want me to come with you?'

She just smiles at me and I smile back. There's no, like, edge to it, no sexual tension or blahdy blahdy blah. It's that look of, like, first love that actually remains long after two people who were basically childhood sweethorts have outgrown each other.

And she says I am *so* an amazing person.

I'm in the sack with Regina, bumping uglies, and, just to let you know, I'm far from disgracing myself. Her nails are tearing the skin from my back and she's screaming the name of the Bethlehem baby.

And no, I've still no interest in her sexually. But four grand a week and an Audi A8? I'm letting her know I'm grateful, that's all.

'Jesus Crayst!' she's going, at the top of her voice. 'That's incradible! Oh may gawd . . . that's focking . . . incradible what you're focking deeing to may.'

Like I said, I'm pulling moves here that I'd nearly pay to watch online.

'Don't stap what you're deeing thor!' she goes. 'Don't yee even thank abite stapping!'

It's at that exact moment, as luck would have it, that my phone storts ringing in my pocket. So I reach down and stort feeling around the floor for my chinos.

'What are you deeing?' Regina – between gasps – goes.

I'm there, 'Don't worry, I'm not going to answer it – I'm just going to check who it is.'

She's like, 'But we're in the maddle of . . .'

'Hey,' I go, 'I can walk *and* chew gum, you know.'

I manage to grab it with my hand – while maintaining my stroke, of course. I check the screen and I end up instantly regretting it. It just says, 'Old dear.'

'Who is it?' Regina goes.

Someone whose ugly mug I didn't exactly *want* in my head at this moment in time.

'Doesn't matter,' I go. 'Let's just get back to the job in hand. You must be nearly there, are you?'

'Jost shot your mithe,' she goes, 'and keep deeing what you were deeing.'

Which is exactly what I do – at the same time, running through a mental checklist of some of my fantasy women, just to make sure I stay afloat. Mila Kunis. Helen Flanagan. Mollie King.

'What the . . .' Regina suddeny goes.

Fock. The air's going out of my tyres. 'Sorry,' I go. 'Just bear with me a sec.'

Rosie Jones. Gabriella Cilmi. Christina Hendricks. Zoe Salmon . . .

'*Ay* told yee to leave your phawn alawn,' she goes, obviously pissed off with me.

'Well, don't write me off yet,' I try to go. 'I think I can get it sea-worthy again.'

Katie Cassidy. Kara Tointon. Doutzen Kroes . . .

'Jost forgat it,' she goes, slipping out from underneath me. 'The moment's gawn.'

I'm there, 'Happens to every goy – that's what they always say, isn't it?' except she doesn't even try to make me feel better. She gets up and has a Jack Bauer, leaving me lying there with a dick like an empty sock, wondering what the fock the old dear could even want at, like, ten o'clock on a Saturday morning.

It turns out she's left a voice message and it ends up totally cheering me up. 'Ross,' she goes, at a pitch so high, it's nearly out of the range of human hearing, 'they're opening – oh, I can barely bring myself to say it – one of these *Cash for Gold* places! Is this what Foxrock has come to? Selling our fillings? Well, you can rest assured that *I* won't be just lying back and taking it. No, I'm going to find out who's behind this. Oh, there'll be a campaign – *that* much I can promise you!'

I hang up, literally laughing.

The sound of the water suddenly stops and I hear Regina's voice from the en suite. She's like, 'What are yee deeing naxt Soturdee, bay the wee?'

I'm there, 'Next Saturday? Er . . .'

Except I don't get a chance to come up with an excuse, because she suddenly steps back into the bedroom, dressed in her bathrobe, drying what's left of her hair with a towel.

'Couple of frands of mane are hoving a wee danner portay. You remambor Levinus and his wafe whoy ay told yee abite?'

I nod, still trying to see an out. 'Okay. And did they invite specifically me? See, they might just want you on your own.'

'They invated *me* plus may boyfrand.'

Boyfriend. Jesus Christ. Do you ever stop and think, how the fock did I end up here?

'Er, *where* is it?'

'What does it motter where it us? Portmornack. Are yee coming or nat?'

'Er, whatever, yeah.'

'Ay told yee, they're all daying to meet yee. May wee toyboy, as they call yee.'

'Jesus.'

'Och, it's nothing to worry abite. They'll all love yee.'

I lie there and watch her get all dressed up – smort suit, the whole bit.

I'm like, 'Where are you going?'

She's there, 'Ay've got tee go into tine – see may solacitor.'

'About your will?'

'Aye. Thot and one or tee other thangs.'

So anyway, off she focks.

I drift off to sleep again. I'm not sure how long I'm *actually* spitting zeds? All I know is that I wake up with a sudden stort, certain that I'm not alone in the gaff.

I lie very still and listen. And that's when I hear it – a creak on the stairs.

Shit.

No, I think. It might be just Regina. Maybe she forgot something and had to come back for it.

But no. Because then I hear another creak and it's obvious that, whoever it is, is basically tiptoeing up the stairs, trying *not* to be heard?

I'm suddenly sweating like a trumpet-player's hole. It's Larry. I'm focking sure of it.

Another floorboard creaks – this one on the landing.

I run through my options like a man who's found himself in a lot of bedrooms he shouldn't have been in over the years. Under the bed. Into the wardrobe. Out the window.

In the end, roysh, I do none of the above, because before I have a chance to even move, the handle of the door moves slowly downwards and I end up doing something which, I have to admit, I'm pretty embarrassed about now. I stort pleading for my actual life.

'Don't hurt me,' I go, as the door slowly opens and I bury my head under the duvet. 'It was sex. Pure and simple. It wasn't even *great* sex, in all fairness. I'm begging you. I've got everything to live for.'

Then I hear a laugh, a female laugh – hord and cruel – and I pull my head out from under the covers.

It's Hedda. She's standing at the bottom of the bed.

'Er, yeah,' she goes, 'I've *no* interest in knowing what you two get up to? *Puke?*'

'Holy fock,' I go, trying to get my breath back. 'I thought you moved out.'

'I *have* moved out? I'm here for more of my clothes. I had to wait until *she* left.'

I'm there, 'Well, take whatever you need, then hit the bricks.'

She's not happy being told what to do – that's teenagers for you. '*Excuse* me?' she goes, hand on her hip 'I don't *need* your permission to be here. This is still my focking home. And I heard about Kathleen, by the way.'

I'm there, 'Who?'

'Kathleen,' she goes. 'Who *you* got fired?'

I laugh. 'Oh, her?'

'She's actually a really, really nice person,' she tries to go. 'Do you know how hord it's going to be for her to get another job in the hotel industry?'

I laugh again. 'Well,' I go, 'she should have maybe kept her passion for me under wraps.'

'You're a focking orsehole. She's an actual friend of mine. I've spent, like, entire summers in that hotel. She told me what happened.'

'Well, the only thing that matters is what your old dear believes.'

'Oh my God, I can't believe she's ended up with someone like you.'

'Someone like me?'

'Yeah – in other words, a sleazebag. Did she buy you that car?'

'Which one?'

'The fucking Audi porked in the drive. She did, didn't she?'

All I do is just smile, which she takes as a yes.

'Are you not ashamed of yourself?'

'Why would I be ashamed?'

'Taking advantage of a widow who's, like, emotionally vulnerable?'

'Hey, we're both getting what we want out of it.'

'She's a fucking drunk as well. She doesn't even know what she's doing. Where's she gone, anyway?'

'To see her solicitor.'

She goes, 'Her solicitor?' except she says it in, like, a *worried* way? I cop it immediately. A moment's weakness. Then – and I know this is seriously cruel, even for me – I go, 'Yeah, it's something to do with her will.'

'Her will?'

'Some, I don't know, change or other that she's talking about making.'

'Don't tell me she's putting you into it.'

I just shrug. 'Could well be that. I mean, the woman's in love – I really think she's capable of anything right now.'

'No way!' she goes, shaking her head, her voice cracking. 'No fucking way!'

Then she storms off, slamming every door on her way out of the house.

'I see Patrick Honohan's put the cost of the Anglo bail-out at €35 billion,' he goes. 'Oh, that'll have them all in a fine old moral lather, won't it? Your Matt Coopers and your Fintan what's-its? I could almost tell you now what they're going to write.'

I end up having to bite my lip. Which I'm becoming pretty good at doing.

'You didn't ring me to tell me that, did you? And I don't mean that in an orsey way. I'm genuinely wondering.'

He makes a big show of clearing his throat, then goes, 'Well, no, as it happens. Always struggled to get one past you, eh, Kicker? No, the reason I'm phoning is to tell you that I'm, well, worried frankly.'

I'm like, 'What did the doctor tell you about worrying?'

'Not to do it,' he goes, 'in so far as that's humanly possible. But I wouldn't be any kind of father – *or* any kind of entrepreneur – if I didn't address one or two concerns that I had.'

I'm like, 'Get on with it. I'm in the cor here, on my way into town. Shit to do.'

'I'll not beat about the, er – inverted commas – bush in that case. The fact is that I've had, well, severals calls of complaint. Customers. One or two them personal friends of mine. And Hennessy's. Saying that their documents haven't been collected. I defended you, naturally – wouldn't be like Ross to miss appointments without a bloody good reason and so forth. And the thing is, old chap, I suspect I know what that reason is.'

He couldn't know. Unless he's stuck one of Hennessy's dodgy private detective mates on my tail.

I'm like, 'Continue.'

'You're growing the business too fast,' he goes. 'Trying to expand too quickly. Too darned hungry for work – that's always been your Achilles, Ross.'

'That, er, might be it, alright.'

'Of course Hennessy would have nothing of it. He has you down as an idler. Said, "He thinks Manual Labour is a Spanish socialist leader." Oh, sharp words were exchanged, Ross, I don't mind telling you. On the sixth in Elm Park. I said, "Sometimes I wonder, Hennessy, whether you even know your godson at all."'

'And what did *he* say to that?'

'Doesn't matter. Suffice it to say that your father mounted a stout defence of your service record – quote-unquote. I said, "It's obvious what's happened, isn't it? He's simply spread himself too thinly."'

I just go with it, of course. 'I have been, er, fairly lashing into the work alright.'

'I expected as much. Why don't you take on more staff?'

'What?'

'Never be too proud to delegate, Ross. One of the most valuable lessons I learned in business.'

'I might actually do that.'

'Because if you miss appointments, companies *will* go elsewhere. Remember, there's a lot of worried people out there. The media are looking for scapegoats to explain why it suddenly looks like we're going to have to go cap in hand to the IMF.'

'Like I said, I'll think about it.'

'A lot of others are going to realize, Ross, that there's money in, let's just say, neutralizing the threat of our guilty secrets coming back to haunt us.'

'Yeah, point taken. Like I said, I'm on the way into town.'

'Well,' he goes, 'there is one more thing.'

'Go on.'

'It's Ronan. He was here this morning. Didn't seem himself at all. Seemed to be carrying the weight of the world on his shoulders. I asked him what was wrong and it seems his mother is – what's this they say? – *dating* Tom McGahy.'

'I know.'

'After his stance on rugby! The bloody nerve of the man!'

'He's a dick. I said it a long time ago.'

'Of course poor Ronan doesn't want the news getting around. You know how cruel teenage boys can be.'

I'm just like, 'Don't worry your head. I'm actually about to sort it now.'

La Mère Zou. For fock's sake. Don't get me wrong, I'm a major fan of the place – always have been. But giving French food to Tina is like feeding truffles to a hog. In other words, a complete and utter waste of time – and possibly even dangerous. Goes to show how little McGahy knows about the whole dating game.

Some people might describe what I'm doing here as, like, stalk-ing? But it's not. I mean, yeah, I sat outside the focker's gaff for an hour, than tailed his cor all the way into town to see where he was taking her tonight. But that was only so I could catch them together – in the act, if you like – and give them the message, loud and fock-ing clear.

I spot them across the floor of the restaurant, in a candlelit corner, holding hands across the table, whispering sweet focking whatevers to each other.

A waiter steps in front of me and asks if I want a table for one.

'Don't worry,' I go, slipping smortly past him, bringing back memories of the glory days, 'I won't be staying.'

It's only as I get closer to the table that I hear what they're even talking about.

He's going, 'I personally think that CRH issuing a profit warning last week is *the* biggest indicator yet of the terminal condition of the Irish economy – I really do.'

Of course *she's* nodding away, not a focking breeze what he's talking about.

'The recession?' I go, butting in. 'That's what you're talking about on a focking date? Jesus, McGahy, it's no wonder they only come around once every forty focking years.'

'What are *you* doin hee-ur?' it's, like, *Tina* who goes?

I'm there, 'I was going to ask you the exact same question,' then I nod at her plate. She's obviously had the *escargots*. 'I mean, when *I* was with you, you thought pizza was foreign food.'

The next thing, roysh – hilarious, this – McGahy picks his napkin off his lap, throws it angrily on the table, then stands up, the legs of his chair scraping across the wooden floor and bringing every conversation in the restaurant to a sudden halt.

Every set of eyes in the place is watching to see what's going to happen. Which is obviously fock-all. He wouldn't dare throw a dig at me.

Instead, roysh, he goes, 'I . . . have had . . . just about . . . enough of you,' spacing his words out, the way teachers always do.

I just laugh in his face. 'You said that back in 1997,' I go. 'And look at me, still giving you hell.'

'This is beginning to border on . . .'

'It's not stalking, if that's what you're about to say.'

'I was going to say harassment.'

'Yeah, whatever.'

'You turn up at my home and you misrepresent yourself to my elderly mother. You steal – yes, *steal* – private family photographs, then you place them on the internet. Now you follow us to a restaurant and you interrupt us while we're having a private conversation . . .'

He's practically in my face while he's saying all of this. I just put my hand on his chest and push him back a step, just to remind him that I'm well capable of decking him if I'm pushed to it.

'I'll make this quick,' I go, 'then you can go back to your *so-called* conversation. You're not taking Ronan to . . . I don't know, whatever city it is.'

'Ross,' *she* goes, 'it's already buked, so it is.'

'Then it's going to have to be *unbuked*, so it is. This supposed *thing* that you two have going on is upsetting him.'

'Well,' McGahy has the actual balls to go, 'he'll have to come to terms with it.'

I decide there's no way I'm taking that. I'm like, 'That's my son you're referring to,' practically jabbing my finger in his face. 'You're going to have to get used to that unfortunate fact.'

Tina goes, 'Ross, we're in luff, so we are.'

I actually laugh at that – you can imagine. I'm like, 'Love? Don't give me that. I was earholing the two of you on the way in. He might as well have been reading the focking business pages to you.'

A waiter – the same one I sold the dummy pass to – arrives over and tells me I'm going to have to leave. McGahy's obviously delighted. He needs back-up, see.

I'm there, 'Don't worry, I'm going,' and then I turn to Tina. 'You're not taking Ronan to Copa whatever-it's-called and that's my final word on the matter. I'm not having *him*,' meaning McGahy, 'of all teachers, playing stepfather to *my* focking kid.'

'We're *going* to Copenhagen,' McGahy goes, with the same look of satisfaction he had when they took away my Leinster Schools Senior Cup medal, 'and there's nothing you can do about it.'

I just shake my head and go, 'Dude, you do *not* want to fock with me – and you can take that as a final warning. Ask around. It's not my first time at the rodeo, Baby.'

To which neither of them has any answer.

'I didn't think Brian Cowen sounded drunk,' Levinus goes. 'Did he sound drunk to you, Regina?'

Regina's like, 'Och, he's always sinded dronk to may.'

She's pretty much mullered herself. She's not wearing a bra under her dress and you can see her bottle rockets.

Levnius puts his knife down and storts, like, tracing circles in the air

325

with his index finger. 'You see, that's my point. This is the new ortho-
doxy. To be a great leader, you have to be a polished media performer.
That's why you have all these columnists – and I'm sorry for saying it,
Maurice, but some of them work for your newspaper – calling for him
to do a televised address to the nation. But to what end? To give the
media something to talk about. It's all part of the dumbing down of
politics.'

'The dumbing down of everything,' Debra goes, rolling her eyes,
then looking around the table for back-up. 'The entire culture.'

Levinus picks up his knife again and goes back to his arrosto misto.
'I mean, I'm no fan of Brian Cowen but, as far as I'm concerned, he's
being pilloried for *not* being Barack Obama.'

These are, like, Regina friends? You could pull up outside an elderly
care home, drag the first four bluehairs you saw into your cor and have
a more fun night than you would in this company.

Sorry, I should introduce you to everyone. Levinus is a senior counsel, who's married to Debra, who's also a senior counsel. It's their
actual house we're having dinner in. *She* seems cool enough – a ringer
for Janice Dickinson – and my guess is she's absolutely filthy with a
few drinks on her. But that's about the nicest thing I can say about
them. *He's* a total cock, in case you haven't already copped it. He's got
one of those what I call *Law* Library personalities? Walks around, you
can tell, with his thumbs in his ormpits, looking at the world along the
length of his nose.

Then Maurice is a columnist with, I *think*, the *Irish Times*? He's, like,
bald, unbelievably serious and he has a really focking irritating habit of
introducing a new topic of conversation by going, 'Sidebar . . .'

Ah, you'll see how it works as the conversation goes on.

He's married to Libby, who *was* a home auctioneer but is now a full-
time mum. Does fock-all, in other words, because her two kids are in
their early to mid twenties, even though they're still living at home.
She's one of those silent types – picture, no sound – although all you
really need to know about her is that she's focking horrendous-looking.

'Maurice,' Debra suddenly goes, 'I really enjoyed your column in
last week's *Times* . . .'

See, I knew it was the focking *Times*.

'We both did. And I reread it this evening, didn't I, Levinus? That bit
where you said that the media-led search for blame figures is preventing

an informed and necessary discourse on how Ireland might recover and avoid making the same mistakes again going forward.'

You can picture me, I'm sure. I might as well be watching doubles tennis on TV. I'm just sat there watching the conversation bounce around the focking table. I'm getting outside the red wine in a serious way as well.

'Well, it *is* a fact,' Maurice goes, 'and psychologists have done studies that will back me up on this, that the expression of indignation and rage gives people a sense of control. A false sense, as it happens. It's easy to hate Sean FitzPatrick. It's easy to hate Michael Fingleton. But we in the media need to see that hatred for what it is – an atavistic human response to what is a complex and multi-layered problem.'

'That was the phrase I loved,' Debra goes.

Levinus – even the name, for fock's sake – is there, 'I certainly believe that the media's coverage of these protest marches on the Anglo-Irish building and all these silly stunts outside the Dáil, has been disproportionate.'

'Yes, it's all just a little bit hysterical,' Maurice goes. 'But the point I was trying to make in my article was that, you know, personalizing the whole thing allows everyone else – and I'm including the media in this – to absolve themselves of blame.'

'There was a Qashqai in the corpork of Mount Anville yesterday,' I suddenly hear myself go. I don't *know* why? Possibly because I'm half wankered. Possibly because I'm being totally ignored and I want to prove that I can punch my weight in any conversation.

It's, like, blank faces all round, though.

'A *Qashqai*?' Debra – in fairness to her – goes.

I'm like, 'Literally. We were dropping my daughter off at school. I mean, I didn't actually see it myself. But it's another sign, you'd have to say, of how focked things really are out there.'

There's, like, silence for a good ten seconds, before Regina finally goes, 'Dabra, this danner is delashious.'

Debra just waves her hand and goes, '*Jamie's Italy*.'

'You can really taste the pancetta,' Maurice goes. 'Sidebar – isn't it great that Fallon & Byrne has survived the recession? Even though I realize what a terrible cliché that is.'

I told you. A total and utter cock.

'You're absolutely right,' Debra gives it. 'It's needed. I really do believe that,' and then she, like, turns to Regina. 'It's baklava for dessert, by the way. I used that recipe you gave me. Love to know what you think of it. Worried it might be rather dry.'

She all of a sudden stands up and, at the same time, indicates the door into the kitchen with her eyes.

Regina gets up then – a bit unsteady on her feet – and goes, 'As long as yee covered the failo peestray with a domp cloth like ay told yee,' following her out of the room, 'it really should be fane.'

So then it's just me, the two goons and Libby – the wreck – left at the table. I help myself to more wine, roysh, which is when Levinus suddenly clears his throat and goes, 'Okay, since no one else is going to acknowledge the pachyderm in the room, then I will . . .'

I haven't a bog, of course, what a pachyderm even is. At first, I'm wondering if it's, like, *racist*? Except then I notice that he's staring directly at me and when I catch his eye, he goes, 'What *is* your game?'

So I go, 'Chill out, Dude. I brought you a bottle, didn't I?'

'Oh, yes, the Australian Chardonnay with the screwcap – I expect you picked it up in an Esso station.'

It was actually Topaz, although I don't say that, because I'm suddenly sensing hostile vibes.

'I'm not talking about the wine that you've been consuming like a teenager all evening. I'm referring to Regina.'

As someone who's been given the old Guantánamo treatment by a lot of parents over the years, I straight away realize where this conversation is headed. I'm like, 'You want to know what my intentions are?'

He goes, 'Oh, I think I can make a reasonable guess as to what your intentions are.'

I suppose you'd *have* to be good at thinking on your feet to be a barrister, always coming up with shit to say.

'How old are you?' he goes.

It's a real nasty atmos. I'm there, 'Thirty.'

'Thirty,' he goes, shaking his head. 'So what's a thirty-year-old *boy* . . . doing with a sixty-year-old woman?'

I drape my hand over the back of the chair, casual-like. 'Every position in the deck,' I go, 'seeing as you're interested,' just letting him know that he's not in focking court now.

Libby tuts. I'm not exaggerating when I say that her face looks like it was eaten by a goat, then shat off a cliff.

Maurice decides to throw his thoughts into the mix then. 'We're just concerned – as long-time friends of both Regina *and* Toddy . . .'

I suddenly realize that this is what the whole evening has been about. As in, get me here, check out the cut of my beef, then as soon as they see what a waste of space I am, get Regina out of the room and warn me off.

'I hear she bought you a car,' Levinus goes.

'Yeah – so what?'

He smiles, I think the word is, like, *inwardly*, like he's got some private joke that he's not sharing with the rest of the room. Then he goes, 'You made an offhand comment the other day, to Hedda, about her mother's will . . .'

I roll my eyes.

'No prizes for guessing who told you about the cor, then.'

'Hedda is my god-daughter. Oh, she's been keeping me updated on what's been going on. It won't be happening, by the way. You won't be getting a cent.'

I'm like, 'Well, that's Regina's decision.'

'No, it isn't. Not if she's deemed to be of unfit mind.'

'She seems fine to me.'

He laughs. 'What, drinking the way she is tonight? With her hair cut short like that and her bloody breasts showing through her dress?'

I give him a big sleazy grin. 'I think it's a look that actually suits her.'

'You pushed Hedda out of her own home,' Libby just blurts out, the first actual words that've come out of the hound's mouth since the focking soup course. I actually laugh. I'm there, 'Welcome to the conversation, Chuckles.'

It's a focking three-way attack, though, because then Maurice is suddenly there, 'Regina buried her husband only ten months ago. She's grieving. This is a time when she needs her daughter around her. And you've driven a wedge between them.'

Levinus looks suddenly smug. Or actually *smugger* if that's suddenly a word? 'Oh, we know who you are. *And* who your sister is.'

'Well done.'

He's good, by the way. Like I said, I've had focking hundreds of conversations like this before – usually with, like, fathers, though, and concerning girls my own age – and their hands would normally be clamped around my focking windpipe right about now. He's as cool as the other side of the pillow, though. Again, he'd have to be in his line.

'Do you think we're just going to sit idly by and watch you destroy our friend's life?'

I'm there, 'We're both getting what we want out of it. I don't think it's any of your beeswax.'

'And what if Regina told you that she'd changed her mind? That she was leaving everything to her daughter? You don't even need to answer that. I can see it in your eyes. You don't spend forty years, as I have, in the courts of this land without learning how to read someone's character. Or lack thereof!'

Debra and Regina arrive back from the kitchen, Debra holding what I *presume* is a baklava, although I've never actually seen one before. Regina just smiles at me, oblivious. She's like, 'Hoy are we all gatting alawng?'

It has to be said, it's some focking turn-out. I honestly haven't seen Foxrock this up in orms since some poor focker storted handing out copies of the *Metro* – tramps bedding, the old dear calls it – at the traffic lights at the bottom of Westminster Road.

There must be, like, fifty of them, all glammed to the gills – Pamela Scott must be staring at just empty focking racks this morning – and they're morching, like, back and forth, in front of the shop, holding placards saying shit like 'Fool's Gold!' and 'Foxrock's NOT going for gold!' their heels clicking along the pavement, the air choked with anger and Coco by Chanel.

And they're chanting as well.

'One, two, three, four – gold shops only draw the poor! Five, six, seven, eight – Foxrock must escape this fate!'

All of the old faces are there. Angela, Delma and all the other veterans of the Move Funderland to the Northside and Ban Poor People from the National Gallery on Tuesday and Thursday Afternoons campaigns. There's, like, no sign of the old dear, though. She'd usually be right at the front, making sure her big, botoxed head gets on TV.

Of course. Why didn't I think of that? All I have to do is look for the focking cameras.

There she is, standing outside Thomas's, talking to Samantha Libreri, who – I've mentioned before – I've always had a major thing for.

Samantha's going, 'There were reports this week that up to two and a half thousand householders per month are having their electricity disconnected due to non-payment of bills. There's evidence that a growing number of people from what would be considered affluent areas such as this are struggling to pay for basic household utilities. Isn't this shop simply meeting a demand that's there?'

Oh, she's a little scrump-nugget – there's no denying.

The old dear just flashes her top veneers at her, then goes, 'No, I don't. These kinds of . . . and I won't afford them the dignity of *calling* them shops, Samantha . . . These kinds of *operations*, as well as drawing undesirables, bring out the dark side in people. And I want to say, Samantha, to any of your viewers who are watching, who might *well* be desperate, that things are never so bad that you have to resort to selling the rings from your fingers – and I don't mind using my celebrity to make sure that message of hope gets out there.'

Samantha's not impressed – you can focking see it. 'Don't you think that, with this recession affecting what were once considered safe, middle-class professions, like architecture and law, people are entitled to do whatever they have to in order to survive?'

She's focking good, the girl.

'Even if that means bringing down the moral tone of the area?' the old dear goes. 'Let me tell you something – some of these girls behind me are suffering terribly in this recession. These are *good* people we're talking about – professional people – and they're forced to wonder what kind of future awaits their children . . .'

Showing off, roysh, I shout, 'Don't listen to her, Samantha. I think some of her collagen has leaked into her focking brain stem.'

It has to be said, they're not impressed with me for interrupting the report. 'We can dub that out,' Samantha goes, without even acknowledging my presence. 'Maybe just continue with what you were saying and we can use some continuity footage to stitch the two pieces together.'

'What I was saying,' the old dear goes, 'is that I hope that we, as a people, can get through this obviously difficult time without resorting to selling our possessions like bloody refugees. Again, I don't mind using my fame in this way, as long as the message gets through, that cash for gold shops are the top of a very slippery slope. First we all pawn our gold. Then there's suddenly no shame in *stewing* beef and methadone clinics on every street corner.'

Samantha seems happy with what she's got and they finish filming. I hear the old dear asking her to describe her as a bestselling author and activist, then going, 'And do you think you could fit the word humanitarian in? How long *are* these captions?'

I go, 'You're a focking disgrace, woman. Making a complete tit of yourself again on national television.'

She's not a happy bunny, by the way. She storms right up to me and goes, 'Why didn't you tell me?'

I'm like, 'Tell you what? Jesus, I'd forgotten how bet-down-looking you were up close.'

'Tell me that this *thing* was opening, firstly. And secondly, who was behind it.' She holds the back her hand to her forehead, like women in black and white movies do before they faint. 'Young JP, Ross! I mean, how many times was he in our home over the years?'

'You should know. You were the one always flirting your hole off with him.'

'I beg your pardon!'

She was, though. The second she heard that he or Oisinn or any of them was coming over, she'd freshen up the lippy and be sat at the piano when they walked through the door, pretending to play 'Song for Guy' or 'Lara's Theme' from *Dr Zhivago*.

She was a focking disgrace – just as she is now.

'Wait a minute,' she suddenly goes, 'where do you think you're going?'

I'm just like, 'Er, into the shop?'

'But, Ross, it's a picket.'

'And this affects me *how* exactly?'

'Well, how's it going to look on *Six One* if the son of the honorary life president of the Foxrock Combined Residents Association sees fit to pass an official picket.'

I'm there, 'Hilarious, I expect,' and I morch straight past the lot of them and into the shop.

Danuta, I probably don't need to tell you, is having a shit-fit inside. She's, like, pacing the floor, muttering what sounds to me very much like threats. JP's trying to talk sense to her, as is Fionn, who I'm actually surprised to find there.

'Told you so,' is my opening line.

I possibly shouldn't twist the knife, except with Danuta, I can't actually *help* it?

She stops pacing and just, like, glowers at me. 'What does zees mean? Fugging . . .'

'Ross!' JP goes, because he knows what I'm doing is basically poking a lion through the bors with a stick.

'Hey, I'm just reminding you all – I did say it. There's no way they were going to let it happen. Fionn, you remember the reaction, don't you, when that ice cream van storted coming around here. The residents blockaded Torquay Road for fourteen days and nights.'

Danuta laughs, I think the word is, like, *bitterly*? 'In Russia, theez eez not allowed. Theez people would be . . . moofed away.'

'Well, you're not in Russia now. You're in Foxrock. Two totally different places.'

'Zat ees your muzzer out zare?'

'With the orse-fat injected into her forehead? Yeah.'

'How much money to stop?'

'What?'

'How much money she want?'

I laugh. 'You won't bribe her. I can tell you that for a fact. She's focking rolling in it.'

'Well, zare are uzzer means of persuasion. Everyone has somesing zey love and don't vont to lose.'

'Find out where they make Grey Goose vodka,' I go. 'Stick a focking bomb in there. That'll get her attention.'

The look she shoots me – see, she knows I'm loving this. JP told me on the Wolfe that they haven't had a single customer since the protest storted.

I turn around to Fionn then. 'What are you doing here anyway?'

I'm going to admit it, he looks well. Being in love obviously suits him, although there's still no way the girl is going to walk up the aisle for him. He's living in dreamland.

'Oh,' he goes, 'JP's offered to give me a hand with the stewarding arrangements for the first battle re-enactment.'

I roll my eyes. 'Don't tell me that's still happening.'

He doesn't take the bait. 'Yeah, the first one's going to be on 22 October. The Battle of the Boyne. I thought we'd start off ambitiously!'

I'm like, 'Yeah, whatever.'

'It's very exciting, Ross. I have to say, Erika did an amazing job selling it to the schools. We've got almost two thousand students coming. From everywhere. Blackrock. Alex. Clongowes. Columba's. Andrew's. Michael's. Gonzaga. Even Tom's bringing fifty students along.'

I'm suddenly all ears. 'Tom? As in, McGahy?'

'Yeah, I know we fell out. He wasn't happy when I left to teach in the Institute. But he thinks it's a great idea. He's been unbelievably supportive.'

I sort of, like, nod for a few seconds. 'Do you know what, Fionn, I kind of feel like maybe *I* haven't been supportive enough?'

'What?'

'Yeah, no, I'm serious. I mean, you're my future possible brother-in-law. Maybe I should have gotten more behind you.'

'Em . . . okay, Ross. Well, thanks.'

'The Battle of the Boyne. That was one of the biggies, was it? As in, a major deal?'

You know me – you know how focking thick I am.

Of course Fionn's biggest weakness – aport from the fact that he can barely focking see – is his enthusiasm. He was, like, born to teach. 'It was *the* most seminal battle in Irish history,' he goes. 'I mean, look at the North, Ross. The outcome still resonates today – what, over three centuries later?'

I just shake my head. 'Do you know what? I think my thirties are going to be my time for, like, improving my mind.'

Danuta snorts. So does JP – some focking mate, he is.

'Yeah, no, definitely,' I go. 'I'm basically going to put my head down and, like, *learn* loads of shit? Now that I know for definite that the rugby thing's possibly not going to happen for me.'

Fionn *doesn't* snort. See, Fionn's like one of those teachers we all had at school, who get the piss ripped out of them constantly by the class, but who never give up, and then one day, one kid expresses, I don't know, a *mild* interest in something he's said and that teacher's on it like a bonnet, happy as a focking Make a Wish kid, thinking the hell he's been through has nonetheless been worth it.

Fionn hasn't got a cynical bone in his body. That's what makes him putty in my hands.

'I can lend you some books,' he goes. 'One or two Antony Beevors to get you started. I mean, some people think they're a bit populist but they're very readable – although I did prefer *The Battle for Spain* to *Stalingrad*.'

'Hey, bring it on,' I go. 'That'd be very much my message. I'll tell you what as well. I think I'd love to find out a bit more about that other battle . . .'

Jesus, I've forgotten the name of it already.

'The Boyne,' he goes.

'The Boyne, exactly. Like, would it be possible for me to tag along? Actually, *I* could help out as well.'

He looks at JP and, whatever look he gets back, he suddenly smells something foul. 'You're not just taking the piss, are you?'

'No.'

'Because this is my business, Ross. This is Erika's and my future.'

'Dude, for once in my life, I'm not ripping the piss.'

He takes a breath, then goes, 'Okay, then, you can come.'

I clench my fist and go, 'Yes!' which is possibly a bit OTT. But I'm happy. Because 22 October is the day before McGahy is supposedly bringing Tina and Ronan away. I still don't know what I'm going to actually do. I don't know if we're going be given fake swords or machine-guns or whatever they actually had back then. But somehow I get the sense that this might be the only opportunity I ever have to, I don't know, at least maim the focker and pass it off as an accident.

Outside, I can hear the old dear leading the protesters in a chorus of 'We Shall Overcome', which was the theme song of the resistance movement she set up to stop the Luas coming to Foxrock. I face the window and put my orm around Danuta's shoulder – that's how suddenly cocky I am.

Do you know what?' I go. 'I think that crowd is getting actually bigger.'

Regina asks me what's wrong and I tell her it's nothing – the same answer I gave her the last time she asked me. *And* the time before that.

She's there, 'Ay *hov* a teenager, remamber – ay know you can say there's nathin wroang when what you mean is the apposite.'

'*I'm* not teenager,' I go.

And she's like, 'Yee could have fooled may.'

This, by the way, is in the middle of Ely Wine Bor.

She says I've been acting weird ever since the dinner that night in

Levinus's gaff. 'Was somethang sad,' she goes, 'when ay was ite of the reem that tame?'

I just shrug. 'Look,' I go, 'they were giving me bad vibes, that's all.'

'Hoy?'

'*Him*. And the other focker. Sidebor. Someone would want to pull him aside, by the way, and tell him what a total and utter cock he sounds with that thing.'

She seems to find the whole thing pretty amusing. 'Ay *thought* there was an otmasphere in the reem when ay came bock in that tame.'

'I'm glad *one* of us finds it funny?'

'Look, they're just worried abite may, that's all. We've all been frands since we were in our twantays. Toddy and ay went on holidays with Levinus and Debra every year for thortay yoors. They loved hum.'

'Even though he did the dirt on you with my sister?'

'For *all* his faults, aye. They thank *ay* should be still sat at home in may dressing gyne and sluppers craying mayself to sleep every nate.'

'Well, they also seem pissed off about you buying me a cor. *And* the whole you-leaving-all-your-money-to-me thing.'

'It's *may* mornay – *ay* can do what *ay* lake with it.'

'Shit.'

'It's nat shit, it's troy.'

'No, I mean . . .'

What I mean is that Hennessy has just walked into Ely. I didn't even know he focking drank in here. He's with, like, one or two other suits, obviously mates of his, and they're up at the bor, bullshitting away.

All I know is that if he sees me in the corner, enjoying a cosy drink with the woman who took my old man for one point seven million, he'll shit focking giblets.

'I, er, wouldn't mind hitting the road,' I suddenly go.

Regina's like, 'What?' because we've literally just opened our second bottle.

She's there, 'Thot's a tee-hondred-and-twanty-euro battle of wane thor.'

'Let's just leave it,' I go. 'Pretend it's still the good old days.'

She still seems in two minds, so I go, 'Look, I'm going to level with you, Regina. I'm horny as fock,' and no sooner are the words out of my mouth than she's grabbed her coat and she's trotting after me like a faithful old hound.

One of Hennessy's mates is saying that the fifteen billion in cuts needed to reduce the deficit is going to lead to a prolonged recession. He's like, 'Even the ESRI is saying it.'

Hennessy says he can't say *how* he knows – he just does – that an IMF bail-out is going to happen. It's already being discussed. It's not a matter of if, but when.

I slip past him and out. I'm already sat in the back of a taxi by the time Regina makes it out in her four-inch heels. She walks around the cor and gets in the other passenger door.

No sooner has she told the driver Malahide than she's got her tongue in my ear and she's rummaging around belowstairs. The driver's getting a good eyeful in the rear-view, wondering at what point does he tell us to kill it.

That's when my phone all of a sudden rings. It's Ronan, so I answer it. I'm like, 'Hey, Ro.'

She carries on giving me hand to gland combat, by the way.

'Rosser,' Ronan goes, 'she's arthur telling me to pack me bags.'

I'm like, 'What?'

'Pack me bags. It's this weekend, Rosser.'

I'm like, 'Ro, don't sweat it. It's *in* hand.'

'Look behind me,' Sorcha goes.

And I do – although I'm not quite sure what I'm supposed to be looking at.

'That woman who's coughing, Ross – is she covering her mouth?'

I face forward again. I'm like, 'Er, no.'

'I didn't think so,' she goes. 'Maybe I should say something.'

I'm like, 'Sorcha, I really don't think you should.'

'Ross, it's how germs *spread*?'

'I think these people have got a lot more to worry about than catching a few germs, Sorcha.'

I have to admit, it's not half as bad as I expected a dole queue to be. Once you get used to the whiff of Adidas Blue Challenge. The people seem cool enough, although there's no telling when a crowd like this might turn.

Luckily, Sorcha drops the subject.

337

'That's a luffely coat,' a woman's voice behind us goes. She's talking about Sorcha's Balmain black crystal-embellished military jacket.

'Thank you,' Sorcha goes, half turning around and fake-smiling her.

See, Sorcha's good with people from all walks.

She's delighted with the compliment as well. What to wear was a major issue this morning, this being one of the few occasions she has literally no experience of dressing for. Real Uggs or fake was a dilemma that took up a good focking hour of our day. '*Actual* ones,' she went, 'might suggest that I don't, like, *need* the money? Claire from Bray lent me, like, her Rocketdog ones? But then when they hear the way I speak, will they think I'm wearing them in, like, a sarcastic way?'

Who'd be a girl, huh? In the end, roysh, she settled for Claire's Fuggs but then her skinny Rock and Republics, which cost, like, four hundred sheets, and the coat, which her old dear paid fock-knows-how-much-for as a commiseration gift when her shop went tits-up.

'Are you sure you're in the right place?' another voice goes, a man's this time.

Sorcha turns around again. 'Yes, thank you,' she goes. 'I'm one of the new unemployed,' and the way she says it – we're talking pure Vico Road – seems to invite a comment from everyone in the place, everything from 'The new unemployed, says she!' to 'I'd bang me fooken back out riding her.'

'Just, er, keep your eyes front,' I go, then I try to take her mind off what's going on around her. 'So are you going to tell Honor?'

'About what?'

'About this – er, what you're *doing*?'

She just shrugs. 'I don't believe in keeping secrets from her,' she goes. 'There's no shame in it, Ross.'

'Well, that's what a lot of people are saying, I suppose. Good luck telling her that.'

'There isn't. I mean, yeah, obviously I'll have to break it to her gently.'

My phone suddenly comes alive in my skyrocket and everyone in the room seems to recognize the ringtone. '*Hawaii Five-O*,' they all just blurt out, like there's a focking prize for guessing. I suppose that's what happens when you watch game shows on TV all day long.

I check the screen and it's, like, Regina.

'Is that her?' Sorcha goes, although if she's asking in a jealous way, she's doing a pretty good job of hiding it. 'As in, your girlfriend?'

'Er, yeah.'

'Why don't you answer it?'

'Nah, I'll talk to her later.'

'Ross, I honestly don't mind.'

It's easier, I know from long experience, to just do what she says. I answer by quietly going, 'Hey. I'm actually in, like, the *middle* of something here?'

'Fanish whatever it us, gat home here and sort may ite – *ay'm* the one who's hornay todee.'

What can I say, standing there in the middle of the focking dole office. 'I'll, er, give you a shout back in ten,' I just go, then I hang up.

'She sounds like she's from the North,' Sorcha goes and it's obvious she heard it.

'She is, yeah.'

She sticks out her bottom lip. 'So I definitely wouldn't know her, then?'

'Yeah, no, I doubt if you would.'

There's, like, silence between us then, the only sound being the muttering of people talking to the, I don't know, desk clerks through half an inch of glass.

'Go to her,' she eventually goes. 'She seems to want you pretty desperately.'

'No, I'm here with you.'

'Ross, I'm actually fine by myself.'

I might have been wrong. She *is* jealous. Or is she just hurt?

'Sorcha,' I for some reason go, 'it's not actually that serious. It's a pretty much use and abuse situation.'

'Ross, I hate that expression, you know that.'

'Well, then it's, like, a convenience thing. It's a case of getting what I want out of it and then . . .'

'Next!'

We're being called.

'You're up,' I go.

'Next!' the dude behind the counter goes again.

339

Sorcha approaches him, dragging her feet along the ground, which is how she always walks in Uggs. There's only, like, a short exchange. Sorcha storts telling him about her shop in the Powerscourt Townhouse Centre that closed and her daughter, who's just storted big school, and how she's never done anything like this before in her life but obviously she can't live on, like, *nothing*?

The dude behind the glass tells her – *I* thought in a nice enough way – that you can't just turn up and expect to be handed money, that you have to be assessed first and for that she'd have to go to, like, hatch number one, down along the line. But Sorcha, for whatever reason, takes offence, bursts into tears and, like, runs straight out of the place.

'The new unemployed is right,' I hear some dude in the queue go, then he sort of, like, chuckles to himself. 'Tell her she'll get used to it.'

I follow her outside and find her stood beside my Audi with her face buried in her hands, bawling her eyes out, her shoulders going up and down like Flipper.

I go over to her and I don't say a word. I just, I don't know, hold her in my orms until she's eventually ready to talk. 'I can't do it,' she goes. 'I was a fool to think I could.'

I'm there, 'Sorcha, you can do anything you put your mind to,' which is the exact same line she's always giving to me. And this is in the middle of, like, Cumberland Street, remember?

'I can't, Ross. I'm not brave like you.'

I'm like, 'Brave?' and I actually laugh in her face. 'You're the bravest person I basically know.'

'I'm not, Ross.'

'Okay, can I just remind you then about Amanda Osbourne, that girl who was in your class in sixth year . . .'

She'd a fantastic pair of sweater muppets on her – that's how I remember her.

'When her old pair couldn't pay the fees, who was it who went to the nuns and pleaded her case?'

She looks off into the distance and sort of, like, smiles. 'She has her own shop now – soft furnishings.'

I go, 'Soft furnishings, Sorcha!' and I somehow resist the temptation to make a crack about her focking jobbers. 'Which she probably wouldn't have if it wasn't for you. I'd say she even accepts that herself.

And just remind me again, who was it who gave birth to our daughter?'

At the mention of Honor, something enters her eyes.

She's like, 'What?'

'Oh, you heard me, Sorcha. When you went into labour at, like, my old dear's *first* book launch? You weren't even a little bit afraid. See, I was always brave when it came to shit like sticking my neck into a ruck. Or holding the likes of Denis Leamy up five yords from the line – ask him and he'll tell you it was like getting hit by a focking eighteen-wheeler. But *real* bravery? The kind you need in, like, everyday life? That was you. And I have to admit, I've always envied that in you.'

She gets that look of sudden determination on her face that those of you with Mounties at home would instantly recognize.

She's like, 'Okay, let's go back in,' and we head inside again and go to the back of the queue.

We're only standing there another few seconds when we hear this tap on glass, roysh, and the bird in hatch one is going, 'You don't need to queue up again – just come down to me,' which is exactly what we do.

She must have seen Sorcha run out of the place, roysh, because she's being especially nice to her. 'It's very simple,' she goes, pushing the form at her under the glass. 'Just a few questions about your circumstances.'

Sorcha goes to take the form, except the woman holds onto it for another second, then goes, 'You know, there's no shame in this.'

Sorcha nods.

I go, 'That's exactly what I told her.'

The woman – who's not great-looking – goes, 'Is this your husband?'

Sorcha's like, 'Er, yeah.'

Then the woman says *the* most amazing thing. 'You're a lucky girl.'

I love a boost, see.

'Well,' Sorcha goes, looking down at the form, smiling sadly, 'we're actually getting divorced.'

'And he's *still* here for you?' the woman goes. 'Then you're even luckier.'

There's some so-called economist on the radio saying that the most important person in Ireland right now, in terms of the country's potential for economic recovery – *in* the short term – isn't Brian Cowen and it isn't Brian Lenihan either. It's actually *X Factor* finalist Meerdy Burden.

If Meerdy succeeds in capturing votes, he says, in the same way that she's captured the horts of a frankly ravaged nation, there's no doubt that she'll be the ultimate winner of this year's *X Factor*, thus generating a sense of elation among Irish people in the days immediately after the delivery of what promises to be *the* most difficult budget in the history of the state. This – let's just call it – feel-good factor, he says, will guarantee an increase in national confidence of the kind not seen since we were routinely winning the *Eurovision Song Contest* in the – let's remember – embryonic years of the Celtic Tiger. And this confidence, in turn, will precipitate a return to consumer spending in the weeks leading up to Christmas.

'In that sense,' he goes, 'Meerdy Burden – a checkout lady, from Ballyfermot, who first entered our consciousness, remember, singing 'I Who Have Nothing' – is very much Ireland's Eva Perón. Or at least the Eva Perón of the Irish retail sector.'

I'm like, 'They're all trying to get in on McWilliams's act these days, aren't they?'

Oisinn and JP laugh, although it might be more at how I look – how we *all* look. We've really made the effort, it has to be said. We're wearing, like, jodhpurs – I borrowed mine, just between us, from Idina Grogan, a heavy-boned bird who used to run an equestrian school in Carlow, who's big-time in love with me and who I've given the occasional jab – thigh-high hooker boots – also Idina's – long black coats and big floppy hats.

I hope Fionn appreciates the effort we've gone to.

Mullinavat, I think it's safe to say, has never seen anything like it. The roads in are, like, clogged with cors and pretty much coaches and, like hundreds of other people, we end up having to pork in the hord shoulder of the N9 and walk the twenty minutes to the field – no easy task in thigh-highs, I can tell you that.

I'm like, 'What side are we on again?'

'King William III,' JP goes, although he could have said literally anything, because I was just, like, staring at my little plastic sword – which isn't slang, by the way – wondering how much actual damage I could do with it. 'I have to admit, I was sceptical when he first came up with the idea, but it looks like Fionn has really pulled it off.'

I pull a face as if to say, yeah, but like the wedding, it could still all go disastrously wrong.

Oisinn's there, 'Erika said they had to stop taking bookings at 2,300. And they've got enough names to do it all again next Friday.'

He looks the funniest of the three of us, because he's wearing a long blond wig that he got from a bird whose dog he walks. And it has to be said, he's the happiest I've ever seen him – he's lost a focking tonne of corgo from all the exercise – and for the first time I don't actually *regret* persuading him to come home and face the music.

As we're walking, roysh, I'm dragging my sword along the ground, shorpening it to a fine point.

'Hey, Ross,' JP, out of the blue, goes, 'is there any chance you might have a word with your old dear?'

I laugh. Her and her mates are obviously still picketing the shop. Must be, like, three weeks now, which is hilarious. I'm there, 'Dude, what makes you think she'd listen to *me*?'

He just goes, 'Danni's upset, Ross,' as if I'm meant to somehow *care*?

I laugh again. 'I'd say she is. I wouldn't say she's had even one customer.'

He doesn't answer that, which means it must be true. He suddenly stops walking, though. So me and Oisinn stop as well. He has a look over his shoulder – I don't *know* why? I mean, she's hordly likely to be behind him – then he goes, 'Ross, she got off the phone to her old man last night and she was talking about . . .'

'About what?'

'About . . . finding ways to get at your mother.'

I crack my hole this time. 'Dude, what's the worst she can do to her? I mean, the woman's mostly collagen, alcohol and black morket organs – I doubt if it's even *possible* to kill her.'

'Ross,' he goes, practically shouting now, 'I'm scared of what she might do! There's a . . . There's a coldness about her. When I look into her eyes sometimes, it's like . . .'

It's Oisinn who asks the obvious question. 'Dude, why don't you finish with her?'

'Exactly,' I go. 'Drop her like honours maths.'

He just shrugs, like he doesn't even know. But *we* both know – as in me and Oisinn. The focker's whipped like a rented mule.

It's portly because I feel sorry for him and portly because I don't want to be late for this thing that I go, 'Okay, I'll have a word with the woman,' even though I've no intention of it. 'Now come on, walk. We're supposed to be, like, stewarding this event, remember?'

I don't think any of us is ready for the sight that greets us when we step off this little – I don't know – boreen, into the field where it's all going to go down. I mean, we *played* in front of bigger crowds back in the glory days, but you've no idea what two-and-however-many-thousand people look like when they're done up in fancy dress and crammed into two ends of a field out in the middle of the sticks.

'Glad you guys could grace us with your presence,' we hear Fionn's voice suddenly go.

It's one of those phrases they must learn in teacher college, like, 'Get your bag and baggage and get out' and 'What do you mean, it's in your locker? We're not having class in your locker, are we?'

We *are* late, in fairness.

I turn around and there he is – you're not going to focking believe this – yeah, done up in fancy dress like the rest of us, but sitting – I swear to fock – on an *actual* horse, which I recognize straight away as Harlow, one of Erika's two white Arabian mares. I don't need to tell you, I'm sure, what a total and utter goon he looks, with the glasses and everything.

'Sorry we're late,' JP goes. 'We got pulled over. Ross was driving like a focking maniac.'

I'm like, 'Hey,' defending myself, 'I flashed my lights at some tosser for hogging the fast lane. He was only doing, like, ninety.'

'It was a focking cop car, Ross. And it wasn't even an *unmarked* one. It had a red light on the roof and the word "Garda" all over it. And I told you not to do it.'

'Hey,' I go, 'I just don't believe that two passes in your Leaving and a certificate from Templemore entitles you to drive like a focking OAP in the speeding lane. That's my belief and I'll take the penalty points for it.'

The next thing I hear is more clippity focking clopping. I look to my right and there's Erika, up on Kelly. She looks incredible on horseback and I mean that in a purely platonic way. Just really, I don't know, powerful and in command.

We get the hellos over with, then she looks at me and goes, 'Idina tells me she had a booty call from you last night.'

The goys all laugh. Like I said, she *is* a bit of a heffer. I actually forgot that Erika stables her horses with her.

I'm like, 'Yeah, whatever,' deciding not to rise to it.

But Erika doesn't leave it at that. 'I knew you were into stealing knickers from your conquests, Ross, but boots and jodhpurs?'

Again, they all laugh. I just shrug. I don't want to get into it. I'm, like, studying the crowd, looking for McGahy's ugly focking mug.

'Okay,' Fionn goes, you can see, really loving the power, 'can you guys help me get everyone organized and maybe get a bit of hush as well, so we can get started.'

So what happens is that we each take a section of our ormy – William the whatever JP said – and we organize them into, like, lines of ten, called columns.

At the other end of the field, there's six or seven more stewards – I recognize one or two of Fionn's nerdy friends from the Maths Olympiad – organizing the other ormy, whatever *they're* called, in exactly the same way.

I'm still looking out for McGahy. I don't even know if he's with us or them. Not that it matters either way. What do they call that when you get attacked by someone on your own side? Is it, like, friendly fire?

There's, like, loads of people who've brought their horses, by the way – maybe forty or fifty on either side. I suppose there *are* a fair few South Dublin girls' schools here. Anyway, it definitely contributes to the whole atmos.

Fionn rides out into what I suppose you'd have to call no man's land? Then, through a loud-hailer, he storts going, 'Okay, can everyone hear me?'

When he's satisfied, roysh, that everyone can, he goes, 'Okay, welcome, students *and* teachers, to the first – and we certainly *hope* not the last – in a series of historical re-enactments that we – that is, my partner, Erika, and I – have organized to try to give you a better understanding of some of the battles that have shaped our history and that appear on the Leaving and/or Junior Cert. syllabi . . .'

Jesus Christ, he'll be lucky if we're not all asleep in the next five minutes.

'Now,' he goes, 'I probably should say at the outset that there will be *no* actual combat today – I hope! – and that when I give the order for the two armies to advance, I want you to do so by walking, at a leisurely pace, towards the point where I am right now. Please do *not* run, as it may startle the horses . . .'

I stort looking around at some of the kids on *our* team and you can see them, like, rolling their eyes, as if to say, we might as well have stayed in focking school for all the crack we're going to have here today.

'Now,' Fionn's giving it, 'the Battle of the Boyne took place on 1 July 1690. The protagonists were two rival claimants to the throne of England, Scotland and Ireland – the Catholic King James II and the Protestant King William III, otherwise known as William of Orange, who had deposed James two years earlier . . .'

I'm still looking around me for McGahy. I'm pretty sure he's not with us, because I can't pick him out. I do notice, though, that a fair few of the kids are wearing their school colours *under* their fancy dress, flying the flag for Mary's, Gonzaga, Belvo, whoever. You'd have to say fair focks.

Fionn's still blabbing on. 'The battle – the key battle in the war between the Williamites and the Jacobites – was fought for control of the ford at Oldbridge, on the River Boyne, near Drogheda. Approximately nine thousand of William's men crossed the river at Oldbridge. In an effort to counter this move, James – fatally, as events transpired – committed almost half of his troop-strength and most of his artillery . . .' and blahdy focking blah blah.

Where the fock *is* McGahy? I'm squinting my eyes across the length of the field, trying to make out his big focking teachery head.

'This is focking boring,' I hear one of the kids mutter. He's Blackrock, but I'm not going to contradict him.

'I thought it was going to be, like, an *actual* fight?' one of the – I *think*? – Belvo goys goes. 'This is like being in focking school.'

There's, like, a definite tension building up. You can sense. They're all thinking, er, a hundred snot? For this? Fionn's still droning on, giving it, '. . . contingent of Huguenot troops . . .' and all the rest of it.

Then – *fatally, as events transpire!* – it storts raining. Not only raining but focking lashing. Everyone's getting soaked. You can hear the kids all turning to their teachers, going, 'Can we go, Sir?' and, 'Miss, can we

346

at least, like, *shelter*?' and of course no one is listening to Fionn any-more.

Erika's not a happy bunny with the situation. She rides over to where I'm standing and storts, like, shushing people. Which doesn't go down well at all. You can hear the kids going, 'Who the fock is she?'

That's when I suddenly cop him. I stort looking at the ormy oppo-site us, the front row, all the way along, inch by focking inch – and there he suddenly is. I don't know *how* I missed him standing there. Typical as well, he's telling some kid to stop acting the dick. Stop enjoying himself, in other words.

I'm automatically thinking, this is the focker who wants to be step-father to my actual son. That's exactly what he'd be like as a dad as well. I'm looking at him – the big focking cross head on him – and I'm going to be honest here, I end up working myself up into a bit of a rage.

'I'm getting the fock out of here,' I hear one of the goys from, I think, CBC Monkstown go.

'You'll stay where you are,' a teacher goes.

Another kid's there, 'Sir, we're getting pissed on,' and he's right. The field *is* turning into a bit of a quagmire.

I'm staring at McGahy, then at my shorpened sword, thinking, okay, how am I going to get at him?

'Ssshhh!' Erika goes. 'Will you please listen!'

'Who are the fock are you to tell me to listen?' the same kid goes.

Another's there, 'This is an actual rip-off!' and there's a bit of a fock-ing cheer for that.

That's when I end up doing it. It's one of those spur of the moment things – as in, the idea pops into my head and I do it without asking myself whether it's even wise. Erika wheels around on her horse and, when I think no one's looking, I give the beast a little jab in the orse with my shorpened sword.

After that, I think it's fair to say, everything happens pretty quickly. Kelly rears up, like horses do in actual westerns. Erika manages to hold on but Harlow gets spooked then and *she* goes up on her hind legs as well.

In the sudden confusion, I just go, 'Chorge!' at the top of my voice. And to my total surprise, everyone *does*?

Well, *our* ormy does first. Then, roysh, when the other side see our crowd coming towards them, *they* decide to chorge as well.

It's that real mob mentality, people are just totally caught up in the moment. You've got, like, two thousand and however many kids – *and* their teachers, by the way, which really surprises me – running towards each other at a fair old pace, waving their swords and hurling angry abuse at each other, most of it school-related.

I just keep my eyes on McGahy, who looks like he's being swept along, against his will, by the tide of bodies – as in, he wants to stop, but he can't, because he'd be pretty much crushed underfoot. Even in all the confusion, I don't lose sight of him. I've always had unbelievable focus, to be fair.

It takes about ten seconds for the two ormies, teams, whatever you want to call them, to close the space between us. Then it ends up being like the battle scene from *Bravehort*, we're talking a serious mill, mud flying, with the sound of plastic swords crossing and cries of 'Blackrock wankers', not to mention 'Fock you, Belvo, and shove your two Taoiseachs, one president, twelve knighthoods, one Victoria Cross, one Olympic gold medal, one signatory on the Proclamation of Independence and thirty-two Irish rugby internationals up your focking northside holes!'

Fionn, still sat on Harlow in the middle of the field, gets swallowed up in the literally pandemonium.

But I still don't let McGahy out of my sight. He doesn't actually notice me until we're, like, ten feet aport. I can only imagine the madness in my eyes, roysh, because his expression changes from one of just fear to one of, like, total terror.

I swing my sword in his general postcode but the focker is surprisingly quick and manages to, I don't know, *evade* the blow by dropping his shoulder and I end up slashing at thin air, then falling face-forward into the mud, as he shoots past me.

I'm up quickly, though, and haring after him. He escapes from the general, I suppose, mêlée and heads for a small wooded area, maybe two hundred yords away, with me still in hot pursuit.

I'm closing on him fast – very few people could live with my pace – he knows it, roysh, because he storts pleading with me over his shoulder. 'Have you taken leave of your senses?' he's going. 'Stop this nonsense at once!'

There's, like, fifty feet between us. Then forty. Then thirty. Shit, though, it looks like he's going to reach the wood before me.

I stort shouting ahead, going, 'You're not going to outpace me, McGahy. You've never played a sport in your life.'

But he carries on running, following the pathway into the woods. I'm, like, five seconds behind him, roysh, but when *I* enter the wood – unbelievably – he's, like, disappeared. I mean, he's literally nowhere to be seen. I decide he must be hiding, either behind a tree or in, like, the undergrowth.

So I stort walking around really quietly – I suppose *tiptoeing*? – while listening out for the rustle of leaves, a twig snapping or basically *any* giveaway noise.

And that's when I hear it. A small voice, going, 'Help! Help! Ross! Please!'

It's coming from somewhere off to my left.

I follow it, pulling back leaves and branches, until I come to, what I know from the tiny bit I learned in McGahy's geography class, is called a ravine. And there, at the bottom, lying on his back, his face twisted in pain, is the man himself.

'Help' he tries to go. 'Please, help me!'

I ease myself down on my orse – it's only, like, twelve feet high – using plants for grips. Then I wander over to him.

'Ross,' he goes, when he sees me. 'I've twisted my ankle. Both my ankles. They might even be broken.'

I crack on to be all full of concern. '*Both* your ankles? What a focking terrible stroke of misfortune. It's shit for you.'

'Well, don't just stand there with your mouth open,' he goes. 'Go and get help!'

Go and get help? Who the fock am I – Lassie?

I'm there, 'Especially with you supposedly going away tomorrow, with Tina and Ro.'

'Ross, this is no time for . . .'

'I don't think you're in any position to tell me what it is and isn't time for, do you?'

It's then that I spot it, out of the corner of my eye. It's McGahy's mobile – a Nokia, by the way, that's been out of date for, like, a decade – lying on the ground, just beyond his reach. Not only do I see it, but he sees that I see it, and as I bend down to pick it up he storts going ballistic, giving it, 'Hand me that phone! Hand me that phone, boy!'

Boy?

I stand there, still looking at him, weighing the thing in my hand. Honest to God, there's been, like, eight or nine models since this focking hunk of shit came out.

'I'm trying to remember,' I go, the power really going to my head now, 'what it was you said to me – that time you tried to make a fool of me in front of the entire class.'

'What?'

'"There are more intelligent life-forms than you crawling blind on the ocean floor."'

'I . . . I don't remember.'

'No? Well, let me jog your memory, then. It was the day I asked you whether it was the Egyptians who built the Pyrenees.'

'Yes!' he goes, practically losing it with me. 'And you were sixteen at the time! How in the name of Hades could you think that the Egyptians built the Pyrenees?'

'Because I was on the S! And Father Fehily put you in your box, didn't he? Said he wouldn't tolerate a member of the Senior Cup team being disrespected by the staff.'

'Hand me my phone.'

'You had it in for me from that day forward. You had it in for rugby, I know, a long time before that.'

'Give it to me.'

'Which is why, when the chance came to get me stripped of my Leinster Schools Senior Cup medal, oh, you took it – you took it with both hands.'

'You won that medal under false pretences.'

'And now you want to act as, like, stepfather to my actual son? Did you really think I was going to just let that happen?'

'I'm in love with Tina!'

He blurts it out, roysh, just like that. I laugh in his face. 'Well,' I go, 'let's see how you feel having something you love taken away from you.'

I wave the phone in his face, then I turn and I stort climbing back up the edge of the – again – ravine.

He's going, 'Where the hell do you think you're going? Come back

352

here this instant!' but I just keep going, then he howls out, as if in pain, presumably from his focked ankles. 'Come back here now!' and then eventually, 'Please! I'm begging you,' except it's very much a case of too little, too late.

I make my way out of the wood and stand there, roysh, just surveying this scene of basically *cornage*? It's a focking battle re-enactment alright. There's a couple of thousand of them down there, beating *all* colours out of each other. I can make out Fionn and Erika in the middle, still on their horses, shouting through their loud-hailers, trying to restore order.

I sit down on, like, a tree stump and look at McGahy's phone. First, I go through his texts – portly out of curiosity, portly to find out the name of that place that he's supposedly taking her and Ronan again. *He* calls *her* Precious, I notice, and *she* calls *him* Bitsy. Focking ridiculous carry-on – the age of them.

Copenhagen. Yeah, no, that was it.

I hit create new message, then I write, 'Sory 2 spring dis on u at d last minute tina but i'm gonna hav 2 pull out of d whol copenhagen ting. Cut a long story short i want 2 end dis relationship – if u cud even call it dat.'

Then I send it.

Twenty seconds later, a text comes back and it's like, 'lol.'

So I end up straight away having to send a second one, except *horsher* this time? 'Tina im serious, i want out, no more bitsy and precious, im sorry : ('

'Are u drunk?' she texts back.

So I text her, going, 'Why wud i b drunk?'

'Cos u never abbreviate ur words! In fact u always mock me 4 doin it. And 4 using numbers 4 words!'

Yeah, that'd be him alright.

'Okay,' I text, 'I'll give it to you in my kind of language. You're dumped. End of.'

The phone *rings* then – Tina trying to get through. I let it ring out, then I text her, going, 'Don't ring me. I don't want to talk to you. I'm serious about this thing. Just accept it and get on with your life :)'

It's a good, like, five minutes before she texts back. 'Tom i dont understand, why are u bein like dis?'

I text her back, going, 'Because Ross was basically right. It was only ever a spite ride situation. I only actually did it to get back at him because I've hated him for years. Although I have to admit now that a lot of that was down to the fact that he was an incredible rugby player and probably the best out-half never to represent Ireland.'

I delete the last line, thinking it might be a bit much, then I change my mind – the old big head getting the better of me – and I stick it back in again. But then there's nothing, roysh, for the next twenty minutes and I'm thinking, shit, she's seen through it.

But as I get back to the cor, having had to practically fight my way through this pitched battle that's still basically raging, my own phone rings and who is it, roysh, only Tina.

She's in absolute tears and she goes, 'You were reet abourrim, Ross. You were reet.'

10. 2G2BT

It's, like, three o'clock on Saturday afternoon and I'm stood outside the Central Bank, looking across the – I think the word is, like, *concourse?*

In my day, it was, like, grunge. Before that, there were, like, goths. Even before them, you had, like, *punks?* Every generation comes up with a name for dressing like shit and thinking your parents are orseholes.

Hedda's in there somewhere, among the hundreds of little clusters of hormonal teenagers, dressed in tight jeans and even tighter band T-shirts – er, T-shirts, *despite* the fact that it's November? – talking about how there's, like, levels to *Napoleon Dynamite* – you just have to watch it again – and how the new Jimmy Eat World album isn't even *worth* downloading.

Picking her out is nearly impossible. It's like looking at one of those focking *Where's Wally?* books.

I spend a good twenty minutes picking my way through the crowd, drawing a lot of funny looks and a fair few comments. I hear someone go, 'He must be someone's dad,' and then some – I *think?* – dude in a black, long-sleeved T-shirt with a logo on it that says 'Bleed just to know you're alive' checks out my Dubes and my sailing jacket and goes, 'Hey, you must be into rugby!' except I know he doesn't mean it in, like, a good way?

'What the fock is wrong with rugby?' I go, genuinely meaning it.

He just sneers.

I'm like, 'It's actually the greatest sport in the world.'

But he just turns his back on me, going, 'Yeah, you're a total noob.'

On any other day, he could consider himself as good as decked. Except today I'm in, like, cracking form. Ronan texted me at ten o'clock this morning – from Dublin, not Copen-blahdy-blah – just going, 'Thanks, Rosser,' which was an amazing thing to hear.

He hasn't a bog what I did, of course, just that Tina came to him in tears this morning saying that Ross was right and the trip was off.

And now I feel I could take on literally anyone or anything.

I suddenly spot her, sitting on the little morble step in front of the building, with her back to the iron railings. The focking state of her as well. She's wearing, like, a tight, pink-and-black-striped mohair cordigan, torn black leggings and wrecked pink Chucks.

I morch straight up to her and go, 'You've some focking mouth on you, do you know that?'

She's like, '*Excuse* me?' all innocence.

I'm there, 'Blabbing to your old dear's mates – about me and the cor and Regina's will and blahdy blahdy blah.'

'Oh! Melancholy! Gazes!' the bird sitting beside her goes. 'This is *him*?' obviously meaning the dude who's throwing her old dear a bone.

Hedda smiles, a rare enough event, I'd imagine. 'Yeah, it's hord to believe, isn't it?'

What the fock is that supposed to mean?

I'm there, 'Look, you've obviously got an issue with me and I can understand that. But when you stort telling tales out of school, especially to tossers like that Levinus, that's when I stort to take shit personally.'

This dude sitting on the other side of her – black, greasy hair, cut at an angle and Buddy Holly glasses – suddenly stands up and goes, 'Sorry, can you fuck off and leave us alone?'

He's right in my face as well. For a weedy little focker, who looks like he hasn't had a good feed in years, he's got a set of nuts on him like focking wrecking balls.

'You're lucky,' I go, 'that I'm in an unbelievable mood today. Who the fock are you anyway?'

Hedda dives in. She's like, 'Don't tell him,' and it's straight away obvious she doesn't want me to have anything *on* her?

Except *he* can't help himself. 'Yeah, I happen to be her boyfriend,' he goes.

I crack my hole laughing, then turn to Hedda. 'I thought you were a virgin?'

He answers *for* her? 'She's celibate,' he goes. 'It's not the same thing.'

'Well, either way, it sounds to me like neither of you is getting any.'

And you can tell, roysh, that he's one of these emotionally sensitive types who develops, like, platonic relationships with birds he fancies

– because he *thinks* he can get to know them on a whole other level – then ends up losing them to goys like me who're only interested in one thing.

'Of course,' he goes, 'because that's all there is to a relationship as far as you're concerned, isn't it? Sex? There can be connection between a man and a woman other than the physical?'

I'm telling you, he's a ballsy little focker, especially for one wearing women's ankle boots.

'Dude,' I go, 'how even old are you – nineteen?'

He's like, 'Twenty, in fact.'

I laugh. 'Twenty? You really need to get wise. Look, take it from someone who's in the know. I've *bought* the chocs and flowers. I've sat through all the romcoms . . .'

I turn and give Hedda the old Come to Papa eyes, just to freak them out. 'And I know that what women really want is the same thing they wanted billions of years before chocolates and flowers and romcoms were even invented.'

I give her a little wink then.

'You're disgusting!' she goes. 'You're *focking* disgusting!'

I'm there, 'And you're a pain in the hole. Stay out of my business – that's my basic message. And stop badmouthing me to your old dear's friends.'

Fionn texts and says he wants to meet me for, like, Sunday brunch. Which is weird, roysh, because it's usually the day after a home international or a big Leinster match that we all get together in Dalkey and each give our analysis of the game over anything from, like, eggs Florentine to a Mexican wrap. But I know for a fact that Ireland aren't playing South Africa until *next* weekend?

I text him back, roysh, and I ask him if JP and Oisinn know and he says no, it's just going to be me and him, which has me immediately thinking that he knows – he *must* know – that it was me who kicked off the riot in Mullinavat.

'Is der sometin specific u want 2 talk 2 me about?' I go and he's straight away back with, 'I need to ask you something. See you at 11, the usual spot,' and then nothing else.

I must read the message, like, a hundred times, trying to decide if he sounds angry, happy or whatever other emotions there are. In the end, roysh, the optimist in me decides that it's probably nothing to do with what happened on Friday. Imagine my shock, though, when I walk through the door of Idle Wilde to see him and Erika sitting side by side at a table facing the door. I end up nearly crapping a lung.

He looks like shit, by the way. Like he hasn't slept. As does she. They both smile when they see me, which is a good sign. Although it *could* still be a trap – lulling me into a false sense of blahdy blah.

They both stand up, like they're being received by royalty. *She* air-kisses me, going, 'It's lovely to see you, Ross,' while he shakes my hand, then sort of, like, pulls me clumsily into an embrace, patting my back, just to let me know it's a man thing, nothing funny.

It's just instinct, roysh, but I don't think they *do* know?

'I, er, meant to you ring yesterday,' I go. 'Make sure you were okay. I got a text from Oisinn. He said you were both thrown off your horses.'

'Fionn's fall was broken by the angry mob surrounding him demanding their hundred euros back,' she goes, smiling at him and holding his hand on the table. 'Luckily, I know *how* to fall. That's my dressage background standing to me.'

'Well, I'm going to have to say fair focks here.'

Her eyes take on a bit of a – I've heard it described as a *yonderly* look? She's there, 'I'd just love to know what it was that spooked Kelly.'

I shake my head slowly. 'It's a genuine mystery that, isn't it?'

'I mean, you've seen me in competition with her, Ross. She's always so calm.'

'We may never know. I think we need to just accept that fact and move on.'

Fionn goes, 'I've been suspended by the Institute. I suppose you heard.'

'No. Fock.'

'Pending a disciplinary hearing. I'm pretty sure I'm going to get the sack.'

'That's horsh.'

He laughs. Well, it's more of a harrumph. 'I don't think it is, in all fairness. Four members of the teaching staff – the entire history faculty – are in hospital. I went to visit John Hent yesterday. He's in Vincent's Private. Anyway, he said he was certain that he heard an order to charge,' and then he makes, like, a book motion to the wait-ress and mouths the word, 'Menus?' to her.

'So,' I go, moving the conversation swiftly along, 'what was the final, er, death toll, if that's what you want to call it?'

He's like, 'Well, none dead, thankfully. Seventy injured. Forty arrested. Have you seen the Sunday papers?'

Erika's there, 'Fionn, I told you not to read them.'

'Front-page headline on *The Sunday World* – The Battle of the Boyne II.'

I throw my eyes skyward. 'Wouldn't you know the papers would blow it out of proportion.'

Our menus arrive.

'Out of proportion? You were there, Ross. It took two hundred Gardaí in riot gear to clear the field. It'd be impossible to blow it out of proportion. In fact, I don't think the papers even came close to captur-ing it.'

'Fair enough. I only really said it to be supportive. I take it that's the end of it, then – as in, there won't be any more re-enactments?'

He laughs. 'You're too right there won't be any more. I spoke to the insurers yesterday – they think we could be looking at up to half a mil-lion euros in personal injury claims.'

'Half a million?' I go. 'That's serious wedge.'

Erika closes her menu. 'Tell him the other thing?'

'Oh yes,' Fionn goes, pushing his glasses up on his nose. 'Tom McGahy has gone missing.'

I'm like, 'Missing? As in?'

'As in, his mother hasn't seen him since Friday. Since he set off for Mullinavat in fact. She's really worried. She can't do much for herself, you see. I think it goes without saying that's very out of character for him.'

I'm suddenly taking a huge interest in the lunch specials. 'I honestly don't know whether I'm going to have the Conquistador scramble or the gingerbread waffles with apple and vanilla bean compote.'

'Hey,' he goes, suddenly remembering something, 'isn't he, I don't know, seeing a lot of Ronan's mother these days? Oisinn said some-thing about it.'

I'm there, 'Yeah, no, now that you say it, I remember they were sup-posedly going to – I think it's pronounced Copenhagen, this weekend.'

'Copenhagen?'

'Is that how you say it?'

'Well, yeah – it's exactly as it's spelt. But he wouldn't go without telling his mother, would he? That doesn't sound like Tom.'

'Well, like you said, she is old. Maybe he did tell her and she forgot. She's in, what, her eighties – she's possibly bonkers.'

'She could be just confused, I suppose.'

'There you are, then. You both look a bit wrecked, I hope you don't mind me saying.'

'Well, we've slept, I think, three hours in the last two nights,' Erika goes. 'We spent the entire day yesterday on the phone to solicitors, school principals, the insurers. And then the newspapers, of course.'

Fionn smiles sadly.

He goes, 'But we *do* have a wedding to plan. So we decided that for the next three days, we're going to forget about Friday and the inevitable court cases and my disciplinary hearing, whatever it's going to end up costing us down the line, and just concentrate on the arrangements.'

I'm there, 'You sound like a man with a plan.'

I might end up doing something totally left field and get the pimento cheese toast.

A definite look passes between them then. Suddenly, Erika stands up. 'I must go and feed the meter,' she goes, which I realize straight away is horseshit because porking is supposedly, like, *free* on a Sunday? Actually, it better be.

It's only when she's out the door that I cop it. She's leaving the two of us alone.

'Ross,' *he* goes, after she's left, 'I've got something to ask you.'

I'm like, 'Er, cool.'

'Okay, I had this little speech planned in my head, but I'm not going to bother with it. I'm just going to ask you straight out. Will you be my best man?'

'Me?'

'Yeah.'

'But . . . Jesus, Fionn, I've given you a seriously hord time over the years. Glasses and all the rest of it.'

He laughs, even though he knows I'm right.

I'm like, 'Why me?'

He's there, 'That's exactly what Erika said. But I just realized something recently. All of the best moments in my life, the best laughs, the best times, they all had one thing in common. You were there at the centre of all of them.'

'I thought your best moments were in the focking library.'

'You see, that's what I mean. There have been days when you've made my life a living hell. And I realize how tragic it is to wake up one day and realize that the best friend you've managed to make in your thirty years on this earth is Ross O'Carroll-Kelly. But there it is. We have had unbelievable times together.'

'There's no denying that.'

'When I tell people – even Erika – about some of the things we got up to . . .'

'She possibly thinks you're making them up.'

'But it's not just the fun times we had. I'll never forget that it was you, more than anyone, who helped me get over Aoife's death.'

Shit. Not my conscience again.

'Dude,' I go, 'we all did our bit, in fairness.'

He's like, 'No. It wasn't JP, Christian or Oisinn who called up to my apartment night after night. Even when I told you that I didn't want to see anyone, you said you'd sit on the step for an hour in case I changed my mind.'

'Most nights I left after ten or fifteen minutes. I'm not going to bull-shit you.'

'There's a kindness in you, Ross. You don't like people acknowledging it. But it's there . . .'

Fock. I don't think I'm going to be able to stop myself from telling him.

'And last year, when I was depressed, asking myself what I'd made of my life and where I was going, who was it who sat me down and told me, in plain terms, that it was time to stop grieving for Aoife.'

Yeah, I end up just blurting it out.

'I know where McGahy is!'

He's like, 'What?'

'Look, I wasn't going to say anything, until *you* started tugging at my focking hort strings there.'

'You're saying he's *not* in Copenhagen?'

'I'm saying that I've actually got a bit of a confession to make . . .'

It's at that exact point that Erika comes back. She immediately picks up on the atmos and asks what's going on. Fionn gestures for her to listen to me.

'Look,' I go, 'they were *supposed* to go to Copenhagen this weekend. For the bank holiday. Ronan, in his defence, wasn't a million percent happy that his headmaster was doing the nasty nasty with his old dear and he asked me to do something about it – like only I can.'

'Ross,' Fionn goes, 'what the fock did you do?'

'I can see you getting ready to judge me there, Fionn. And bear in mind that I'm only telling you this because that was all great shit you were saying to me earlier on. Okay, when the whole – I suppose – riot kicked off, I chorged like everyone else. I mean, you get caught up in it, don't you? That's what these psychologists always say. Anyway, that's when I copped McGahy and I found myself thrown into a, I have to admit it, *rage?* Anyway, to cut long story short, I chased him into the woods and he ended up falling down this – basically? – ravine.'

'A ravine?'

'I'm pretty sure. You'd possibly have to see it yourself to judge.'

'So what happened after that?'

'Not a huge amount. He broke both his ankles.'

Erika has to get involved then. 'So you're saying he's in hospital?' she goes.

'Er, not exactly, no.'

Fionn's there, 'Ross, where is he?'

I have to say it – no choice, with the pressure they're putting me under here.

'I left him there.'

'You *left* him there?'

'Yeah.'

'At the bottom of a ravine?'

'Again, some people might consider it just a high drop.'

'You left him there to die?' He raises his voice this time.

I just roll my eyes. He can be such a focking drama queen. 'I wasn't going to let him die. No, I was going to just leave him there for the weekend, then I was going to make a unanimous phone call to the cops.'

'For the entire weekend?'

'Yeah. See, I thought if I called them yesterday, his ankles might end up not *being* broken, then they could still get a flight out at some stage today. Like I said, it's a bank holiday weekend, which would have still given them the Sunday and Monday out there.'

The next thing anyone hears is the sound of Fionn's chair legs scraping across the floor as he stands up and sticks his finger practically in my face. 'You'll be very lucky if he hasn't died from exposure.'

I'm there, 'Ah, leave it, Fionn – how long has that focker had it coming from me? And can I just remind you that you two left me in a pretty similar situation not so long ago. I ended up in, like, an open grave.'

But he's just like, 'Erika, we'll go in your car.'

Except Erika doesn't even stir. She's just, like, staring at me, although glowering is possibly *more* the word?

She's there, 'It was you, wasn't it?'

I'm like, 'What?'

'It was you! *You* caused the entire thing!'

There's no point in me even denying it.

I'm like, 'No,' going through the motions anyway.

'What did you do,' she goes, 'to startle Kelly?'

I just shake my head, like the whole thing is ridiculous.

'What did you do, Ross?'

'Look, I might have given her a jab in the orse with my plastic sword. And, yeah, I possibly shouted, "Chorge!" as well.'

Now, I've seen Erika pissed off with me many times down through the years but never more than at that moment. There's, like, no withering comment from her. No witty put-down line. For once she's, like, totally speechless. She doesn't even look at the waitress when she arrives over to ask us if we've decided what we're having. She just follows Fionn out the door – all *his* fine words from just a few minutes ago already forgotten, by the way.

I tell the waitress I'm going to, like, pass on breakfast myself. Because I know there's somewhere I need to urgently be. See, it's like when you're playing rugby against Mungret or any of the Limerick schools – it's a case of getting your retaliation in first.

An hour later, I'm sitting in Tina's living-room – the *lounge*, as they call it in this port of the world – with my orm around her shoulder, listening to her sobbing her hort out, telling her, at the same time, that I know how much she was looking forward to going away for the weekend but that she can do, like, way better than McGahy – and we're talking *way*?

I end up sitting with her all day and half the night. We watch the previous night's *X Factor*, which she Sky Plussed. Simon Cowell is telling Meerdy Burden that no matter what happens in this competition, she will not be going back to Tescos.

'Yeah, it'll be focking Morks & Spencers,' I go and Tina laughs, probably for the first time this weekend. 'The important thing,' I go, while I've got her where I want her, 'is not to believe his bullshit when he rings.'

Her face instantly lights up. 'Do you tink he'll ring?'

I'm there, 'Of course he'll focking ring – when he realizes what he's lost? What he let go? Jesus! But the important thing is not to listen to whatever bullshit excuse he tries to give you. In fact, if he rings, just let me do the talking.'

'But maybe I owe him at least a heardin.'

'Tina, he's a player.'

'Dat's whor I can't believe. He seemed like such a gentleman.'

'That's his act. In fact, knowing him like I do, he'll probably try to blame me in some way. Honestly, Tina, if he rings, I'll answer.'

Ronan arrives home at nine o'clock. God knows where he's been. He asks Tina if she's okay and she says she will be. He smiles at me and I have to say that smile totally makes up for Fionn and Erika's big-time overreaction.

He can maybe have another crack at giving up the cigarettes now.

It's, like, ten past ten when Tina's mobile finally rings. I'm thinking, fock, it must have taken them a long time to find him. He's ringing from an obviously payphone, roysh, because I can hear the pips. Then in the background, there's, like, *hospital* noises? I answer without even saying a word.

'Tina!' he goes. 'Thank God. Oh, I'm sorry. I'm so, so sorry. You wouldn't believe the forty-eight hours I've had. I didn't think I'd live to speak to you again. It was Ross. He chased me. I fell down a ravine . . .'

See, I *said* it was a ravine.

'And he left me for dead. Both my ankles were broken. I couldn't move. For two days and nights, I survived on nothing but Silvermints and dew sucked from the morning grass. Then last night the temperature dropped and I thought I'd freeze to death. I'd nearly have almost preferred death to another night in the open. The only thing that kept me alive was the thought of seeing you again.'

'I'm very flattered,' I just go. And you can actually hear his shock on the other end of the phone. I'm like, 'That was some focking story, by the way. I told her it'd be a cracker. It'd *have* to be.'

He's there, 'You little shit. You put me onto Tina. You put me onto her this instant.'

'I'm sorry,' I go, giving Tina my best sympathetic look, 'she doesn't want to talk to you.'

'Ay hod a word with Levinus,' Regina goes, 'abite what he said.'

There's a dude measuring my inside leg, by the way, while this conversation is taking place. 'Keep looking straight ahead,' he tells me, through a mouthful of pins.

'Ay hope yee don't maind,' *she* goes. 'It's just *ay* knew high upsat yee were.'

I'm there, 'No, it's cool. Can I expect an apology from him, then?'

She laughs. 'Och, *yee'd* be lockay. No, he's stacking tee his gons. We'd a terrible roy on the phone. Fortay years of frandshup – gawn, just lake thot.'

'Well,' I go, 'thanks for taking my side. What kind of shit was he saying about me?'

'Och, the usual – he's only anthrested in yee for yeer mornay.'

'The focking nerve!'

'It was more what he was seeing abite may. Said he couldn't believe ay'd take the sade of a total streenger over may own flash and blood.'

'She *is* a bitch, though – you said it yourself.'

'Oh, ay *know* what she is. He called may salfish, though. Said ay've been thanking abite mayself and may own needs and ignoring the fact that may daughter's grieving for her doddy.'

The dude wraps the tape around my chest then and I watch him scribble down the measurement in his little pad.

I go, 'Good?' but he doesn't give me an opinion either way.

The snotty focker just goes, 'As I said, it wasn't necessary for Sir to remove his shirt.'

I think *his* issue is that he used to be Toddy's tailor – he *was* for, like, twenty-something years? I sensed his sudden – you *could* say – disapproval, the second he copped that I wasn't her nephew. This is, like, twenty Ks' worth of a suit that Regina's splashing out on here. You'd think he'd be happy, especially in the whole current economic.

'I don't know why people can't mind their own focking business,' I make sure to go, as he's measuring my orms. 'Keep their focking opinions to themselves.'

Regina, of course, thinks I'm still talking about Levinus. 'Well, then I finde ite yasterdee thot he's been talking tee Kathleen.'

'As in Kathleen who came onto me in the hotel?'

'Aye. Wee whore.'

'You said it. I mean, she was seriously gagging for me. I told you that, didn't I?'

'Well, she's threatening noy to sue may. Unforr dismassal. And Levinus is going tee rapresant her.'

'What?'

'Thot's what *ay* said. Couldn't believe it when may solicitor told may. Ay *rong* Levinus street awee. Says ay, "What are yee deeing?"'

'And did you *mention* the fact that she was the one who was gagging?'

'Course ay dud. But Hedda's filled his head with *all* sorts of lays.'

'The little . . . There's words I could use here, Regina, but I won't.'

'Ay'm really scurred of her, Ross.'

'Scared? Of Hedda?'

'Aye – *ay* thank she'd dee onythang to breek us op.'

'Well, she's not going to succeed – I can tell you that now. And that Levinus dude, he can't be serious about actually suing you. Especially after everything you've been already *through*?'

'Oh, he's dadlay serious. Says he, "*Ay'm* deeing this for *your* own gid. Ay'm gonna get you to see what kaind of a fellay yee've got yourself maxed op wuth – even if thot means putting the tee of them in a watness box and seeing whose storay a juray believes."'

Oh, shit.

'Ay thank the grey plaid is really gonna seet yee,' she goes. 'It was always Toddy's favourite as well, wasn't it, Nacholas?'

Nicholas – that's the focker's name – he doesn't answer her, though, he just fake-smiles, then disappears into his little back room with his notebook.

'He's another one,' I go, flicking my thumb in his general postcode. 'Did you pick up on the – again – disapproval?'

She sort of, like, waves her hand. 'Look, *ay* don't curr what anyone says anymore. Ay'm hoppay – that's all *ay* know.'

She kisses me, then runs a hand over my pecs and gives me a look – and you know the look I'm talking about.

'Och,' she goes, suddenly remembering something, 'what are yee deeing on Soturdee?'

'Saturday?'

'Ay've got tackets for Meekle Beeblay.'

'Bublé?'

'Aye – he's in the Oy Tee.'

'The O2? Er, yeah, cool – whatever.'

I'm onto you.

He says it just like that.

He goes, 'I'm onto you.'

I'm there, 'What's that supposed to mean?'

'Means you might have your old man fooled – but I didn't just come down the river on a rubber fucking ducky.'

I'm like, 'Hennessy . . .'

But he just cuts me off. 'Hennessy nothing!' he practically roars down the phone. 'Where are you now?'

He doesn't give me a chance to even answer.

'You're in bed,' he goes. 'Two o'clock on a Monday afternoon and you're in fucking bed.'

I mute *Home and Away*.

'Sorry, do you mind me asking how that's any of your beeswax?'

'Beeswax? I'll tell you how it's my beeswax. One of my best clients is looking at five years in the big house because you didn't make a pickup. That's how it's my beeswax, you little prick.'

'And did the old man not explain to you that I got this really weird vibe that the place was about to be raided?'

'Like I said, you've got *him* fooled – but not me. There's an old proverb, says you can't shit a shitter.'

'I've heard it loads of times.'

'So are you going to tell me what's going on?'

'There's nothing to tell.'

'All Charlie's old clients – they can't get you on the phone anymore.'

'I've been rushed off my feet.'

'When they do get you, you're telling them to try Slash & Byrne or Des Troy Evidence Services.'

'Like the old man says, there's a lot of people out there with a lot of shit to hide.'

'So if you're so busy, how comes I ain't seen the van around town – not for months.'

'To be fair to me, I've been doing a lot of heavy back-work out on the northside direction.'

Which, at least, is *kind* of true?

'There's something,' he goes. 'Something you *ain't* saying. I'm going to start asking questions.'

'Ask all you want.'

'I'll find out what it is. And you *know* I'll find out.'

It storts with, like, an explosion of fireworks.

I'm telling you, they'd want to be careful, given the age profile of the audience. There must be, like, one St John's Ambulance man for every three punters.

He opens with 'Crazy Love' and the people go literally ballistic. I *say* people, but I *mean* women, because that's what they pretty much nearly all are – drunk and drooling fifty- and sixty-year-old desperados, reeking of *Flower by Kenzo* and dressed a good thirty years too young for their age.

And I'm *including* Regina in that. She's wearing, like, a black cat-suit with sporkling sequins and four-inch Loubs and she's belting out what lines she can remember through a fog of three or four Bacordi Breez-ers too many.

'*Ay* love hum!' she goes. I'm standing immediately behind her with my orms wrapped around her waist. 'Ay jost *love* hum!'

I'm there, 'He's certainly the consummate showman. You always hear people say that, don't you?' and at the same time, roysh, I'm hav-ing a good look around me. There's a lot of women in here who've had a lot of work done. In fact, if you collected up all the loose skin that's been surgically removed from the faces in the O2 tonight, you'd have enough to stick a focking retractable roof on the place.

'Toddy and ay used tee love the whole big bond thang,' she goes. 'Shorley Bossay. Tam Joins. We saw Frank Sinatra in Caesar's in Vegas in 1974.'

I just shake my head. 'Jesus, that was before I was even . . .'

She turns around shorply and puts a red-painted finger over my lips. 'Don't even thank abite seeing what you were abite to see.'

I laugh, then she takes her finger away and just kisses me. The feel of her lips on mine – being honest – disgusts me now.

There's a little huddle of women about twenty or thirty feet away and they're, like, checking us out in a major way. I remember them from Milano's earlier. They were staring at us then as well – you could nearly hear them thinking, yeah, no woman gets *that* lucky – it *must* be her money.

Too focking right it's her money.

Regina cops them having a good eyeful and whispering among themselves and she put her orms around my shoulders and storts pretty much getting off with me to basically make a point. I can taste the melanzane parmigiana off her tongue as she practically tickles my tonsils and old Mickey Bubbles launches into 'Georgia on My Mind'.

She pulls away – point made – then turns to face the front again, pulling my orms back around her waist. The women are still staring, licking their lips, like four dogs looking in a butcher's window. I can tell, roysh, that Regina loves the way it makes her feel. I look at them and just give them a wink. There's going to be some amount of cougar action in the bors of Dawson Street tonight – a lot of post-menopausal women knocking boots, a lot of goys in their twenties waking up tomorrow to an excellent breakfast and a day of self-loathing.

He dedicates the next song – 'All I Do is Dream of You' – to his fiancée, we're talking Luisana Loreley Lopilato de la Torre, and the crowd turns suddenly sour, all booing, until the band strikes up the first note and everyone gets suddenly into it, singing alone. Including me. It's amazing to discover how many Michael Bublé songs you actually know – even just from shopping in Superquinn.

'Ay'm hornay.'

It comes out of literally nowhere.

I'm like, 'What?'

She turns fully around to me again, a big drunken smile on her face. '*Ay'm* sorious,' she goes. 'Ay'm hornay as hell.'

I give her one of my nice and sleazy looks. 'Well,' I go, 'we'll have to see what we can do about that later on, won't we?'

'*Ay* con't weet thot long.'

I actually laugh 'We can't leave now, Regina. He's only, like, four songs in.'

And this look comes into her eyes – the let's-do-it-in-the-toilets look that I remember only too well from my time in UCD.

I just smile. Then she turns and, practically running, leads the way to the jacks.

She drags me into trap two.

'Be quack,' she goes. 'Ay don't want to muss "Cray Me a Ruvver".'

Quick, of course, is my speciality.

As I mentioned – and as a lot of you no doubt already know – I'm no stranger to performing in ladies rooms and other, let's just say, confined spaces. It's pretty difficult, though, to do it with a woman wearing a cat-suit – and even more difficult when you're sitting on a toilet with a focking sensor flush.

Somehow, we manage to manoeuvre our various bits and pieces into position and suddenly she's bouncing up and down on me like she's on her Wii Fit, getting a good sweat up and stopping every thirty seconds, between screams of ecstasy, to go, 'What song is thot?'

Through the door, roysh, we can hear the mutters of, like, disgust – women tutting that it's a disgrace – an *absolute* disgrace – and it wouldn't happen in the RDS, except obviously during Horse Show Week. I still manage to keep my stroke, though, even *with* the toilet flushing every time my back touches the wall behind me.

'Quack,' she suddenly goes. 'That's "Ay Jost Hoven't Mat Yee Yat" he's sanging. He alwees does "Cray Me a Ruvver" naxt.'

So I finish the business, then we sort of, like, separate ourselves from each other. Regina fixes her cat-suit, touches up her hair and – with no hint of shame whatsoever – opens the door of the trap, to face a sea of, like, goggling faces.

And that's when my bowels pretty much give out. Because there, stood in the middle of them – in her old reliable black bustier-and-trousers combo, flashing her big wrinkly décolletage that she imagines is attractive – is my old dear.

Her jaw, as you can imagine, is on the focking floor and a fart silently slips my orse.

Regina walks straight past her, over to the washbasins, to check out her big flushed face. The old dear just stares at me, like she's waiting for an explanation.

I decide to just brazen it out.

'Close your mouth,' I go. 'You look like something that's been pulled out of the focking sea.'

Delma and Angela, I notice, are stood either side of her.

'I told you it was him,' Delma goes and that's when I suddenly realize – that's who it was staring at us in Milano's earlier. I possibly need to get the old mince pies checked out.

'What the hell kind of way is that to behave?' is all the old dear can think to go. '*Here,* Ross? At Michael Bublé!'

She has so much make-up on, she's practically slurring her words.

I just laugh in her face.

There's, like, ten or fifteen other women standing around, enjoying the show.

She's there, 'Have you no shame?' which is focking hilarious, you'd have to admit.

I'm there, 'Er, given who my mother is, strangely not.'

'I beg your pardon!'

'Yeah. Whatever.'

Regina comes over then to see what the scene's all about. 'Is overythang okee?'

The old dear doesn't even look at her. She just goes, '*Her?* I mean, of all the people . . .'

That gets Regina's back immediately up. 'Hoy the holl are yee?' she goes.

People from the North are always spoiling for a fight.

The old dear doesn't answer her – wouldn't give her the pleasure. '*You* should know better,' she goes, without even looking at her, 'a woman of your age.'

'A woman of *may* eege? Do *yee* thank that botox meeks yee look younger or somethang? Because it doesn't. Big shany feece on yee – meeks yee look lake yee've been embalmed.'

I crack my hole laughing. Regina obviously thinks she's just some randomer who's basically *jealous?*

The old dear gives her the elevator eyes. 'You should be at home, in your house-coat, watching reruns of old Miss Marple,' which is a weak comeback and that's not me being biased.

'*Ay* should? Teak a look in the marror over thor. Are yee onder the ampression somehoy that thot cleavage is in some wee saxy? You look lake you've gat a scrotum splashed acrass your chast.'

You can imagine me, at this stage. I'm nearly on the floor laughing. 'Regina,' I go, somehow managing to hold it together for five seconds, 'this is my mother.'

'Yeer *mother*?' she goes, unimpressed. It might also be the Breezers and the half a bottle of, like, Pinot Noir talking. 'Och, ay recognaze her noy.'

'And I recognize *you*,' the old dear goes. Then she turns to Angela. 'She's just like that destination spa hotel of hers. Looks fancy. But underneath? Cheap, nasty and falling apart.'

That ups the definite stakes.

'*Ay've* read one or toy of those beaks of years,' Regina goes. 'Talk abite sexual frostration. I thank *yee* could dee with gatting some yeersalf.'

I laugh my balls off. 'That's an *actually* spot-on assessment,' I go.

Delma tries to come between them then. 'Just walk away, Fionnuala – come on, it's Bublé.'

Except the old dear gets this really, like, bitchy look on her face, that you'd know well if you spent any time in the Weavers. 'You see, that's the type of people you are,' she goes. 'Crude. Your husband was no better, of course.'

'Yee leave Toddy ite of thus.'

'He was just like you – much as I hate to speak ill of the dead. Happy to take advantage of the young and impressionable.'

Jesus Christ, I'd hordly call me *or* Erika that.

'If yee weren't Ross's mother,' Regina goes, '*ay'd* slop yeer feece for yee. Come on, Ross – thot's *may* song coming awn.'

She walks out. I go to follow her, roysh, with a big focking smirk on my face, because it's supposed to be the old dear's favourite song as well.

'I'm telling your father,' she calls after me.

I turn around and look at her. 'You wouldn't.'

'One point seven million euros, she took from him. She was more responsible for his heart attack than anything else.'

'That's why you won't tell him.'

'Oh, I will.'

'You definitely won't.'

★ ★ ★

The old man rings at, like, quarter to eleven in the morning. 'Ross, I just heard the news,' he goes.

I haven't even properly woken up here. I'm like, 'That *focking* bitch.'

'Ross,' he goes, 'I'm referring to this four-year, fifteen-billion-euro adjustment plan of Brian Lenihan's.'

'Oh.'

'He's saying now that it might have to be somewhat frontloaded – quote-unquote. What did *you* think I was talking about?'

'Er – nothing.'

'Somewhat frontloaded, eh? I never thought I'd hear such a thing. Unprecedented times, indeed. Still, it's an ill wind that doesn't blow for someone. As *you've* discovered with the success you're making of Shred Focking Everything.'

'That's, er, true.'

'And as *I* discovered about fifteen minutes ago.'

'What are you talking about?'

'Brace yourself, Ross. I've got some news. You may have wondered – as I did – when Anglo-Irish was going through its painful death throes, what would become of its corporate box in the new Aviva Stadium.'

'Er, not really – but continue.'

'I bought it, Ross.'

'What?'

'Private bar. Full catering. Two dedicated hostesses. Superior service. Etcetera, etcetera. And fifty seats with the best available view of the pitch. Oh, you heard me right, Ross.'

I laugh. 'That's incredible. Will you have it for the All Blacks?'

'You're damn right I'll have it for the All Blacks. And bring all your pals. JP and the chaps. I'm going to ring Hennessy – tell him the joyous news!'

I'm about to hang up when goes, 'By the way, Ross, have you done something to upset Erika?'

I'm like, 'Erika?'

I've tried to ring her *and* Fionn once or twice but they won't, like, talk to me. I'm not even sure if the whole best man offer still stands.

'Look,' he goes, 'I know it's been difficult for you two, discovering after all these years that you are in fact brother and sister. Trying to – inverted commas – re-imagine your relationship . . .'

'Was something said?'

'No, nothing. It's just, well, Helen and I were out with her and young Fionn yesterday. Scouting venues for their proverbial big day. And it's just they both clammed up, the moment your name was mentioned. Well, what Helen and I managed to glean from them was that they, in some way, blame *you* for what happened at this battle re-enactment of theirs. I'm sure you've seen it in the newspapers – the Siege of Mullinavat and so forth.'

The thing is, roysh, I'm pretty certain they've told him the full story – about me jabbing Erika's horse with my sword, shouting 'Chorge', even leaving McGahy in the woods – *their* words – *to die*? It's just he doesn't want to believe it. He doesn't want to see the wrong in me.

So all he can say is, 'It'll blow over. I said it to Helen. I'm sure it's all a big misunderstanding.'

Some dude on TV3 says that both Reuters and Bloomberg are reporting this morning that Ireland is in talks with the IMF about a bail-out for the economy. Taoiseach Brian Cowen has strenuously denied the reports.

I continue flicking until I find ITV, then I run my eye over today's field. Lynda Bellingham. Sherrie Hewson. Carol McGiffin. Denise Welch.

It's far from a classic. Looks like it's Kate Thornton again so.

'Oh my God,' I suddenly hear a voice go, 'you're wanking!'

I open my eyes to find Hedda stood at the door of the bedroom.

'You're wanking over *Loose Women!*'

I'm not even going to bother denying it. 'Hey, *I'm* in touch with my sexuality,' I go.

She laughs. She doesn't laugh actually – she sort of, like, huffs. 'Oh, you're that alright. I could hear the focking bed squeaking from downstairs.'

I laugh, though, just to let her know that she's not getting to me. 'What are you doing back here anyway? I think you're having trouble staying away from me.'

She doesn't respond to that. She just goes, 'Where's *she*?' meaning her old dear.

'I'm pretty sure she said Fletcher Pilates.'

'How long has she been gone?'

'Half an hour? How's, er, what's his name? The skinny little focker.'

'Don't give me that. His name happens to be Villette.'

'Jesus!'

'His mother loved Charlotte Brontë.'

'Well, it's no wonder he's so pissed off with the world.'

'I happen to think it's really sweet.'

She does something that really surprises me then. She sits on the edge of the bed.

'You know,' she goes, 'I think you could be alright if you weren't such an asshole.'

I laugh. 'If I'd a yoyo for every time I've heard that . . .'

She crosses her legs and runs her hand along her sheer purple leggings. I'd be lying if I said I wasn't thinking the obvious.

She goes, 'What would you think of the idea of calling a truce?'

'A truce?'

'Look, I've been doing some thinking. Maybe this *thing* between you and my mum is something I need to come to, like, *terms* with?'

'Okay.'

'I mean, if you *are* going to be together, then maybe it's important that you and I start getting along.'

'Hey, I'm *all* for getting along – ask around.'

'I mean, we're obviously never going to be close.'

I give her the eyes. You know the eyes I'm talking about. 'Me and you can be as close as you want,' I go.

She doesn't say anything. I'm wondering did she maybe miss the double meaning.

Which is why I decide to rephrase it. 'How close would you like to get to me?'

I'm horder than a mother-in-law's love, by the way – and I can tell you that it has fock-all to do with Kate Thornton.

She goes all bashful then. She's there, 'I . . . I don't know.'

But I make it easy for her. I reach for her hand and pull her a little bit closer to me.

I'm like, 'How about this close?' except I say it in a real, I suppose, *seductive* voice?

She tries to look away then but we both know why she came here this morning.

So I pull her all the way over to me. 'Or how about this?' I go.

377

That's all she needs. She's suddenly all over me like the focking Revenue. She throws the duvet back and storts sucking the lips off me, her hands moving up and down my abs like she's frisking me for explosives.

At the same time, roysh, she's making a sound like she can't breathe, like it's a choice between, I don't know, oxygen and my lips and she wants my lips more.

I pull my head away – *I* need air, even if *she* doesn't – and I unzip her black and white chequered hoodie and cop a bit of upstairs-outside action, over her white camisole with the Manga characters on it.

The moo moos aren't great, in all fairness – feeling her up is like going on a focking Easter egg hunt.

'Oh God!' she goes, loving it. 'I've wanted you since the very first time I saw you.'

I'm there, 'I know. I knew from the way you looked at me. You were screaming for it.'

She storts going at me again – working like a focking mush dog. It sounds like a weird thing to say, roysh, but she actually kisses very like her mother.

'Wait,' I go, stopping her dead in her tracks. 'Can you do something for me first?'

She looks worried. It's amazing how many girls in that situation presume they *know* what you're going to ask?

'Not that,' I go. 'I was actually going to ask would you mind just washing your make-up off?'

'What?'

'Well, the eye make-up especially. I find it a bit, I don't know, off-putting. I'm sorry if that sounds weird.'

'Er, no, it's cool.'

'It's just the whole emo thing. It sort of, like, freaks me out? Plus, I think you can actually look like Summer Glau when you make the effort. And that's a compliment.'

'Okay,' she goes, then she disappears into the *en suite* to get busy with the cleansing wipes.

Sixty seconds later, she's back, having lost not only the slap but the rest of her threads as well, standing in front of me, totally naked, with two big hungry eyes and her chitty chittys hanging down like two wet teabags.

'I hate to gloat,' I go, giving her the old James Bond smile, 'but I *was* right – about birds only wanting one thing?'

'Shut the fock up,' she goes, crawling across the bed. 'I want sex.'

I laugh. I'm there, 'What about the whole celibacy thing?'

'Fock celibacy.'

I laugh again, slipping off my boxers and my Boss Orange T-shirt. 'And Villette?'

'Fock Villette as well. Yes, you were right, if that's what you want to hear. I want a real man. A rugby man. A man who can make me basic-ally *feel* things?'

Now, you know me when it comes to diverging details. I've never been one to kiss and tell. But one thing becomes obvious during the course of the hour that follows. Hedda might well have *been* celibate, but she's no plastic surgeon, not with *her* understanding of the male anatomy. And, if I might be allowed to throw in a word for myself, I end up putting in a performance that would swear anyone off abstin-ence for life.

When all the heavy lifting is done, we end up just lying there in a sweaty pile, trying to get our breaths back. Some dude on the lunch-time news says that well-placed sources within Ireland's Central Bank insist that the country *is* in discussions with the IMF – contrary to the claims of Irish prime minister Brian Cowen – and that the extent of the bail-out is likely to be very, very large.

'That was fantastic,' I go. 'You've got a real gift there. Don't waste it.'

'You know,' she goes, pushing me off her, 'you are such a focking sucker.'

I'm like, 'Excuse me?'

She laughs – one with, like, real badness in it. 'Why do you think I just did that?'

'Did what?'

'Er, *seduced* you?'

I don't even get the chance to answer because she ends up just laughing again. 'I only did it so I could get my mum to see what you're like.'

She climbs off the bed, still laughing. Then she's stood in the door-way to the *en suite* again, pulling on her clothes.

I'm there, 'You're not going to tell her, are you?'

'Oh, I am. Let's see what she thinks of you after that.'

'She won't believe you.'

'We'll see. Oh, and by the way, I probably don't need to tell you that I faked that orgasm.'

'I should have guessed.'

She laughs. She's sitting on the end of the bed with her back to me now, putting her Vans back on. 'There's no way you *would* have guessed, Ross, because you think with your dick.'

'Not always.'

'You were, like, totally obsessed with me being celibate. I knew that if I offered myself to you, you'd fall for it.'

'I didn't fall for anything,' I go. And of course she doesn't know what to think when she turns around to find me grinning like a cheddar cat. 'I *knew* what you were here for. See, that's why I sent you into the jacks to wash that shit off your face. When you were gone, I took your phone out of the pocket of your hoodie and dialled Villette's number. Then I left it on the bed.'

'Empty seats at an Ireland versus All Blacks match!' the old man goes, stood at the window with an unlit cigor in his mouth, staring across the pitch at the stand opposite.

JP's old man is sat in what should have been Sean FitzPatrick's chair, a big black leather job. 'Never thought I'd see the day,' he goes.

'Well,' the old man goes, stepping behind the bor and helping himself to a Diet 7-Up, 'I only hope that our new friend Ajai Chopra isn't down there somewhere. Because he'll think, hello! Here's a country that's bloody well given up.'

I think it goes without saying that I have literally no idea who Ajai focking Chopra is.

The teams walk out and we all wander over to the window to watch them line up. The old man checks his watch. 'Hennessy had better get a move on,' he goes. 'Otherwise he'll miss the bloody haka.'

Then it's suddenly the anthems. During 'Ireland's Call', Oisinn hands me a can of the old Preparation H and asks if I'm okay.

I'm like, 'Yeah, why?'

'I was talking to Fionn,' he goes. 'Shit the bed, Ross, it was you?'

'What?'

'You kicked off the riot.'

'Oh, that. Dude, it's not even near the top of my worry list at the moment.'

'What do you mean?'

'It's just, have you ever got the sudden feeling that there's one almighty shit-storm blowing your way?'

He laughs. It's a stupid question to ask him of all people.

'It passes,' he goes. 'That's one thing I've learned, Ross, from being around dogs. They don't worry about what might or might not happen tomorrow. It's the moment. Sometimes, you just have to accept the inevitable.'

JP suddenly arrives with Danuta. *She's* got a face as long as January. I'm telling you, good looks are, like, totally wasted on the girl. 'Did you speak weez your muzzer?' she goes, in my face straight away.

I'm there, 'What?' trying to see the haka over her focking shoulder.

'JP asks you to speak weez your muzzer – she *must* stop zees protest.'

'Yeah,' I go, 'I, er, had a word,' which is total horseshit, of course. 'And it's no dice.'

I'll tell you something, Johnny Sexton doesn't look even a bit intimidated.

'She say zees? *No dice?*'

Johnny Sexton ends up being my inspiration. I just decide, there's no way I'm putting up with *her* shit anymore.

'No, her exact words were, tell that mental mafia bitch to fock off back to Russia. And that's, like, a *direct* quote?'

'You can tell her zer wheel be consequences!' she goes, totally losing it with me. 'She wheel suffer! I *wheel* make sure of zees!'

JP goes, 'Danni, let's, er, go get ourselves a drink,' and he sort of, like, ushers her off in the direction of the bor, at the same time making soothing noises to her, trying to basically calm her *down*?

I notice JP's old man having a bit of a chuckle to himself. *My* old man is too entranced by what's happening down on the pitch to even notice.

'Is it to be an Ireland victory,' he goes, 'at the twenty-fourth time of asking?'

Dan Corter kicks the ball high into the air and a roar goes up. And it's at that exact moment that Hennessy walks in.

'There you are!' the old man goes. 'History crooks its index finger at Ireland once again – eh, old scout?'

Except Hennessy doesn't answer. He doesn't move either. He just stands at the door, staring straight at me, looking like he could put his fist down my throat and choke the life out of me, right here in this premium-level, fully serviced, corporate hospitality box.

He goes, 'Why don't you tell you father a little bit of what you've been up to lately?'

'Come on,' the old man tries to go. 'The game has started. I've kept you David Drumm's seat here, look.'

'Oh, believe me,' Hennessy goes, 'this is far more entertaining than anything happening down there on the pitch. Do *you* want to tell him, Ross?'

At this stage, everyone in the box is looking my way.

'No,' I go, 'you tell him,' because I've no idea at this stage what *exactly* he knows?

He's there, 'Shred Focking Everything no longer exists as a business. This little fuckpiece hasn't fulfilled a single order since May, when – according an old Garda friend of mine – the van was found abandoned and burnt out in Blackrock.'

Shit.

'Burnt out?' the old man goes, looking at me, waiting for me to deny it. 'Who could have done such a thing? Ross?'

I end up having to sit down. 'It was Terry and Larry,' I go, deciding to come a little bit clean.

The old man looks at me, totally clueless. 'But I thought they were your friends. Good Lord, were they demanding – inverted commas – protection money from you, Kicker? For the business?'

I'm right on the point of saying yes when Hennessy goes, 'I'd bet ten grand to your one that the reason somehow involves his dick. Tell your father who you've been sharing a pillow with.'

Oh, bollocks.

I'm like, 'Er . . .'

'Tell him.'

When I don't answer, *he* says it *for* me.

'Regina Rathfriland.'

There's, like, a collective gasp from everyone in the room. Except the old man. He just looks confused – that's how much he still *wants* to see the good in me? 'I'm afraid the only Regina Rathfriland *I* know is that awful woman who . . .'

Hennessy's there, 'It's her, Charlie.'

The old man's like, 'No. No, you're wrong . . . Ross, he's mistaken isn't he?'

I'm right on the point of saying yes again when Hennessy goes, 'I'm not mistaken. This comes on the very best authority . . .'

I'm thinking, that big-mouthed bitch.

'Do you want me to tell them, Ross, how comes I know?'

But I decide, roysh, that I'm not going to give *him* the pleasure of saying it. Which is why I say it myself. 'The old dear caught us having sex in the shitter at Michael Bublé.'

There's, like, another huge intake of breath. I look around the room. There's genuine shock – and this from an audience that pretty much *knows* my previous? And that's when I realize that Hennessy looks as surprised as anyone else.

The old man turns to him. 'Are you saying,' he goes, 'that Fionnuala knew about this?'

Hennessy shakes his head. 'I never heard it from Fionnuala,' he goes. 'I heard it from Levinus Leonard. I know him from the Law Library.'

I hear Danuta laugh. She's loving this, of course.

I watch the colour literally drain from the old man's face. 'I'm afraid I feel rather unwell,' he goes.

He genuinely looks like he's about to keel over. He feels behind him for a seat. JP's old man jumps out and shoves one underneath him.

Outside, the crowd whistles and howls as Dan Corter kicks the All Blacks three points ahead. 'That does *not* sound good,' I go, as much to break the tension as anything else.

'Ross,' the old man goes, looking more disappointed in me than he ever has, 'I really would prefer it if you left now.'

Then a few seconds later, when I haven't actually moved, he just roars it again. 'Now!'

I'm in, like, Malahide, playing Guitor Hero on the PS3 that Regina bought me this morning, except my hort, if I'm being honest, isn't really in it.

Regina is sat in the corner, drinking her third gin and tonic of the afternoon and reading *Mom, They Said They'd Never Heard of Sundried Tomatoes* – I don't *know* why? Presumably for material on my old dear.

Every, like, thirty seconds, I hear her basically tut and go, 'Hoy does she gat awee with wrating shate lake thos.'

I'm there, 'Because she fools people. That's what she does. Been doing it all her life.'

The doorbell all of a sudden rings. Regina puts the book face-down on the coffee table and gets up to answer it.

I do one or two more songs – 'Take Me Out, November Rain', then a little bit of 'Layla' – before I suddenly realize that fifteen minutes have passed and she still isn't back.

And I get this instantly bad feeling.

I put the guitar down and I tip out into the hall, where I can hear raised voices coming from, like, the kitchen. It's actually Regina. And she sounds seriously pissed off about something.

I tiptoe down and listen at the door. She's going, '*Ay'm* asheemed of yee – ay really om. Yeer fawther would be, tee, if he was alave.'

Then another voice goes, 'Don't you mention him! What do you think he'd say about you! You're a drunken slapper.'

'Yee're a laying lattle batch!'

I just push the door.

Regina and Hedda are stood facing each other across the freestanding range. They're both crying. Hedda's mascara is all over the shop – her face looks like a focking Google map.

They both look at me at the exact same time.

Hedda wipes her face with her open palm, then goes, 'Go on, then,' nodding her head in my direction, 'why don't you ask him?'

I'm like, 'Ask me what?' even though, deep down, I already know.

'Is it troy,' Regina goes, 'what she's traying to tell may?'

I'm there, 'Depends what she's trying to tell you,' trying to buy myself some time here.

'Did yee sleep with hor?'

I'm like, '*Sleep* with her?' all innocence.

'Aye.'

I put on my best confused face and shake my head slowly, like I've no idea where a story like that might have even come from.

'You focking liar!' Hedda roars at me. 'We did it in your bed, Mum! While you were at Fletcher Pilates.'

I'm there just smiling, going, 'I think it's very sad that you'd resort to something like this to try to break us up.'

She goes, 'He even dialled Villette on my phone before we did it. He sent me into the bathroom to wash my make-up off, then he rang him on, like, my *phone*? Villette heard the entire thing. And he dumped me,' and then she loses it for a second and ends up just roaring at me. 'Are you happy with that? He focking dumped me!'

Unfortunately, one of my biggest problems in life has always been that, even when I'm on top, I can never resist the temptation to focking showboat. I'm stood behind Regina, roysh, and I'm pretending to take her from behind – all for Hedda's benefit – while pulling that face that you do when you're about five seconds away from blowing your muck.

It ends up being my undoing.

'You weren't even any good!' Hedda roars at me.

I keep it up, this time grinning at her.

That's when she says it. *'Ham and eggs, Baby! Ham and eggs!'*

It's a pretty spot-on impersonation as well. Regina all of a sudden reels around and looks at me, her face in total shock.

Hedda, of course, picks up on it straight away. 'Oh my God!' she goes. 'He's used that line on you, hasn't he?'

'Regina,' I go and I try put my hand on her shoulder. She won't even look at me, though. She just turns her head and stares off in the direction of the conservatory.

'You know I'm telling the truth,' Hedda goes.

That's when *I* end up losing it with *her*? 'You're a shit-stirrer,' I go. 'And a total one.'

But she just blanks me. Instead, roysh, she tries to grab Regina by the sleeve of her yoga wrap. 'I told you, didn't I? I told you what would happen! But you were too busy trying to relive your youth to listen.'

'Stop it!' Regina goes.

'Too flattered that *anyone* would be interested in you after Dad.'

'I said stop!'

'You couldn't see that all he was *ever* really interested in was your money.'

Regina turns around and lets a sudden roar out of her. 'There *is* no money!'

She looks from Hedda to me, then back to Hedda again. Then she shakes her head. 'There *is* nay mornay.'

Now it's Hedda's turn to look confused. 'What do you mean, there's no money?'

'Whay do *yee* thank yeer doddy kalled himsalf?'

Hedda goes to, like, point at me. 'Because of his . . .'

'It was nathing to *dee* with *hus* suster. He kalled himsalf because . . . because we were in dat. Tens of mallions in dat.'

Regina looks at me then, as if searching my face for something.

Hedda just shakes her head. 'How could we be tens of millions in debt?'

Regina just laughs. 'Jesus Craist, Hedda, teek a look arinde yee. Whoy usn't?'

'What about the hotel? The restaurants? They must be worth something.'

I was thinking the exact same thing.

'See, thot's yee, laving in a wee bobble. Where did yee thank the monay came from? It was all borrowed, on the onderstonding that occupancy would always be hoy, that profits would always be what they wurr. Banks owned averything we hod. Ay've *no* chance of *aver* peeing back what we borrowed . . .'

She looks at *me* then.

'All our dats – all the loans that may and Toddy took ite – they're all going tee NAMA. A yurr from noy – tee at the most – *ay'm* gonna be bankropt. Lake a lot of others.'

My eyes stray automatically to the door. It's, like, a *reflex* thing? There's a port of me that just wants out of here. Gone like Maud.

Hedda just shakes her head – like me, not really knowing *what* to say? In the end, roysh, she settles for, 'You focked up my life!' which she aims first at Regina, before then including me in it. 'You've both focked up my life.'

Then she storms off out of the room, then out of the house, leaving me alone with her mother.

You *know*, of course, how much I focking hate awkward silences. Which is possibly why I reach for the kettle and go, 'Yeah, no, I'm wondering where she picked up that ham and eggs thing. She could have heard it from a lot of people, I suppose. It's a line I'd be famous for.'

She smiles at me – you'd have to say sadly. 'Yee're nat going tee ask may to believe thot, are yee?'

There's probably no point in saying yes.

I'm like, 'Yes.'

All she does, though, is shake her head. 'Yee know, it's nat that yee slapt with her, Ross. Ay suspacted she mait tray something lake thot onywee and ay *knee* yee probably wouldn't fate her off – yee're a mon, aren't yee? Ay could forgav yee all thot. But ay saw yeer feece, Ross, when ay said there was no mornay – it jost said *overythang* ay needed to knoy.'

She takes the kettle from me, then takes my two hands in hers. That's probably how I know it's *actually* over? For the first time, she doesn't give a shit about me seeing her actual hands. I look down at them, sort of, like, cupping mine and I understand why she was so keen to hide them now. She has hands like focking baseball mitts.

'Ay'm sorray,' she goes. '*Ay* shouldn't hov told yee there was mornay. That was bod of may. It's jost, ay knew yee were gonna fanish ut – thot dee, iteside in the gorden . . .'

'I just felt bad about doing it – doing you, I suppose – behind the old man's back.'

'And *ay* knee ay needed to see something to gat yee to stee. Ay shouldn't hov done ut.'

'So that day you went to see your solicitor about your, supposedly, will?'

'It was abite NAMA teeking over may loans. He thanks ay'm gonnay be in the thord tronche.'

I just nod. We both know that this is goodbye. It's just that the actual word doesn't get said.

'Ay'm gonnae go opsturs noy,' she goes, 'and pock a fee thangs in a bog – ay'm gonna go awee for a fee dees.'

The understanding, obviously, is that I'll be gone with all my shit by the time she comes home.

I'm presuming it's the end of my four Ks a week as well.

'If it's any consolation,' I go, 'it happened exactly like you thought it would – as in, she pretty much hopped me.'

She doesn't respond to that. Probably doesn't matter either way at this stage.

She walks as far as the door of the kitchen, where the entire – I suppose – *affair* first storted. She stops and looks back at me. 'Toddy used to see, if somethang seems tee gid to be troy, it's usually because it *uz* tee gid to be troy. Ay suppose we *all* forgat thot, dudn't way?'

And they end up being the last words I ever hear her say.

I sit there for a good ten minutes, listening to her moving about upstairs, dragging around what I'm presuming is luggage. I'm about to go when my phone all of a sudden rings. I answer it without even checking who it is. It turns out to be JP and he's in, like, a total panic.

'Dude,' I end up having to go, 'say it again – but just calm down before you do.'

He goes, 'They know where you are, Ross.'

I'm just like, 'Who?'

He's there, 'Terry and Larry.'

I end up nearly crapping my chinos, there and then. 'What do you mean?'

He takes a breath. 'Danni told them.'

I'm like, 'Dude, tell me you're shitting me.'

'She did it to get at your old dear,' he goes.

'My old dear doesn't give a fock what happens to me.'

'And, well, Terry and Larry did send all that gold her way. They're the only clients she's had.'

I wander over to the CCTV screen in the corner of the kitchen and I stare at a grainy, black-and-white image of two men in baseball caps looking up at the perimeter wall, trying to decide the best way over.

'I'm sorry,' JP goes. 'If it's any consolation – which I'm sure it isn't – I told her that I never want to see her again.'

I hang up and continue watching. One of the men grabs the gates and gives them a bit of a rattle, then looks back at his – presumably stolen – Land Rover. They're obviously going to try to drive *through* them?

The other man reaches into his jacket and pulls out his phone, which he then holds up to his ear.

'Larry,' I go. 'How the hell are you?'

He's like, 'There ye are, Rosser. Suren didn't I say we'd foyunt ye.'

'Where are you?' I go.

I'm bluffing, obviously.

He's there, 'Don't gimme that where-are-ye ould shite. We're out-soyut your boord's gaff. Ine gonna ram these fooken gates less you open them, reet this second.'

I'm just like, 'Dude, *I'm* in Blackrock.'

'What?'

'I'm *in* Blackrock. I'm actually having a coffee here, reading Wardy's verdict on our performance against the All Blacks.'

I hear Larry tell his brother what I said – except the bit about Wardy, obviously.

'He is in he's bollocks,' Terry goes. 'He's insoyut de gaff there. Come on, let's go troo dem gates.'

I can't let them, for Regina's sake. She's already found her husband dead with a bullet in his head. I can't let history repeat itself. This famous conscience of mine is telling me that I possibly owe her that much.

'Look, I'll meet you,' I go.

That grabs Larry's sudden attention. 'What?'

'I'll meet you. Man to man. To be totally honest with you, I'm sick and tired of running.'

'Ye caddent run for ever in anyhow.'

'I know. I realize that now. Can you just promise me one thing?'

'What?'

'You'll hear me out.'

Larry laughs. 'Reet.'

I'm there, 'I mean it, Larry. And I'm talking about a *fair* hearing? See, I remember that thing you were saying before about the whole honour thing. And, to be honest, it impressed me.'

'Feerd enuff,' he goes. 'So where do you wanna meerup?'

'What about where I'm sitting right this second – as in, Bucky's on the Main Street?'

'Would *you* ever fuck off ourra dat. Steerbucks, me bollicks. What, a hundred-and-odd peers of eyes steerding arrus. CCTV – de lot.'

'Okay, you name somewhere, then.'

'Wharra bout the bats?'

'The what?'

'The old bats. Blackrock bats.'

'The baths?' I laugh. 'You must think *I'm* stupid. Nice and deserted, huh? No one around to hear me scream.'

'Okay,' he goes, 'wharra bout the Deert station.'

'The Dort station?'

'Yeah.'

'Okay, that sounds better.'

'What toyum – seven?'

'Seven, tonight?'

'Yeah.'

'Okay, seven is cool. But you have to promise me in advance, Larry, that you're going to listen to what I have to say.'

He laughs, then goes, 'I will, Rosser.'

Then he just hangs up.

I've no idea *what* I'm going to say, of course. All I'm trying to do here is buy myself some time.

I throw on my jacket and grab my cor keys off the hook in the kitchen. Then I end up having a whole dilemma in the hallway, over whether the cor even belongs to me anymore.

I suppose it *was* an actual gift.

So I tip around to the garage. And it's as I'm opening the electric door that I suddenly remember something. It's in the tool cabinet.

Toddy's gun.

Sorcha asks me if watched the six o'clock news. I tell her no, I missed it unfortunately, because it's a lot quicker than pointing out what a ridiculous focking question it is.

Sixty-seven point five billion. She says that's how much it's going to cost the IMF to bail this country out. She says our great-grandchildren are going to end up paying the price for our folly.

'Well, thank God for that,' I happen to go.

She looks at me, roysh, like I've offended her in some deep way – this is, like, stood in the hallway in Newtownpork Avenue. 'What's that supposed to mean?'

'Look, all I'm saying is that at least it's not going to be us.'

She's about to react to that statement – draw me into one of her famous arguments that I can't possibly win – when she suddenly spots something over my left hammer. 'Oh my God, is it, like, *snowing* out there?'

I follow her line of vision through the glass panel in the front door. 'Yeah,' I go, 'it storted coming down about half an hour ago. I don't know if it's going to stick, though.'

She smiles. 'Well, after the day that's just gone, this will really cheer the country up. It's the distraction we all need,' and she turns her head and shouts up the stairs.

'Honor, Princess – it's snowing outside!'

Honor's little voice comes from upstairs. '4COL, Mom!'

Sorcha looks at me, bewildered.

I'm there, 'I think it means for crying out loud.'

'You're being lame again,' Honor goes. 'I've already told you twice, I'm watching *Glee*.'

Sorcha smiles sadly at me, embarrassed – no, actually, *hurt*?

'I told her about me signing on.'

'I take it that it didn't go down well.'

She just shakes her head.

'So,' she just goes, trying to change the subject, 'we finally found out who this mystery woman of yours was.'

I'm like, 'We?'

'Oh my God, everyone's talking about it, Ross.'

'Yeah, I can imagine. I'd say Fionn and Erika are focking delighted.'

'I actually don't think it's that bad. There's, like, no taboo about age-inappropriate relationships anymore, especially between an older woman and a younger man. I was reading this – oh my God – amazing article the other day about the whole OW/YM phenomenon and how it worked for, like, Tim Robbins and Susan Sarandon. *And* Madonna and Guy Ritchie. *And* Demi Moore and Ashton Kutcher. Although it *was* an old article – I found it at the bottom of the recycling bin.'

She looks incredible, by the way – I might have already mentioned.

I'm like, 'It's over, by the way. Between me and her.'

She tries not to give me the reaction I'm looking for. 'That's a pity,' she goes.

'Well, I just thought I'd say it.'

'Erika told me what happened in Mullinavat. That's, like, oh my God, Ross.'

'Do you not think I realize that?'

'She says she's never going to speak to you again.'

'Never is a long time. I seem to remember you said the same thing once or twice. You look incredible, by the way. And I'm only saying that as a statement of fact.'

She gets embarrassed then, so she calls up the stairs again. 'Come on, Honor – your daddy's here to say hello.'

'Are you, like, *totally* retorded?' Honor shouts down. 'I've told you three times now – I'll be down when this is finished.'

I watch Sorcha's face suddenly fill with – I think the word is, like, *resolve*? She goes, 'Excuse me a minute, Ross. Go in and sit down,' which is exactly what I do.

I tip into the kitchen and whip out my phone. I think about it for a few seconds, then I end up just doing it. I dial the old man's number.

It rings twice but it's, like, Helen who answers. She's there, 'Hi, Ross,' except she says it in, like, a whisper.

I go, 'Is he there?'

She's like, 'He still doesn't want to talk to you,' except she actually says it in a really nice way. She's an amazing person.

'Oh,' I just go.

'He'll come round, Ross. Just give him a few more days.'

I laugh, roysh, because I can hear him ranting and raving in the background, going, 'Oh, I can just hear them now – your Fintans and your whoever else. Was it for this the Wild Geese, etcetera, etcetera . . .'

I'm there, 'He certainly sounds excited about *something*.'

'Yes, it's this bail-out.'

'Oh. It's all anyone seems to be talking about all of a sudden. Will you just tell him – I don't know what it is you're supposed to say in these situations – maybe that I'm sorry. The thing is, Helen . . . Look, I'm as focking useless as tits on a bowling ball. I always was. His problem was that he just could never see it.'

'He'll calm down, Ross.'

She hangs up just as Sorcha arrives into the kitchen with Honor. There's suddenly a lot of shouting. Sorcha's going, 'Three times, I called you.'

Honor looks up at me, her hand on her hip. 'Will you tell this dolite,' she goes, 'to take an actual chill pill.'

I'm like, 'What?' genuinely meaning it.

Honor goes, 'Er, *dolite*? It's, like, a nicer way of saying dole scrounger.'

Sorcha puts both hands up to her face. Her eyes instantly fill up with tears. She looks as unhappy as I've ever seen her.

And I end up literally exploding.

I go, 'Don't you ever speak about her like that again!'

Honor's in, like, shock. See, this is a side of me she's never seen before. It's about time she did, a lot of people might say.

She's like, 'Dad . . .'

But I'm there, 'Dad nothing!' and I'm practically roaring at her, jabbing my finger in her general direction. '*She* is your mother! You have no idea what she has gone through the last couple of years to put food in your mouth and designer clothes on your back. She goes down to that dole office and she focking dies down there for you. And I don't want to hear you ever – ever! – disrespect her like that again!'

I leave her standing there with her mouth wide open.

Sorcha follows me out to the front door. She's like, 'Thank you.'

I turn around on the doorstep. I'm there, 'Make sure she always gives you the respect you deserve but basically don't always get. I know I didn't set her a very good example.'

She shakes her head. 'Ross, why are you talking to me like we're saying goodbye?'

I shrug.

'Father Fehily used to say we should always treat people like it's the last time we're ever going to see them. Because one day it will be.'

'Ross, you're scaring me.'

'Don't be scared. I'm just saying, basically, I'm sorry – for being a shit boyfriend slash husband.'

She just shakes her head and goes, 'The ride with you was worth the fall, my friend.'

I smile. 'Who *is* that?'

'It's actually Whitney Houston. "Didn't We Almost Have It All".'

The poor focking girl. She must have, like, fifty or sixty break-up songs for me.

'Anyway,' I go, 'I'll hopefully see you soon.'

On my way out the gate, I hear Honor shout something. And I laugh. Because I'm pretty sure she called me Knob Features.

Five minutes later, I'm pulling up on, like, Idrone Terrace. It'll tell you how all over the place my mind is that I can't decide whether or not I should even bother feeding the meter.

In the end, I do, then I walk around to the back of the cor and open the boot. It's in there – wrapped up tightly in a white sheet.

I take a deep breath, then I unwrap it, watching the light from the street lamp overhead glint off the metal. This is it. It's a sad day but I realize that this is my only chance of surviving to see the end of it.

I pick it up in both hands and I stort walking towards the Dort station with it held out in front of me. It obviously draws quite a bit of attention. It's not a sight that people in this port of the world would be used to. People are looking at me with their mouths open, going, 'What the hell is he doing with that thing?'

One or two women even scream.

Of course, I know what you're all presuming. That it's the gun. But it's actually a crate of Galahad Premium.

See, I have this, like, scene in my head where the three of us – me, Larry and Terry – sit down on the wall opposite the station and we basically talk it out and by the time the twelve cans are drunk everything just seems, hopefully, different.

I take up my position on the wall, with the snow coming down heavily now, and check my watch. It's, like, five past seven already and still no sign of them.

I listen to the trains rattling through the station. Cors pulling up outside. People being collected after a hord day's whatever. Others heading for pints in O'Rourke's or the Wolf. The snow makes it feel like it's Christmas come early. All anyone seems to be talking about, though, is Ireland's sovereignty.

Your guess is as good as mine.

It's suddenly, like, twenty past seven and still nothing. Did we definitely *say* the station? Maybe they think I said yes to the baths. Maybe I should tip around there.

But then maybe that's what they want me to do. Maybe they're waiting for me where they know there'll be no witnesses.

My phone suddenly rings. I get such a fright, I end up practically levitating.

Is it them?

I check.

No, it's actually Ronan.

'Thanks for finally returning my call,' I go.

He's just like, 'Where are you, Rosser?'

'Freezing my balls off in Blackrock, waiting for someone who still hasn't shown.'

'Ah, reet. Here, did you leave McGahy in a forest to die.'

I just laugh. 'Who's been saying that?'

'Me ma.'

'He finally got to her, then.'

'Yeah. They're back togedder, Rosser.'

'I'm sorry, Ro. Look, I did my best.'

'Ah, maybe it's just something Ine gonna have to get used to. Unless you can come up with anudder plan.'

I look at the crate of cheap beer on the wall beside me. We'll probably go to drink it and it'll be frozen focking solid. I laugh. I'm like, 'I think plans are one thing I'm all out of, Ro.'

He gets all of a sudden excited about something. 'Here, did you see the news tonight?'

I just shake my head. 'What's this big fascination with the news all of a sudden? So we've been bailed out. Am I only one who thinks that's an actual good thing?'

'Ine talking about Terry and Larry Tuhill,' he goes.

I'm like, 'What about them?'

'Thee were mordered,' he goes. 'This arthur noon. Riddled with bullets, so thee were. At a traffic light on the Portmeernock Road.'

Epilogue

The snow is coming down out there like I don't *know* what? I can hordly see through the windscreen. And at the same time it's, like, hypnotic – if that's the word. Millions and millions of white flakes just flashing in the dorkness in front of me and making me want to just go to sleep.

There's some dude on the radio saying that it's not a time to be talking about the GPO and Ireland's dead mortyrs. That, whether we like it or not, we surrendered our sovereignty the day we signed up to join a Europe that was something more than the small economic association originally envisaged. Anyone who thinks we can exist in this world alone is kidding themselves.

I take the coast road towards Malahide. Strange thoughts go through my head. I think about Terry and Larry. Nothing bad. I think about how much I'm going to, like, miss them. Not the way they were the last few months but the way they used to be.

I think maybe I'll adopt Rooney – as, like, a tribute to them. I know he's a Rottweiller and he supposedly has a thing for me. But once he's desexed, I think we could be actually friends.

Ronan exaggerated, by the way. The cor wasn't peppered or showered or whatever word it was he used. There were six shots fired. They took three each, according to the news, and the Gordaí said the gunman was a professional. They were pronounced dead at the scene.

I think about the two of them, not screaming threats down the phone at me or hanging off the back of the van, threatening to cut my balls off, on the Blackrock Bypass. I think about them in, like, happy times, summoning me to one of their porties, sticking a joint and a can of cheap beer in my hand and making me sing some focking UB40 song with them.

It said on the news that they were known to Gordaí. Nowhere did it say that they were two of the most generous goys you could ever meet. Yeah, they were ruthless gangsters who were responsible for God knows how many deaths and how much human misery. But it's like Father Fehily used to say – at the little porties he used throw once a year to celebrate Hitler's anniversary – no one is only one thing.

The snow is *really* coming down out there now. It's, like, *blinding*?

Like my old man a year ago, I feel like I've been given a second chance. And because of that I feel that I can do anything now. I might spend the time between now Christmas trying to make things right.

The old man will forgive me. He'll definitely forgive me. So will Erika and Fionn. They have to. They're, like, family. I'm going to be an amazing best man as well – no more cracks about him punching above his weight. Even though he is. I'm going to just go along with the whole charade.

And if Tina wants to get it on with – fock's sake – McGahy, then I can accept it, as long as Ronan can.

Maybe I'll ring the old dear and totally shock her by telling her that she's doing Foxrock proud with her protests against the cash for gold shop and that her book isn't nearly as shit as I told her it was. I might end up even reading it. That *could* happen. Might even be the first thing I do.

Maybe I'll put some manners on that daughter of mine. Knob Features. I laugh to myself. Well, there's no denying where she picked that one up.

Maybe I'll tell her mother how I really feel about her. Beg her not to divorce me. Tell her that I'm done with the whole, I don't know, indiscriminate sex thing and I'm ready to maybe settle down – one goy, one girl.

I have a little chuckle to myself. Who am I focking kidding?

I press the button on the little remote and the gates swing open. The old windscreen wipers are fighting a losing battle with the snow at this stage, which is why I drive slowly up to the front of the house.

I'm returning the cor to Regina. I think about just slipping the keys through the letterbox. But then I think, no, that wouldn't be right. One thing no one's ever been able to say about me is that I lack class.

So I go in and I make my way down the hall to the kitchen. There's no sign of Regina. She's obviously already gone. Urlingford would be my bet.

I leave the keys on the island, then I think about maybe leaving a note. But then I think, what would it say? What is there left that *needs* to be said?

It's only then that I realize that I've no way of getting back across

397

the city. I whip out my phone with the intention of ringing Oisinn. See, I know he'd come for me like I came for him.

It's then that the kitchen door swings open and I'm suddenly stood staring at Hedda. Her face is, like, an angry shade of red and she's holding – it's very difficult *not* to notice – her father's shotgun.

'You focking orsehole!' she goes.

She looks like she's actually *lost* it? I try to come up with a line to maybe calm her down.

'Can I just remind you,' I go, 'that emos are supposed to be, like, *non*-violent?'

Shit, I think. That's not going to be enough.

'You've focking ruined everything!' she goes.

And I go, 'Hedda, put the gun down.'

'You focking bastard!'

'Hedda, please put the gun down.'

'You focking . . .'

I don't actually *hear* the explosion? Although I'm sure there must *be* one. I feel myself being suddenly thrown backwards against the wall, then falling flat on my face. The next thing I'm aware of is screaming – Hedda screaming, like she can't believe what she's just done.

Then I must black out, roysh, because when I come around again, Hedda's on the phone and I can hear her – totally frantic – telling someone the address, then going, 'Quick. Focking quick.'

Then I must black out a second time, for longer this time, because I don't actually hear an ambulance arrive. But I'm suddenly aware of, like, voices echoing in the kitchen – all men's.

One of them goes, 'Jesus Christ!' which – considering the kind of shit they usually see – means it must be bad. I hear a voice say I've lost too much blood, then another says no, he's going to be alright, then another says it's going to be touch and go.

Then one of them slips, I'm presuming on my blood. Then a voice goes, 'Okay, we're going to have to transfuse him here.'

And the last thing I see? Across the floor of the kitchen, sitting side by side on the mat at the back door, are Regina's MBTs. That's when the borders of my vision stort getting dorker and dorker, until suddenly everything is black.

Acknowledgements

Thanks, as usual, to all the team. My brilliant editor Rachel Pierce, extraordinary agent Faith O'Grady and the artist Alan Clarke, whose renderings of Ross and his world continue to leave me agog. Thank you, Michael McLoughlin, Patricia Deevy, Cliona Lewis, Patricia McVeigh, Brian Walker and everyone at Penguin Ireland for all your support. Thanks, as ever, to my father, David, and my brothers, Vincent and Richard. And to my wife, Mary, thanks that can never be adequately expressed.

Shall